D0752814

JILLIAN HART

A Love Worth Waiting For

Heaven Knows

Steeple
Hill®

Published by Steeple Hill Books™

STEEPLE HILL BOOKS

Steeple
Hill®

Recycling programs
for this product may
not exist in your area.

ISBN-13: 978-0-373-65140-5

A LOVE WORTH WAITING FOR AND HEAVEN KNOWS

www.SteepleHill.com

Printed in U.S.A.

CONTENTS

Books by Jillian Hart

Love Inspired

A Love Worth Waiting For
Heaven Knows
*The Sweetest Gift
*Almost Heaven
*A Soldier for Christmas
*Precious Blessings
*Every Kind of Heaven
*Everyday Blessings
*A McKaslin Homecoming
A Holiday to Remember
*Her Wedding Wish
*Her Perfect Man
Homefront Holiday
*A Soldier for Keeps
*Blind-Date Bride
†The Soldier's Holiday Vow
†The Rancher's Promise
Klondike Hero

Love Inspired Historical

*Homespun Bride
*High Country Bride
In a Mother's Arms
  "Finally a Family"
**Gingham Bride
**Patchwork Bride

*The McKaslin Clan
†The Granger Family Ranch
**Buttons & Bobbins

JILLIAN HART

grew up on her family's homestead, where she helped raise cattle, rode horses and scribbled stories in her spare time. After earning her English degree from Whitman College, she worked in travel and advertising before selling her first novel. When Jillian isn't working on her next story, she can be found puttering in her rose garden, curled up with a good book or spending quiet evenings at home with her family.

A LOVE WORTH
WAITING FOR

Your word is a lamp for my feet
and a light for my path.

—*Psalms* 119:105

To Cheryl McGee and Jolene Haskins—
extraordinary women, writers and friends.
The writingchicks rule.

Chapter One

"Noah!"

She was in his arms the second he'd stepped away from the crowded gate. Noah Ashton couldn't get over it. His little sister, Hope, married and glowing, flung her arms around his neck, squeezed tight and then stepped back to look him over.

Her brows furrowed and her mouth pursed downward as she scanned him from head to toe. Noah liked that about Hope, that she fussed over him. Not that he needed it and not that it made a bit of difference. She always had the same complaints when it came to his lifestyle.

"Do I meet with your approval?"

"You most certainly do not, and you know it, mister." She scowled, eyes flashing. "You look like death warmed over."

"I'm just tired, that's all. Long day, long night, long flight." Noah brushed aside her concern with a wave of one hand. "I'm good as gold."

"Gold is a lifeless mineral."

"Ah, but it's of great value."

"You know what I mean." She slipped her slim arm around his, steering him down the small breezeway in the tiny Montana airport. "You work too hard. Our grandmother is worried about you."

"Nanna hasn't seen me since your wedding. For all she knows, I'm still as good-looking as ever."

"Good-looking?" Hope's smile dazzled, teasing him right back. "There *is* something wrong with you, brother dear. You're delusional."

"Hey, women tell me I'm handsome all the time."

"What kind of women have you been hanging around? They obviously have terrible taste when it comes to men." Her dark eyes sparkled with humor.

Hope loved teasing him, he knew it, but he was a good guy. Did he deserve being hassled? "Hey, wait a minute. Not five minutes off that plane and you're torturing me. I'm a billionaire. I don't need to put up with this."

"You're only getting what you deserve." She winked at him. "You've hardly spoken to me since my wedding. I've been busy, but never too busy to talk with you."

"I've been overburdened with this takeover, and

I figured being a newlywed, you needed time with your husband." Noah shrugged, not sure how to feel about his sister's decision to marry. Good luck in marriage genes just didn't run in their family. "Are you doing all right? Married life agrees with you?"

"It sure does. Why, are you thinking about trying it?"

"Not in this lifetime." Noah swung his carry-on over his shoulder, steering Hope toward baggage claim. "I want you to be happy—don't get me wrong—but after watching our parents year in and year out, I still can't believe you're giving marriage a try."

"I'm not giving it a try. I'm in for life. And don't give me that look. Not every marriage was like our parents'." She led the way through the doors and into the crisp weather. "I never thought I could be so blessed."

She *did* look happy. She sparkled when she smiled. It was as if she'd found her heart's desire. Now there was a concept—the words *happy* and *married* in the same thought.

Remembering the chaos of his childhood, Noah shivered. If true love *were* possible, it had to be a rare occurrence—like a total eclipse of the sun.

Great that his sister was happy as a newlywed, but he wasn't about to be led astray from the path he'd chosen—a single, unattached bachelor's life.

He wasn't about to wish there could be a woman out there who would love him just the way he was.

"Nanna is so excited you've come," Hope told him after he'd grabbed his luggage, and when they were weaving between cars in the parking lot. "It means so much to her that you'll be at the party tonight."

"I wouldn't miss it—you know that." Tenderness filled his chest at the thought of their grandmother. "How's she doing?"

"Fantastic." Hope pressed her remote key chain and the side door on her minivan slid open. "Getting married at her stage in life is an exciting event. She wants to make sure she does it right."

"And the engagement party is the kick-off event?"

"It's a celebration, Noah, not a football game." Hope stole his briefcase from him and set it on the floor of her van. "Tell me it isn't so, that you didn't bring work."

"Of course I did. You know I have to. I have a company to keep afloat while I'm here."

"Haven't you ever heard of a vacation? You know, where you leave your desk and phone behind and go someplace and enjoy recreation?"

"I've heard of it. Never tried it myself. Could be addictive and destroy my carefully guarded work ethic."

"No wonder you look like death warmed over. You really don't look well."

She'd hit a nerve, but he didn't want her to know

that. Whatever his problems were, they were his. That's the way he was made—he could solve his own troubles. "I'm jet-lagged. Just came back from Japan."

"That would explain it. Okay, you're off the hook. For now."

He deposited his suitcase and garment bag on the floor. Now what? How did he tell his sister, who loved him and thought she was doing the best for him, that he didn't know about the state of his health? When he'd flown in from Tokyo last week, he'd spent the night in the emergency room.

He opted not to tell her and snapped the seat belt into place instead.

Hope negotiated her minivan through the airport traffic and soon they were pulling onto the freeway. The Christian country music on the radio mumbled in the background as the miles sped by. Noah stared out the window at the road ribboning between gently rolling fields. The rugged snow-capped mountains, dead ahead, rose up from the horizon to touch the enormous blue sky.

Peace. For a brief moment, the restlessness within him stilled. What would it be like to live here, spend each day absorbing the beauty and the quiet, letting serenity settle over like the sun from above?

Then his cell phone rang, and Hope glared at him in that sisterly way that said she was still worried about him.

Not able to tell her why he had to work, why there would be no peace for him, he took the call.

The church hall was warm and friendly despite the darkening storm outside, and the heater clicked on just as Julie Renton was stretching on tiptoe on the second-to-the-top step on the ladder. The crepe paper rustled as she pressed it to the ceiling. The air current from the nearby duct tore the streamer of pink from her fingers and sent it fluttering to the carpeted floor.

On the other end of the streamer, Susan Whitly cried out in protest as the end she was securing to the opposite corner popped out of her grip.

"Sorry." Laughing, Julie scurried down the stepladder to rescue the crepe paper. "Doom strikes again."

"The more you say the word *doom,* the more it's going to follow you around like a dark cloud," Misty Collins called from the corner where she was draping the last of the tables with beautiful shimmery pink cloths. "Everything's coming along fine. We'll be done in time for the party."

"I can't help seeing disaster." Julie glanced around the large hall, already half-decorated thanks to her very best friends. "Granddad's had it tough over the past few years. Now that he's found happiness, I want this party to be perfect. To sort of kick off this exciting new phase of his life."

"With all the hard work you've done and the plans you've made, it will be beautiful," Susan assured her from high atop the other ladder. "Your grandfather is going to have a wonderful time."

"I'm praying that you're right!"

The party *had* to be perfect for him, Julie thought as she climbed up the rickety ladder. It wasn't every day a girl's grandfather got engaged. After being a widower for so long, Granddad deserved as much joy as he could get.

He'd been the only close family she'd had after Mom left.

"They say Nora's grandson is coming tonight." Misty smoothed wrinkles from the tablecloth. "You know, the really rich one."

Julie inwardly groaned. She was under enough pressure with this party going well. "I don't want to think about the billionaire."

"Why not?" Misty opened a package of lace place mats. "I mean, he's a billionaire. You know. With billions of dollars."

"That doesn't mean he's nice." Julie pressed the streamer into place. "Just because he's rich doesn't mean he's gracious or polite or even understanding about a party for his grandmother. He's probably used to events far more lavish than we could ever dream of. What if he doesn't think our efforts are good enough and isn't afraid to say so?"

"Julie, don't worry." Susan leaned the ladder

safely against the wall. "This Mr. Ashton may be rich, but he's got to have a heart. He has to want his grandmother to be happy."

"What if he thinks my grandfather isn't good enough for his grandmother?" Julie's throat felt tight as she tossed the tape roll into the cardboard box she'd brought all her supplies in.

"Who knows? Rich Mr. James Noah Ashton the Third *was* on the cover of some magazine I was reading at the dentist's office. He lives a grand lifestyle," Misty argued. "I wouldn't mind some of that."

"Hey, I saw that picture and I thought he was to-die-for," Susan added. "He looked really nice. Like a real gentleman."

Hmm, a gentleman? Julie wasn't too sure about that. "Can you really tell from a magazine picture? Especially where they airbrushed away all his flaws?"

"What flaws? Judging by the picture, I don't think the man has one itty-bitty imperfection."

Julie sighed and didn't say a word. The indentation on her left ring finger remained from the engagement ring she'd worn for over a year. She definitely knew about men's imperfections. Specifically their unwillingness to commit.

"Maybe this Ashton guy isn't so bad," Misty argued. "Even if he does have blemishes or scars or something. His coming here to our little town, don't you think it's like a fairy tale? He could be my Prince Charming come to rescue me."

Julie helped Misty with the last of the candlesticks. "I love that you're an optimist, but believe me, I don't think Prince Charming exists."

"They do on my daily soap opera," she insisted. "Don't mess with my dreams."

Everyone laughed, even Julie. Okay, so she was a little disillusioned. She didn't mean to be. It had been a difficult year, learning to set aside her long-cherished dreams of a husband and children of her own. Her heart still ached.

Maybe someday her own prince would come, a man who wouldn't leave her, who'd never let her down.

It was a prayer, a wish really, and Julie knew deep in her heart it was one wish that would never come true.

The sound of the car door closing shot like a bullet in the quiet. Probably Granddad. Right on time, as always.

"Is that our promised pizza?"

"And our reliable deliveryman," Julie confirmed. "I'd better go help him. You guys stay here and put up your feet."

Cold wind hit her face, reminding her that winter was on its way. Soon, Granddad's wedding would be here, and she'd be celebrating the holidays alone.

But it's good for him, Julie reminded herself, and let the cold wind blow over her, chasing away the heaviness of lost dreams. She had friends, and she still had her grandfather, who was heading her way, awkwardly balancing a couple of pizza cartons.

"Julie!" he called out, his voice deep and robust, the way an old cowboy should sound. "I hope I got the order right. Good thing is they're still hot."

"You're my favorite granddad for doing this." She ducked his Stetson brim to kiss him on the cheek, cool from the chilly air.

"Least I could do for the girls who are making my Nora's party special."

"Let me take these." She lifted the boxes from his arms. "Everyone's done a great job. The hall looks so nice. Do you want to come see?"

He looked sheepish—and a little panicked. "An old rustler like me dining with fine young women like you? Nope. Somethin' tells me I'd best be on my way."

"Shy, are you?" She tucked a twenty-dollar bill into his pocket and argued when he tried he give it back to her. "I'll let you get away with running out on us this time, because I know you have a beautiful woman waiting for you."

"Nora's grandson's gonna be there, you know." Granddad pulled his Stetson low over his brows. His mouth pressed into a tight, worried line. "Not sure how I feel about meeting him, though. My

Nora puts a lot of stock in that grandson of hers. Thinks anything he says is as good as gold."

"Well, if he doesn't take one look at you and see what a decent, honorable man you are, then I can teach him a lesson or two. I didn't win state in calf roping two years in a row for nothing."

"That's my girl." Laughing, Granddad tipped his hat and backed away. "Wish me a bucket of luck, girl, cuz I'm fairly certain I'm going to need it. If I need help, I'll give you a call."

"You can count on me, Granddad."

"I know I can. You take care, now, you hear?" He climbed into his classic pickup and started the engine. He tipped his hat again as he drove away.

The church's side door swung open with a squeak. It was Susan. "Hey, I thought we lost you. We're some seriously hungry women. I don't think you should keep us waiting."

"I've got the goods right here." Julie held the boxes level as she headed for the open door.

The warmth of the church beckoned her, but the cold kept hold on her. She wished she could do something to take away her grandfather's troubles.

She watched the red taillights of his pickup fade from sight. "They don't make men like Granddad anymore."

"Oh, there's a few good ones around. The tough part is finding them."

"Tough? How about impossible? I've been

trying to find one to call my own, and I've given up."

"That's when it happens, you know." Susan held the door wide. "When you've given up all hope and you don't think you'll ever find love, love finds you."

Not me, Julie wanted to say, but what was the point? Susan had her beliefs, and Julie had hers. Three failed engagements that had taken more of her heart and her confidence each time she gave back the diamond ring.

She didn't have a lot of heart and confidence left to risk on another man, another dream, another chance for happily-ever-after.

She'd make the most of the life God had given her—and that was easy. Look at all the blessings she had—a wonderful grandfather and soon a new grandmother, and lifelong friends she loved like sisters. What a beautiful life she had.

"We're starving," Misty called from inside the hall. "Is that pepperoni I smell?"

Because anyone holding a pepperoni pizza was popular, Julie hurried into the hall to share the meal with her friends.

Chapter Two

"Consider this fair warning."

"Warning for what?" Noah bounced in the seat as his sister navigated her minivan along the stretch of dirt that passed for a driveway. "Maybe I should see that this road gets paved."

Hope shot him a withering look. "Forget the driveway. It's been newly graveled. I'm trying to look out for your best interests. Nanna has her agenda."

"Believe me, I know. She hits me over the head with it every week when I call her." Noah squared his shoulders. "Don't worry, I can handle her. I'm bigger and stronger. I have a will of steel."

"Hey, Superman, I give Nanna two minutes before she brings up the subject of marriage."

"Marriage is like kryptonite to a man like me."

Noah winked at her. "One and a half minutes, I say. She's gotten pushy since she's become engaged. Wants to spread the torture around I guess."

"Misery loves company." Hope winked right back at him. "I can handle Nanna. She's not going to marry me off."

"We'll see about that." Hope brought the vehicle to a stop in the gravel driveway, beneath the shelter of a mighty oak. Rain sputtered from the sky, making the wipers skid on the windshield. "Did you want me to pick you up? Or are you taking Nanna to the party?"

"I have no idea. I'm just along for the ride." He opened the door. The cool and damp air rushing over him was enough to make him shiver as he stepped onto Montana soil. "Go home to your husband and kids. Thanks for the ride."

"Anytime."

He grabbed his bags and briefcase. His sister drove away, leaving him standing in the noontime rain.

The windows of the old white farmhouse glowed like a promise of shelter from the storm. The front door swung wide, casting a generous swatch of light onto the old-fashioned porch. Noah's chest warmed at the sight of the woman framed in the doorway.

"There you are." Nanna opened her arms wide, and he stepped into them. "I should have known my

Noah would be here right on time. Oh, it's good to see my boy."

He hadn't been a boy in over twenty years, but he didn't correct her. "You're looking as lovely as ever. I guess being in love agrees with you."

"And why shouldn't it? Love is one of God's greatest blessings and one day you're going to discover it for yourself. I've been praying, so you'd better watch out, my boy." She broke away and nudged him into the threshold. "Let me take a good look at you."

"I'm fine."

"Fine, my foot! Why, James Noah Ashton you look terrible. Simply terrible. What have you been doing to yourself?" Nanna shook her head, her mouth tight with disapproval. "I know what you've been up to, lying to me on the phone!"

"I wasn't lying—" He was being selective. He didn't know for sure if anything was wrong.

"Letting me think you're better off than you are! I can take one look at you and see that you've been working day and night, not getting enough sleep. Not taking care of yourself. Eating restaurant food."

"There's nothing wrong with restaurant food."

"Have you looked in a mirror lately? And why aren't you wearing a coat? Come inside out of this cold." She grabbed him by the arm and hauled him into her living room. "Now sit down and warm up in front of the fire."

She had every right to scold, he figured. And as long as she went on about his lifestyle, she wasn't bringing up the word *marriage*. He checked his watch. Two minutes and counting.

"It breaks my heart to see you alone," Nanna called from the kitchen, not sounding heartbroken at all. Oh, no, she sounded like a four-star general on the eve of battle. "I had so hoped you would bring along a date. It's not good for a man to be alone."

"I've heard that before. Somewhere, I just can't think where—" He strolled into the kitchen in time to see her wave her hand at him.

"Oh, you. Don't blame a poor old woman for wanting to see her only grandson happy."

"I am happy." He kissed her cheek and stole the oven mitt from her. "Move aside and let the master work."

"Master? You can't cook, young man." She chuckled, her laughter as sweet as a meadowlark's song.

"That's what you think. I bought this video series by some gourmet chef on how to cook. So you see, I can feed myself and I do know how to get stuff from the oven."

"Just be careful. The pan is plumb full—"

"I won't spill," he told her gently, because he loved her. Noah lifted the heavy pan from the oven and set her culinary masterpiece on the trivet to cool. The delicious scents of Italian herbs made his mouth water. "Hey, I just thought of something. You could give me the recipe and maybe I can make it when I'm at home."

"That I'd pay good money to see." Nanna squeezed his arm. "The lasagna needs to cool. Come sit down and I'll get you some of that lemonade you like. And no, I certainly will not give you my recipe. It has been a guarded secret in my family for generations."

"Nanna, I *am* family."

"When you have a wife and children of your own, then I'll give you the recipe. How's that?" Eyes twinkling, she led him to the round oak table near the windows.

"Maybe I'll have to charm the recipe out of you because, face the truth, Nanna, I'm not getting married. Read my lips."

"Oh, what you don't know." She tugged at his tie. "Sit down and relax. I've made up my mind to treat you so well, you're never going to want to go back to the big city and the job that's making you so unhappy."

"I'm not unhappy," he reminded her, and because he knew he could distract her, took her by the hand and pulled out a wooden chair. "My grandmother taught me to treat beautiful women with respect, so here, have a seat. I won't take no for an answer."

"There you go, charming me again. You're trouble."

"Don't I know it. Now, sit."

She slipped onto the cushioned seat with great resignation, but her eyes sparkled with pleasure. "It's so *good* to have you here. Now my engagement party will be perfect."

"It's good to be here." He found a pitcher of lemonade in the refrigerator. "Tell me more about this man you're going to marry. When do I get to meet him?"

"Harold?" Nanna clasped her hands together. "Why, you're going to love him!"

Noah snared two glasses from the cupboard. "He must be quite a man to win your heart."

"He is! Oh, the plans we've been making. We've hired an architect and we're going to build a new home, can you imagine? It's a terrible big project, but oh, what fun I've been having. I've even decided on the house plan I want. It took a lot of looking, I tell you."

A cold sensation settled in the pit of his stomach. "Will you be building here on your land?"

"Oh, no. Harold owns a large spread. A simply beautiful place. The mountain views he has are a sight to behold. I've got a place for the house picked out on a rise, so we'll have views in four directions. There's nice afternoon shade for a rose garden."

Nanna's eyes sparkled with pure happiness, lit

from behind. Noah hated having to ask the next question, but it was for her benefit. Clearly she was so much in love, she might not see this Harold's hidden agenda.

"So, what will you do with this place?" He said it casually as he set the glass of lemonade in front of her.

"Oh, I thought about renting, but you know how that is. I'd worry someone wouldn't take care of this house I love so much. Your sister has her own home and I'm sure as can be you don't want this land—" She stopped midsentence and squinted at him. "Do you?"

"You know I love New York."

"I just knew you were going to say that. Well, you said it yourself, so I guess my only choice is to sell."

"Sell?" Noah didn't like the sound of that. "Is this your idea?"

"And whose would it be? It's just common sense, young man." She took a sip of lemonade. "Now, before you start, I realize there'd be taxes to pay, but that's your job, handling my finances for me the way you do."

"But you don't want to sell?" he asked carefully.

"How could I *want* to sell? I have wonderful memories in this house, but it's time to start something new for me. Maybe what this old place needs is a nice young family to fill these empty rooms. What do you think?"

"You'd make money off the place." A few million, Noah didn't add. "I suppose you and this Harold have talked about that."

"No, we truly haven't. We haven't had the time. With the new house and our wedding plans, I've been a busy bee, I tell you."

Just as he expected. Nanna didn't suspect a thing. She didn't even consider that the Harold she loved could be a fortune hunter.

"Would you be using the money from the sale to build the new house?"

"Noah, you and that finance mind of yours." Nanna stood, and her chair scraped on the linoleum. Her hand settled on his arm. "I swear you've been working so hard and so long, you don't know how to take it easy. '...all our busy rushing ends in nothing.' My dear boy, stop trying to accomplish so much. When you're in this house, you don't need to prove anything to me. I love you just as you are. Perfect."

She planted a kiss on his cheek.

His heart filled with tenderness for this spry, lively woman who loved him without condition. As he loved her.

"All right, I know you're dying to tell me about bridesmaid dresses and colors of tablecloths or whatever it is you brides get to decide." He took her hand and led her back to the table. "Are you happy now?"

"Overjoyed." Nanna sparkled like a rare gem. "Sit and let me grab my books. I'll show you the picture of the wedding dress I picked only yesterday."

"I'd love to see it."

For his grandmother, he'd do anything.

Noah took a sip of lemonade, wishing it was a double latte, and watched his grandmother hurry from the room in search of her wedding magazines. Alone in the kitchen, with the rain tapping at the windows, a rare peace swept over him. A comfort so strong, he was sure he was doing the right thing, watching out for his grandmother.

The pink and gold decorations were airy and romantic. The glitter streamers winked like stardust. Candles waited, ready to be lit, and the fresh flowers emitted a gentle, rose scent that made the room a dream.

Julie took a final look at their handiwork and satisfaction filled her. "This is like something out of a fairy tale. I couldn't have done this without my friends."

"Your grandfather is going to love it." Susan put her arm around Julie and gave her a quick hug.

"Everyone is going to be wowed," Misty added. "And speaking of impressing people, I've got to fly. If I want to impress the handsome, rich bachelor who's going to be in this very room in just over two hours, I've got to beautify. I'm wearing that blue silk swirly dress I bought in Missoula. It's the best thing I own."

"Thank goodness I got my red shift dry-cleaned last week," Susan enthused.

Julie couldn't believe it. All this fuss over one man? "Just because he's rich doesn't mean he's nice."

"He *could* be nice. We don't know that he isn't," Misty reasoned. "He might be a good dancer."

"It's an engagement party, not singles' night."

"It's a Friday night. There'll be a band. That means we'll have to dance with him."

"It'll be tough, but someone's got to do it." Susan looked determined to suffer. "My theory is that you never know what God has in store for you. In my case, why not a billionaire?"

Julie laughed, she couldn't help it. "Okay, believe Mr. Ashton is going to be your knight in shining armor. I'll make sure to introduce you to the billionaire. Satisfied?"

"Absolutely." Susan waggled her brows, looking full of trouble. "Maybe I'll get my hair done, too. Since I'm getting dressed up, it wouldn't hurt to dazzle him."

"Why bother? I'm sure Mr. James Ashton has his pick of beautiful women," Misty teased.

"You don't think he'll take a second look at me. Is that it?" Susan pretended to be offended.

"He could be looking at me instead." Misty

flicked her hair behind her shoulder. "Maybe the billionaire likes blondes."

Susan and Misty laughed together, and Misty said goodbye. The outside door clicked shut as Julie snapped off the lights.

"I'll be back in an hour to direct the caterers." Susan grabbed her coat and purse from the dark corner. "Don't you worry about a thing. You just make sure your grandfather is here on time."

"You can count on that. Thanks, Susan."

"Don't mention it."

Together they turned off the rest of the lights and closed the doors behind them. The fat raindrops became a downpour the minute they stepped into the parking lot.

"I hope this is just a temporary thing," Julie called over a sudden gust of wind. "I'd hate to have to row people across the parking lot."

"Joke all you want, but it'll all work out." Susan shouted to be heard over the drum of rain as she headed to her car. "Drive safely."

"You, too!"

The sky let loose with a violent torrent of icy rain. Great. Just when she didn't think it could get worse… She took off running. Gravel crunched at her feet and rain knifed through her thin jacket. She flung open her truck's door and collapsed on the seat. With hands stiff from the cold, she found her keys and started the engine.

"Please, don't tell me it's going to be like this all afternoon." She flicked the defroster on high, but only chilly air sputtered from the air vents.

Rain pinged on the roof and streamed down her windshield. She shivered and swiped a circle of fog from the glass. Tree branches swayed violently in the wind. Twin beams cut through the downpour as Susan's car eased out of the parking lot and out of sight.

With her mind on the party, her grandfather and the billionaire showing up, Julie put her truck in gear and crept through the storm, keeping a close eye on the road.

"It was good to finally meet you, Mr. Renton." Noah shook the older man's hand. He hadn't found any obvious reason not to trust the man.

There was an honest glint in Harold's eye, that was for sure, as he grabbed his battered Stetson and headed for the door.

Harold may appear to be kind and decent, but Noah had learned the hard way that people were not often what they appeared.

"I'll look forward to seeing you at the party, son." Harold nodded in the way men from the country did, his drawl unassuming as he tugged open the door. "Looks like the storm isn't about to let up. Hey, that's Helen's car in the driveway. She must have just pulled up."

"Wonderful!" Nanna clasped her hands together, obviously overjoyed. "She's going to help me fix my hair. You drive safe, Harold, my love. Guess I'll be seeing you in a few hours."

"I don't see how you can get much prettier, but I'll be lookin' forward to it." Blushing, head down, the older man cleared his throat.

Noah blushed, too, realizing Nanna and Harold were waiting for him to leave so they could be alone. Well, he could take a hint. He headed for the living room to give the couple privacy.

Okay, so he sort of liked Harold. He was a well-preserved man, who spent his retirement running his ranch and seemed to love doing it. And the way Harold looked at Nanna—well, it *did* look like true love.

Don't jump to conclusions, Noah warned himself, pacing the room, listening to the fire pop low in the grate and the bushes scraping against the windows.

Trying not to listen to the murmur of his grandmother's voice in the entry hall, Noah whipped out his handheld computer. The little electronic notebook was his life support, and somewhere in the files he'd begun a list of everything he had to remember for today—

There it was. He scrolled down the list. Flowers. He'd forgotten flowers for his grandmother.

There was plenty of time. He'd just take Nanna's car and zip into town. It wasn't that far away.

Hadn't Nanna shown him pictures of the bridal flowers she'd selected? This town, as small as it was, had a florist shop.

"Where are you going?" Nanna demanded when she caught up with him in the kitchen. "My friend Helen is here, and your sister will be by any second to help me get ready for the party. Are those my car keys?"

"If you let me borrow them, I'll bring you home a surprise."

"All right, then, fine. Take my car, but you be careful, young man. My Chevy is older than you are, so show her some respect. And absolutely no speeding."

"I'm not a teenager, remember?" He kissed her cheek. "I'll be good. I promise."

He said hello to Nanna's friend, pocketed the car keys and escaped out the back door while he had the chance.

The defroster in her pickup couldn't keep up with the fog. Julie swiped at the windshield with the cuff of her jacket sleeve, watching the endless curtain of gray rain that obscured the road ahead. What was that up ahead? She squinted to make out the faintest red glow flashing in the thick gray mists. Taillights. Someone was in trouble.

Julie braked, easing to a stop in the road behind an old sedan. She hit her flasher as thunder cracked overhead. Her pulse kicked high and fast in fear, and she reached for her purse, feeling for her cell phone.

There was no sign of anyone anywhere. Maybe the driver was hurt. Maybe—

A movement in the shadows caught her attention. The tall, broad-shouldered form became a man, rain drenched and awesome, as the lightning cracked behind him, zagging like a crooked finger from the sky to the top of a nearby knoll.

What was he doing out there? Didn't he know it was dangerous?

As thunder clapped, Julie bolted into the storm, ignoring the cut of ice through her jacket and the sting of rain on her face. "Hey! Get back in your car—"

Lightning splintered the sky the same second the man turned. The earth began to shake like a hundred earthquakes beneath her feet. As the thunder boomed like cannon fire, Julie saw it all in an instant. The bright streak of light overhead, the man leaping toward her and the spark of fire as a tree beside the road flashed with flames.

All she could feel was the steel-hard impact of his shoulder, the dizzying spin of rain as it knifed from the sky and the drum of cattle racing by. She hit the muddy earth with a breath-stealing thud.

Pain rocketed through her body and her head smacked on the rocky earth. The man's hand curled around the back of her head, cushioning the shock. Fighting for air, she was only dimly aware of the lightning and thunder, the cold and wet. The man's face was a blur as he crouched over her. A tree limb crashed to the ground at her side. Fire licked at the leaves, even as the rain made the flames smoke and die.

"Are you all right?" he asked in a voice as deep as night, as powerful as the storm.

She gasped for air but couldn't draw it into her lungs. Fighting panic, she knew she wasn't hurt seriously. All she had to do was relax—

"You've had the wind knocked out of you. You're going to be fine." The rumble of his voice was comforting as he lifted her from the ground and leaned her against his chest.

What a strong chest it was, too. Sitting up, Julie felt a little better. Cold air rushed in as her lungs began to relax.

Thankful, she breathed in and out. She felt nauseated, but she wasn't going to be sick. Icy rain stung her face, the wind buffeted her and thunder hurt her ears.

"We'd better get you inside your truck." He took her hand, helping her to her feet. "You'll be warm there. I don't want you to drive, just sit and get your bearings, okay?"

Her toe caught the edge of pavement and she stumbled. His iron-strong hand curled around her elbow, catching her before she could fall. "I can make it."

"Good. I'd help you, but I think someone is in trouble. That's why I got out of my car." He let go of her hand. "You'll be all right?"

"Who's in trouble? What did you see?"

"All I know is that there's a horse with an empty saddle in that field. I was going to take a look when you pulled up."

"I'll come with you."

"I don't think that's a good idea." Lightning flashed the same moment thunder pealed. "It's dangerous. I want you safe in your truck so I can go help who's in trouble."

"Safe? Well, *you'd* be safer if you stayed in your car, too."

"I'm a risk taker," he told her. "A dangerous sort of guy. I don't need safety."

Thunder rattled the ground beneath her feet and seemed to shake her very bones, but it didn't distract her from the man's dazzling grin.

Dangerous? Oh, yes. He was handsome and confident and a complete stranger. There would be time later to ask who he was and where he was from. Right now someone might be in trouble. She scanned the field. "Where did you see the horse?"

"There." He gestured toward the far rise as lightning singed the air around them.

Julie could barely make out the bay pony in the

downpour. "I know that horse. That horse wouldn't run off and leave his rider."

She took off at a run as the rain turned to hard balls of hail. Ice struck her like boxer's gloves as she raced across the field and over a knoll to the creek below rapidly swelling with runoff. The bay wheeled with fear as lightning and thunder resounded across the sky.

"Hailey!" Julie called, snaring hold of the gelding's reins. She couldn't make out anything in the gray and white storm.

"There." He spotted the child first, a small dark shadow on the other side of the creek. "That water's rising fast."

"We can cross it." Julie saw the gelding was in good shape and uninjured, but too panicked to ride through the fast-moving current. She tied him quickly to a willow branch, so he wouldn't injure himself further. He'd be safe, for now.

"Be careful," she shouted. "The water's rising and it's more dangerous than it looks."

The stranger was already at the steep bank. "Stay here where it's safe. I'm going in."

"No, wait!" Julie called, running full out, but the effects of her earlier fall held her back. She wasn't up to one hundred percent. "The current's fast—"

As if he didn't hear her or understand the danger, he plunged off the bank and disappeared beneath the muddy water coursing dark and deep.

Chapter Three

Knowing the flooded creek was powerful enough to knock a man down and keep him there, Julie grabbed the rope from the saddle and ran. She could feel her lungs straining—they were still tight—and air gasped in and out of her throat, but she pushed harder.

She wasn't about to let him drown.

The water pulled at her shoes as she secured the rope to a fence post. Her fingers felt clumsy as she tested the knot, but it held. The creek licked at the rope, sucking it out of her hands. She wrestled it back, held tight and leaped into the rising creek.

The shock of the water turned her skin to ice. Lightning flared so close she could feel the crackle in the air. Thunder crashed, rattling her very bones. Above the hammering hail, she heard the thin wail of a frightened child.

"It's okay, Hailey," she called to the little girl, but the wind snatched her words and tore them apart.

"Where is he?" The current pushed like a bulldozer at her ankles, then her knees. He'd fallen in right here. Where was he? What if she couldn't find him? What if the current had swept him downstream? *Lord, please help me find him....*

"Toss me the rope!" a deep voice boomed above the roaring storm. "I can get across, I know it."

Julie stumbled. Thank God! There he was, climbing out of the water onto a snagged stump in the middle of the creek. The powerful current buckled around him. He looked muddy, soaking wet and blood oozed from a cut on his forehead, but from where she stood, he looked invincible.

Since she wasn't a blue-ribbon roper for nothing, she tossed the line, watching it uncoil as it sailed through the air and into the man's outstretched hand.

"Good throw!" he shouted. "Stay there where it's safe."

One thing about this stranger was really starting to annoy her. He was bossy, and she wasn't staying anywhere. "If Hailey's hurt, you'll need my help."

He glanced over his shoulder at her. Through the driving wind and thick hail, she could see surprise flash in his dark eyes.

Handsome guy. She didn't get the chance to think on that any further because the current knocked her feet out from under her. The rope held her as she kicked her way across the swollen creek. She surfaced just in time to see the big man kneel on the ground beside the fallen child.

"Are you all right, little girl?" His voice was kind, and it was amazing to watch how calm he was, how steady. "I'm Noah. What's your name?"

"H-Hailey," the child sobbed.

Julie secured the rope and dropped to the girl's other side. "Hi, there, cutie. What are you doing out here in the storm?"

"Miss Renton!" Hailey flew off the ground, burrowing into Julie's middle. "I wasn't supposed to be riding Bandit, but I didn't know it was gonna storm. Honest. He fell real hard. Is he hurt?"

"He looks perfectly fine to me." Julie soothed the little girl who'd been in her kindergarten class two years ago.

"Are you hurt anywhere, Hailey?" The man—Noah—leaned close, dripping mud and creek water on Julie's sleeve. "Tell me what hurts."

She cried. "My arm."

"Sounds like it's pretty bad." He leaned close, and even though he'd been at the bottom of a creek, he smelled wonderful—like an expensive aftershave, spice and molasses rich. "Let me take a look."

"Are you a doctor?" Hailey sniffled.

"No, but I broke my wrist once, so I consider

myself an authority." Noah gently cradled Hailey's thin forearm and pushed her sleeve up over her elbow.

"Ow," she cried again.

"That could be a break. Look at the swelling." Noah's eyes met Julie's and there was concern in them. "It would be best if we can stabilize it."

"Just what I was going to say. We can use small branches from one of the cottonwoods." Julie cradled the girl in her lap, protecting her from the wind and hail. "Do you hurt anywhere else, Hailey?"

"Nope." She snuggled closer, whining a little in pain.

"Good. We'll get you home soon, I promise."

"Here." Noah reappeared with two fairly straight branches, stout-looking enough to stabilize Hailey's arm.

They worked together, as the wind strengthened and the temperature dipped. The hail turned to ice. Freezing wherever it fell, it turned the landscape to a white wintry world.

"Here, give her to me." Noah took the child in his arms as easily as if she were a doll, and tucked her beneath his jacket. Snug against his chest, at least Hailey would be as warm as possible.

The creek had risen to a dangerous level. There was no way to go around, so they went straight through. Noah held on to the rope, and Julie helped him keep Hailey out of the water. Julie fell once and

Noah slipped, but the taut line kept them both upright. Exhausted, they made it to the opposite bank.

"Is there a hospital nearby?" Noah shouted to be heard over the fierce storm. "She's cold. Too cold."

"Her grandmother lives just up the road. We'll take her there." Julie slipped and slid through the icy field until the pavement was safely under their feet.

She took one look at the sedan off to the side of the road, taillights flashing eerily through the thick white curtain of snow. "Let's get her into my truck. I've got four-wheel drive."

"Something tells me we might need it." Noah cradled the child out of the wind.

Julie yanked open the door, threw the seat back to grab a couple blankets stashed there.

"You get the truck started." He stole the blankets from her. "We've got to get her warm."

That was what she was about to do, but she didn't waste time arguing. She ducked her head into the wind, scrambled across the snow and ice to the driver's side, and turned the key in the ignition. The engine leaped to life and tepid air puffed out of the vents. Julie turned the heater on high. At least the engine hadn't cooled off completely—she was thankful for that.

Hailey's tears echoed in the cab. Wrapped in two blankets, shivering in Noah's strong arms, she looked small and vulnerable. But safe.

Julie smoothed the girl's tangled curls. "You're going to be warm soon, I promise."

"Want my d-daddy."

"We'll get you to him, I promise." Julie tugged the cell phone from her purse and tried dialing. "With the luck I've been having, I should have known this wouldn't work. It's the storm. I've got to scrape the windshield—"

She got out of the truck and slammed the door shut, not needing his instruction. Cold had settled like pain in her midsection and, being wet to the skin, she actually couldn't get much colder. As she dug the scraper into the stubborn frozen mess on her windshield, she fought the driving ice with each swipe. Her hands were numb and she kept working until she'd pried the windshield wipers free.

The truck was mildly warm, but she couldn't feel the heat or her feet as she pushed in the clutch. "Hailey, how are you doing?"

"Still want my d-daddy."

"We'll find him for you, don't you worry." With a prayer on her lips, Julie backed onto the road. She couldn't see much, but there were no headlights coming her way.

Everything she'd fretted over and worried about today was insignificant now as she clenched her teeth to keep them from rattling. She wrapped her numb fingers around the steering wheel and peered through the veil of white hiding the road from her sight.

All that mattered was getting Hailey home.

Over the rasp of the wipers on the windshield and the whir of the heater, Noah's low, melted-chocolate voice seemed to drive away the fury of the storm. He was talking to Hailey, assuring her that her horse would be all right, and asking her questions about the animal. What was his name? How old was he? Was he a good horse?

Hailey answered quietly in a trembling voice. As the minutes passed and warmth filled the cab, the girl stopped shaking and climbed onto the seat between them. She told how she'd been racing Bandit for home to beat the lightning, but he got real scared.

Out of the corner of her eye, Julie couldn't help watching the big man who seemed to fill up half the cab. He had to be well over six foot, by the way his knees were bent to keep from hitting the glove box. It had been something how he'd taken care of Hailey.

"I had a pony once, too," Noah told the girl. "I rode him to play polo."

"Polo?" Julie had to question him on that. "No respectable Montanan plays polo. Rides broncos, maybe, ropes calf, definitely. But polo?"

"I was only a kid at the time, so don't hold it against me. Now I like baseball. Do Montanans like baseball?"

"What kind of question is that?" She nodded toward the minor league cap on the dash. "Okay, so I won't toss you out on your ear, but only if you never mention polo again."

"You drive a hard bargain, Miss Renton." He winked at her.

With his hair wet and slicked away from his face, and his jacket clinging to every contour of his remarkable chest, he looked like a dream come true.

He's trouble, Julie. Big-time, one-hundred-percent trouble. A sensible woman would keep the Continental Divide between them—and that's exactly what she was going to do.

As soon as she got Hailey home.

Heaven was kind to her, because she spotted the Coreys' driveway and eased off the road. The tires churned up the steep lane. No sooner had she slid to a stop in front of the carport, there was Mrs. Corey, arms outstretched, taking Hailey from Noah's arms.

"I can't believe you found her. Praise be, Julie, you're a lifesaver."

"Not me. I just did the driving," Julie gestured toward the strong man, holding the back door open for Mrs. Corey. "Noah here is the hero. He saw Hailey fall from her horse and stopped to help."

"No! Say you didn't." Mrs. Corey paled as she set Hailey down on the chair in front of the pellet stove and turned to stare at the handsome stranger. "Aren't you Noah? Of course, I've heard of you.

Goodness, won't this be a story to tell. Hailey, my girl, you're hurt."

Noah knelt down, carefully taking the wet blankets. "We splinted her arm just to be safe. She should see a doctor."

"I'll call my nephew. He's a medical doctor and he's out looking for this little one, right along with the others. I've got to run and get hot water started. Julie, be a dear and call them on the radio."

"Sure thing. I'll send someone after Hailey's horse, too." As she left the room, she smoothed wet locks of hair out of her face and tucked them behind her ear.

A graceful gesture, and Noah couldn't look away as she crossed the room. Her jeans and sweatshirt were baggy and stained with mud from the creek.

She was no fashion statement, but there was something that made him look and keep looking. She was simply beautiful. Not made up or artificial, but genuine.

"Miss Renton's awful nice," Hailey whispered to him while they were alone. "She got a broken heart."

"A broken heart?"

"'Cuz she had to give the ring back. A *really* pretty one. It sparkled and everything."

Hmm. A broken engagement, huh? Noah couldn't help turning his attention to Julie. She stood in the kitchen, visible above the countertops, where she was signing off on a handheld radio.

"Mrs. Corey, do you mind if I borrow your phone?" she called down the hall. "I've got to get a hold of Pastor Bill. I'm guessing that the party is canceled."

"What? You can't let the storm get in the way of an important celebration." Mrs. Corey marched into view, with a warm blanket outstretched. "Look, the snow's already stopping."

Julie Renton. Noah thought about that. She had to be related to Harold Renton, the man he'd met today. The man ready to marry his grandmother and her money.

"I've got a bath running." Mrs. Corey tapped into the room and scooped Hailey from the warm chair. "We'll warm you up and get you into some clean clothes, and by that time the doctor will be here. Thank you again, Mr. Ashton."

"No problem, ma'am." He straightened. "Just make sure Hailey's going to be all right."

"She will be. Thanks to you and Julie."

Julie appeared, frowning. "Pastor Bill has promised to clear the walkways right away. I guess the party is still on."

"We'll try to make it, dear. You drive safely now, and thanks again." Mrs. Corey gave her a hug and, carrying Hailey deeper into the house, disappeared from sight.

"Did I hear her right?" Julie asked the minute they were in the truck. "Did she call you 'Mr. Ashton'?"

"Some people have been known to do that."

"Why?"

"Because it's my name."

The gleam of the dash lights showed the shock on her face. "You're Nora's grandson, the billionaire."

"True."

"James Noah Ashton the Third." She closed her mouth and put the truck into reverse. "What should have been my first clue? That you know how to play polo?"

"You're Harold's granddaughter, the one he kept calling his angel."

"I'm no angel. Granddad is just—" She wiped the fog from the rear window and backed up. "You wouldn't understand."

"Why not?"

"Because he's simply wonderful. And I'm telling you right here, if you don't treat him with respect, you and I are going to have serious problems."

"I'm not looking for trouble." He did his best to sound innocent. "Not unless it's already there."

"What does that mean?" She jammed the gearshift into first and held it while she eased out the clutch. "I knew it. This is what I've been afraid of all along. You're going to cause trouble because you don't think my decent, wonderful grandfather is good enough for a billionaire's grandmother."

"Where did you get an idea like that? I only want what's best for Nanna."

Only want what's best? Julie didn't like the sound of that. "Then you mean my granddad isn't?"

"That's not what I said. I'm trying to keep an open mind."

"Trying?" She popped the truck out of gear on the steep slope, gripping the steering wheel so tightly, her knuckles were white. "Tell me you haven't come to try to stop the wedding."

"Why would I do that? I won't break my grandmother's heart unless there's a good reason. If your grandfather is the decent man you say he is, there will be no problem. You have my word on that."

Something troubled her, but Julie couldn't figure out what as she applied steady pressure to the brakes and turned into the spin as the truck slid. "Then you're here only to help celebrate this engagement? You're not against it? You don't dislike my granddad?"

"I came all the way from New York just to make my grandmother happy by attending her party. That's all for now. You can't blame me for wanting to protect her. Aside from my sister, Nanna's the only family I have."

"Then you understand how I feel about Granddad." Julie's blood pressure crept back down to normal, and she didn't hold the wheel quite so hard as she pulled onto the main road. "All my life he's been there for me. Supportive. Understanding. Someone I could depend on. I don't intend to let anyone hurt him."

"Then we agree." The deep lines etched in Noah's forehead vanished and he relaxed against the seat. "No mother or father?"

"No. Mom ran off when I was in eighth grade, and three years later my dad was thrown from a horse and killed." She swallowed hard, but the pain after all those years was still there. Would always be.

"I'm sorry for your losses. That had to be tough."

"With the Lord's help and my granddad, I managed to get through all right." She didn't tell him how lonely she'd been, living with relatives, always feeling as if she didn't belong. "Granddad's guidance made all the difference in the world to me when I was growing up."

"I know just how you feel." He nodded once, his gaze pinning hers.

She felt an odd connection between them. Suddenly the truck's passenger cab seemed to shrink and he was way too close. She was alone with one of the richest men in the country—probably on the planet—and he wasn't at all what she expected or what she would have predicted him to be.

"There's Nanna's car. It's a classic, she tells me. I think she's fooling herself because a refrigerator would be warmer than that heater she has."

Julie shifted into neutral and coasted to a stop.

"If you want, I can give you a ride to her house. You're as wet and cold as I am."

"I'm tough." He flashed her a megawatt smile. "I guess I'll see you in a few. At the party. Save me a dance, will you?"

"Sure. No problem. I'll fit you in between the corporate raider millionaire I'm seeing and my supermodel ex-boyfriend."

He laughed, deep and rich, and there was something about him. He was like a flawless diamond and she was a cubic zirconia.

"Later." He'd meant it as goodbye, but it sounded more like a promise.

The door slicked shut. The fog and ice on the windshield had completely cleared away, giving her a perfect view of Noah's confident, powerful gait. As if the cold couldn't touch him, he moved easily, without hurry, and stopped to fish the keys from his trouser pocket.

She waited until the car had started before she put her truck in gear. As she passed by, Noah rolled down his window and waved to her.

Her pulse skipped an entire beat. And why was that? she asked herself as she negotiated the icy road. What she felt was *not* attraction. She simply refused to be attracted. Hadn't she learned her lesson? Hadn't her heart been broken enough?

True love wasn't God's will for her, and she accepted it. Plain and simple.

As for that little skip in her vital signs, she'd simply forget it ever happened. She had a party to host. A grandfather to see married. For the first time in a year, she was standing on level ground. She was happy. She wasn't going to mess that up by wishing for a man who was out of her league.

Chapter Four

Noah turned off the ignition in the church's packed parking lot. *Lord, please let this engagement be right for Nanna.* He wanted nothing more than the absolute best for his grandmother, but with his opinions of marriage…well, what if she were making a mistake?

The possibility that she might sell her land and that Harold Renton, no matter how kind he looked, could strip Nanna of her sizable financial assets burned like a sickness in Noah's stomach.

Please, let this man she's marrying be good enough for her. Noah wished he could stop worrying, but since he'd accumulated his own sizable fortune, he'd learned how far ruthless people would go to get their hands on easy money. Even people who looked perfectly nice and who had perfectly nice relatives.

Sitting in the stillness of his grandmother's sedan, he felt no reassurances. Snow beat on the windshield and the wind buffeted the side of the car, driving the cold in. Even through the lacy accumulation on the windshield, he could see that the church hall was lit up like a Christmas tree, decorations visible in the windows.

It looked like the party was in full swing, and that meant it was about time for him to make an appearance. Luckily, he wouldn't have to stay long. He'd greet his sister, congratulate his grandmother and hit the road. There were a lot of women in that room, judging by what he could see through the window.

His stomach blazed with anxiety. Since his last romantic disaster years ago, he avoided most social situations. He'd learned the hard way there was no such thing as true love. He had his own fortune to protect.

Well, he couldn't sit in the car all evening.

A blast of cold air lashed through him when he climbed from the heated interior. At least the ice storm had tamed into a peaceful snowfall. White flakes tumbled all around him, accumulating quickly on the freshly shoveled sidewalk. His shoes slid, but he managed to make it to the door okay.

The chorus of "Blue Moon" drew him down the well-lit hall, and the warm blast from the furnace chased away the chill from outside. His stomach still burned. He decided to ignore it.

"Hey, stranger."

Heels tapped in the corridor behind him. He spotted Julie Renton closing in on him.

She tossed him that dazzling smile of hers as she looked him up and down. "You sure clean up nice."

"So do you." Very nice. She looked dynamite in an off-white gown with long, slim sleeves and a narrow waist. The skirt flared softly around her to skim the floor. Classic. "I've come with a peace offering."

"I didn't know we were at war."

"Maybe we should call it a limited skirmish. Over you wanting to protect your grandfather." He tugged the small plastic box from his jacket pocket. "I didn't know what was appropriate, but when I saw white roses, I thought of you."

She took the box in her slim hands. Surprise made her sparkle. "A corsage. I'm speechless."

"Lucky for you, no words are necessary." He opened the top of the plastic container and lifted the single rose, wrapped in baby's breath and a silk ivory ribbon, from its bed. He withdrew the pin. "Remember the promise you made me?"

"What promise?"

"To save me a dance."

Okay, so he was a lot nicer than she first thought. Julie couldn't quite look him in the eye as she held the collar of her dress so he could pin on the flower. It smelled lovely, sweet and soft.

It was perfect and thoughtful. She never should have judged this man before she met him.

He fumbled with the pin. So, he wasn't experienced at corsage pinning. Neither was she. She held her breath, aware of their closeness.

"This is trickier than it looks," he confessed with a lopsided grin. "There. I think that should do it."

She glanced down. "I like my peace offering. Does this mean I should give you something? Isn't that expected in peace time negotiations?"

"I'm holding out for that dance you promised me."

"What am I going to do with you? A man who brings gifts and likes to dance?" She slipped her arm around his, liking the friendly, solid feel of him. "I suppose I could agree to your terms, but it's going to cost you more than a flower."

"Fine. I can afford it." He opened one of the double doors. "Name your price."

"If you want to dance with me, then you also have to dance with my two good friends."

"Friends. I should have known." He didn't seem offended as he guided her through the room. "Playing matchmaker, are you?"

"Against my better judgment," she admitted, because it made him laugh again. "They begged and pleaded."

"I don't mind at all," he agreed pleasantly, scanning the crowded room. "You did a great job, Julie. I'm sure my grandmother is pleased."

That meant a lot, coming from the only billionaire in the room. From the man who'd given her a corsage.

"There's Nanna." He nodded in the direction of the dance floor. "It's good to see my grandmother happy."

There was no doubt he meant it, and that he loved his grandmother. Julie knew just how that felt. Her heart ached at the sweet sight of her granddad and his grandmother swaying to the last chorus, gazing into each other's eyes as if they'd found true love.

True love. She knew from firsthand experience exactly how rare that precious gift was. She prayed her grandfather would know nothing but joy for the rest of his days. "They're a perfect couple. They light up from inside when they're together."

"They make you want to believe." He held out his hand, palm up, as the piano belted out the first strains of "Strangers in Paradise." "Remember our deal?"

"How could I forget?" She placed her fingers on his palm, featherlight.

A sharp sensation wedged hard beneath his sternum and stayed there. He ignored it, closed his fingers over Julie's and led her through the tables to the area in front of the band. It was hard to miss all the people turning in their seats to watch him pass. He tried not to think about it or the sharpness in his chest.

Just stress—that's what it was. He'd take a deep breath and… Pain pierced his sternum, as hot as fire and razor sharp. He missed a step, and Julie's grip on his arm tightened.

"Noah, are you all right?"

He was still standing, but he felt like a fool, so he kept dancing. "Yep. Just overwhelmed by my dance partner's beauty."

"Good try, but you can't fool me." Her fingers remained a firm presence on his arm. She squinted up at him, narrowing her pretty eyes, as if she wasn't about to be tricked by the likes of him. "You need to sit down before you fall down. You're breathing funny. Are you having any chest pain?"

"It's my weak ankle, that's all." He didn't want her to know the truth. "It's an old polo match injury."

"The fib would have gone over better if you'd used a baseball game instead of polo. You keep forgetting. You're in Montana now."

He rolled his eyes, pretending to be annoyed. "It's hard to forget where I am with so many Stetsons around."

"Not your typical Lower Manhattan attire, huh? Watch out. If you stay here too long, you'll be wearing a hat and boots and learning to ride."

"I'm heading back to New York first thing tomorrow morning."

"You work on Saturdays?"

"Sure. Got a busy week to look forward to." He was already starting to feel better. Maybe the pain was going to go away now.

She allowed him to pull her close—not too close—and whirl her to the Frank Sinatra tune. She'd almost made him forget the pain. Almost. It returned in a sharp lash through his chest, doubled in intensity.

Breathe deep. It will go away. At least, he was praying it would. "Really, I'm fine."

Julie froze in his arms. "That's it. Something *is* wrong. You look practically gray. You're sitting down. *Now.*"

"It's nothing to worry about. Probably just the clean air out here. I'm not used to such purity." I refuse to be sick. I'm not sick. *Please don't let me be sick, Lord.* Not at Nanna's party.

"You and your excuses. Unfortunately for you, I'm a teacher. I'm immune to them." Julie frowned and pressed her hand to his forehead. Her skin was cool and soothing. "I also have lots of practice with sick kids, so I can recognize the signs."

"I'm no kindergartner." Okay, now he was getting annoyed. "I don't get sick."

"Everyone gets sick now and then." With the way she bit her lip, she looked as if she was trying not to laugh. "Fine, have it your way. Come with me. *I'm* feeling sick."

Well, if she was feeling ill, he'd go along with her. "Maybe you need some fresh air, too."

"How did you know?" She was teasing him now, and he wasn't sure if he liked it. Miss Julie Renton seemed far too sure of herself as she hauled him out the back door and into a dark room.

"I'll be right back," she promised like the angel she was, disappearing through the door, leaving him alone.

The tightness in his chest was worse. Much worse. He just had to breathe deep. Relax. This was stress, that was all. It had to be. He was too young to have a heart attack, right?

Blade-sharp pain sliced from back to front, leaving him panting. He tugged loose his tie and popped the top buttons on his shirt. This is only stress. Just a lot of stress. So that meant he could will the pain away….

The door swung open, and warm air spilled across him where he sat on the concrete floor, clutching his chest. He saw Julie's eyes widen and the shock on her face, then the door slammed shut, leaving them alone in the empty room.

She sank to the step next to him and pressed a plastic cup in his hands. "You're not looking so good."

"Then I'm looking better than I feel." The punch was sweet and cold. It tasted great, but didn't do a thing for the pain in his chest. It hurt to breathe. It hurt to move. It hurt to do anything. He set the cup on the step behind him.

"I'm going to go fetch Dr. Corey." Julie's touch

on his shoulder felt like a rare comfort. One he wouldn't mind hanging on to.

"No doctor." He cut off a groan of pain. Sweat broke out on his face. "This isn't anything."

"Sure, you mean, the way a heart attack isn't anything?" She slipped the tie from beneath his collar. "Let's get you lying down."

He caught her by the wrist, holding her tightly so she would understand. "I'm not having a heart attack."

"If you want to stay in denial, fine." She pulled a worn blanket from a nearby shelf. "There's a doctor on the other side of that door. I won't be gone a minute."

"Don't leave, Julie. It's not a heart attack." At least, he thought it wasn't. "It's some kind of stress thing. I've already been to the emergency room over this."

"Same symptoms?"

He nodded, pain hitting him like a sledgehammer. It left him helpless, struggling to breathe. He hated this.

Julie's cool fingers pressed the inside of his wrist. "You swear that you're not going to die on me?"

"Didn't last time."

"Great. That's comforting." She shook the blanket out and draped it over his shoulders. "I'll go get your grandmother."

"Don't tell Nanna." He choked on the words. The air in his lungs turned to fire. He couldn't say anything more. He couldn't tell her how important this was. To keep this secret from his grandmother. Please, he silently begged.

"What am I going to do with you if you have a heart attack on me?" She said it as though he was bothering her, but he could see the fear tight at her mouth. The worry furrowed lines into her forehead. "I should go get the doctor, call the ambulance and make them wheel you out of here."

"That would ruin my grandmother's party."

"I'm sure she wouldn't see it that way."

"I don't care. You're not calling anyone." More pain spliced through his chest. He leaned his forehead on his knees. His palms felt clammy. Just like last time.

He flashed back to last week. To being trapped in the emergency room, the monitors beeping, voices above him blurring, the ceiling tiles too bright and his fears too enormous.

The same fears whipped through him now. "Please."

What was she going to do? Julie knew she had to get him help. How could she go against his wishes? She understood exactly how important his grandmother was to him. "Can you make it to the parking lot?"

"I will make it." His hand found hers and squeezed.

She felt the need in his touch. Strong and stark, as if he had no one else to turn to. Maybe he wasn't used to relying on others.

She knew how that felt.

She helped him up. When he couldn't straighten, she almost pushed him back down. He needed a doctor. Now, not later. But he took one limping step out of her reach. He was one determined man. His back was slightly stooped and his shoulders slouched from the pain. His face was ash-gray.

The poor man. Julie grabbed the heavy back door before he could, and pushed it open. The wind roared in, snatching the blanket from his shoulders.

She caught hold of the wool and smoothed it back into place. A fierce desire took root in her heart, one she didn't understand. She needed to take care of him, to make sure he came through this all right. She'd give Misty or Susan a call and ask them to take care of things. The party would go on just fine.

All that mattered was this man at her side. The one who seemed so alone.

She knew how that felt, too.

Noah swore hours had passed, but he'd been watching the clock on the pickup's dash so he knew it was exactly seventeen minutes later when Julie pulled into the well-lit driveway. The red flash of ambulance lights glowed eerily in the snowfall. Pain seized him up so tight he could only breathe in little puffs.

Noah was dimly aware of a cold gust of air when she opened the door. She called out to someone by name, and the next thing he knew he was being hauled from the passenger seat and laid on a gurney.

He searched for Julie, but couldn't find her. Strangers' faces stared down at him as the world around him blurred and the gurney bumped over the concrete and through the electric doors. The ceiling tiles flashed above him like lines on a highway.

I don't want to be here. I'll do anything, Lord, if I can come out of this all right. I'll work less. I'll eat better. I'll take a vacation. I'll listen to my sister. I'll do everything my grandmother says. Just get me through this.

He knew he was bargaining. Pain roared like an erupting volcano in his chest, and he didn't know what else to do. He only wanted the pain to stop.

More strangers crowded around him. A needle pricked his arm. Cables tugged at the skin on his chest. Monitors beeped too fast, or it sounded that way. He worried about that, too.

We need to run some tests, the doctor back home had told him. But there had been meetings that couldn't be delayed, deadlines that had to be met and a business to tend to.

It was easy to put off a few tests, because a lot of people depended on him for their jobs. Jobs that made their lives better. That was important, and the attack he'd had was due to stress, so it was nothing to worry about.

Now he wasn't so certain.

As the people worked around him, grim and efficient, he had to admit it. Something was wrong. He couldn't deny it any longer.

"Your EKG looks good." The doctor jotted something down on a clipboard. "We need a few tests."

Relief left him feeling numb. That meant it wasn't a heart attack, right? He'd been fairly certain it wasn't—it hadn't been last time. But the pain had been so fierce, he'd started to wonder. It was probably just stress again. He would stop working on weekends maybe and get more exercise. That ought to take care of it, right?

A light tap of heeled shoes sounded on the tile floor near the door. Julie? He hoped so. This place was feeling lonely, and he wouldn't mind seeing a familiar face.

The shoes hesitated on the other side of the blue curtain, then a chair rasped against the floor. "Sarah," a stranger's voice said to someone else on the other side of the curtain on the other bed.

Noah stared at the partition. So, it wasn't Julie. He wasn't disappointed, really. He didn't mind being alone. She'd probably become bored and went back to the party.

That was okay. Alone was *his* choice. It was much better than the alternative. He believed that with his whole heart. All he had to do was remember his parents and their marriage. Their fighting and their constant discord.

They'd been so polished in public, because appearance was everything, that no one outside the family would ever have guessed the truth. Noah suspected many marriages were like that—pleasant on the outside, but painful on the inside.

A soft voice broke through his thoughts. "Hey, they said the drugs are helping."

"The pain is better." He opened his eyes to see Julie at his side, looking out of place in her beautiful party dress. "What are you still doing here? I thought you'd want to go looking for excitement."

"I called my friends, and they're taking care of everything at the party. You just close your eyes and relax. I'll stay right here with you." Her hand curled around his. Her gentle touch was sweeter than anything he'd ever known.

He held on tight. "What about your boyfriend?"

"I don't have a boyfriend. I decided you men weren't worth the hassle."

That's right. The broken engagement. "You should be dating someone, a pretty woman like you."

"Me? What about you? A smooth-talker like

you has to have five girlfriends on a string. Do you want me to call one of them so she can play your angel of mercy?"

"I'll leave that to you."

"I'm terrible at mercy, but I can teach you the alphabet."

"I already know it."

"How about finger painting? How to color between the lines?"

"Already mastered both." He could picture her, firmly guiding a classroom of small children. Her students probably adored her. "I'm hooked up to all these monitors, but I am cognizant enough to notice you changed the subject."

"Which subject?"

She looked to be all innocence, but she didn't fool him. He hadn't built his company from a basement operation by luck alone. "Your boyfriend. He's probably pining for you, brokenhearted."

"I'm not dating anyone, Mr. Nosy. I think they gave you too many painkillers. If you were in more pain, you wouldn't have the energy to interrogate me."

"It helps pass the time."

"Then maybe I should torture you?" She lifted her chin, all challenge, all sparkle. "I guess I don't have the time. They've come to take you away."

An orderly pulled back the curtain. "They're ready for you down at X ray."

X ray. That didn't sound too painful.

Julie's squeezed his hand before she stepped away, a final show of comfort, and then they were wheeling him away, leaving her behind.

He'd never felt more alone in his life.

Chapter Five

The glow from the church windows seemed to light up the parking lot, reflecting off the falling snow. Noah took another swig from the water bottle he'd picked up at the drugstore. The pain pills were in his breast pocket, unopened. He was hurting, but it was getting better.

It looked as though tomorrow morning he'd be going in for more tests. He'd talked the doctor out of an overnight hospital stay, but a flight back tonight was out. Whatever the problem was, it needed to be dealt with. Noah clamped his jaw tight. He hated doctors.

"Are you sure you can make it home?" Julie pulled the parking brake, leaving the engine idling. "I can drive you. Granddad can return Nora's car tomorrow morning."

What was with Julie? Why was she helping him? Nobody was *that* nice. That was the lesson life always seemed to teach him. Every time he trusted a woman, she turned out to be someone different. Someone who wanted something from him. Every single time.

The glow from the dash lights illuminated the concern on her heart-shaped face. A genuine concern, no different from what she'd shown the little girl they'd rescued in the storm. Julie Renton was a bona fide nice person. There was no other explanation for it.

"You can stop helping me, now." He tugged the tie from his pocket and shook the folds from it. "Because of me, you missed most of the party you planned and paid for. You missed being with your friends. You didn't get dinner or dessert."

"True, but I got a lovely tour of the hospital and a new friend. That's not a bad deal."

"Thanks for hanging out with me." He didn't know quite how to say it. How did you tell someone you hardly knew how alone you were? "You made things better for me."

"You really scared me, Noah."

"I scared me, too." Words caught in his throat. He wasn't used to speaking honestly about his fears.

"I'd better get in there." He grabbed the door handle. Didn't want to go. "About the E.R. visit. You won't say anything to my grandmother?"

"It's yours to tell. Or not."

He leaned across the seat and kissed her cheek. Her hair smelled as fresh as strawberries. Her sweetness clung to him as he opened the door. "Thank you."

His chest felt tight with emotions. He couldn't begin to sort them out, so he stepped into the cold and dark. The snow was slick beneath his shoes as he circled the truck.

He caught her elbow as she was climbing from the cab, her long skirt swirling in the wind. "Couldn't wait for me to open your door, could you? Whoever the guy was who broke your heart, he was no gentleman."

"So, you've already heard about that? Nothing's a secret in a small town." Snow clung to her hair, shimmering like priceless diamonds in the light, this friend the Lord had sent to him on this night. "No, he wasn't. If he'd been more like you, I might have kept him."

"If he were rich, you mean." Noah wasn't fooled. He knew the way the world worked. Love always had its price.

"No." Julie sounded angry, and she looked angry, too. "If he were as nice as you. Kind beats out rich any day."

She was a kindergarten teacher. He had to remember that. Julie Renton spent her days reading stories to little kids and teaching the alphabet. She probably drew happy faces in the dots over her *i*'s and put gold stars on every child's school page. She wore rose-colored glasses to view the world, but it was a nice outlook. It made him like her more.

"The caterer's truck is still here." Julie pointed through the hazy snow to a white van parked at the edge of the crowded lot. "I'm going to go scare up a couple plates of food. There has to be leftovers."

"See if there's any cake left. Chocolate, if they have it."

"Chocolate, huh? I may be forced to raise my opinion of you."

"Of me? What? Do you think I'm an undesirable city slicker?"

"With those shoes? You betcha. Any self-respecting Montanan wears boots."

"You're in heels."

"True, but I couldn't find a pair of boots to match my dress."

"I had the same problem, so I went with trousers." He held the door, wincing a bit. His chest was still sore, but it hardly mattered. Julie was chuckling at him, and it had been a long while since he'd had anyone to laugh with.

Julie couldn't believe it. Noah was standing up straight. Except for the strain at his jaw and the dark circles beneath his eyes, no one would ever know he was hurting. He moved slowly, holding his grandmother tenderly, making her laugh as they danced to a Cole Porter tune.

She set Noah's plate on the table.

"Julie, what happened?" Misty circled the table. "I've been worried about you. Susan said she thought you were at the hospital. She heard sirens in the background. Are you okay?"

"I'm fine." She'd sworn to keep Noah's secret, so she didn't elaborate. "You're wonderful for managing all this. I owe you and Susan a dinner out, my treat."

"I would hope so." Susan joined them, feigning distress. "It was a nightmare. One disaster after another."

Misty winked. "That's right. Maybe you should spring for lunch *and* dinner."

"Funny." Julie collapsed into the closest chair. "Everything went all right?"

"Perfect. You had everything done ahead of time." Susan dropped into the chair next to her. "You and Mr. Billionaire left about the same time."

"Mysteriously," Misty added. "Is he nice?"

"Very." He had been terribly ill, but he danced the last dance of the night with his grandmother. Without a single word of complaint. That was nice, in her book.

Susan slipped off one high heel and rubbed her toes. "Is it true what everyone's saying? Did he really rescue the little Corey girl?"

"He did." The image of him wading through the

harsh storm-tossed creek with little Hailey safe in his arms remained. She'd never forget it. "I saw it with my own two eyes."

"You were alone with him then, too." Susan's gaze narrowed. "Is there something you want to tell us? Did you go steal that handsome rich man right out from under us?"

"I wish." Julie clamped her hand over her mouth. Where had that come from?

"I knew it!" Misty clapped her hands with glee. "Fine, if I have to lose him to someone, it may as well be to my best friend. As long as you let me come stay at your Hawaii beach house."

"Yeah. And at your New York penthouse," Susan chimed in.

"And sail on your multimillion-dollar yacht."

Julie's face flamed. "Enough, you two. Heaven's sake, I played chauffeur for the man. I didn't propose to him."

"Why not?" Susan demanded with a wink.

"I would have." Misty waggled her brows.

"Ladies." A man's pleasant baritone broke through their laughter—Noah. "I couldn't help noticing the beautiful women at this table."

Julie's face burned hotter. How much of their conversation had Noah heard? He stood there, humor curving his mouth, a little too pale and very tired looking. But every bit a gentleman as he took Susan by the elbow and swept her out of her seat.

"Did you see that?" Misty drained all the lemon-lime punch from her glass. "He simply whisked her away. Just like on my favorite soap, when Pierce whisked Jessica away and they fell in love. Oh, this is too unbelievable."

"Unbelievable." There was no other word for it.

"Is he a good dancer?"

"Oh, yeah." Julie couldn't help sighing a little as she watched Noah spin Susan around, slow and sweet. She knew exactly what it felt like to be swept away by him.

"Look at your grandfather," Misty whispered. "He was pretty worried where you went, but I smoothed things over. Look at the way Nora is gazing into his eyes. Now, *that's* true love."

Absolutely. Granddad held Nora tenderly, distinguished in his dark jacket and white shirt, joy transforming him. See? True love did exist. She couldn't wish for more for her granddad. *Thank you, Father, for bringing love into his life again.*

"Since I'm not needed here, I'll go help clean up." Julie climbed to her feet, stealing one more look in Noah's direction. He had Susan laughing and the attention of every woman in the room.

Misty pushed out of her chair. "I'll give you a hand, too, since Susan has the billionaire all to herself."

"Stay put. I happen to know you're next."

"Really? Oh, thank you!"

Several people stopped Julie on the way to the kitchen to ask where she'd been or to comment on the lovely party. It was beautiful. Candles flickered gentle and low. The decorations sparkled like stardust. Flowers scented the air as she pushed open the kitchen door.

"The caterers are almost done." Her friend Karen, who owned the town coffee shop, plunged her hands into the sink. Water sloshed as she scrubbed a pot. "Thought I'd pitch in, so we wouldn't be here cleaning up all night."

"You're an angel." Julie took a dish towel from a nearby shelf and grabbed a soup kettle from the drying rack.

She and Karen talked while they washed and dried. The music from the band kept them entertained, and so did the caterers who dropped nearly everything as they packed their van.

Susan poked her head in after a while. "Harold and Nora are getting ready to leave."

Julie left the dishes and joined the crowd in a long line down the hallway. Shouts of good wishes and congratulations rang in the corridor as Nora and Granddad paraded by. Julie called out her good wishes along with everyone else.

"Hey, beautiful."

"Noah!" She spun around, startled to see him there, looking pallid. "Why are you still here?"

"I'm ready to leave. Just wanted to see them off."

The party was dispersing, voices ringing out in the hallway so loud, it was hard to hear. Julie leaned closer. "This is why you were in the emergency room. I bet you weren't feeling well all day, and you ignored it."

"I refuse to answer that. I'm pleading the Fifth."

For the first time, she got a really good look at Noah Ashton. He wasn't perfect like some air-brushed magazine-cover photograph. Not flawless like a dreamed-up perfect man. He was real and strong and vulnerable all at once, and a man who kept his promises.

That mattered to her. "You didn't have to dance with my friends tonight."

"I wanted to. You see, there's this very nice person who helped me tonight. I didn't want to let her down."

"You do that a lot, I bet. Try not to let people down."

"I try." His gaze strayed to the doorway, where Nora was waving out the passenger window of Harold's pickup.

Noah was so different from the man she expected. Julie touched his sleeve. "I'll be inside if you need anything. Like a ride home. You can't drive if you take painkillers."

"I know." He nodded, in control. "I'm fine."

She watched him take a few steps. "You're limping."

"I'm not." He shuffled forward. "My ankle is tired from all that dancing."

"You're hurting. You should take a pill and let me drive you home."

"My knee's tired, too. I'll just take it slow down the hall. I'm fine."

"You keep saying that."

"Maybe that'll make it true." He tossed her a wink before shouldering through the door.

Julie watched him limp all the way to his grandmother's car.

A handful of kids ran down the hallway, coats dragging, shouting as they went. A cold draft from the open door breezed over her, reminding her that she had work to do. She could still see Noah through the glass in the door, digging car keys from his pocket.

Nice man. Not at all what she'd expected and exactly the kind of man she liked. Didn't that spell trouble?

He'd made it home. Noah took a deep breath, said a prayer of thanks and turned off the engine. Snow pelted the windshield as he sat in the silence. The pain was coming back in slow but steady increments. Probably because the drugs he'd received in the emergency room were wearing off.

Maybe he would take one of the pills from the brown plastic bottle in his jacket pocket. Just to make it through until morning. More tests were awaiting him, starting at 8:00 a.m., when he was supposed to be flying home. There was a finance meeting on Monday morning. He couldn't miss it.

Pain pulsed in the middle of his diaphragm, as if someone was trying to tell him to pay attention. Okay, maybe he'd keep the doctor's appointment. Then he'd worry about his company.

Moving carefully, he climbed out into the winter weather. The night was bitter cold and dark. Driving snow blew him off course. A lilac bush tried to ambush him on the way to the front porch, but he escaped up the steps.

"Noah, come in," Nanna called the instant he opened the door. "My stars, look at you. You're all alone. I can't believe it. I saw you dancing with so many lovely young ladies, why, I kept hoping you'd find my future granddaughter-in-law."

"Keep dreaming, gorgeous." He leaned stiffly, trying not to wince, to kiss her cheek, and noticed the distinguished gentleman sitting on the couch. "Good evening, Harold. You two look as if you need to be alone. I'll just head upstairs."

"Some awfully pretty girls." Nanna bounded up from the sofa, refusing to be distracted. "And what did you do? You made yourself scarce. A business call came up, and that was more important than dancing with eligible young women."

He couldn't lie to her, but he couldn't tell her

about the emergency room. "I was otherwise engaged, it's true, but how can you blame me? After dancing with the loveliest lady in the room, those other women paled by comparison."

"You stop trying to charm me." Nanna blushed, pleasure wreathing her face. "I know I ought to be mad at you, running off the way you did, but dancing with you was such a treat, I'll have to forgive you this once. When will you learn that your work isn't everything? Even our good Lord rested on the seventh day."

"I've heard that somewhere before." He let his grandmother wrap him in a warm hug. She felt so small and fragile, so much love and goodness. Tenderness warmed him, and he wanted to protect her. He'd do anything to make her world right.

Nanna stepped away, leaving the scent of her violet perfume on his jacket. "It's cold tonight, and if this wind keeps up, we're likely to lose power. I'll run upstairs and fetch a few blankets, just in case."

"I can do it, Nanna. I'm a big boy."

"Stuff and nonsense." She was already heading toward the stairs. "You two can get to know each other while I'm gone."

He did want to get to know Harold Renton, just not right now. Exhaustion weighed him down, and he eyed Mr. Renton warily.

Harold nodded in the way men from the country

did, his drawl unassuming. "Counted on seeing you at the dinner tonight. My granddaughter went to some trouble to seat you at our table. You hurt your grandmother when you didn't show."

There was no accusation to the man's words. Just hard plain fact. Noah couldn't find fault with that. He had missed dinner. "I can only apologize."

"Might be good to consider her feelings for a change. She thinks the sun rises and sets by you."

"I think the same of her. If you don't know that, then you and I have nothing to say." Pain curled deep in his chest, but Noah didn't back down. This man was a stranger. Maybe good, maybe bad. Noah didn't know for sure. But he'd had a long day, and he wasn't in the mood.

The kitchen was quiet and welcoming, with a light over the sink guiding his way. He filled a cup with water and popped it into the microwave. While the machine hummed, he lifted the lid from the cookie jar and rummaged inside.

What was he going to do about Harold? Noah tugged two cookies from the ceramic beehive cookie jar and replaced the lid. Because of the medical tests, he'd be staying here for at least another day. That gave him plenty of time to find a detective.

That felt kinda sneaky, but how else was he going to protect his grandmother? He'd seen her tonight, alight with love for this Harold guy. She was too trusting. Noah had to take care of her. All that mattered was her welfare.

The microwave beeped, drawing him back to the room. He took a bite out of the cookie—raisin oatmeal—and removed the cup out of the microwave. Steam wafted off the heated water as he went in search of a tea bag.

"I didn't have a chance to buy any more of that fancy tea you like." Nanna tapped into the kitchen. "Some nice chamomile ought to help what ails you."

"I'm fine." It wasn't a lie. He was suffering from stress, like any businessman in his position. That's all the doctors were going to find out come morning—stress. He'd start working out regularly, and he'd be all right. No need to worry his grandmother.

"You can't blame me for fussing over my only grandson." She swept a jar from the counter and dug out a tea bag. "Here, try this. It's not fancy, but it will help you sleep. You look exhausted, Noah. No doubt from that lifestyle of yours."

"Here we go again." He loved his grandmother. That's why he wasn't going to argue with her, so he took the tea bag and dunked it into his cup. "Fine. I'll drink this tea that smells like weeds, to make you happy."

"Wonderful! That's my boy." She squeezed his arm in approval. "I hope you won't be up late on that computer of yours. You need a good night's rest. I'll feel better when I see those dark circles of yours gone for good."

"I like it when a beautiful woman fusses over me." He doused the tea bag a few more times. "That's why I'm not even going to argue with you tonight."

"Wise man." She beamed her approval. "I'd better see your light off when I come up to bed, or they'll be trouble to pay."

"Yes, ma'am."

"And drink every last drop of that tea, you hear?"

She cared. It felt good. Noah couldn't disappoint her. "I'll drink every last drop. Even if it tastes as bad as it smells."

"Sleep well, my Noah." She blew him a kiss across the kitchen. When she disappeared down the hall, he stood listening to her steps, missing her.

She'd been his to care for, for as long as he'd been grown up enough to do things for her. Manage her finances and make sure she had everything she desired. He'd watched out for her, flown her out for holidays and vacations. Called her faithfully every week.

And now there was this Harold. This man who was going to be responsible for Nanna. Who wanted to marry her.

Marriage. That single word could cinch up Noah's stomach tighter than anything could. What if Harold didn't treat Nanna right? What if he hurt her? Ran off with her money, or broke her dreams right along with her heart?

In Noah's view, those outcomes were more probable than the happily-ever-after other people imagined.

Noah's guts burned. Pain pounded in his chest. This had to be upsetting him more than he realized.

Taking the weed tea and the remaining cookie, he climbed the steps to the cooler second story. Boards squeaked beneath his shoes. A dim light lit his way to the top.

One thing for sure, this house needed a remodel. Nanna could trip and fall on these stairs. And what about that draft? She could catch pneumonia, and at her age that was a concern.

He'd talk to her about it at breakfast. But for now, he'd check his messages and his e-mail. Make sure no crisis was brewing back home.

The door whispered on old hinges in the guest room at the end of the hall. Lamplight glowed from the night table near an old fashioned, four-poster bed. Several of Nanna's afghans were folded at the foot of the bed, topped by her page-worn Bible. A yellow ribbon marked one of the pages.

Leave it to Nanna to speak to him, even when she wasn't in the room. Noah set aside the tea and cookie and opened the precious book. Nanna had chosen a passage from Psalms. "Lord, remind me how brief my time on earth will be. Remind me that my days are numbered, and that my life is fleeing away."

He sat down on the bed. Okay, he could see where she was going with this. He kept reading. "We are merely moving shadows, and all our busy rushing ends in nothing."

Like an arrow hitting its target, Noah felt the words take root in his heart. Fine, he knew he was unhappy. Stress was taking a toll. He had an appointment in the morning for blood tests, a CT scan and an MRI. Pain roared like a jackhammer in his chest.

He took the bottle of pills from his jacket pocket and studied them. There were only a few, enough to get him through until morning. He wasn't going to take one. He knew, as had happened last time, the pain was winding down. By morning, he'd feel okay. Not great, but not horrible, either.

"We need more tests." That's what the doctor had told him when Julie had gone to find a pay phone. "We could be looking at a real problem."

Help me, Lord. Noah bowed his head and prayed.

Chapter Six

Julie yawned, refusing to think about how late she'd been out last night. She was no night owl, and she was paying for it this morning. Her alarm clock had rousted her from sleep hours ago, and she was still in the sweats she'd pulled on over her nightshirt.

Caffeine was bound to help. She took a sip from her steaming cup of coffee and flipped open the book in front of her. Were they making the print smaller today? No, her eyes were tired. The cleanup had gone later than she'd planned, but that wasn't the real reason she was tired. She'd tossed and turned half the night.

She'd been worried about Noah Ashton. He'd been in so much pain. She'd been afraid for him, and she still was.

Maybe she ought to call, after all. It was a few minutes past nine. Surely Nora had been up for hours. With any luck, Noah was back from his early-morning appointment.

A knock at the door echoed through the house. Julie leaned in her chair to get a good view out the door. There was a green pickup visible through the glass door. Granddad! What was he doing here?

Probably come to plow her driveway. She turned the dead bolt and yanked open the door. "Perfect timing. The coffee just finished brewing."

"I'll take you up on that offer." Granddad knocked the snow off his boots on the small deck before venturing inside. "Whew, it's cold out there. We've got a good ten inches out there, and it's still falling. Thought I'd warm up before I clear your driveway."

"Want some muffins?" Julie snatched a ceramic mug from the cupboard and reached for the glass carafe.

"Don't go to any trouble for me." He went straight to the pink baker's box on the corner of her kitchen island. "That was some party. You did a good job, girl. Sure made my Nora happy."

"I think you make her happy." Julie filled the cup with steaming coffee. "You want sugar with this?"

"Takin' it black today." Granddad kicked out a chair and plopped into it. "That's a nice flower you got there."

"What flower?" Julie turned from the counter.

"That one, right there."

There, in the center of the table, right next to her devotional, was Noah's corsage. The single white rose looked as perfect as ever.

"It's nothing." She gave Granddad his coffee and snatched the flower from its place on her table. "And since it's nothing and means nothing at all, I'm going to go put this in the fridge."

"Are you gonna fess up? Tell me who bought it for you?"

"It's top secret. Classified by the government and everything."

"You're fibbing, girl, and that tells me what I need to know." Granddad looked proud of himself. "Who's your new beau?"

"Nosy, aren't you?"

"Just looking out for my granddaughter. It's a grandfather's job."

"Well, it's a granddaughter's job to keep you guessing." Julie grabbed a plate from the shelf and carried it to the table. "There is no boyfriend. You know why."

"You just need time to find the right one, that's all." Granddad unwrapped his blueberry muffin. "Look at me, getting married at this time in my life. Figured I'd be alone for the rest of my days, and the Good Lord saw fit to send Nora my way. Only He knows what's in store for you."

"I think God has already told me that." The empty place on her left ring finger still remained both a memory and a humiliation. Only Granddad knew how much. Determined to change the subject, Julie slid the plate in front of him. "I noticed your lights were on late when I drove by last night. What were you doing up?"

Granddad reached for the butter dish. "Couldn't get to sleep. Guess the party had me all charged up."

"You don't look happy when you say that." Julie pushed a clean knife across the table for him. It was there in the crinkle of his brow and the exhaustion dark beneath his eyes. Something was making him unhappy. "What happened?"

"Nora and I had a little disagreement." Granddad dropped the muffin on his plate and left it there. He sighed, looking miserable.

Julie wanted to comfort him, to reassure him that everything would be all right, and that he and Nora would work out their problems. But she'd been in this same place, and it hadn't turned out okay. Wedding plans were easy enough to cancel, but the cost to the heart was staggering.

"I'm sorry." It was all she could say. "Is there anything I can do?"

"Yep. Help that grandson of hers pack up and get the blazes out of here." Granddad rubbed his brow. "Pardon me for sayin' that. I get my back up when I talk about that young man."

"What happened?"

"I just spoke my mind. Should've thought about it first, but I figured it needed to be said. It wasn't right the way he left the party like that. He's always off doing what he wants to do. Nora won't admit it, but it hurt her when he left. I can't stand her hurting. I told him about it, but he didn't apologize. Just told me I didn't know a thing."

Julie bit her bottom lip. So, Noah had decided to keep his condition secret. What should she say now? She'd given her word to him. She couldn't break it, but she couldn't stand to see her grandfather hurting. "I think Noah had a good reason to leave, and he *did* return to the dance."

"She forgives him for anything."

"That reminds me of another grandparent I know. Let me think who it would be…."

"Not me." Granddad blushed a little, relaxing as he reached for the coffee mug. "That's different. I don't indulge you. I don't look the other way or make excuses. You're a good, responsible girl, nothing at all like…" Granddad sighed. "No, I've vowed not to say an unkind word. I shouldn't be making judgments, but if he makes Nora sad one more time…"

"The trouble is when you really love someone, you hurt for them, too." Julie knew something about that. "I know how you feel. You want to protect Nora. That's wonderful. But you don't know what happened last night."

"And you do? I noticed you were missing. Your friends made a few excuses, how you'd just ran out on an errand and whatnot. Don't think I didn't notice how you left about the same time he did. And came back, too."

"You can say his name, Granddad. Noah's different from what I expected. You should get to know him."

"When? He's probably halfway to New York by now."

Julie glanced at the clock. Noah's pain was so severe, what if there was something terribly wrong? No one else knew where he was or what he was going through. "I like Noah, Granddad. You might, too, if you gave him half a chance."

"I don't need advice from you, missy." He winked, to soften the impact of his words. "What I need is to finish this coffee so I can get back to work. He gave you that flower, did he?"

"If he did, that would make him a nice guy. Mean guys don't go around giving corsages to women they don't know."

"He got one for Nora, too. Giving her flowers is *my* job."

Mystery solved. Julie reached across the table for her grandfather's muffin. "Noah's been looking after his grandmother for a long time. It's probably going to be hard for him to step aside and let someone else take over. Even someone as wonderful as you."

"You're takin' his side."

"No way. I'm firmly on yours." She grabbed the knife and buttered the muffin. "You can't let anything stand in the way of your special love for your bride. It's that simple. Noah adores his grandmother."

"Adores her, or her money?"

"Granddad!"

He looked fierce and protective and every bit a hard, seasoned cowboy. He looked ready for a fight. Her gentle granddad! He fisted his hands. "He's the one who takes care of her finances. Nora has no idea of her net worth. She has to call him to transfer money if she needs it. He's generous and says he takes care of her, but who knows if he's taking advantage of her."

"Noah wouldn't do that." She was certain of it. The man who'd risked his life in an electrical storm and crossed a flooding creek to save a child, had to have a good heart. A man who'd suffer pain and fear alone, so he wouldn't worry his grandmother, had to be protecting her, not out to hurt her. "Noah wouldn't, Granddad. Trust me."

"I'd sure like to, but the truth is, you don't know Noah Ashton any more than I do. Thought I could get to know him last night. Talk to him a bit, but then he ran off."

"He had a good reason. He wouldn't travel all the way from New York just to stand up his grandmother."

Granddad's fists relaxed. "Maybe you're right, and maybe that grandson of hers is overprotective."

"No one I know is like that."

Granddad blushed a little, taking a bite of muffin. "Didn't come here to hear the truth. Would've rather gotten some sympathy for my wounded pride. Not told I was wrong."

"You're not wrong. You're in love." Julie pushed the sugar bowl across the table. "Forget plowing the driveway. I'll take care of it. You go find Nora and apologize."

"Maybe I can use your phone. Give her a call or something."

"You know where it is."

Julie flipped open her devotional as he left the room. She wanted happiness for him, more than anything. This would work itself out. Noah was a good man, and he hadn't come here to interfere. He'd given his word.

In the living room, at the far side of the house, she heard Granddad's rumbling voice as he spoke to his fiancée. The furnace kicked on, breezing warm air across her slippered feet. The cat, curled in his cat bed next to the vent, stretched and yawned, content. The storm outside buffeted the windows but couldn't touch him.

Julie turned her attention to the opened page in her devotional. "As a face is reflected in water, so the heart reflects the man."

She thought of Noah. Maybe, she'd give him a call. Find out if he was back from his appointment, see if he needed a friend.

Tough morning. Noah spotted the neon window sign that read Espresso in blue lettering and pulled off the main road through town. There wasn't any traffic so he didn't need to wait. Snow crunched beneath the tires as he slid to a slow stop against the curb.

His hands were still shaking. The doctor will be in touch, they'd said. What did that mean? Good news? Bad news? Either way, he was forced to wait for it.

How was he going to go home to Nanna like this? She'd see through him this time, for sure. Two weeks ago, he'd been able to write this off as a bad case of stress and too many chili peppers in his enchilada. He couldn't make excuses today. The visit to the doctor was as real as it got. They'd taken blood tests to detect invasive cancer.

Please don't let it be that. Noah rubbed at the sudden pain behind his temple. It was too much to think about. He wasn't going to do it, tear himself up inside worrying over what was out of his control.

No, he was going to be proactive. Go about his life as usual until he heard from the doctor. He'd stay in Montana at least another day. Maybe spend time with his grandmother, or give his sister a call…

That wouldn't work. Nanna and Hope would take one look at him and know something was wrong. He took a deep breath and let it out slowly, trying to figure out what to do. He could get ahold of Julie and see what she was up to today. She'd been great to him last night. He owed her. Big-time.

Thank goodness he'd gotten ahold of her. He'd buy her a cup of coffee and thank her again. It was the least he could do.

Taking it easy, he climbed out of the car. This small piece of Montana seemed like another world. Right here, in the middle of town, silence met his ears. Peace filtered around him. The air smelled fresh and crisp, like something wonderful that could never be bottled or packaged. Snow shifted over him as he locked the car door.

"Hey, city slicker." Julie Renton tromped through the snowy street without even looking for traffic. Her hiking boots kept her from slipping as she headed his way. "Around here nobody locks their doors."

"Guess I'm not blending in." He tucked the keys into his wool trousers. "I didn't have time to hit the Western store and buy a Stetson and jeans."

"And boots."

"Are you ready for some coffee?"

She tossed the fringed end of her scarf over her

shoulder. "Are you kidding? I'm always ready for coffee."

"My kind of girl." Noah headed for the shoveled sidewalk.

"So, are you going to tell me what happened this morning?" Julie led the way up the sidewalk, where the coffee shop gleamed like a beacon of light and modern heating. "What did the doctor say?"

"Since it's Saturday, he'll have to get back to me." Saying it that way didn't sound scary at all. He could be awaiting the results of a sore throat or a rapidly growing wart. It didn't have to be anything as grave as cancer. "They told me he'd get back to me by Monday."

"Monday? That's too long to wait. I saw you last night, Noah. I can't believe they let you walk out of Emergency."

"I'm a persuasive man when I want to be."

"I bet you can be, Mr. Billionaire."

"The way you say that sounds as if you don't like billionaires."

"I can't be that judgmental—it goes against my faith. You are the only billionaire I've ever met, and all I can say, is *frightening*."

"I'm that bad?"

"Absolutely."

He grabbed the door for her, the bell tinkling merrily as she swept past him.

She smelled of strawberries and vanilla and

snow—awesome and sweet. With the faint scent of strawberries lingering on his coat, he followed her into the shop.

"You're nice to your grandmother, kind to strangers and you're buying me a latte. What's not to like?"

"I'm buying you a latte? I thought you were buying."

"No, no. I'm sure you said you were paying." She was laughing as she reached in her coat pocket. She sauntered up to the counter and called to the young woman behind the counter. "Michelle, I'll have a special, please."

A little white eraser board was propped up behind the cash register. Apple Pie Latte, 2.00, it said in curly handwriting. "Sounds good," he added. "Make it two."

Julie unsnapped her wallet.

He tugged a bill from his pocket and laid it on the counter. "My treat. I mean it. You've done enough for me. It's time I started doing something for you."

"We're even, Noah." Her hand brushed his forearm with the gentlest of touches. "Let's find a table."

He dropped another bill in the tip jar as Julie wove through the nearly empty room, calling out a hello to a group of women in the corner.

What would it be like to know everyone in the coffee shop by name? It was an alien concept.

Julie chose a table along the long wall of windows. "How about this?"

"Looks good." He could see the main street, cloaked in peaceful snow. Couldn't be more than four blocks to the town. It looked like something out of a Western movie. "What do you people do here? There's no sports arena. No museums—"

"Hey, we have the historical museum directly across the street. Except it's closed today."

"I must have missed seeing the sign on the way in to town."

"It happens." Julie shrugged out of her coat. "For your information, buster, there are a lot of things to do here. Wonderful, exciting things you can't find in your basic major city."

"And that would be…"

She rose to the challenge, all fire and life. "Aside from our historical museum, you mean? Well, there is every winter sport you can think of."

"The luge? Bobsled? Curling?"

She gave him her schoolteacher look. "I expect you to behave, Mr. Ashton, and stop thinking you're so smart. I'm talking about cross-country skiing. Downhill skiing. Snowshoeing. Snowmobiling. There's the weekend high school basketball game, but it was away this week."

"You're living the high life, Julie." Noah slung his coat over the back of his chair. "I'm not sure I can keep up with you."

"Is that a challenge?" She lifted her chin, as if she wasn't afraid of him. Not one bit.

"Sure. Exactly what are you challenging me to? A wild walk down Main Street?"

Her schoolteacher look darkened. "I think you definitely need to be taught a lesson, Mr. Ashton. Do you ski at all?"

"Downhill, but I haven't been in years. I never have the time to fly to Colorado for the weekend."

"Well, I'm one up on you. I don't have to fly anywhere for the best skiing I've ever found."

He couldn't resist asking. "Have you ever been out of Montana?"

"Once, when I went to Yellowstone Park, which is about a hundred miles south of here. It's in Wyoming." Her eyes sparkled at him, full of mirth and humor and real friendship.

That was something he didn't get often. "The best skiing, huh? I'm there."

"Great. I'll take you home with me. You can borrow Granddad's skis. You two are about the same height."

"You live with your grandfather?"

"Near him." Julie turned to talk to the waitress who brought their coffee in tall white paper cups.

"Thanks for the great tip, Mr. Ashton." The waitress was probably just out of college. She looked so young.

His ten-year college reunion had been a few summers ago. Over a dozen years had passed since he was that age. Where had the time gone? Noah didn't know. His life had become a blur of work, meetings and loneliness.

It felt pretty great sitting here with Julie. She chatted with the waitress a few minutes. He didn't notice what she was saying. Only the friendly way she treated everyone. It was the same way she treated him, and he liked it.

Noah popped the top off the cup and tossed the slim red straws onto a napkin. He drank from the brim. The sweet, apple-and-cinnamon-flavored coffee was different. He always ordered his latte without flavoring. Change was nice, he decided. Different, but nice.

"Okay, your time off for good behavior is up." They were alone, and Julie swirled the plastic straws around in her drink. "Confess."

"Maybe I don't want to."

"Then I'll have to torture it out of you." She looked angelic in a soft cable-knit sweater. Her dark hair was drawn back into a bouncy ponytail, leaving airy wisps to frame her heart-shaped face. "Don't smirk at me like that. I'm tough enough to get the truth out of you, mister."

"I'm sure you are." Noah tried not to laugh. She was a pushover—anyone could see that—and in the nicest way. He liked that about her, too. "I'm not smirking. I'm trembling with fear. Don't torture me. I'll tell you anything you want to know."

"I thought so. When my kids misbehave, they

have to put their heads down on their desks until I say they can get up."

"Brutal. I wouldn't want that happening to me." Noah winked at her, more charming than any man had the right to be. Then his cell phone rang and he reached into his coat pocket for the phone. "Wait— it's not the doctor. I'll let the voice mail get it."

"They didn't give you any hint about what was going on?"

He shook his head. Dark shocks of hair tumbled over his brow as he leaned forward to tuck the small phone into his coat pocket. "They didn't say anything, and I'm a pretty persuasive guy."

Julie could hear the low, quiet tone of fear in his voice. The humor on his face had drained away, leaving lines around his eyes and mouth, and showing how pale he was. "Are you still in pain?"

"Not much. It's down to a low throb. I keep telling myself it's just an attack of some kind. Like heartburn or something, but..." He shrugged, falling silent. What he didn't say rang loud and clear between them.

He was afraid. She understood. "If you need anything, ask."

"I appreciate that." He swirled the foam around in his cup. "Do you know what I need?"

"I'm clueless. What?"

"To get my mind off this." He squared his wide shoulders. "Want to teach me how to cross-country ski?"

"It's going to cost you. Big."

"How big?"

"Huge. Enormous. I'm a teacher, sure, but right now I'm off-hours. I don't just teach anyone anything for free."

"How about another cup of coffee to go?"

"You're on." Julie reached for her coat. "But first, prepare yourself. You're in for the time of your life."

Chapter Seven

Julie wasn't kidding. Noah stopped at a turnout on the path between tall, snow-bound firs. His breath rose in great clouds in the cold air as he trekked close to the edge.

Wow. Those were some of the best views he'd ever seen. Mountain peaks close enough to touch rose straight up into the clouds. Snow fell in a misty curtain from sky to valley floor, far below, draping endless stands of trees. He breathed in the cold air and felt peace.

Out here, there were no demands. No deadlines. No pressure. Nothing. Just God's beauty.

Julie glided up next to him, stopping expertly with a slight turn. "How are you holding up?"

"Great." Better than great. "I know this pain attack I had is just stress. I get away from my problems for an hour, and every bit of pain is gone."

"I'm glad." Julie knocked snow off her cap. "Can I make a suggestion? Get rid of your stress."

"I'll take that under consideration." He couldn't get enough of this view. Of this peace shifting over him like the snow. Or maybe it was because of Julie. He couldn't tell. He only knew that he felt as light as the snow tumbling from the sky when she smiled at him.

"Are you ready to go? Or do you need more rest, city boy?"

"This city boy can beat you any day of the week." Noah wasn't sure about that, but he liked the way challenge gleamed in Julie's eyes as she tugged her cap lower over her ears.

"You're on. I'll race you over to that meadow down there. See? The one *waaay* down there?" She pointed with her mittened hand, leaning close.

His chest tightened, quick and hard, like a punch to his midsection. For a split second he thought the pain was coming back, faster than before. But it wasn't pain. It was something else.

"Come on. I'll give you a head start." Julie trudged back to the trail, leading the way. Pine boughs rocked, heavy with snow, in her wake and knocked against him.

"I'm such a fantastic skier, *you're* the one who's going to need a head start." He winked, and she laughed.

"Right. Fine. We start together, but you're going to be sorry, Mr. Billionaire. C'mon. Line up." She motioned him close, digging in at an imaginary starting line. "Ready?"

"Ready." He dug in beside her.

And they were off at the same moment, shoulder to shoulder. The silence shattered as they crashed along the tree-lined path, knocking limbs. Snow tumbled to the ground. Noah tried to cut over, but he couldn't. Julie was right there, arm braced to keep him right where she wanted him.

She was pulling ahead! "You come back here." He caught her by the back of the jacket and stopped her just enough to take the lead.

"Cheater!" She was laughing.

A snowball pelted him in the middle of the back. "Good aim."

"That was a warm-up, so watch out." She was behind him, skiing hard. One pole was tucked under her arm because there was another snowball in her hand.

He recognized the look in her eye. Okay, he hadn't grabbed her to cheat. He just wanted to grab her. Now he was going to pay for it. "I'm in trouble."

"You bet your bootstraps, buster." She took aim like a major-league pitcher with the bases loaded. Total concentration. Complete confidence.

There was nothing he could do but take the hit like a man. The snowball caught him square in the back of the knee. He went down in an instant, skis flying into the trees, rolling in the snow. He didn't mind the cold creeping down the back of his collar as he climbed onto his feet.

Julie dug in and stopped. "Cheaters never prosper."

"I wasn't cheating." The snow gathered naturally in the palm of his hand. As if it was meant to be. It sailed in a perfect arch, as if he were meant to throw that snowball at this exact moment in time. At this one woman.

The snow broke apart in midair, showering her before impact. Icy crystals rained over her head and knocked her cap off to the side.

"You want trouble? You just got it." She tossed her poles and filled her gloves with snow.

He was on his feet, but it wasn't fast enough. Cold powder hit him square in the face.

"Oops. I didn't mean—" She shrieked as he took off after her.

She was quick, but he was faster. He tackled her from behind, bringing her down in the soft snow. Powder flew as they hit. Her skis shot into the trees as they rolled to a stop.

She landed beside him, laughing. "No fair. You can't tackle me to keep me from winning. Just because you were clumsy and fell down—"

"Clumsy, huh?" He didn't feel like teasing her back. His heart was thundering, he was breathing hard, exhilarated from the cold and the exercise. He reached out and brushed snow from her face with his thumb.

Warmth filled him. Tenderness burned in his chest so hard it almost hurt. It was great being here with her. Having fun. Letting go of his troubles and his responsibilities. And it was because of Julie. He felt real with her. He felt as though she saw the real Noah, when no one else did.

"I'm glad we're friends." He meant it. Down deep. Because he felt a connection to her, he stroked his hand over the curve of her face.

"Me, too." He couldn't interpret the gleam of emotion in her eyes. She climbed to her feet and brushed at the snow caked to her jacket. "As my friend, you'll help me find my skis. Right?"

"Don't be too sure about that." Because one of her skis wasn't that far away from him, he snagged it before she could circle around him. "We're still racing. I intend to win."

"What are you going to do? Hold my ski hostage?"

"Knowing you, it wouldn't stop you. You can probably take this hill on one ski." He handed the thing to her, as he'd planned to do all along.

It was incredible, this way he felt inside. And the scenery… The wind ebbed away, leaving silence in its wake. It was like finding a corner of heaven, new and beautiful and untouched. So far from every unhappiness he felt in his life. So close to the nicest woman he'd ever known.

Noah believed that everything happened for God's reason. The Lord had given him this day, so what was He trying to say?

Noah thought that maybe he already knew.

He caught Julie before she could climb into the thick stand of trees to retrieve her other ski. "Let me. I have a way with firs."

"Those are pines."

He liked that she didn't have a problem putting him in his place. "Fine. I have a way with trees. Stand aside."

Snow-laden boughs slapped him in the face and beat him in the arm as he climbed deeper into the forest. But seizing the lone ski made it all worthwhile. Even more rewarding was the feel of Julie's touch on his arm. It was a real connection. She was a real friend.

He hadn't had one of those in a long time.

He found his skis while Julie waited, and then they were off together, battling it down the mountainside. The wind buffeted him and the cold stung his eyes. It was like flying, wild and fast and thrilling. He fought hard, but at the bottom of the steep hill, Julie inched ahead of him for the win.

Losing had never felt better.

As they skied back to the road, through the forest that edged her property, Julie could still feel the brush of Noah's thumb on her cheek and the touch of his glove to her face. The cold air may have numbed her skin, but that didn't seem to matter. She tried to think of a dozen different things. That didn't help, either. She could remember the look in his eyes. *I'm glad we're friends,* he'd said.

Friends. Yep, that's what they were. Friends. She wouldn't deny it. Didn't expect anything else. But why did men always have to emphasize it, as if she wasn't good enough or attractive enough or special enough to be anything else?

She'd been around the romantic block too many times to mistake friendship for romance. So why were her feelings hurt? Why was she yearning for tenderness from him? It made no sense. It wasn't as if Noah was going to fall for her. He was a billionaire. She was a small-town girl. A few hours of recreation did not make a romance.

Still, disappointment washed over her when she glided across a knoll and the road came into view. Their excursion was over.

He puffed, a little out of breath. "You're slowing down."

So she was. It had been a fun day, and she hated to have it end. The sun was beginning to sink into the western mountains. "Every time I'm out here, I'm never ready for it to end."

Yep, that was it. She just loved skiing so much. It had nothing to do with Noah.

"You were right. This is the best skiing I've

ever found." Noah tossed her that grin of his, the one that could make a woman forget every word she'd ever learned. "I can't remember when I've had a better day."

"If that's true, you need to get out more."

"What do you mean *if?* This is pretty special, what you have here. It's amazing. If I want to ski, I have to fly there first."

Julie rolled her eyes. "I hate it when I have to fuel up the Learjet just to go skiing."

"There you go, teasing me again. I don't deserve it."

"That's one theory." She glided around their vehicles parked in her driveway and kept going.

"Just because I have my own jet, doesn't mean I'm a bad guy." He followed her. "Hey, where are you going?"

"That's my house." She took the snow-covered driveway at a fast pace, the wind whistling past her ears.

"*Your* house? Not your grandfather's?"

"I know what you're thinking." She wedge-turned onto the front lawn and circled the house. "How can a kindergarten teacher afford this on her salary?"

"Something like that." It was a little different skiing right through her yard as if it were a trail, but the snow was thick and perfect, leading them to her wood deck in the back.

Julie knelt to release her bindings, and her dark ponytail brushed over her shoulder to touch her face. Her skin was pink from the cold, and Noah had never seen a woman so beautiful. His chest tightened in that strange way again, and he felt…

He didn't know how he felt. He only knew that he liked her.

She straightened, hauling her skis up the steps and leaning them against the side of her house. "A few years ago, Granddad gifted land to each of his grandkids and built us each a house of our choice. This cabin and the eighty acres we just skied on are mine."

"He did what?" Noah leaned the borrowed skis next to Julie's. "He gifted this to you?"

"I know. Pretty great, isn't he?" There was no mistaking the affection in her voice. "He wanted to give us all a better start in life than he had. His ranch is just up the road. You probably saw the house when you drove out here."

Noah hadn't noticed. He was too busy looking around at the incredible view. What she called a cabin was really a two-story log house. Not extravagant, but nice. Very nice. And the land, why, it had to be seriously valuable. Something a man just didn't give away…. "I see where you're going with this. You must have heard Harold and I didn't exactly become best friends."

"I did hear a version of that." She opened one of

the glass doors—no keys, she must have left it unlocked—and stomped the snow off her boots. "You could keep an open mind the next time you meet him. Give him half a chance."

"Yeah, yeah. If I wanted a lecture, I could have let Nanna do it." With a wink, he followed Julie inside.

"I'm not lecturing, and *you* asked about the house. What do you think?" She held her arms wide, gesturing to the home she was obviously proud of.

"What's not to like?" He took in the golden honey floors and walls. The open beam ceilings that made the kitchen and eating nook feel spacious. Glass windows stretched from floor to ceiling, showcasing the perfect view of shrouded forest and mountains. "I wouldn't mind looking out at this every day when I come home from work."

"It's great stress reduction. I put up my feet, look out the window and every trouble melts away." She put cups of water in the microwave. "Want to try it? The recliner in the living room is to die for. Once you get in it, it will take an act of Congress to get you out."

In the living room, a gray striped cat took one look at him and raced up the stairs in a blur. He should have figured Julie for a pet person. A blanket was folded on the couch cushion, with telltale cat hair on it. It wasn't too hard to imagine her curled up on the couch watching television at night, with the cat at her side.

It was a pretty big place for one person. He could see his reflection in the living room windows as the sun peeked out, streaking through the glass. The view was even better from here. A man who'd given this to his granddaughter probably wasn't short on cash.

"How many grandkids are there?"

"Ten of us." Julie sounded pleased with herself.

She ought to be. He'd been determined to find out Harold's true motives. True love was possible, but there were other more likely reasons.

Greed. He saw every day what people would do for the almighty dollar, as if that was what truly mattered. Women he'd dated and he'd thought he'd been in love with. Friends that wound up betraying him. Even his family. Whenever Mom or Dad gave him a call, as rare as that was, it was because they needed a few hundred grand to get them by.

"I hope you like hot chocolate with lots of marshmallows." Julie breezed into the room in her stocking feet, the hem of her jeans wet with snow. She carried two brimming mugs and thrust one at him. "You don't look like a marshmallow kind of guy, but too bad. You're getting them anyway."

"What does that mean? I am a marshmallow kind of guy." The cup was hot against his fingers, the chocolate aroma rich and sweet. The marshmallows melted into a foamy froth. "As sweet as can be."

"Do I look gullible?" She grabbed a remote and pressed a button. The fireplace in the corner roared to life. "You're a self-made man, according to all my friends who read that recent magazine article about you."

"I inherited my first million, but made the rest myself." He took the recliner. "That doesn't make me ruthless. Maybe I made my fortune by accident."

"By accident? How do you do that, I'd like to know. I love teaching—don't get me wrong—but I wouldn't mind being accidentally wealthy." She sat on the edge of the wide coffee table, chin up, all challenge.

She didn't believe him when he'd said his success was an accident. Fine. She would.

"This is something you won't read in any magazine. I never admit this to anyone else. Probably because then I'd look like an incompetent who shouldn't be in charge of a company."

"Ooh, now I'm curious." She leaned forward, and he felt as if he could tell her anything.

"I was fresh out of business school with my MBA in hand. The last thing I wanted to do was work with my father. He has a consulting firm and he was pressuring me to join him. But I'd come into my money that summer, so I rented office space in the basement of this old building in Queens. I set up shop and wrote code with a buddy of mine. By

Christmas, we had a financial software package on the market, for trading stocks electronically. By spring, I quadrupled my inheritance."

"I thought you ran this huge electronics conglomerate."

"It started out as a small software venture. I was just doing what I loved to do. It snowballed. No, it exploded like a ton of dynamite and buried my life." He felt a sense of loss he couldn't explain and didn't know where it came from. "So I made billions and built a huge company, and I never intended to do it."

He took a sip of hot chocolate, and the sweetness soothed that unsettled feeling in his stomach. "Julie, promise me something. Don't tell the stockholders I admitted that."

"Cross my heart." She said it like a promise she would keep for the rest of her days.

She was too good to be true, and he was thankful she was his friend.

She took a sip of hot chocolate. Marshmallow clung to her upper lip. The tip of her tongue swiped the sweetness away.

Before he knew what he was doing, he reached across the distance between them. Her lips felt like warmed satin against his fingertip. "You missed a spot."

"I bet the women you spend time with don't spill marshmallow fluff all over themselves."

"No, they don't." His fingers stroked the corner of her mouth. His touch felt tender and amazing.

She sparkled all the way down to her toes. No man had ever made her feel like this.

He withdrew, but he didn't ease back into the chair. He placed his elbows on his knees, remaining close. So close she could see the black flecks in his dark eyes. It would take nothing at all for him to lean forward and kiss her. She almost wanted him to.

Romantic doom, remember? It was hard, but she managed to slide away from him without spilling her hot chocolate or letting her feelings show.

The microwave dinged, saving her. Instead of running away from being so close to him, it looked as if she were leaving for completely valid reasons.

Noah seemed unaware as he straightened, stood up and paced to the far window. The sunlight was waning, the world outside somber and brooding.

Friends, he had said wisely, and she wholeheartedly agreed. A man like Noah Ashton was wrong for her.

The chili was steaming, and she gave it a good stir.

"Smells good." Noah wandered into the kitchen, stretching. "Homemade?"

"The only kind." She slipped a plate piled with cornbread slices into the microwave and hit the start button. "What do you want to drink? I have vanilla soda or root beer."

"You pick." He sidled past her to the sink and turned on the faucet. The scent of berries filled the air as he pumped out a few dollops of soft soap.

There was a jingling sound, but it wasn't the microwave.

"My cell." Noah's hands were in the water. "It's in my coat. Can you grab it?"

It could be the doctor. She could feel his urgency. She dashed to the table, where his jacket was hanging over the back of a chair, and found the phone by feel.

"If it's from area code 212, let the voice mail get it." He turned off the faucet. "I can always get back—"

Kline Detective Agency, it said on the caller ID screen. Julie stared at it for a moment, and the ringing stopped.

"Is it the doctor?" Noah was dripping water on the floor. He grabbed the phone with his wet hands, worry harsh on his face as he read the screen.

Julie turned away. It was none of her business who was calling Noah. It could be a wrong number. It could be anything.

Then why was he so quiet?

"I'll return that call later." He tucked the phone back into his coat pocket.

"Sure." She carried the bowls to the table. She wasn't going to make any judgments or any conclusions. The pit of her stomach felt oddly empty.

Noah wouldn't have Granddad investigated, right? That was something people only did on television.

Noah punched open the microwave door and brought the cornbread to the table for her.

The silence in the kitchen felt enormous. He could hear every footstep. The scrape of wood against the tile floor seemed so loud. Or maybe it was his guilty conscience.

He shouldn't have asked Julie to catch the phone. He didn't think the detective would get back to him so fast. The doctor was supposed to be the one calling, and no way had Noah wanted to hear bad news on his voice mail.

Now, he regretted his impatience. Julie was very quiet as she set spoons and knives on the table. She pushed aside a neat pile of construction paper. Looked as if she'd been cutting out big block letters for a classroom bulletin board.

She waited until she was seated to say grace. He muttered "Amen," and reached for the paper napkin.

She looked upset, and he was a smart enough man to steer clear of the phone call topic. So he said what was on his mind. "What do you think of marriage?"

Her spoon hit the bowl with a clatter. "Do you mean the upcoming wedding or are you talking about marriage in general?"

Uh-oh. She sounded really angry. He started

backpedaling. "Marriage in general. It sounds like your parents divorced, too."

"I didn't know that was any of your business." She said it nicely, but there was no mistaking the way she glared at him.

Yep, she was mad. He wasn't going to get out of this unscathed. He may as well face up to it. "I didn't mean for you to know about the detective."

"Why should I? You aren't investigating my grandfather, right?" She folded her hands neatly on the table in front of her. "That detective was calling about something else, right?"

"No." He felt really bad, so he took a bite of chili. He was amazingly hungry. "After being with you today, I decided I didn't need a P.I."

"So, you thought you had the right to investigate him?"

It was perfectly legal, he wanted to point out, but he decided to take the diplomatic course. Because he really did feel guilty. "I made a mistake. I'll pay the detective what I owe him, but I won't ask for the information."

"I see. That makes it all right?"

"No." He didn't want to hurt her. "I'm sorry. My grandmother is a very wealthy woman, and I have the right to protect her."

"You've come to stop the wedding, haven't you? You're just not going to admit it."

"I admit it. I don't think marriage is a good idea in

general, but Harold seems to make Nanna happier than I've ever seen her. Ever. That's worth something."

She pushed away from the table. How could she have been so wrong about Noah? "You took one look at my grandfather and thought, 'Now there's someone to suspect.' Look at the way he helps his grandchildren and attends church on Sunday and donates his time at Young Life. It's all a front. He's really a romancer of rich women."

"Julie." Noah stood, and looked pained, his hands held out as if he wasn't sure he should touch her or defend himself from her. "It wasn't like that. Really. Could you let me apologize?"

"Apologize? That won't change anything." She couldn't believe she'd been so gullible. She'd been taken in by Noah, too. She'd *trusted* him, and he'd been using her! "You spent the day with me to gather information on my grandfather."

"No! That's not true."

"How can I believe you after this?" It felt as if her heart were being torn in two. "I want you out of my house. Now."

He bowed his head. All the fight seemed to go out of him. "Fine. I'll go. But you're wrong, Julie. I didn't use you."

"Sure." She refused to believe him. He was no different than any other man she'd liked. She was a magnet for deceitful men, and Noah was no exception.

He did look so alone standing there. He didn't argue or lose his temper. She saw the regret on his handsome face before he turned, grabbed his coat and walked out her door.

Good riddance. The last thing she needed was a spying, suspicious man out to use her.

And she'd mistaken him for a friend.

"Noah, is that you, dear boy?" Nanna called out from the living room.

"Yes, but I could be anyone since you don't keep your door locked." Noah shut the door behind him. The cold had leaked into his bones, and he felt as if he'd never get warm. Plunging his hands in his coat pockets, he wandered into the hallway. "Want anything from the kitchen?"

"I have all I need."

Did she have to sound so happy? As if she had the answers to everything? She probably did, but that didn't help his situation. He'd messed up the first friendship he'd made in a long time. He felt guilty.

"Did Julie get ahold of you? She called here looking for you this morning."

Noah yanked open the refrigerator. "I met up with her in town."

"Good. She's such a nice girl, don't you think?"

Sure. And he'd made her nice and mad. He felt horrible. He'd hurt her.

"See that Crock-Pot simmering on the counter? I made a nice beef stew. We'll eat in a bit." Nanna was unstoppable. "Don't you go spoiling your supper."

He grabbed a carton of milk. "I'll be good."

"You will be, because I'm watching you, young man." Heels tapped on hardwood as she approached, all smile and charm. "You look much healthier after one day in my care. See what good, clean Montana air can do?"

"I know where you're going with this." He stole a glass from the cupboard. "You think I'm looking for business property."

"In case you decide to relocate." She handed him a clean glass. "It never hurts to keep your options open. Who knows? You might decide you love it here and never want to leave."

"Yeah, sure, right after I find a bride. Neither one is going to happen. Trust me."

"You think you know everything, young man. You just wait. The love bug is going to bite you hard. You'll be helpless against it."

"The love bug? I graduated magna cum laude from Harvard and never once did I learn about the love bug concept." He filled the glass. "It must not be an academically recognized term."

"I should never have spared the rod with you."

She pinched his earlobe and held on tight, but it was an affectionate hold. "You are accompanying me to church tomorrow, aren't you? I have to show off my handsome grandson to all my friends at the Ladies' Aid."

"I'd be honored. It's not every day I get to escort such a beautiful lady to church."

"Oh, you take after your grandfather, boy. A charmer to the core, he was. And ambitious, too." She released him, only to fish a handful of cookies from the ceramic jar. "About tomorrow. Will I need to give you a talking-to?"

He kissed her cheek and stole the cookies. "I already know what you're going to say. I'll be nice to Harold. I'll turn off my cell phone in church. I'll go to bed early."

"That wasn't what I was going to say, smarty." She patted the back of his hand, not willing to let him go upstairs, where his computer and e-mail were waiting. "It's so good to see you here. I love you so very much."

"I love you, too, Nanna." He hugged her tight and didn't want to let go.

But the Crock-Pot bubbled and the oven timer buzzed. She spun away to grab her oven mitt. Outside, dusk began stealing the daylight from the sky, but inside the kitchen, and in his heart, it was warm and bright.

Chapter Eight

It was just her luck. The first person she saw the exact second she stepped foot inside the church was Noah. He was standing in the aisle next to his grandmother and three of her friends. He shook each woman's hand, giving Nanna a kiss on the cheek. Winning their hearts, no doubt.

Yesterday, he'd been busy winning hers. Determined not to let it bother her, she tucked her purse strap higher up on her shoulder and lifted her chin. If she sat far enough in the back, she probably wouldn't be able to see him through the entire service.

Especially if she slumped down in the pew.

"Julie!" Susan scrambled up the aisle from the door. "Come help me figure out where he's going to sit."

Hopefully in the front row. "I was planning to hide out in the back."

"What for? You'll never be able to see him that way."

Julie opened her mouth to argue, but it was too late. Susan had spotted Misty, in the middle of the church, who was waving to catch their attention.

"I saved the best spot for us," Misty whispered breathlessly as they crowded onto the bench, a stone's throw from where Noah stood, still busily charming those kind, unsuspecting ladies.

"A perfect view," Susan agreed.

Too perfect. Julie deliberately kept her back to him. Noah wasn't her friend. He'd used her, and that hurt. She still didn't understand it. He'd seemed so nice. Kind, funny and wonderful. Unbelievably wonderful. She'd been up half the night, tossing and turning, troubled by his betrayal.

"Ooh, he's looking this way." Misty was nearly bursting with excitement. "Quick, smile and wave."

Julie couldn't resist a quick look at him, but she most certainly was not going to smile and wave. She felt his gaze like a bitter wind in her direction. Her heart ached, remembering his touch, his steady kindness, the way she'd sparkled on the inside when he said her name.

The aisle between them felt as wide as the Grand Canyon. Yesterday had changed everything for him, too. There was no easy grin on his face when his gaze met hers. He looked uncomfortable and sad. So was she.

"Wow, to think we danced with him." Misty leaned close, whispering to keep from being over-heard. "He keeps looking our way."

"Mesmerized by the two of us. *Not* Julie." Susan winked.

"That's right. It's a shame how he ignores her. *Not.*" Misty winked. "I don't think he sees anyone else in the entire church."

Oh, no. Julie covered her face with her hands. "Is he really watching me?"

"Oh, yeah." Noah's voice at her ear, and his touch on her sleeve. "My grandmother wanted me to invite you and your friends to come sit with us."

He did look contrite, and that made it easier to be civil. "Thank you, but my friends and I are fine right where we are."

"Julie!" Susan admonished.

"Julie, please," Misty whispered.

Noah's eyes glinted with amusement. "Yeah, Julie. Please. I promise I'll behave."

"I don't care if you behave. I'm not budging."

"You're mad at me, I know. You have the right. But maybe you could put our differences aside for an hour, for my grandmother's sake. Would it help if I let you kick me in the shin? Flog me with the hymnal?"

"I'd like that. Do you want to stand up? Or should I kick you from here?"

"Ouch. I guess you're serious. Okay, I'll take the flogging. I deserve it. I was bad. Can you forgive me?"

"Not if you paid me." She wanted to, but he'd used her to get information on her grandfather. He'd found a private detective to dig into Granddad's life. "You can't charm me. I'm immune to it."

"I'm not," Susan spoke up.

"Thank you." Noah flashed the grin that could dazzle a shopping mall full of women in half a second. "You don't have to forgive me, Julie. You can jab me with your elbow through the entire service until my ribs are bruised. You can drop the hymnal on my toe until it swells and I can't take off my shoe. You can fire death-ray glares of disapproval at me for the rest of my life, but please, reconsider. My grandmother really wants you to join her."

"Maybe you should explain to her why I don't want to sit anywhere near you."

"Let's not. She'd get mad at me."

Julie was weakening. Noah could sense it. Victory was close at hand. "You don't want to disappoint your granddad. He's over there, sitting next to Nanna. See him? And what about your friends?"

Bingo. He'd used the right leverage. Her knuckles turned white, she was gripping her purse so hard. Good, because he wanted the chance to make things right with her. She was a good person.

One of the nicest he'd ever known. He wanted to apologize. And he'd keep apologizing until she forgave him.

"All right," she relented. "But I want this perfectly clear. I'm not happy with you."

"I can accept those terms of our peace accord." He winked at her, hoping it would make her smile.

Utter failure, but he'd keep working at it. He wanted to clear up this misunderstanding. He refused to lose Julie as a friend.

He led the way across the aisle and made sure he scooted next to her on the hard wooden bench. Her friends crowded on his other side, but they were nice enough and he didn't mind chatting with them for a few minutes. As long as he could feel the solid heat of Julie's arm pressed against his.

"Stop trying to change my opinion of you," she informed him. "Making nice to my friends isn't going to make me dislike you less."

"Then I'll have to try another tact. Did you hear? Today's sermon is on forgiveness."

Her jaw snapped closed and she glared straight ahead. She looked mad at him, but her mouth was crinkled in the corners, as if she were fighting to keep ahold of her anger.

Yep, she was weakening. He was thankful.

Julie set the brim-full gravy boat on the corner of Nora's dining room table. It was impossible to keep from noticing the man on the other side of the table, setting knives and forks and spoons in place around the pretty china plates. Harder still to ignore the charming grin that he was sending her way.

He was trying to soften her up, and it wasn't going to work. Nothing on this green earth could make her forget what he'd done. He could wink, he could smile, he could dance on the ceiling for all she cared, and better than Fred Astaire, but it wouldn't change what he'd done.

Or how foolish she'd been.

"Did you enjoy today's sermon?" he asked. "I enjoyed it immensely. Made me really decide to reevaluate the grudges I've been holding against people."

"Really? I don't see anything wrong with holding resentment and hostility toward a person, if they truly deserve it," she quipped.

"That's not what I got out of the sermon."

"You must not have been paying attention." She turned on her heel.

She'd taken Pastor Bill's sermon to heart, and it was troubling her. Noah had hurt her, and yet, she didn't want to hold a grudge, didn't want to let the sun set on her anger. What should she do? Maybe the Lord would guide her.

"Just in time." Nora laid a thick slice of old-fashioned ham on the heaping platter. "If you take this for me, I'll grab the bowl of potatoes and we should be ready to eat, dear."

"Thank you for inviting us over." Julie took the platter, eager to help. "I'm glad you're marrying my granddad. He loves you so much."

"As I love him." Nora looked like the happiest woman in Montana as she fished a hot pad out of a drawer.

Granddad lumbered into the room, his boots knelling on the hardwood, his hands jammed into his pockets. He looked uncomfortable. "Smells awful good in here. Need any help?"

Julie took one look at him, then at Nora's loving expression. She could take a hint. "I'll leave you two lovebirds alone."

She grabbed the bowl of potatoes, too. Granddad looked smitten as he stood there in the center of the room. Yep, they definitely needed to be alone.

She found Noah was halfway around the dining room table, doling out forks, spoons and knives like cards in a Go Fish game. "Hey. Have you forgiven me yet?"

"I need to hold on to my grudge until dinner's over, at the very earliest."

"Will that be before or after dessert? I just want to know how much time I have to perfect my apology to you."

"I hope it's a well-thought-out apology. A glib one is likely to make me toss a potato at you." She set the heavy platter and bowl in the center of the table. "I'm a pretty good aim."

"I remember. But I'm not afraid, because I've got a killer apology prepared." Noah sidled close to slide the last set of silverware into place. "I'm enjoying this, you know."

"I've noticed. Maybe I should pelt you with potatoes right now because it's not nice to hurt people's feelings."

"I know, and I deserve it. You might want to lash me with a few ham slices while you're at it," Noah joked, because he knew he could wear her down. Soon he'd have her laughing.

She was so close, he could smell the strawberry shampoo in her hair. It was nothing at all to reach out and brush his knuckles down the side of her face, his fingers tangling in her hair. Petal-soft skin, and satin-soft curls.

Her eyes widened like a doe caught in a semi's headlights. "I'd better go check on Granddad. He—"

"They need their privacy, just as we do." He didn't want her to go. "I hate that I hurt you. Absolutely hate it."

"Me, too."

Pain was there, revealed in the dark shadows of her eyes, and he had to fix it. Had to repair every bit of harm he'd caused her. He had to tell her what lay in his heart. "I've had a lot of people betray me,

Julie. People I trusted, and who were close to me. When I heard my grandmother was getting married, I feared the worst. Because I've had the worst happen to me once too often."

"And that's why you hired the private detective?" Julie's jaw looked tighter. "You couldn't come here with an open mind and decide for yourself, after meeting Granddad?"

"I can see you're getting angry again." He sighed. "Look, I don't want you mad at me. I like you. I want you to like me. I just need you to understand."

"I don't understand." She yanked open the drawer on the big glass cabinet thingy on the wall. The glass windows rattled. Silverware chimed. She grabbed a spoon and dug it into the potato bowl. She plunged a ladle into the gravy.

Good going, Noah. Looks like you messed that up.

"Good, you're both here." Nanna clipped into the room, carrying a basket of bread, sounding unusually strained.

That worried him. Maybe she was tired. He took the basket from her. "Let me get your chair for you. I love coming to a beautiful woman's assistance."

"You can stop laying it on so thick, young man, and ask Julie what she'll have to drink. I forgot the lemonade pitcher—" She snapped her fingers. "I just don't know what's come over me today. I'm forgetting everything."

"That's because a woman in love has a lot on her mind. It's perfectly natural." He kissed his grandmother's cheek, courteous and adoring, before he helped her scoot in her chair.

Julie's heart melted. Right when she'd been ready to stay mad at him, he had to go and do something like this. So sweet and affectionate, he made it impossible to stay mad at him.

Noah returned to the room with a pitcher of lemonade. Granddad followed him in and took a seat, cleared his throat. Nora said grace. After a round of "amens," Granddad lifted the bowl of peas and passed them to Julie.

It was so quiet. Nora was busy ladling gravy on her potatoes. Granddad spent a lot of time breaking a roll apart and buttering it. Not a word was spoken.

There was definitely something wrong. Nora and Granddad refused to meet gazes as Noah offered them each a first shot at the ham platter.

"Julie?" He nudged the meat-laden platter across the table. He lifted one brow as if asking a question, then looked at their grandparents seated at opposite ends of the table. About as far apart as they could be.

"Thanks." She forked a slice onto her plate, and gave him a shrug. She didn't know what was going on.

"Noah, I got a chance to speak with your sister after the service." His grandmother didn't look up as she broke the silence. Her voice sounded strained. "She couldn't come over—one of the little boys has an earache, poor dear—but she does want to drive you to the airport tomorrow."

"Goin' back so soon?" Granddad asked.

What about the doctor? Julie bit her tongue before she could ask the question out loud. She knew Noah wouldn't want his grandmother to know.

A chair scraped against the wood floor as Nora straightened in her seat. "We can just ask him, Harold. Noah, we have a meeting with the builder tomorrow. Now, it's a lot for us to take in. Why, I've lived in this house for most of my life. Harold is sure of himself, but, well, I would feel better if you sat in on the meeting with us."

Julie watched Noah's face fall. She knew there was still the matter of the doctor's call.

"You really need me, huh?" He glanced at Harold, then back at his grandmother.

Granddad looked surprised. "Why, I won't say we need you, but it would make your grandmother happy."

"I may as well leave a little later. Sure. I'd be happy to."

"Oh, I feel better already." Nora looked relieved as she cut into a slice of homemade bread. "It's such a big project. Our own home, together. It's a new start for us, isn't it, Harold?"

"Yes it is, sweetheart—" Harold blushed, apparently embarrassed by his feelings.

Noah was starting to like the man. As if Julie realized it, she lifted one brow in a question. So, she was still blaming him, was she? Still angry?

He'd have to fix that, and quick.

"Harold, come help me with the tea water." Nora took her dessert plate with her as she rose from the table.

"Sure thing, honey." Granddad grabbed his plate and headed after her.

Julie blinked as they disappeared from sight. "Do you know what that was about?"

"No, but I think they want to be alone." Noah rubbed his brow, because this was too much. "Okay, I'm starting to see it for myself. Harold really does love her."

"You've taken care of her for a long while. It has to be hard to let someone else take over. He'll be good to her."

"I'm figuring that out."

"Didn't need an investigator's report for that, huh?"

"Not this time. I already admitted I was wrong."

"I heard you." Julie snared her plate and rose from her chair.

"I didn't use you. That's what you think, isn't it?" His dark gaze searched hers, forthright and unflinching. Beneath the steel was tenderness.

Julie's chest tightened. Her throat ached. What

did she do now? She stared at her plate, no longer hungry, but it was a better place to focus her attention than Noah. She was no longer angry with him. It would be easier if she was.

"I know. I chose the wrong words. I do that sometimes."

"You're a billionaire. You're a chairman of the board. You're supposed to know what words to use."

"Sure, rub it in." He took the plate from her, his fingertips lingering over hers. Masculine and warm and amazing. "I'm just a man."

He walked away, leaving his confession to echo in the shadows. Just a man, he'd said. A man who made mistakes and apologized for them. A man who'd asked for her forgiveness.

She found him in the living room, where the fire was crackling in the fireplace and the cheerful atmosphere seemed at odds with their mood.

Noah hadn't touched the thick slice of chocolate cake on his plate. He didn't look up, not even when she settled onto the couch next to him.

She set her plate on the coffee table. "Going back home tomorrow?"

"Yep. I've got a meeting that I'll do by telephone. Probably on the jet on my way home."

"I always do tons of phone calls on my Learjet, too. It's a time-saver."

The tiniest hint of a grin tugged at the corner of his mouth. "I've always thought so."

"If the doctor does get ahold of you on your plane, then you'll be alone. You need your family with you, or your friends."

He relaxed a little, trouble starting to twinkle in his eyes. "I prefer being alone. It's easier than having women get mad at you right and left."

"That's your own fault, buster. Why haven't you told your grandmother? She would want to be there for you."

"Because there's nothing really wrong, that's why. I'm not going to upset her for no reason."

He seemed so sure of himself, but Julie wasn't fooled. Not by a long shot. She'd seen his face change. He didn't like being alone any more than she did. Most of all, he didn't want to be seriously ill and alone.

"I saw you in the emergency room. I witnessed how much pain you were in—"

"It was nothing," he interrupted, holding up one hand to stop her. "Look how good I'm doing. I feel great. My chest hasn't hurt since we went skiing. If something were really wrong, it wouldn't have vanished like that. I had fun, exercised and, surprise, no pain."

"Have you ever heard of a fool's paradise? Of the ignorant's bliss? You should tell your grandmother and stay here until you hear from the doctor."

"Why? I think those tests are going to come up negative, for whatever it is the doctors are looking for. I live a stressful life. Stressful enough that it's made me unhappy for a long time. I just need to make some changes, that's all. The attack I had was some sort of wake-up call."

"I hope so." She truly did, but she couldn't shake the bad feeling deep inside. "I hope you're never in that kind of pain again."

"You care about me, huh?"

"I thought we were friends."

"We are." His hand covered hers. "A lot of people I know want something from me. A job, a better job, a loan, a wedding ring and no prenuptial. I learned to keep to myself. It's easier on the heart."

"I know what you mean, about protecting your heart." Her confession came rough as she twined her fingers through his bigger ones, holding on. "That's the reason I've vowed never to let myself think about finding a man to love me. It only leads to disaster, and my heart can't take much more breaking."

"I heard about the ring you returned," he confessed.

"Everyone knows. That's the problem with being left at the altar. The church is full of people who can't help but notice the groom's missing." She tried to make light of it.

He heard the pain anyway. "What kind of man would leave you at the altar?"

"He was a fertilizer salesman."

"You dated a man who sold fertilizer? I'm not even going to comment on that."

"He was nice to me. I thought that was enough. I just thought…" She looked so vulnerable and alone. Her ponytail brushed the slender column of her neck, so dark against her soft skin. "He didn't love me, and his best man told me so. In front of half the town."

Noah gently squeezed her fingers, offering her comfort. "What kind of man couldn't love you? Wait, don't answer that."

"A fertilizer salesman." She swiped dark tendrils out of her eyes, sad and trying not to be. "It still hurts. Maybe worse because it wasn't the first time."

"Someone else jilted you at the altar?"

"No, but I did have two other broken engagements, and I don't want to talk about them." Her eyes were glassy, as if she were holding back tears. She yanked her fingers from his and leaned forward and away, breaking contact and all the connection between them. She grabbed his plate and thrust it at him.

Heartbreak. He knew how deep it cut, how much it hurt. He could imagine her in a pretty white gown of satin and lace, alone in that crowded church. Abandoned by the man who'd said he loved her. She didn't deserve that.

"What about you?" Her silver fork scraped on the china.

"Love and I don't mix."

"Ever?"

"I tried it once, but I didn't have any better luck than you did." He speared a piece of frosted cake and chewed. He refused to discuss what had happened the one time he'd been weak enough, and foolish, to fall in love.

"Hey, I told you my heartache. You ought to be as brave."

"It's not a matter of courage. It just doesn't matter."

"If it hurt you, it matters."

She meant it. It was there in her eyes. "I came out all right, so don't worry about me."

"I don't like the way that sounds." She licked the frosting off her fork. "What are you? In your mid-thirties, and you've never been married. Do you have that fear of commitment thing?"

"Not me. I'm about as committed as a man can get. I work twenty-hour days, six days a week. Just about every day of the year. That's responsibility."

"You're rich. Why do you work so much? I mean, you could retire. Then you'd have lots of time to spend with your girlfriends. You know, the ones you've got dangling on a string, pining away for you."

"Is this your roundabout way of asking if I do a lot of dating?"

"Your social life is none of my business. I'm just saying…" Her face was burning hot. She didn't want to think about Noah and dating. He'd go for a wealthy, sophisticated woman. The sort who wore designer labels and who wouldn't be caught dead in a pair of department store sneakers.

"I saw the way the women at the party were ogling you. You were magnetic."

"It had nothing to do with me and everything to do with my bank account. As nice as your friends are, they don't see me. Who I am. What I stand for. If I were a poor man, they'd never look at me twice."

His sadness touched her. "Some woman really hurt you, didn't she?"

"I'm not going to talk about it."

Whatever happened, she sensed he had been hurt worse than she had in life. Tenderness filled her up, tenderness she didn't have the right to feel. Tomorrow he'd be jetting away in his plane to the East Coast, where he ran one of the most successful companies in the country.

And she'd return to her classroom that smelled of crayons and finger paint and chocolate chip cookies.

A teapot whistled in the kitchen down the hall, and Julie could just make out the low rumble of her grandfather's chuckle.

"They're so happy," she whispered. "It's adorable."

Noah didn't answer. "You have faith in marriage, do you?"

"Marriage is no different from life, I figure. It's what you make of it. Are you worried that your grandmother is going to be unhappy? My granddad will do anything it takes to make her happy."

"She's had one good marriage. I guess that means she knows how to make another good one. Marriage seems perilous to me."

"Me, too, and I've only been as far as the altar," she quipped, making light of the feelings she was too afraid to acknowledge.

Two sets of footsteps padded down the hall and into the dining room. The faint creak of a chair told her the happy couple was sitting down to enjoy their tea and conversation. The low, contented buzz of their conversation filled the house with their happiness.

Noah put his empty plate on the coffee table. The clink of the silverware on china echoed in the quiet. He looked weary as he climbed to his feet and paced to the fire. "Want to know why I really hired that detective?"

She set her plate aside and moved close, so they could keep their voices low. "Does this have to do with the woman who broke your heart?"

"She did more than that." He crouched in front of the fire, staring into the flames.

Why would anyone hurt this man? Julie hunkered down on the floor and waited for Noah to say more.

"Her name was Vanessa and she went to my church. Still does, actually." He curled up next to her. "Sure you want to hear this?"

"Do you want to talk about it?"

"I never talk about it." He hung his head, dark shocks tumbling forward to hide his face. "But I need you to understand. I'm a man who would never mean to hurt anyone, and I feel bad about the P.I."

"I'm beginning to know that about you."

"Good. I hired the detective because that's what I should have done for myself, about five years ago. I trusted someone I shouldn't. Vanessa was kind and beautiful and seemed to understand me. I was lonely, and many of my friends were married, some happily. I thought, maybe that could be me, with a gentle wife who loved me. I really wanted someone to love me. Foolish, I guess."

"What's wrong with wanting to love and be loved?" Julie took his bigger hand in hers. Held him tight, so he would know that he wasn't alone.

He slipped his arm around her shoulders, drawing her close. Tenderly, sweetly.

How could anyone not love this man?

"Your parents divorced, as mine did. You have to know what it's like. The fighting. The conflict.

The constant hurting. Words become weapons that hurt more than fists."

"Yes." She knew exactly what he meant. "But not every marriage is like that."

"That's what I told myself. I figured Vanessa was as nice as could be. Soft-spoken. Gentle. She never had an unkind word to say to me. Unlike you, she never showed her anger with me. That should have been a clue, in retrospect."

"What does that mean? You liked that I became angry with you?"

"You were honest with me. You were angry. There's nothing wrong with that. She hid every honest emotion from me, and I didn't know it. I thought no discord, no problems. I couldn't have been more wrong. She was sleeping with another man—my best friend."

"Noah, I'm sorry she betrayed you."

"I'm a Christian. I respect my faith. I wasn't sleeping with her. I guess that made it easier for her to pretend to be in love with me. When I proposed, I gave her a five-carat flawless diamond for an engagement ring and pledged to her my undying love. I was a fool." He'd lost more than his heart that day.

"I'm so sorry. You didn't deserve that." Julie wrapped her arms around him, in comfort and friendship.

He buried his face in her shoulder, her sweater

soft against his skin, and held her. Held her, gently and gratefully, until the hurt deep in his soul ebbed away.

Chapter Nine

Noah padded down the hallway, following the single light shining in the dark house. "Nanna? Are you down here?"

"Just finishing up my reading." Nanna glanced over the top of her bifocals at him, from her place at the small kitchen table. Her Bible was open before her. "I thought I told you to get to bed early, young man."

"I was on my computer. Lost track of time." Noah turned a wood chair around and swung onto the seat. Getting comfortable, he leaned his forearms on the chair back. "Aren't you up pretty late?"

"Seems I have too much on my mind to fall asleep easy these days." Nanna swiped her hands over her face, looking weary. So very weary. "Between the wedding and the new house. It's a balancing act, I tell you. Hope and Julie are helping me with everything, but some days I can't stop worrying if my dress will arrive on time. Oh, and now the meeting with the builder."

"I'll be there, Nanna. I'll help you as much as I can."

"I know you will. Oh, I'm not complaining. I just need another cup of chamomile tea and to spend a few more peaceful moments with my reading." She touched her Bible. "What about you? Will you be flying off in that jet of yours the moment our little meeting is over?"

"You know I have to get back to work. If there's anything more I can do while I'm here, I'll do it."

"My dear boy, one day, you are going to realize what you're missing in life. Then you'll stop working every waking hour of the day. You'll be running to your family instead of away."

Her words hit their mark. Noah looked away. It was easier to stare at the floor than at the understanding on his grandmother's face. "I've been the cause of this discord between you and Harold. I should have been more welcoming to him."

"You were polite."

"You're defending me, and I love you for it. But you're right. We both know it."

He thought of the story he'd told Julie tonight. The truth he'd never told anyone else, except for his attorney. Not even Nanna understood the true reason why he couldn't stomach the idea of marrying.

He'd closed off his heart so completely, he couldn't let himself trust the people he loved. People who had never let him down.

He should confess. He should tell her about the stress attacks. They were over now, and he'd make sure it stayed that way. Nothing would cast a shadow over her upcoming wedding....

"You're the sunshine of my life." Nanna caught hold of his hand, her grip strong and faithful, loving and loyal. "It would be a great help to me if you'd give me your opinion of the construction bid. You and Harold could look it over together. Why, it would give you the perfect chance to get to know one another."

"So, everything really is all right?" He worried about her. He couldn't help it. "You were pretty upset."

"I know, but Harold gave me his word that he'd try harder. Now I'll need the same from you."

"Ah, you know I will."

"Fine, then, enough said. The meeting with the builder is at nine sharp. I know I'll make the right decision with my two favorite men to help me. I'm so pleased that you decided to change your plans out of your love for me."

"Bribery. Guilt. Manipulation." He kissed her cheek. "I didn't have any choice, but I don't mind."

"That's my dear boy." She caught his cheek and gave him a pinch. "Now off to bed with you. It's far too late as it is. Go. Scoot."

He stood and swung the chair into place. How could he tell her about those stress attacks, or whatever they were? She'd be worrying about the doctor and when he'd be calling and what he might say, during her meeting with the builder. A woman didn't get a new house, custom-built, every day.

It was only a stress attack. It wasn't as if it would be happening again. There was no need to tell her. Problem solved.

Noah's story troubled Julie most of the night. She woke up thinking about him, as the morning dawned bitterly cold. She had failed relationships that hurt to this day, but nothing like that. No wonder he'd given up trusting in people.

Well, he could trust her.

She added him to her morning prayers, hoping for a good answer from the doctor. He had looked healthier last night, almost as if the painful attack had never happened. Maybe Noah was right—it was stress. He certainly had a stressful lifestyle.

Snow began falling on the way to school. By the time she reached town to grab her morning latte at the coffee shop, the roads were slick. School buses with chains on their tires clunked down the main street, heading out on their routes.

"Hey!" Susan popped into Julie's classroom, her own latte in hand. "How was Sunday dinner with Mr. Billionaire?"

It felt private, all that had happened between her and Noah. "Fine."

"Fine? Misty and I have a theory." She tapped into the room with complete confidence. "Mr. Ashton the Third is sweet on you."

"On me? No, we're friends. And before you say one more word, remember that he lives in New York City. I live in Montana. And it's not only the miles that separate us."

"Aha! I knew it. You like him, too, or you wouldn't have thought this out so much. Admit it."

"His grandmother is marrying my grandfather. We have to be nice to each other. It's like a rule." Julie searched through the file folder open on her desk for the bright red *H*. "I'm a potato farmer's daughter. I have nothing but a string of failed relationships, so I don't think that makes me a prime candidate for a relationship with a wealthy, handsome and perfect man like Noah."

Susan nodded sagely. "Perfect, huh? Well, I guess that means he's available, after all. You don't mind if Misty or I try to charm him the next time he's in town."

"Go right ahead. Neither of you are victims of romantic doom." She grabbed the stapler and attached the *A* in place above the friendly-looking snowman.

"Sure that you're not feeling a little jealous? A little possessive?"

"No, why should I?" Julie stapled a *P* next to the *A*.

"Can we say the word *denial?* C'mon, Julie. You forget who you're talking to. I was standing right beside you when Keith told us that Chet decided not to marry you. I stayed with you when you cried long into the night. I sent back the wedding gifts for you, so you wouldn't have to face doing it. I know how much that hurt."

"You're a great friend, Susan. The best." Julie stared at the stapler in her hand, feeling lost and confused. "I know what you're going to say. You're going to tell me that I should take a risk again. That being jilted once doesn't guarantee it will happen again."

"So? What's holding you back?"

Julie thought of Noah. Of all the wonderful things he was. How he treated her. How much fun they'd had together skiing. How he'd apologized to her when he was wrong, and he opened up to her later. He told her his most painful secret. He held her in his arms, just held her.

"Noah is not the right man for me." She couldn't afford to let him be.

But that didn't stop her from thinking about him after school, when her room was quiet and silence echoed in the hallway as she closed her classroom door behind her. Had he heard from the doctor? Was he back home in New York by now and going about his normal life?

"Julie, I sure enjoyed the engagement party," the principal's secretary called the minute Julie stepped foot inside the front office. "I haven't had that much fun in ages. Your granddad sure looked happy."

"He is, thanks. I'm glad you had a good time." Julie looked in her box—the usual stuff—and jammed the paper into her book bag.

"My favorite part was seeing you dance with the billionaire," her cousin, Jenna, commented from behind a nearby computer. "Is there something going on? I had to help keep an eye on the caterers because you ran off with him."

"I'm pleading the Fifth."

"You took him to the hospital, didn't you? My brother saw you two in the hallway. He's an EMT, remember?" Jenna nodded sagely. "I bet Mr. Ashton was injured rescuing the little Corey girl."

"He's quite the hero," the secretary agreed. "Isn't that him waiting out there by your car, Julie?"

Every head in the office turned toward the window that looked over the lawn to the parking lot. Sure enough, there was Noah leaning against her truck fender. What was he still doing here?

His smile was genuine when he noticed she was marching across the grass in his direction. She had no idea what he was doing there, but he looked good doing it. He could have been a page torn from a men's fashion magazine with the way his longer black coat was unbuttoned to show a glimpse of the black suit beneath and a matching silk tie. He looked like a man who didn't belong in this small Montana town.

"Hey, beautiful. I saw the school buses pulling down the street and all the kids running down the sidewalk, and I figured you might be through with work for the day." He stole her heavy book bag and carried it for her. "Can I bum a ride from you? I need to get to the airport."

"What happened to your sister? Wasn't she going to take you?"

"Her little boy's earache is worse, so I told her to stay home. Nanna and Harold met with the builder today and dragged me along. I escaped after we'd gone over the contract, but they're still talking over the finer details of the house. Since I don't have a car, I'm stranded. So, here I am, hoping some pretty lady will take pity on me."

"It's your lucky day. I have an available vehicle, and I happen to have the rest of the afternoon free. You look good, so I take it the morning brought good news. What did the doctor say?"

"He hasn't called yet." Noah opened the truck door for her. "He's been stuck in surgery all day, but his nurse swore an oath that he would call me before four."

"It's been a tough wait?"

"No. I don't think it's bad news. It's just the waiting so I can hear those words for sure." He took her elbow to help her into the truck. "I don't want to be an imposition. Do you mind playing taxi for me?"

"Not at all. That's what friends are for."

"Thanks." He shut the door for her, pure gentleman.

She liked him, far too much. Good thing she didn't have to worry about a romance developing between them. And if a part of her wondered what it would be like to be in love with Noah, she would simply ignore it.

He hopped in the passenger door and tucked her book bag on the floor. "I'm sure your granddad will tell you all about it, but he and Nanna have finally settled on a house plan. They break ground as soon as the weather changes. I looked over the contract for them, that's why I'm staying in town longer than I planned."

She started the engine and backed out of the spot. "How did it go?"

"With your granddad, you mean? Well enough. I think he was glad enough to have someone who could read contracts for them." A shrill jingle sounded from his coat pocket. He tossed her a slightly worried look as he fished out the phone.

Hadn't he distinctly said he wasn't worried?

"I can do this." He took a deep breath, released it and punched a button. "Hello?"

Julie pulled up against the curb in the residential district. With the engine idling, she could hear the mumble of the doctor's voice.

"I see." Noah sounded…different. Strained. "Of course. I'll think about it. Thanks."

Her heart felt as if it stopped beating. Her blood turned to ice. The news wasn't good. Noah had turned completely pale as he punched the button that turned off the phone.

He was so silent. She wanted more than anything for him to turn to her and say, "The tests came out perfect." Anything to put the color back in his face and to sweep away the lines digging into his brow. This was not good news at all.

She didn't know what to say. No words came to mind, so she reached across the small distance between them to touch his sleeve. Noah didn't acknowledge her touch as he gazed out the side window. Snow tumbled in fluffy pieces to melt on the hood and cling to the windshield.

"I really thought it was nothing." He sounded so far away. "I'd talked myself into it. Nothing but denial, I suppose. After you took me skiing, I felt so great. I thought I'd dodged a bullet, that nothing was really wrong. If I started working out more and taking some time off, that would do the trick."

"What did the doctor say?"

"They found a suspicious mass in my abdomen." He felt wooden. Shock coursed through his veins, turning his blood to ice.

Tumor. He couldn't say the word aloud to Julie. Cancer at the worst. Gallstones at the least. The doctors wouldn't know until it was removed, and that meant surgery.

He buried his face in his hands. How could this be happening to him? It couldn't. The scans had to be wrong. He felt fine. He felt healthier than he had in years. It couldn't be cancer. Look at how he'd reduced his stress for one afternoon and the pain disappeared. That had to mean he was going to be all right. Right?

Lord, please let the tests be wrong.

He knew deep down they were not. The doctor wouldn't have called until he was certain.

"Noah, I'm so sorry. Did they say anything else?"

"Only that I had to have it removed as soon as possible."

"Do they know if it's benign?"

He shook his head. She was asking in a polite way if he had cancer, and he couldn't say that word out loud. What if it was that serious? He might be looking at the end of his life.

It couldn't be that bad, could it? This couldn't be happening to him.

160A Love Worth Waiting For

"We can pray that it's benign. Will that help?"

He nodded. Her hand on his sleeve was the only thing that felt real right now. His head was spinning. His heart was thundering. But the steady warmth of her hand was like a connection that kept him grounded, that kept him from panicking. Her words were soothing as she began to pray.

He bowed his head, hardly able to hear her through the rush of his pulse. The gentle words of her prayer reminded him that whatever happened, the Lord was watching over him. He would be all right.

He took a deep breath, calmer, stronger. *Thank you for Julie,* he added silently to the prayer before he murmured his amen.

He opened his eyes. Julie's face was all he could see. Her dark hair escaping in wispy tendrils from the ponytail to frame her face. The curve of her cheek, the light of her spirit in her eyes, the delicate cut of her chin that made him reach out and cup her jaw in the palm of his hand.

"Your friendship is the best blessing I've received in a long while." He'd never spoken so honestly. Overwhelmed with tenderness, he brushed his lips to her cheek. Sweetness filled him, and he felt heartened. Uplifted.

"You're a blessing to me, too." Her voice came rough with emotion.

He rubbed his thumb across the soft line of her jaw. She was so amazing to him. He'd never met anyone like her, so full of convictions and life and spirit. The caring that shone in her eyes seemed genuine. It really did. That amazed him, too, because he didn't see it very often.

"Do you want me to take you back to your grandmother?" she offered.

"No, I'm not ready for that, and I don't want her to know right now."

"I don't think you should be alone. I can call your sister. Or, I know, I could take you skiing again. Or we could just go to my place and talk. I'll even make hot chocolate. We'll do whatever you need, Noah."

His instincts told him to be sensible. He didn't need to talk. He didn't need anyone. His jet was waiting. They were expecting him at the office. While he was sitting here, work was piling up on his desks. There would be memos, phone calls, e-mails and faxes all needing his attention, and more problems to solve than the day was long.

He had every reason to ask her to take him to the airport.

Only one reason to stay.

She was waiting for an answer, half in and half out of her seat belt, her sweater rumpled and a blue paint smear on her sleeve. His thoughts should be focused on the doctor's news. His emotions centered on the fear or panic or whatever it was that he was going to feel once the numbness and shock wore off.

Instead, he wanted to go skiing with her. They'd had so much fun. No one had ever teased him like that. And she'd raced him, and beat him. Man, he'd had a great time.

The wind gusted against the side of the truck, rocking the vehicle just enough to jostle him out of his thoughts. A lot of snow had fallen, he was only now noticing, and it completely covered the windshield except for a tiny row at the top. Giving him a glimpse of the white-mantled maple overhead and the ice-gray sky above. The sight of that sky made him yearn for something he couldn't name.

Or maybe it was this feeling Julie was creating in him.

Logic told him he had to leave. There was work waiting for him. It was the responsible thing to do. But that wasn't the real reason.

"I have to get back." He hated seeing the flash of disappointment on her beautiful face. He'd let her down, and he hadn't meant to. "Can I call you sometime, just to talk, friend to friend?"

"Absolutely. I should give you my e-mail address, too." She went to reach for her book bag, as if nothing were wrong, as if he hadn't just rejected her.

He pulled a card from his pocket. "Here's mine. Call me anytime, Julie. I mean that."

"That goes both ways." She ran her thumb over the embossed letters on the thin business card. "We're still friends, right?"

"Very good friends." He really liked her. He liked that she understood about romantic doom, since he'd had a lot of that in his life. He loved that she was his friend.

Out of the blue, he needed her, and she was there. She had to be a gift from heaven, a blessing wrapped up in a blue jacket and topped with a rainbow-striped cap. She'd reminded him there was more to life than work. Maybe even more to him.

What if this was cancer? He stopped his thoughts right there. One step at a time. He needed to contact a doctor back home. There would be appointments and surgery and… His stomach clenched tight with fear. He really didn't want to think about what happened then.

What mattered was the present. This moment. With Julie.

"Maybe next time I'll take you skiing." Yes, that's what he'd do. He loved skiing, and it *was* wintertime. Colorado was really something this time of year.

"Next time, huh?" She climbed back into her seat belt, trouble twinkling in her eyes. "I could be persuaded to ski with you again. For the right price."

"Wow. The right price, huh? How about a cup of hot chocolate?"

"Add marshmallows and you have a deal, mister."

How she made him shine inside, like the sun

dawning in the dark night of his heart, bringing a fresh start and new possibilities.

He reached across the seat and twined his fingers through hers. He cared about her. How fortunate he was that she'd walked into his life.

At the small municipal airport, Julie watched Noah wave a final time before he disappeared behind the glass windows. The scent of his after-shave lingered in the cab and on her clothes. She felt lonely, knowing he was gone.

Way to go, Julie. You're starting to like him way too much. And what good would come of that? Not one thing. Noah was rich, handsome, kind and a good Christian. Pretty much everything she'd ever dreamed of in a man.

As if he'd ever be interested in her.

Julie could see the small private planes through the security fencing. Without a doubt, she knew the pretty white-and-gold plane, the one that shouted "lavishly expensive" was Noah's. In a few minutes he'd be boarding that plane and probably settling down in seats of the finest leather. He'd snack on caviar and call Tokyo on his air phone.

Yep, she'd surely fit into his lifestyle. No problem. Her Chevy truck could compete with his jet anyday. So, she hadn't gone for the leather seats, and she didn't have satellite positioning. She could always upgrade, right?

Wrong. She shifted, pulling onto the highway. Snow scudded across the pavement, driven by the harsh wind. She felt like the road, laid bare by powers beyond her control. Her heart felt exposed, raw and aching.

He'd touched her. He'd been so sweet to her in the truck. Looking into his eyes, seeing the real Noah made her like him way too much.

It was his fault, for being so terrific, so gentle and kind and good and funny. He was to blame for going skiing with her and liking hot chocolate and caring so much for his grandmother. That would make any woman adore him.

He was at fault for being so wonderful.

Then he'd cupped her face with his big hand. "Your friendship is the best blessing I've received in a long while." And then he'd kissed her.

How had she let this happen? Wasn't being abandoned in front of her friends and family enough to prove to her that she'd always be alone? It didn't matter how wonderful everyone had been or how sympathetic and sorry, the truth was still the truth. Chet had tried to love her, and couldn't. He couldn't stand before God and take her as his wife. She wasn't someone he could love like that.

And Ray, the fiancé before that, had felt the same way. He'd fallen in love with one of her bridesmaids and they'd eloped. At least Ray had called her from Pocatello, Idaho, so she'd had time to cancel the wedding.

And her very first fiancé, when she'd been a tender nineteen, had been too young, just as she'd been. They'd made a mess of their romance because they had different values and different wishes for their lives. The breakup had been sensible, but it had left her feeling as if she wasn't good enough. That she'd never find a love of her own.

Three strikes, you're out. Isn't that the way it was? She often made light of it, but not even Susan or Misty or Granddad knew the real anguish in her soul. What was wrong with her, that love never worked out? That the men who said they loved her enough to offer her an engagement ring couldn't stick around? They, like her mother, didn't see enough in her to want to stay.

How on earth could she ever expect anything more from Noah? He had his choice of women, and he'd been horribly hurt in love, but…all you had to do was look at him. He was perfect in every way. When he chose to risk his heart again, it would probably be to fall in love with some slender, leggy supermodel, the kind that graduated from Harvard and launched her own charity foundation and did good deeds for humanity between photo shoots.

He deserved the best. Julie wanted that for him. It was humbling and it hurt, but she was no supermodel, that was for sure. She merely had a teaching degree from the local university, and she hadn't graduated with honors. She wasn't photogenic, her charitable work was done through the church's annual food drive for the holidays and she'd be lost in a big city like New York.

And why was she even thinking like that? The man wasn't interested in her. He wasn't going to propose to her. He hadn't bought a tux for their wedding. He just wanted to go skiing again—that was all.

At the edge of town, she slowed to the posted twenty-five miles per hour, waving at the local sheriff, who was in his patrol car checking radar beside the road. They'd gone to school together, and his little boy was in her morning class. He saluted, as he always did, with a friendly smile. They'd dated briefly in high school. He'd been her date to Junior Prom. Now he was married and a father.

Some people were very blessed.

Feeling extralonely, she followed an impulse and pulled into an available parking spot in front of the town grocery. Tonight she would make Granddad's favorite meal and invite both him and Nora over for supper. Since she had her cell phone handy, she made a few calls to arrange it.

By the time she snagged her own cart from the front of the store and started through the aisles, she was feeling better. Her momentary lapse of sadness was gone. She had blessings she was immensely grateful for.

"Miss Renton! Mama, there's Miss Renton!" a little girl's voice rang out from the produce aisle.

Julie recognized a student from her afternoon class. "Hello, Brittany."

"We're shoppin' for the turkey." The little girl's ringlets bounced as she skipped to a stop in the middle of the aisle, leaving her mother's side and the brimming shopping cart. "Mommy's gonna make yams just the way I like 'em."

"With the sugary stuff?" Julie asked, as Brittany's mom bagged a head of lettuce before heading their way. "Those are my favorite kind of yams, too. Is your mommy baking a pie?"

"Three pies." Brittany held up the appropriate number of fingers. "My baby brother's too little to eat 'em."

"We're having the whole family over," Carol explained as she shoved the heavy cart to a stop, the new baby belted safely in the seat. "Oh, I had the best time at the engagement party. I haven't danced in so long and my feet still hurt from it, but I don't mind a bit."

"I'm glad you had a good time. How's your new baby?"

"Not sleeping through the nights, yet. Look, he's wearing the sleeper you gave him at the shower." Carol tugged down the blanket to show a blue romper. They chatted for a few more minutes, before Julie went on her way.

As she selected onions and bagged them, a baby began crying in the next aisle. Probably Carol's baby. The principal's wife whisked by with a basket and said hello, and later Julie waved at a friend from church in the bakery section. Kids were plastered in front of the glass display case of decorated cookies. Mothers were everywhere, hurrying to buy what they needed for supper, or shopping early for the upcoming holidays.

Julie checked off the last item on her list and headed for the checkout. She paid for her purchases, carried the two bags of groceries to her truck and headed home.

Alone.

Noah heard the phone ringing in the hall. Was it Julie? He didn't know why, but he hoped so. Maybe she'd call to see if he made it home safe. That would be just like her.

Hurrying as the phone continued to shrill, he punched off his security and raced through the room, dropping his keys and briefcase as he went. He couldn't wait to hear her voice.

He snatched up the phone in midring. "Hey."

"I'm mad as a wet hornet at you, young man," Nanna scolded. "You didn't tell me what happened, oh, no. I had to hear about my only grandson from my friends at the weekly Ladies' Aid meeting."

How had Nanna found out? Nobody knew about his test results. No one but Julie, and he hoped she hadn't told. How was he going to protect his grandmother from this? Her wedding was two weeks away, and he could be facing a cancer diagnosis. "Nanna, I'm sorry. I meant to tell you."

"Well, I should hope so. I asked Julie if it was true, when she invited Harold and me out to her lovely home for supper tonight, and she said it was. Whatever am I to do with you, my dear boy?"

"*Julie* told you?" He broke a little inside. He'd thought she was the kind of person he could trust.

"Trying to keep it a secret from your own grandmother. Don't you know how I like to brag about my Noah? Goodness' sake, how can I take pride in you if I'm always the last to know about your latest good deed?"

"Good deed?" Noah stopped in his tracks. Nanna wasn't taking about the medical tests? Then what was this about?

"Saving that little girl from the creek. I heard how she was drowning and you dove in to save her." Nanna's voice radiated pride.

"Not true. The kid had fallen from her horse. Both Julie and I happened to be driving by when it happened. We stopped and found the girl in the field. We both took her home. End of story."

"Hmm, I didn't know that about Julie. She conveniently left that piece of information out of our conversation. Now I'm fed up with the both of you! Next time, you tell your grandmother what you've been up to. Do you hear me?"

"Loud and clear, ma'am. I promise I'll be good. So, you saw Julie tonight." Julie. He was glad she hadn't betrayed his trust.

"She cooked the most wonderful spaghetti sauce. I had to beg for the recipe from her. She baked bread and fixed up a fancy salad. My, it was a treat. She even made cheesecake for dessert. She's such a fine cook, I can't imagine why some man hasn't come along and snapped her up."

"Neither can I, Nanna." He rolled his eyes.

He loved his grandmother dearly, but she believed everyone should be married! Why? He'd never figure that out. Just because she had good fortune with her first marriage, she looked at love through rose-colored glasses. He adored that about her, but it wasn't realistic.

Although, to be honest, he liked to think people were happy together somewhere. That some marriages were about building one another up with love and caring. That was the kind of love television would have you believe. The trouble was, he'd seen the other side. He'd endured his parents' troubled marriage, and had the scars to prove it.

Chapter Ten

Julie couldn't sleep. She tossed off her down comforter and searched around on the floor for her fuzzy bunny slippers. She found them by touch and jammed her feet into them. Shivering, she groped in the dark for more clothing. She found a thick sweatshirt on the back of the chair in the corner and tugged it on over her flannel pajamas. The cat nestled in the chair cushion meowed his disapproval.

"Sorry, Wilbur." She rubbed his ears in apology and grabbed the book from the night table.

The wind whipped against the eaves. A storm must be blowing in. The downstairs was cold, too, and she headed straight to the kitchen. Popping a cup of water into the microwave took a second. In a few minutes, she had boiling hot peppermint tea steeping.

The cat slinked through the shadows to inspect

his food dish, just in case. He sat in front of his kitty bowl expectantly.

"It's not even close to breakfast time, and you know it." She tried to be firm with him, but he flicked his tail. Displeased with his human, Wilbur sauntered over to her and wound around her ankles, as sweet as can be.

"Turning on the charm, are you?" She lifted him into her arms to scratch him properly. He purred, leaning his chin against her fingers.

See, she wasn't alone. She had Wilbur. The happiness from the evening's dinner party seemed to remain in the kitchen, where Nora's hostess gift of silk flowers sat on the island, soft and colorful against the beige Formica. She had so many blessings, it felt wrong to wish for what she couldn't have.

Not knowing what to do, she carried her cat, her book and her steaming cup of tea to the living room. The fabric blinds were closed tight against the windows, blocking out the night and the draft. She hit the remote and the gas fireplace flared to life.

Wilbur, apparently having all the adoration he could tolerate, climbed onto his blanket and curled into a contented ball. Julie brushed the cat hair off her sleeve before flipping open her book. She would read, drink her tea—and in no time she'd be sleepy again. Insomnia wasn't going to trouble her for long.

Except she kept reading the same three lines over and over again. The inspirational romance that had kept her riveted an hour before bedtime couldn't hold her attention now. The words she kept staring at seemed to have no meaning. It wasn't the book, it was her. She *wanted* to think about Noah. She'd vowed *not* to think about Noah. And so she couldn't think of anything else.

If she closed her eyes, she could still feel his touch. His warm, steady hand cradling her chin. His feather-soft kiss on her cheek. She'd tried to forget the emotional closeness they'd shared, but it was impossible. All she had to do was think of him, and in her thoughts she was back in her truck, with his aftershave scenting the recirculated air and snow landing on the windshield.

I'm concerned about his health, that's all this is, she tried to tell herself. She would worry about anyone diagnosed with an abdominal tumor. But that wasn't the whole truth. She had so wanted Noah to stay with her, instead of leaving on his jet. She wished she had the chance to comfort him.

Okay, now that sounded a little selfish, and it wasn't how she meant it. She only knew that she wanted to mean something to him. She wished that when he was hurting, and when he needed someone to hold on to, he would reach for her.

But he'd gone back to New York. Returned to the world he preferred. He probably had tons of friends and an active life. Broadway plays and football games and museums to wander through on a rainy weekend afternoon.

It was a few minutes past midnight. It would be just after two in the morning in New York. He'd be fast asleep, and in a few hours his alarm would go off and he'd start his day. It would be a day without her. A day when he wouldn't think of her once.

But she would think of him.

Noah couldn't sleep. He opened one eye to get a brief view of the clock—2:14, the green lights proclaimed. Great. He'd been asleep for an hour and two minutes. His chest was burning, and that wasn't a good sign. He prayed it wasn't the start of another attack. He had pain pills the doctor had prescribed for him, but he didn't want to take them.

Maybe what he needed was a glass of warm milk. With any luck, he was only experiencing heartburn. Indigestion. A pulled muscle between his ribs. Okay, he was reaching, but he was doing fine not thinking about the result of those tests.

If he didn't think about it, he didn't have to deal with it. If he didn't have to deal with it, then he wouldn't be afraid. He wouldn't wind up taking a look at what was really bothering him.

He figured staying in denial was a better alternative. He'd go along as he had, and in a few weeks his chauffeur would drive him to the hospital. With any luck, he'd be given anesthetics right away and he'd never have to think about the possibilities of cancer.

Cancer. Great, he'd been avoiding that word until now, and it made a cold fear wash him, from head to toe. He nearly dropped his robe on the floor. He couldn't find his slippers so he padded barefoot across the plush carpet, his step loud in the silence. A single sconce in the hallway guided him past a row of doors, all belonging to empty bedrooms, past the foyer and into the gourmet kitchen.

He hit the switch over the eating bar and the track lighting shone off polished stainless-steel appliances and marble countertops. The marble floor was cool on his bare feet as he trudged to the stainless-steel-fronted refrigerator and pulled out a gallon of milk. He tore the plastic loop and removed the cap. After locating a saucepan in the bottom cupboards, he set it on the stove.

Boy, the place felt empty tonight. His movements rattled around in the shadows, making the apartment feel enormous. Too big for just one person. He'd bought this place because it was a good investment and because it was close to work. That was before Vanessa, when he'd held out the smallest hope that he might get married one day and have kids of his own. A family that would fill the rooms with their laughter and toys and stuff to trip over in the hallway.

He hadn't thought of that in years, and it was

because of those test results. The doctor had used the word *cancer,* and Noah felt as if the earth had fallen out from beneath his feet. Everything was uncertain. What would happen at his next doctor's appointment? How serious would the operation be? Would he be able to return to his work? And his health… Would he be all right? Or was this something so serious, it would take his life? What if the time he had left on this earth was much shorter than he thought?

That was a scary notion. He'd spent the last decade working long, hard days. Shouldering responsibilities to the board, the stockholders and the employees who received a check every two weeks. He'd given all he had to this company, and there hadn't been much time left for friends. Or family. Or doing anything he might enjoy.

What if he had one year to live? How would he spend it?

The milk bubbled, and he grabbed the pan from the heat. He filled a porcelain mug. He'd work— that's what he'd do. He'd put everything in order so someone else could take over the responsibilities of the company he'd built.

Work? No, that didn't seem like the right answer. He carried the mug to the shadowed table. The light over the sink cast a reflection on the black windows. He hadn't bothered to pull the shades. Rain smeared the glass, distorting his reflection.

He'd had a blast this weekend skiing with Julie.

Being out in those foothills, where the mountains were so rugged and huge, they were close enough to touch. That was paradise.

He loved skiing. He didn't go as often as he could. And why was that? Because he was busy working for a company that didn't care about him. That wouldn't miss him when he was gone and buried. Whether that was in a year or fifty years. He didn't love his company.

Trouble was, he didn't have a family of his own to love.

Sure, his sister and grandmother. But they were extended family. What he craved was a wife, kind in the way Julie was, who would love him and never let him down.

He'd never felt more alone than he did right now. Sure, he could pick up the phone and call Hope or Nanna. But Hope was married and truly happy. She had a husband and children, a real family of her own.

He couldn't tell Nanna about this tumor. Not after seeing her so happy this weekend. She and Harold had been adorable—there was no other word for it. The joy in her voice and the love in her eyes… No, he refused to take those away from her.

Maybe it was better this way. He really didn't need anyone. Really. This was supposed to be the best time of Nanna's life. He remembered how her face had lit with undiluted joy when she'd shown him the picture of her wedding dress. It has been light gray, beaded and embroidered and lacy—all the things a bride wanted. The bridesmaid dresses would be an emerald-green. She'd showed him that picture, too, of the simple and elegant dresses, exactly something Nanna would pick out to adorn her beautiful bridesmaids.

Would Julie be one of them? He didn't know, but his thoughts turned to her. Maybe it was her presence he was missing tonight. The uncanny way she had of making him feel so deeply and so much. With her he felt real. As if his work and responsibilities vanished like smoke, and she was there. She'd been hurt, too. She knew what kind of scars a shattered relationship could leave.

He didn't know why she was the one. Why was it that she could simply sit with him in a snowstorm when he received the worst news of his life, and the constant aloneness he carried inside him disappeared.

What he wanted to do was to call her and hear the warmth of her voice. Julie was the only person he could talk to about this. The only one he trusted that much. It was past midnight in Montana. She'd be fast asleep, safe and at peace, tucked away in her cozy log home for the night. He couldn't wake her, but he wanted to.

That wasn't like him. He didn't need anyone, remember?

For the first time in his adult life, he felt off balance. As if someone had pulled the rug out from beneath his feet and left him to fall. In one moment on the phone with the doctor, his entire world had tipped on its side. Everything had changed.

He felt lost as the rain pattered against the windows and the wind gusted around the corner of the building. The warmed milk didn't soothe him. The thought of Julie only unsettled him. The burning pain in his chest was stronger. It hurt to breathe.

"When I am afraid, I will trust in you." The verse from Psalms came into his mind, and he felt comforted. Noah *did* trust the Lord to show him the way through this shadowed valley that had become his life.

Julie couldn't believe her eyes. There was Noah's e-mail address right there on her computer screen. He'd written! She clicked open the letter, not knowing what to expect. Now that he was back at home, surrounded by his friends and his busy life, she didn't expect him to think of her at all.

Wait a minute. Just because he'd dropped her an e-mail didn't mean he was feeling the same growing affection she felt. He'd probably typed a few lines in a friendly way. A short correspondence to a long-distance acquaintance. She shouldn't expect anything too personal or emotionally intimate.

"Dear Julie," she read. "I can't sleep and it's too late to call you, so I thought I'd write. I miss you."

She stopped reading and studied that sentence again. He missed her friendship? She certainly missed his. Her life felt empty without him. That didn't make any sense because she'd only known him for a short while. In their time together, he had made an impact on her heart.

"I meant what I said in the truck on the way to the airport. You've been a true friend."

A true friend, huh? Julie sighed. He kept using that word *friend*. Okay, she could take a hint. She knew he wasn't looking for love. Good thing, too, because neither was she.

Think of what a terrible complication it would be if he wanted to be more than good friends? Oh, he'd buy her gifts and ask her on dates. He'd be calling her and doting on her, and frankly, who needed that kind of attention?

No, she was better off sticking to being friends. A friend couldn't leave you at the altar. A friend couldn't offer you a dream of a happy family, only to snatch it away.

As for these bright, sparkling feelings growing stronger in her heart, it was platonic affection and nothing else. She refused to love one more man who was wrong for her.

"Dear Noah," Julie's e-mail began. "I hope you're enjoying your busy life in the city. Want to know what I did today? While you were probably in meetings in a room with hardly any windows, I was out on my skis. Enjoying nature. Watching the sun set into the snowcapped Rockies."

"You're torturing me." He twisted the top off the iced tea bottle and took a sip. He had been in meetings all morning and had spent the rest of the afternoon on the phone. Sure, he had a great view from his office, but what could compete with Julie's view? And to think she could step off her back porch and start skiing, well, he would love to live like that.

And come to think of it, why wasn't he?

He ignored his assistant's knock at the door and the buzz of the telephone so he could keep reading.

"I had to keep out of the backcountry, because of avalanche warnings. We had a major storm blow through and dump a ton of snow. Maybe you'll want to schedule in a spare day when you come for the wedding. I'll take you up into the mountains and, trust me, you'll never want to leave."

She'd gone skiing—and had the nerve to write about it. Remembering the cool air rushing across his face, the exhilaration of gliding on untouched snow beneath mountains too beautiful to describe made the tension melt from his shoulders. The problems piled on his desk—messages and file folders and a heap of paperwork in the in basket— lost their importance.

"Noah?" Kate hesitated in the threshold. "There's a call from a doctor's office holding."

The surgeon? Cold fear washed over him, leaving him weak. Noah leaned back in his chair, took a deep breath and tried to calm down. It would be all right. Whatever happened, the Lord was with him. He wasn't alone.

He lifted the receiver. "Noah Ashton here."

"Mr. Ashton, this is Margie, Dr. Reynolds's nurse. We'll need to schedule a consultation this week. You'll have a chance to meet with your surgeon and go over the procedure. Looking at your blood tests, we can't rule out cancer. The doctor is quite concerned."

"Yeah." That's what the Montana doctor had said, too. Suspecting cancer wasn't actually having cancer, but this time it was harder to rationalize it away. He'd been numb before, so the words hadn't really sunk in. Hearing "abdominal mass" had been enough to send him into a state of shock, but this…

Woodenly, he answered the nurse as best he could and scheduled an appointment, and then stepped into Kate's office to tell her to clear his Thursday afternoon.

"But that's the day you're leaving for Japan." She pushed back her glasses, frowning at her computer screen. "Is this about the doctor's office? Is something wrong?"

He couldn't answer that. As much as he respected his assistant and how well she did her work, he liked things kept professional, not personal. Of course, if he *did* have a terminal illness, that would affect his professional life and everyone in it.

Don't think about it. He'd deal with that problem later. Right now, he had a takeover to handle, lenders to appease and the latest crisis that had taken up his entire day.

"Just clear the afternoon." He told Kate and headed straight out her door.

In fact, it was hard not to keep going. It was almost five. It wasn't an uncommon time of day for people to stop working and head home.

He dug in his heels to keep from marching straight down that hall to the elevator. A desk heaped with work was waiting, and it was his responsibility. He'd agreed to do it. Every person in this building was counting on him to run this company well and right. They had families to support, kids to raise, mortgages to pay.

And what did he have? Nothing. No one waiting for him. No family, no kids. The only person he'd let get close to him since his breakup with Vanessa was in Montana, probably finishing up her afternoon kindergarten class and getting more paint smudges on her clothes.

She may as well be a world away.

"If you're through with me for the day," Kate announced as she breezed by, carting a heavy briefcase, "I'm outta here. See you bright and early."

Was he really standing in the middle of the

hallway, staring into space? He decided to do his ruminating in the privacy of his office.

Julie's note was still on his screen. It was amazing to him how much he missed her. He sat down at his desk, pushed aside the audit from the company he absolutely had to have three weeks ago and read the rest of her message.

Julie swept last night's powdery snowfall from her front steps. Saturday morning was still, the landscape sugary perfect. A deep mantle of snow hugged the world like a cozy blanket, and the only movement was a pair of bucks, wading through the drifts along her driveway.

The sun was slow to rise, casting long low fingers of golden light through the mountain peaks and across the glittering meadows. Perfect skiing weather, but she didn't feel up to it. Noah wouldn't be with her. She was a sad, sorry case, letting a man affect her like that. Without his companionship, not even skiing was the same.

Inside the house, the phone rang. Probably Granddad checking up on her. She'd cherish his concern for her while she could. Soon his life would be changing. He'd be married with little time to spare, which would be good for him. She suspected he called so often because he was lonely.

Leaving the broom on the porch, she shot in the

door and snatched the receiver before he could hang up. "Good morning."

"Good morning to you," answered a familiar voice.

Not Granddad at all. "Noah! What are you doing calling me? I know you work on your weekends. Aren't you in the middle of a takeover or something?"

"I'm never too busy for you. I meant to answer your e-mail, but I decided to call instead. Are you going to torment me with more tales of your skiing adventures?"

"I could if you wanted me to." She didn't want to tell him how her favorite thing to do on a winter's day now seemed to make her feel lonelier than ever.

How could she admit something like that to him? He probably had a busy day planned between work and friends and his city lifestyle. "I'm going downhill skiing at the Bridger Bowl, a few miles up the road, with Susan and Misty. What about you?"

Good question. Noah put his feet on the glass coffee table and leaned back in the leather sofa. What was he going to do today? The pile of work in his home office needed attention. He could always work out in the health club across the street until he forgot about the upcoming surgery he'd scheduled.

But he didn't want to tell her that. He would

sound…pathetic, needy, like a man who didn't know what he wanted out of life. He didn't want to admit that to anyone, even Julie. "I've got a load of work to do. It'll keep me busy all day."

"Weren't you going to cut back on your stress?"

"Well, after I have control of this microchip company, I'll take it easy."

"I can tell when you're fibbing. I bet you're the kind of man who never takes it easy, even when your health is an issue. Is there a lesson here? What could it be, I wonder?"

"I'm going to do some relaxing tonight. Does that make you happy?"

"*You?* Relax? I don't believe it. Tell me the truth this time."

"I got some movies." He snatched up the DVD cases from the bag on the floor. "Arnold's latest action adventure, and a subtitled one about crouching tigers that says right on the front it won a lot of awards. That ought to be good."

"You don't get out much, do you? Tell me you're as worldly as any other billionaire on this planet."

She was laughing at him! "I work a lot."

"You do get out of your office to go to movies, shows, plays. A museum now and then?"

"I mean to, but there's always something I have to do first."

"You could be living in a cardboard box and you wouldn't know the difference."

"Sure I would. A cardboard box would be drafty. I'd notice that." He felt a hundred times better hearing her voice, knowing her friendship was still there. "Remember the day I left for Montana? I promised that I'd take you skiing."

"Oh, so you have a few acres of mountain property?"

"Who doesn't have a few acres of mountain property?" He loved making her laugh. Her warm chuckle rumbled in his ear. "I have a cabin in the Rockies. I bought it a while ago thinking that I would start taking time off to do lots of skiing, but I was always too busy. I used to think I had plenty of time later to do the things I really wanted to do. Now I have to accept that I could be running out of time. If I want to do something, then I'd better do it."

He'd been wrong, hiding in his work for so long. He was realizing it only now. How many days did he have left? How was he going to spend them?

Not sitting in his office, that was for certain.

He would savor every moment. He'd treasure every minute of being alive on this earth. God's gift of life was precious, and Noah was beginning to realize how much.

When Julie checked her e-mail the next morning, there was a new message from Noah. He'd listed a time and flight number. "I'll meet you on the slopes," he'd written.

The Colorado Rockies! Talk about exciting. She hadn't been out of state since she was in high school.

Noah hadn't given her much time. She'd have to talk to the principal, type up instructions for the substitute and pack. Pack? What did she have to wear? Okay, now she had to go shopping, too.

The cat flicked his tail in great disapproval when she sprinted up the stairs.

Oh, right. She'd have to ask Granddad to feed Wilbur while she was gone.

I'm going to Colorado, she wanted to shout out loud. The chance to go on a trip absolutely thrilled her.

And maybe the man did, too. Just a little, tiny bit. And only in a strictly *friendly* way.

Chapter Eleven

The first-class ticket waiting for her at the local airport should have been a clue. Even the limo waiting for her at the private airstrip in the posh skiing village should have made her stop and think, but she was too distracted by the incredible view and the impressive homes tucked into the mountainside. And knowing she was about to see Noah again didn't help.

She was blown away by the "little cabin" he owned. There was nothing little about it. Made of log and stone and glass, it blended perfectly with the surrounding forest. It was a picture from an architectural magazine come to life.

The limo rolled to a stop in the sloping driveway, and she couldn't move. She was still gaping, in awe of that house. Noah owned this. When he was sipping hot chocolate in her house and skiing on her land, he had almost seemed like any other guy. A really great guy, but still, as normal as could be.

This was not normal.

The etched-glass front door swung open, and there was Noah bounding down the inlaid stone steps to open her car door. He looked great in a dark blue sweater and jeans, his hair blowing up in the wind.

"Julie, it's good to see you." He said it so warmly, she knew he meant it.

He had missed her that much? As if in answer, he held his arms wide in welcome. She bolted to her feet and flew into his arms, feeling his solid chest against her cheek as he held her tenderly.

I missed you, too. She held back the words she didn't dare say. Her hands settled on his broad shoulders, and the wool of his sweater tickled her. Holding him like this felt right. Sweetness swept through her as gentle as a winter's dawn. She could stay like this forever, tucked in his arms, feeling his heartbeat against her cheek and be perfectly content.

But this was a friendly hug, she reminded herself, and stepped away from his embrace. "Little cabin, huh?"

"Well, I call it the cabin."

"As opposed to the penthouse and the Hawaii beach house?"

"No beach house, although I've always thought that would be a good investment."

"Yeah, me, too."

A dimple cut into his cheek as he grabbed her bags from the trunk. "Great. You brought your skis. Want to go grab lunch at the inn and then hit the slopes?"

"The *inn?* You mean that elaborate and expensive-looking hotel down the road?"

"It's just over the rise. We can ski there." He hefted her ski cases out of the trunk, acting as if this was completely normal.

For him, it probably was. Well, when in Rome... "Sure, let's ski over to the little inn down the road and grab a bite." Which probably meant filet mignon, lobster and caviar.

"This place has better skiing than Telluride." Noah manhandled her bags up the stairs. "Did you have a good flight?"

"It was a first-class seat. I don't think flying gets much better than that."

"Wait until you see my jet." He waggled his brows; it was the Noah she knew and loved. Okay, so he was rich. He was still a guy who loved his power toys.

But she saw the man. The real Noah who walked into a house where sounds echoed around him. There were no family pictures hung on the walls, no personal treasures stashed on the cherry wood shelves in the living room and not one favorite shirt slung over the back of the leather sofa.

They were not so different, the two of them, both living in houses with too many empty rooms.

He'd forgotten how sweet the air was at this altitude. Sweet enough to make his eyes sting, not from the cold but from something else. He didn't know what it was, but it made his chest ache deep.

He wasn't like this when he was alone. It was Julie. She was creating this feeling inside him. Her beauty, and her goodness and her friendship.

Who was he kidding? Friendship was too small of a word for what she was to him. She was like the only buoy in a storm-tossed sea to a lone survivor of a shipwreck.

"Hey, handsome. Are you ready to go?" Julie tugged her rainbow-colored cap down low over her ears, her poles waggling in the air.

"Where do you get a hat like that?" He tugged on the pom-pom on the top of her head.

"What's wrong with my hat? Okay, so it's not a designer one, like everyone else's. But at least it stays over my ears in the wind." She flashed him that smile, the one that made his heart lighten. "I bought it at the church bazaar. One of the women on the Ladies' Aid made it."

"I've never been to a church bazaar."

"You're one strange cookie, Noah Ashton." She

lit up when she laughed, and made him brighten, too. "I suppose you buy your stuff from some ritzy tailor shop."

"No. I have a personal shopper."

"Oh, me, too. Doesn't everyone?"

"Are you laughing at me again? I suppose I deserve that for commenting on your hat. It's cute." It was Julie, bright and cheerful and sensible. In fact, he liked her hat so much, he grabbed it by the pom-pom and yanked it off her head.

"Hey, give that back!" She stumbled over her skis, swiping wind-tousled curls from her face.

Her lovely face that he wanted to gaze at forever.

"My ears are freezing. Noah!" She jumped, surprisingly agile on those skis, but she couldn't reach.

"You can have it when you catch me." He knew he was in trouble, because she could outski him, but he was no slouch. He double-poled, shooting onto the groomed trail. Soft snow powdered up behind him as he flew with Julie hot on his tails.

"You'll have to try harder," he taunted her, but didn't dare take the time to glance over his shoulder. He kept his concentration on the course, because she was on his heels. He could see the smudge of her blue jacket in his peripheral vision.

"Seemed to have overestimated your abilities, Ashton." She closed in on him, nudging around him like a thoroughbred going for a Triple Crown win. "Didn't think I could beat you twice, did you?"

"True. I thought your win last time was a fluke. Luck. Nothing more." He was breathing hard. Pushing hard. They were neck and neck.

"Nothing more, huh? Just luck?" She matched his pace, not even breathing hard. "Then explain this."

He saw her arm shoot out, and he yanked the rainbow-striped cap out of her reach just in time. The trouble was, she wasn't after her own hat.

He felt a tug on his head and a cold rush of wind over his ears. "Hey! That's mine. Give that back."

"Come and take it." She was off, kicking fast, leaving him in the dust.

He loved competition. He kicked hard, gliding far and fast on his newly waxed skis. She was still ahead of him, but not as distant. Come on, push harder, he coached himself. There was no way he was going to let Julie get away with his hat.

"Know what I think?" he called, his voice bouncing off the endless snow and miles of trees. "I think you have beginner's luck. That's why you keep winning."

"Ha! I'm no beginner. I've been skiing since I was four."

"You're a beginner. When it comes to competing with me." He was gaining, his strategy all along. "Got a little overconfident, did you?"

She was licked, and she knew it. They were neck and neck, stride for stride, hugging the narrow trail together. "The course is narrowing up ahead. It's getting steep, too."

"Really? I'm not afraid. I'm a downhill kind of man." He kept equal to her, although he had to work for it. "I've heard it's tricky up ahead. Skiers take a tumble all the time. Maybe you want to make a deal."

"There is something I want."

"Your cap." He was breathing hard, and his lungs burned from the cold. His legs felt as heavy as lead. He was more than happy to negotiate. "How about we call it a tie and trade hats?"

"That's a sensible solution, and it proves why you're successful in business." She wasn't winded, tossing him an easy, gorgeous smile that made him stumble.

A man couldn't look at a pretty woman and ski well at the same time. He kept his pace, but she eked ahead a few inches. He recognized that glint in her eye.

She was sure of success.

"I think I'll keep your hat," she informed him. "It *is* a designer label, after all."

"No way. I won't permit it." His ears were freezing, but that wasn't the worst part as she cut ahead of him, just out of his reach. He couldn't gain on her. He was doing his best, but he couldn't catch her.

The course tilted downward, the wind hit his ears and his skis glided across the snow like a dream. Exhilaration filled him as he stared down the face of the jagged mountain, the big slope miles wide and incredible. Not that he was paying much attention to it.

What was he looking at?

Julie as she glided down the slope ahead of him, taking the steep terrain like an expert. She was only a blur of blue through the blazing light and the glittering snow. She was grace and goodness, beauty and speed, and she filled his heart up in a way he didn't understand. She made his world tilt on end....

No, that was just his skis. He lost control, lost his balance and tumbled headlong into the powdery whiteness. He rolled, feeling the bindings give, and sat up, wiping snow out of his eyes.

"Are you okay?" Her angel's voice bounced across the expansive mountainside separating them.

"My ears are cold," he answered back.

It was clear she had no sympathy for him. She was busily adjusting his hat on top of her pretty head.

He was really starting to like her, more than he would ever have thought possible. She made him laugh and feel and ski full out on an incredible mountain slope until he felt alive. He was aware of every sense—the crumbling cold creeping down his neck, the fresh winter scent of the forest, the strange open sound of the mountains and the taste of snow on his tongue.

He'd never been so aware. Shaken, he managed to get back on his skis. Sure enough, Julie was still there, waiting for him, making certain he was okay.

Just as she always did.

"Hey, the last one to finish has to buy dinner tonight." Her confidence rang in her voice, in her stance, and he loved that. "A really nice dinner."

"Do I get my hat back?"

"I don't think so."

He loved a challenge. He pulled her cap on his head. It was snug, but it felt like bliss against his freezing-cold ears.

Her laughter rang on the wind, light and merry. "I'm sorry. I shouldn't laugh. It's just…pom-poms aren't you, Noah."

"When a man has cold ears, he has to lower his pride a bit."

"A bit?" She doubled over, laughing.

Okay, she was going to be sorry now. He took off, full power, hitting the slope just right, sailing toward her before she could straighten up. Her last chuckle lingered in the chilly air as he soared past.

He had the advantage now, but he suspected not for long. When he glanced over his shoulder, there she was, gaining ground. He looked forward to the rest of the race.

And the finish.

* * *

The sun was sinking low between the snowy peaks, their jagged faces shot through with cool lemony light, making Julie squint as she trekked up the slope steep enough to need a rope tow. Every muscle she owned burned as if she'd been lit on fire from the inside. Her lungs hurt. Her feet felt like forty-pound dumbbells.

What she really wanted to do was collapse in a heap, let the cold snow cool her down and never move again.

"Slowing down a little?"

How did he still have enough energy to be saucy? Ooh, she was gonna make him pay. Come suppertime, she'd order the most expensive thing on the menu.

Not that it would begin to put a dent in his wallet, but it was the principle of the thing. He'd tortured her every single yard of this marathon course. She couldn't let him get away without some sort of penalty, right?

"Careful. I'm catching up."

"It's those long legs of yours." She had to work twice as hard, and he was right there, trying to push past her. *Again.* She had to dig deeper and find just enough strength to keep ahead of him. Air rushed into her chest. A stitch dug into her left side. Her thigh muscles felt as wobbly as jelly.

No, she couldn't let him win! He was at her

elbow, then pulling ahead as the trail end marker came into sight around the last bend. She couldn't do it. He nosed ahead, fighting just as hard, and the tip of his ski slid across the shadow made by the end post, a mere inch in front of hers.

"I can't believe I beat you." Panting heavily, Noah tumbled into the snow on his back. "I'll never move again, but, wow. I won."

"Yes, you did." His skis stuck up, in her way, and she skidded to a stop before colliding into him. "Congratulations, pom-pom man."

"Glad I've got your respect. I know I'm dashing in this hat. I'm gonna keep it." He was kidding, but he was charming and wonderful and made her happy, so she didn't care if she ever saw her hat again.

All she wanted was the man in it. She loved him. How could that be? She'd vowed not to love him, but the affection in her heart was too strong to hold back.

It was hard to keep the emotion from her voice as she held out her hand. "You look like you need some help."

"Thanks. I think I can move now." He sat up and climbed onto his skis under his own power. "You made me work for it. I haven't tried so hard since…" He shook his head, scattering powdery snow. "I can't remember when. I've won a free dinner. Wow."

"Wait, don't say it—"

"And I'm ordering the most expensive meal in the house," he interrupted. "Isn't that what you planned to do?"

"Me? Never. Well, maybe."

Laughing, victorious and exhausted, Noah led the way to the lodge. He felt so alive. And he knew whom to thank. So he helped her with her skis and let her choose a table close to the crackling fire.

"This place serves the best hot chocolate on the planet." He told her, as he tugged the pom-pom hat from his head. "And it's my treat."

"Oh, I thought the loser had to pay."

"Right, but even losers deserve chocolate." He kissed her cheek, light and sweet.

The sunshine streaming through the window seemed a little brighter when Julie smiled.

Armed with movies for their movie marathon, to be held in Noah's living room after dinner, Julie waited as he held the video store's heavy glass door.

"I notice you're guarding the bag," Noah commented as he followed her onto the covered sidewalk. "Not a bad plan, considering if I accidentally misplaced those movies, then we could get those action flicks I wanted to see."

"I did offer, but you said losers deserved to pick out the movies. It's your own fault." She swung the plastic bag, sporting four movies. "Winners deserve to be tormented by chick flicks."

"Torture by romantic comedy. I think I can take it like a man." He winked, limping a little from their hard day on the snow.

"What's wrong with a little romance?"

"Not one thing." Trouble flickered in his eyes. "We've got a few minutes before our reservation. You sit right here."

"On that bench?" A cast-iron bench leaned against the wall of the florist shop. "No way. That is one cold bench. I'd be frozen solid in an hour if I sat there."

"Then stand here looking gorgeous." Noah brushed his lips against her cheek in a brief kiss, breathing in the strawberry scent of her hair and her skin. "I'll be right back."

"Ditching me already?"

"Not a chance of that. You wait and see." Because a woman who was buying him dinner deserved flowers, he stepped into the florist shop.

A bell jangled overhead, and a cheerful clerk stepped up to the counter. "Can I help you, sir?"

"What kind of roses do you have?" He waited while the clerk returned with samples of various roses. He considered the rich colors, yellow and red and pink and orange, but he kept going back to the white rose. Good and pure and true. It seemed the right choice.

While the clerk rang up the purchase, he could see Julie through the front window. She was leaning against a wood post, watching the activity on the street. The breeze had tangled her dark hair hopelessly and she looked…good and pure and true.

He took the flowers, wrapped in pink paper, and left. The bell jangled above the door, and Julie turned at the sound. He watched her gaze snap to the flowers.

Delight lit her up. "For me?"

"For the loveliest woman I know."

The delicate fragrance filled the air between them as she took the bouquet. The daylight was fading, shrouding them in blue-gray shadows. "Movies, compliments and flowers. It doesn't get much better than this."

"That's the idea." He brushed tangles from her face with his leather gloves, a gentle brush that made Julie love him, again, a little bit more until there was nothing but the shining brightness of it, filling her up.

"Now," he said, steering her toward the finest restaurant in the village, "I'm getting hungry for my lobster dinner."

"Lobster? Sure you don't want bread and water?"

"As long as I'm with you, water would taste like hot chocolate." He resisted the urge to steal back his hat, for she was wearing it, and took her hand instead.

* * *

"Popcorn's ready," Noah called from down-stairs. "How about you?"

"I'll be there in two seconds." Julie found her bunny slippers in the bottom of the suitcase she borrowed from Granddad and slipped her feet into them.

She felt like warm, melted butter from an hour spent in the hot tub. Her muscles had hurt something fierce when she'd tried to get up from the dinner table, so the jetted hot water was exactly what she needed.

It was so incredibly relaxing as they sat together in the huge Jacuzzi with the deliciously hot water bubbling between them. Sipping on lemon-flavored mineral water, they watched the full moon slip behind dark clouds. As they talked, snow began to fall. Big white flakes tumbled over them to melt in the steam.

So she was feeling better, and her favorite pair of sweats felt like pure bliss on her skin. But it wasn't the time spent in the hot tub or the fabulous bedroom of Noah's sister's that she was in or the luxurious house or the sumptuous dinner of lobster and filet mignon. All the expensive and wonderful things in the world couldn't matter to her.

Just Noah. He made her feel this way. As if she were so happy, she would burst. As if there were so much love in her heart, it would lift her off the ground like a giant helium balloon. Every moment she spent with him made her love him more. Every time he made her laugh. Every time he smiled at her.

If only he loved her in return.

How was she going to hide her love for him? How could she go downstairs, sit on the couch at his side, share a bowl of popcorn and pretend that he was only her friend, just a skiing buddy?

I can do this. She paused at the door, pressed off the light switch and followed the row of elegant wall sconces to the wide, curving staircase. The sound of the television grew louder as she went. There, in the great room below, was Noah slipping a DVD into the player.

"Hey, you look ready to relax." Crouched on one knee, the lamplight burnished the wide span on his shoulders and the curve of his rugged face, a face that had become so dear to her. "Love the slippers."

"Thanks." She skipped down the stairs, keeping a tight hold of her heart. "The popcorn smells perfect. Light, fluffy. Buttery."

"Of course it's perfect. Did you have any doubts? I excel in many fields. Business. Computers. And the most important one of all, the fine art of popcorn popping." He held out his hand, palm up, inviting her close. "I used extra butter, just for you."

It was impossible to resist placing her hand on his. Her feet moved of their own volition, drawing her to him. She was hardly aware of settling down on the incredibly comfortable sofa or Noah moving away to dim the lights as the movie started. She could tell herself a thousand times that Noah Ashton wasn't the man for her. But it didn't matter. Not one bit. She still loved him.

"Lemon or raspberry?" He held out two chilled bottles of tea. "Wait, I bet you want raspberry. There are napkins on the coffee table. Go ahead and put your feet up on the coffee table. I do."

The leather made the softest rustle as he sat next to her. Not right next to her, but close enough to make her wish he would sit closer. If only she had the right to snuggle against his side and feel the weight of his arm across her shoulders.

Some dreams were simply not meant for her.

Every leg muscle Noah owned protested as he limped down the hall. Maybe his body was protesting the extremely early hour, but it was more likely the exertion from yesterday's skiing contest. Remembering the pleasant and companionable dinner Julie had bought him, made the pain worth it. He loved spending time with her, just talking about little things or nothing at all.

"Julie?" He rapped his knuckles against the paneled door. "Are you up?"

"My spirit is willing, but the rest of me isn't," came the muffled answer.

"Well, tell your spirit to drag the rest of you out here. We're running out of time." He knocked again. "Don't you want to help me realize one of my dreams?"

"No." There was a smile in the sound of her voice, if he wasn't mistaken. "No one has the right to dream after only four hours of sleep."

"Who needs sleep?" Their movie marathon had lasted well past midnight. "Do I have to come in there with a vat of cold water?"

"A vat, huh? That I'd like to see." The door opened, and she was there, dressed in jeans and a sweater. Her rainbow scarf was slung around her neck, and her hair was sleep tousled and wildly framing her face. "I'm ready and willing. I'm not sure about being able, but I'll try."

"Have a few sore muscles?"

"Why, do you?"

He limped after her. "About a hundred."

"Me, too." They limped down the hall together.

In the kitchen, he helped her slip into her warm jacket. The scent of strawberries clung faintly to the fabric and to the tousled strands of her hair. He found her mittens for her and knelt down to help her with her boots. His muscles protested, but he didn't mind. Any woman who'd get up with him this early in the morning deserved a little first-class treatment.

"A double latte with hazelnut flavoring, as you

requested." He held out the insulated mug, the black plastic cover locked in place. "And one for me."

"You must want to get me out of the house pretty badly." She wrapped her scarf around her neck and worked her jacket's zipper up to her throat. "To help me with my boots and make my coffee."

"Yep. I've done this only once before, but I remember how fantastic it was. You wait and see. Getting up this early and halfway freezing to death is going to be worth it." He opened the door for her. "Trust me."

Trust him? She did. With all her heart.

The snow was crusty. The minus-degree temperatures felt bitterly cold on her face. She nudged the scarf so it covered her nose, and followed Noah down the icy steps and through the dark, silent trees.

"Careful. It's slick." Noah took her free hand, his fingers lacing through hers, holding her steady so she would not fall. "Look."

She couldn't see anything but him. He was her entire world, the dark rim of night and the stars winking out were nothing compared to the warm solid feel of his hand linked with hers. Then he gestured toward the eastern rim, where the faintest gray had replaced the inky blackness of night. The glacier-capped mountains glowed dark and mysterious.

Slowly the light changed. Gray became purple, then blue and crimson. Peach and pink crept over the horizon to brush subtle strokes across the cloudless sky and hushed peaks.

"This is what I wanted to see." Noah's voice came rough and raw, and he didn't bother to hide the emotion gleaming in his eyes. "This is the one thing I wanted to see one last time."

"You wanted to see the sun rise? Doesn't it do that every day in New York?"

"Just keep watching. I promise. It's going to be spectacular. A once-in-a-lifetime view." He whispered, because the peace of the morning strengthened, like a symphony's crescendo.

There. The first ray of golden light stabbed through the jagged peak of the lowest mountain. Bright, eye-stinging light that was bold enough to chase the darkness across the width of the sky. As if gathering courage, more light punched above the craggy peaks, illuminating the valleys and slopes of the mountains. All at once, the top curve of the sun thrust into the sky, changing the gray to blue and the shadowed world into a thousand shades of color.

"'The Lord is the light by which we see,'" Julie whispered.

"Yes. I thought of that verse, too." He tightened his grip on her, holding her tight, drawing her close. Too many emotions warred deep within him to begin to name them all. He only knew that he was moved beyond words. That his faith in the Lord was stronger now. Strong enough to help him face the hardships ahead; powerful enough to be a light for his path.

"I saw this by accident on one of the few times I ever came here." He set his coffee on a boulder tucked into the slope behind them and took Julie's other hand. So small, so *right,* in his. "I was up early to make a conference call, and I saw this from the living room window. There was too much glare inside the house—I had the lights on—so I grabbed my coat, left the phone and went outside. I felt called to it. I don't know why…."

He held on to her so tightly. "I watched the sun rise into the sky like a promise of life, and I was too afraid to let it move through me and change me. So I went back inside and found the phone and picked up practically where I'd left off. I lived my life as if it had never happened. I don't want to make that mistake again. Whatever time I have left, I'm going to make count."

"Sounds like the right path." Julie heard the affection in her voice. The love she could no longer hide. It swept her away, lifted her up, so beautiful and infinite and true.

He had to know it. His eyes grew dark as he turned to her, reaching out. The first brush of his gloved fingertips felt like a dream against her cheek. He nudged her scarf down, so it drooped beneath her chin, exposing half her face to the crisp mountain air.

He's going to kiss me, she realized, and everything inside her stilled. It didn't seem real as he leaned forward, his gaze searching hers so deeply, she felt her soul stir. Felt as if he saw everything inside her, all her love, all her fears, all her needs.

Then his hand cupped her jaw tenderly, such a welcome touch, and his lips slanted over hers. His kiss was warm and gentle, as sure as a kept promise. She'd found her Prince Charming, the one man who could make her spirit complete and heal the broken places in her heart.

Noah's kiss was like a dream, something too precious and rare to be real. He didn't love her, of course. He was simply carried away by the moment and his regrets, that was all. She couldn't take this kiss seriously. She couldn't begin to start dreaming. Noah Ashton was never going to love her, never going to slip a wedding ring on her finger, never going to hold their baby in his arms. And why was this happening? Why was she wanting everything she could never have?

She broke away, quietly burying the love in her heart. Noah didn't want her, not truly. How could he?

Help me, Father. Please help me protect my heart. Help me to do this the right way. She *would* be strong.

Noah gazed down at her, his hand at her jaw, his emotions tender in his eyes, in his voice, in his touch. "What a beautiful way to start the day."

He broke her heart wide open with his words, and she couldn't speak. It struck her like the cold wind, and she felt it all the way to the marrow of her bones. She would love him. Always.

"Are you hungry?" Noah asked, as courteous as always. "Let's hike down to the inn."

"Sure."

It took all her courage to follow him down the trail past the house of wood and stone, as his *friend* and not as the woman who loved him.

Noah couldn't seem to make his hands stop shaking. Nothing like this had ever happened to him before. He folded the last sweater into his suitcase and went in search for the rest of his socks. Packing to leave wasn't what was important, but he felt as if he had to find every last sock. Maybe because it was easier to be unsettled over misplaced articles of clothing than the real, honest-to-goodness fact that he'd kissed Julie. A full-fledged kiss that continued to affect him—he glanced at the alarm clock by the bed—seventy-three minutes later.

She'd tasted like spun sugar, made him feel as bright as the sunrise, like a day newly dawning. Everything was changing around him—what he wanted, what he believed, what he'd always done to keep his heart safe. There was nothing to protect him from this ache in his heart. It wasn't from his medical condition, because that low burning pain was a daily occurrence, but this was something bigger and greater. Something he didn't understand. Something he had no success with.

He was in love with Julie Renton. The kneel-down-on-one-knee-and-propose kind of love. The love that came soul deep. It was more exhilarating than taking an ungroomed slope at full speed. What he'd felt for Vanessa was nothing compared to this.

He was in love for the first time.

Light footsteps padded down the hall. There she was, so beautiful he couldn't breathe, leaning against the doorframe, looking amazing in a pair of black jeans, riding boots and another of her fuzzy sweaters. This one was a soft yellow that brought out the luster of her porcelain skin and the rich red tones in her dark hair. It wasn't just her physical beauty that captivated him, but all of her—her goodness, her spirit, her faith.

"The limo's here." She winked at him. "That was really fun to say. I'm going to do it again. The limo is waiting for me. That's hysterical. I suppose the Learjet is, too?"

"You're having fun at my expense. I'm not sure I can permit that, not unless I make you pay." Forgetting the socks, he snapped the suitcase shut. "I'll have to keep your hat as compensation."

"It's a one-of-a-kind original. Ought to bring in a good bid at Sotheby's. Okay, maybe on eBay."

He loved that she made him laugh. To feel this way, to be this lucky, seemed too good to be true.

Chapter Twelve

I can do this, Julie vowed as the limo whisked them along the icy, narrow road past the village. I can keep this platonic. I can be the friend Noah needs.

He was talking on his phone—it had shrilled while the driver was stowing their bags in the trunk—and it sounded like a business crisis. On the seat beside her, dressed in jeans and an expensive green sweatshirt, he looked like the down-to-earth man she'd come to know so well. But his voice, dark and booming with authority, made it clear he was no ordinary man. He was powerful enough to run a multibillion-dollar company with ease.

"Sorry about that." He punched off the phone. "I'm heading back to Japan anyway, but now it's ASAP. I need to get this all squared away before my surgery."

"You're going to have jet lag going into the operating room."

"They'll give me an anesthetic, and I won't notice the time difference," he quipped, because she'd hit a nerve.

Then again, he was already on edge. The way he felt about her was new and overwhelming. He didn't know what to do about it. Did she love him back? Or did she feel only friendship for him? How did he figure out which, because he'd finally figured it out. He wanted more than friendship.

He loved her. Not just for today, but for always. He needed her. More than the life he'd built in New York. More than the money he'd made and the luxuries he enjoyed.

And because he loved her, he should tell her. Let her know how he felt. And how much he needed her by his side.

What if she didn't feel the same way?

What was he doing? He was a confirmed bachelor. Why were his thoughts running away from him? Why was he imagining a future that included love and marriage? He didn't believe marriage was a good thing. There were bad-luck marriage genes in his family. The only thing he'd ever failed at was love.

He was terrified. The thought of marriage scared him more than the possible cancer did. He couldn't make promises. He couldn't offer her a ring she might not want.

The one thing he would never allow is for Julie to be as unhappy as his mother had been. That was what he knew of marriage, and just because Nanna and Hope had found joyful marriages, didn't mean he could.

No, he couldn't romance her. Besides, there was the surgery, and the possible cancer. He had to see how that turned out first.

So, now what? He had intended to ask Julie to come for his operation. He needed her by his side when he walked through the hospital doors. He wanted to know she would be waiting for him when he opened his eyes in his private room.

Was it wise to ask her?

His chest tightened. Pain seared through his lungs. Just another attack trying to gain strength. He took a deep breath and dug in his briefcase for his pain pills.

"How are you feeling? Do we need to take a detour to the hospital?" She didn't look at him when she said it.

"The pills have helped. I don't like to take them, but I haven't had a full-blown attack since Nanna's engagement party."

He took the pill without water, swallowing it down. He wanted the pain to subside.

"Look." She eased across to the far edge of the seat to peer out the tinted window. "There's your plane."

Was it his imagination, or did she feel so far away?

* * *

Julie gazed up at Noah's white-and-gold plane that looked as expensive as it had to be, glinting in the morning sun on perfectly groomed tarmac. She'd taken a commercial flight here, to Colorado, because Noah had been rushing back from Japan. Didn't he say there was a change of plans, that he had to return to Tokyo?

For some reason her feet slowed down. When he'd been with her in Montana, it was easy enough to pretend that he wasn't much different than she was. That he was an ordinary man. Yet, when she stepped into the shadow of that sleek jet, one of many on the tarmac, she could no longer deny the truth. Ordinary men drove pickups and didn't have vacation homes in the Rockies with a million-dollar view.

Above the whir of another small plane's engines rose a woman's voice. "Yoo-hoo! Noah Ashton, is that you?"

A woman trotted into sight on heeled boots, her long legs encased in taupe leather. Her matching duster draped her perfectly. Diamonds winked at her throat, on her ears and on every finger, except her left ring finger. "Noah! It is you. Where have you been? I haven't seen you since Daddy's birthday party, and you were there ten minutes before you slipped away."

"Hi, Marley." Noah nodded a polite greeting. "I'd like you to meet my friend Julie."

Friend. There was that word again. And it hurt. It hurt to greet the gorgeous woman, who was really very nice. Julie learned that Marley was the daughter of the CFO of Noah's company. She was poised and graceful and had just returned from two months in Paris. She had a jet like Noah's, except it was red and white.

"It's very good to meet you, Julie." Marley's welcome seemed genuine. "Isn't the skiing here fantastic?"

"Absolutely. It's nice meeting you." She felt plain next to this woman who was so beautiful. Perfect from her rich blond hair to the tips of her polished designer boots. Yep, Julie definitely felt plain, and out of place, and that wasn't Marley's fault or Noah's.

"We're on a time schedule, but it was good seeing you, Marley," Noah said politely. "Tell your father he needs to call me."

"Sure thing. You know he'll be calling to see that I'm here safe and sound." She tapped away, waving her long, slender, perfectly manicured fingers. "Good seeing you, Noah," she called out, and was gone, followed by two men each pushing a huge cart of luggage.

Marley was the kind of woman Noah would marry one day. Julie wasn't jealous of that, no.

Just brokenhearted.

"Come on," Noah told her. "Let me show you my plane."

"You like your plane, do you?"

"Hardly at all." He held out his hand, taking her elbow to help her make the first step.

Always the gentleman. To his CFO's daughter, and to his friends. That's what she was—one of his friends. With each step Julie took, her hopes tumbled more and more until there was only a terrible sense of shame. What had she been thinking? Noah was never going to love her.

He needed a friend. He'd never said anything differently. As for the kiss, she'd misinterpreted that. He'd called her his friend often enough to make it clear. He wasn't going to fall in love with her.

And why would he? He was wealthy. Not just rich, but megawealthy. He would never want a country girl in jeans and a homemade sweater. He'd never marry a woman who wore a knit cap with a pom-pom on it bought for two dollars at the yearly church fund-raiser.

She'd asked the Lord for a sign, and He had answered her. He had shown her how very far apart Noah's world was from hers. The last thing she wanted was to fall in love with a man who couldn't love her in return. *Again.*

Tears burned in her eyes and blurred the lovely décor of Noah's plane. She knew he was coming up the steps behind her, and she had only seconds to pull herself together. To swallow her grief and her heartache and blink the bothersome tears from her eyes. To tuck away her dreams of what could never be.

He was a fine man. Her soul stilled at the sight of him. Wind-tousled like a pirate, as graceful as an athlete and powerful as the self-made man he was.

He would never be hers.

"You want anything to drink?" Noah grabbed a bottle of Perrier from the minibar. "I've got soda, tea, water. What's your pleasure, my lady?"

"You don't need to wait on me, thanks."

"It won't be long until we touch down in Bozeman. Think you're going to be able to walk out of here?" He made light talk as he crossed over to her. "I don't know about you, but my muscles are hurting. This fantastic skier I was with really pushed me to the limit."

"At least I won't be suffering alone." She tossed him a smile, dimpled and stunning.

That was the smile he wanted to see forever. He jerked his gaze away, staring out the window. He wished he could tell her how much he needed her. What this trip had meant to him. He wanted to open up to her so much that it hurt.

He took a long drink, staring out the window at the gray, misty clouds below. Jumping from the plane without a parachute would be less terrifying.

"Do you have a busy week ahead at school?" he asked instead, because that was easier. Keep the conversation light and on the surface.

"I'm on recess duty all week, and that's going to be a challenge with all the snow we've been having. Snowball fights," she explained when Noah raised an eyebrow in question. "One or two break out every recess to keep things interesting. Plus it's the last full week before Christmas vacation. The kids tend to be high-energy."

"You love teaching, don't you? You light up when you talk about it."

She wanted to tell him about her love of teaching, but what good would it do? Her chest felt so tight, it was hard to breathe. The truth was, he didn't love her. He was sitting here, so close she could reach out and kiss him if she wanted. He saw her as his skiing buddy. She couldn't keep doing this, pretending to be his friend. It tore her apart.

"I enjoy teaching. I wouldn't do anything else." That's right, keep it light. Don't let him know how much you're hurting. "When I went to apply at the elementary school, the kindergarten teacher had suddenly retired. I was lucky."

"Teaching kindergarten is a pretty competitive job, then?"

"Not like yours, but it can be, in the world of teaching." She averted her gaze and started digging through her purse.

Something was wrong. She seemed distant.

There was no banter and no cute quips to make him chuckle. Noah picked the wrapper off the water bottle, wondering how to take this.

He ought to rejoice. After this weekend, she'd spent time with him, and realized she didn't like him. Why else would she sit there, dragging a book from her purse, when they'd been close only this morning…

It was the kiss. While kissing her full on the lips had made him realize he loved her. It made her decide to put distance between them.

See? It was a good thing he was keeping his strictly bachelor status.

Julie didn't love him.

Pain tore at his chest, but it wasn't anything a pill could ease. It didn't make any sense, because hadn't he decided not to pursue a romance with her?

He tugged his computer from its protective case and hit the power button. Good thing he had work to do. Something else to concentrate on. To make himself useful.

But he couldn't concentrate. The numbers on the spreadsheet meant nothing, so he closed the document and opened Solitaire. He played the game, trying to pretend that he was all right when Julie was at his elbow, so beautiful and perfect. With her bouncy hair and her elegant profile and the way she bit her bottom lip when she thought.

She didn't look up once for the duration of the flight.

* * *

The forward momentum stopped, and Julie hit the buckle so fast, she couldn't hear the click as the seat belt released. She was on her feet, jamming her book into the depths of her purse.

"In a hurry, huh?" A muscle in his jaw jumped. "Wait two seconds. I want to thank you for a fun ski trip."

"It was fun." She'd had a great time, but not because of the skiing. Because of the man.

If she could, she'd pray for time to turn around and run backward and return them to Colorado. Where the air was thin and clear and the beauty breathtaking. She wanted to hold on to that time forever. The way Noah had laughed. How he'd looked wearing her hat. The cozy evening spent together watching movies.

But she had to move forward. Get back to the life she loved.

As hard as it was to descend those steps into the icy Montana wind, she did it. When her feet touched Montana ground, she'd never been so relieved. She'd done it. Finished this trip with her dignity intact. No one would ever know how close she'd come to making a big mistake.

"Hey, Julie!" Noah called, taking the steps two at a time. "I got something for you."

Not a present, she prayed. Please, not a memento of this trip.

"Thought you might need this, since it's a one-of-a-kind original." He held out her hat. "Whatever happens, at least I've seen the sun rise in the Rockies. Thank you for sharing that with me. So I didn't have to go alone."

She took a shaky breath, because that was all the proof she would ever need. He hadn't wanted to be alone; that's why he'd invited her along. His words made her throat ache, and she hated that her hand trembled when she reached for the hat. "You take good care of yourself, and I'll be praying for you every night."

"I appreciate that. More than you know."

Then he was gone, climbing the steps into the jet, disappearing into the mist of snow and wind swirling around him, her Prince Charming in a white-and-gold Learjet.

Noah watched Montana fall away below as the jet climbed through the clouds. It felt as if he were falling, too, spiraling toward earth. His chest felt empty and hollow.

The more he thought about Julie's behavior, the more it troubled him. How could they go back to being friends after this? Every time he looked at her, he'd see the one woman he would always love.

Chapter Thirteen

I'm late. Late, late, late. Julie tossed a banana and a container of yogurt into her book bag. No time to cook breakfast. No time to pack a lunch. With the way her feet were dragging, and the new snowfall, she'd be lucky to get to school before her kids did.

Okay, keys? Check. Wallet? Check. Lights off? Check. Iron unplugged… She leaned around the corner to peer through the laundry room door. Check. Jacket? There it was, slung over the back of the chair, right where she left it after coming home from the ski trip.

She rushed through the back door, zipping her jacket as she went, wading through ankle-deep snow. There was a familiar green pickup parked to one side of her driveway, a plow attached to the front end.

There was Granddad shuffling through the snowfall, away from her open garage door. "I got your truck warming up. You're normally long gone by now."

She kissed his cheek. "I'm way behind this morning. You shouldn't be here clearing my drive. I have my own plow, you know."

"Keeps an old cowboy like me busy." He winked, jamming his hands into his coat pockets. "Did you have a good time on that skiing trip?"

"The best time." It hurt too much to think about. "What about you? Getting married next week. Are you nervous?"

"After all these years of bein' alone? I'm lookin' forward to it." He knuckled back his Stetson. "You have a good day, now."

"Want to come over for supper?"

"I'm eating at Nora's."

"Sure you are. I'm going to have to get used to that." She sprinted into her garage where her truck was waiting, the heater almost blowing tepid air.

She put the vehicle in gear and backed out of the garage. Alone, driving down the country road, the realization dawned. She was on her way to work. Her life would go on as it had. Nothing had changed. There was work and friends, and Sunday dinner with her family after church.

The only difference in her life was a big, yawning emptiness in her soul.

Her mother had left. Each man Julie committed her heart to changed his mind. Over the span of a lifetime, it was a message she heard loud and clear. But had she listened to it?

No. She'd gone right ahead and given her heart away a final time. She'd known better. She knew how it was going to turn out if she fell in love with Mr. Wrong.

And now look at her. Crying on the way to work when she could have protected herself. Could have turned down Noah's offer to go to Colorado. Could have turned away from his kiss. She could have thrown away his flowers instead of putting them in a vase in the middle of her table. Because a part of her couldn't stop wishing. Still.

Pulling to the side of the road, she let the pain wash over her, the horrible grief that broke like a dam. And she couldn't stop it. She didn't even try.

"Noah?" Kate rapped on the desk. "Earth to Noah. Did you want me to fax the documents?"

"Sure." He shook his head, realizing he'd been staring off into space. Again. He couldn't seem to keep his mind on anything.

The truth was, not even work was absorbing enough to distract him from the loneliness. It couldn't disguise the truth anymore. He was lonely and unhappy and a coward. He loved Julie. He couldn't stop thinking about her, couldn't stop daydreaming about her and replaying in his mind every second of every minute he'd spent with her.

"I'll cover your meeting in Washington tomorrow." Kate, efficient as always, tapped on her small handheld computer, studying the screen. "Your notes are thorough, as always. I'll drop you an e-mail, let you know how it went. Hope your procedure goes well tomorrow."

"Thanks." It was hard, knowing tomorrow would be a day of reckoning.

He was ready. There wasn't much he could do but face it head-on. And if he was scared, well, he knew whatever happened, he would be okay. His life, as it always had been, was in the Lord's hands.

There were last-minute calls to make. Loose ends to tie up so he could be gone for a few days. He tried to work hard, but his mind kept wandering and his heart wasn't in it. Being at this desk used to thrill him. Gave him a sense of purpose. Made him feel as if his life had some significance.

So, why did he suddenly feel as if he were trapped by four walls? As if he could never be happy unless he was zooming down a mountainside at full speed.

It was the skiing he missed, he insisted stubbornly. Vacations were bad things, see? It made a person not want to work as hard when the vacation was over.

It had nothing to do with Julie. So, she hadn't wanted him. She hadn't wanted his kiss. It was probably just as well. Think of the heartache a romance caused. And marriage…

His stomach twisted and his mind spun him backward to the dark of night in his bedroom, and the harsh, angry voices of his parents. The crash of a glass against a wall. Mom's furious litany of words that made him crawl out from beneath his baseball-motif bedspread and huddle on the floor in the corner, next to the giant-size teddy bear. He curled up tight.

He could smell the grass and dirt on his baseball cleats from the game. Dad hadn't made it. He had a meeting, like always. Mom hadn't come, either, but his game wasn't what they were fighting about. They were fighting about him. Mom wanted him out from underfoot because he demanded too much attention.

Pain tore through him like a thunderclap, bringing him back to the present. Back to the peace of his office, where the hum of the computer and the whir of the heating system were the only sounds. He was breathing hard, and sweat beaded on his forehead. *Lord, please make these memories stop.* But they remained there, like a shadow behind his thoughts for most of the afternoon.

By the end of the day, he couldn't take it anymore. Maybe the surgery was bothering him more than he thought—more than he was letting himself feel. One thing was certain, the past seemed too close, as if he could reach out and touch it. He worked late and grabbed takeout from his favorite deli on the way home.

His building was quiet, the security team reading the day's newspaper as he picked up his mail. Bills. Junk mail. A letter from Nanna.

Great. He'd been planning to call her tonight. He wanted to know how the wedding plans were progressing and if her beautiful gown had arrived today as promised. Mostly, he just wanted to hear her voice before tomorrow. She was a great comfort to him.

The Lord had blessed him greatly in giving him such a fine, loving grandmother.

Why hadn't he really considered that before? The Lord had given him a loving grandmother and a loyal sister, and what did he do? Noah didn't trust anyone—not even God—with his heart. Not his grandmother or his sister. And not Julie.

He kept everyone at a distance, and the minute they got too close, off he went. Jetting away to Japan or New York, and never returning phone calls or e-mails. And why was that? Because of that memory he had today, that's why. That little boy rejected by his parents over and over again had grown up into a man who allowed no one to reject him.

Maybe there wasn't a bad-luck marriage gene. Only a man too afraid to love anyone completely.

In protecting his heart, he'd really been turning

his back on some of the Lord's most important blessings. What kind of Christian did that make him? What kind of man?

Tomorrow he was facing surgery. When the doctors removed the tumor, they were going to test it for cancer. There would be no one in the waiting room, or in his hospital room or there to hold his hand while he waited for the lab results.

It wasn't what he wanted. He hated being alone. He hated that he was afraid to depend on anyone. Worst of all, he was running out of time to change things. If he didn't do it now, then he might never have another chance.

He unlocked his door and marched straight to the phone.

"Miss Renton, I can't get this on." Emily trudged up to the edge of the desk and peered up at her, pleadingly. "Mommy said if I don't wear my mittens, I don't get Twinkies. They's my favorite."

"Mine, too. Let me see what's wrong here." Julie circled around her desk and knelt to inspect the problem. Emily's mom had sewn buttons to the sleeves in order to secure the mittens, and one mitten had come unbuttoned. "I can fix this. Stand still for me, okay?"

Disaster averted. With a smile, she sent Emily to the door to take her place in the lineup. When every kid was accounted for, coats buttoned and little backpacks claimed, she led them in double rows down the hallway and out to the loading zone where a half-dozen bright yellow buses waited patiently in the blowing wind and cold. A long line of cars hugged the curb behind the buses, full of mothers waiting for their children.

"Thanks, Miss Renton!" Emily skipped in the direction of the cars. Her black curls bounced in time with her gait. Her mittened hand reached out for her mother, a plump smiling woman who knelt down to take a look at the beautiful cotton-ball snowman her daughter had made.

"Bye-bye, Miss Renton!" Marc offered shyly, his cotton-ball snowman a boyish wad that looked more like a football than anything else. He had a mother, too, who balanced a baby on her hip, and who listened to him patiently while he led the way to their minivan.

Such lucky families. A yearning so strong nearly knocked her to her knees. She'd prayed for days now, trying to stop this ache in her heart. Why had God brought her down this path, just to break her heart? Why had Noah come into her life at all?

His surgery was tomorrow. Had it been a coincidence that she'd met Noah the same night his health came to a crisis? No, Julie didn't believe in coincidences, but she did believe in the Lord. *And we know that God causes everything to work together for the good of those who love Him and are called by Him.*

By turning away from Noah, was she stepping off the path God had made for her? What if this was God's will for her?

I don't know what to do, Lord. How had everything become so complicated? Was she turning her back on a friend? Or simply being realistic? How did she know?

When the last of her charges had safely boarded their buses, Julie turned heel and headed back inside. Susan caught up with her. Susan had blueberry muffins and was willing to share. She'd grab the bakery box and be right over.

Who could argue with blueberry muffins? Julie stopped by the teachers' lounge, grabbed two vanilla sodas from her stash in the back of the refrigerator, her contribution to the impromptu get-together.

Thankfully, the heat had kicked on and her room was toasty warm as she deposited the bottles on her worktable in back and grabbed an eraser from the chalk tray.

A ring came from inside her desk drawer. With chalk dust on her hands, she dug out her cell phone. "Hello?"

"Figured you'd be done teachin' your class by now." It was Granddad. "Are you sittin' down?"

"Close enough." Since she still had a hold of the eraser, she started cleaning the board. "What's up?"

"Got a call from Nora a few minutes ago. Seems

that grandson of hers needs her to come out there, and she's askin' me to go with her."

"You should be at her side, Granddad." Julie kept her voice as steady as possible.

"You don't seem too surprised, girl. You've been spending time with that billionaire. Do you know what's going on?"

"Yes, I do." She hadn't realized she was holding her breath, but she felt tension melt away as she exhaled. She was glad Noah had told his family.

"Nora said to bring you along, if you can go. Her granddaughter is making the travel arrangements for us right now. Are you comin'? I suppose you were probably gonna be headin' out to be with him anyway?"

She heard the question in his voice. He was asking more than that—he wanted to know if she and Noah were romantically involved. "No, Granddad. Well, I wasn't sure."

"Then should I have Hope make a reservation for you?"

Yes, her heart said. But she couldn't go. He hadn't asked her to go. She couldn't fly out uninvited just because she was worried for him—no, afraid for him.

"It sure would mean a lot to Nora if you came," Granddad persisted. "Sounds like a pretty serious situation he's in. If somethin' were to go wrong, it wouldn't be right not to be there."

Exactly.

"I'll take care of my own reservation." There, it was decided. Julie promised she would ask the neighbor to look after Granddad's dog, and hung up.

She stared at her cell phone and the board she'd cleaned without noticing. Well, one dilemma solved. She was going to New York.

Noah heard them in the hall and yanked open the door. It was two in the morning, and he was in his robe and slippers, but he didn't care. Nanna led the way, with his sister on her heels. Harold was hauling luggage out of the elevator.

"Noah!" His grandmother pulled him into her arms, holding him tight. "You shouldn't be up. Hope has a set of keys. The last thing I wanted to do was wake you at this hour."

"I haven't been able to sleep anyway, so I decided to wait for you." He didn't tell her that he'd spent hours poring over his Bible, trying to stay hopeful. That he had a thousand worries and more regrets. "Come in. Let me help with your luggage."

"Harold will handle it." Nanna's touch was a comfort as she took his hand, leading him toward the living room. "This place hasn't changed much since I've been here. There's no wife. No children."

"I found a matched set of a wife and kids at

Bloomingdale's in my price range, but they clashed with the furniture so I took them back. Got a nice floor lamp instead."

"Very funny." Hope hugged him, too, holding him extra tight. "How are you? What time do you have to be at the hospital? Nanna and I have come to take charge of you, since you can't seem to take care of yourself."

"That's right," Nanna agreed like a no-nonsense general. "You'd better follow my orders, too, young man. You'll say hello and get to bed. Where do you want Harold to put the luggage?"

"Hello, son." Harold looked exhausted but stood as straight as ever, not weighed down too much by the luggage he carried. "You tell me where you want this."

"Down the hall, second door on your left." He was surprised that Harold had come, too. They hadn't exactly gotten along. "It's good of you to be here."

"You're family now, or will be once I get your grandmother to wear my wedding ring. There's nowhere else I'd be." With that, he disappeared down the hall.

Okay, so Harold wasn't a bad guy, after all. Definitely good enough for Nanna.

"It's too late to scold you properly for not telling me about this sooner," Nanna scolded anyway. "So all I'm going to say is shame on you, and leave it at that. Now get to bed, because morning will be here before you know it. Hope, would you mind heating some tea water for me? I always get lost in that big fancy kitchen."

"Sure thing." Hope hugged him one last time, and he felt what she didn't say.

They were a family. They would stand by him no matter what the prognosis. They were there to lean on, if he needed them.

He'd spent the night with his Bible, preparing for the worst possible outcome. Now, with his family here, he was ready for the best.

Chapter Fourteen

"Julie." It was Hope Ashton Sheridan standing in the hallway, closing the door to Noah's hospital room. "I'm glad you made it. Noah's out of recovery. The mass was even bigger than they thought, and they wound up taking out his entire gallbladder, but he's doing great."

"Thank God." Julie hadn't realized how worried she'd been. No, *worried* wasn't the word. *Terrified.* "I wanted to be here earlier, but my flight was delayed. I'm just so thankful he's okay."

Her knees were strangely weak. She had to sit down. Stumbling, she made it into the nearby waiting room and found a chair. Her overnight bag slid from her shoulder and hit the floor. The tiny vase she held felt as if it were made of iron, so she set it on the nearby magazine table. Boy, was she shaky or what?

"I'm tired," she explained to Hope. "It was a tough flight."

"I understand." Was that sympathy in her eyes?

Okay, so that's one person I haven't fooled. Julie rubbed her hands over her face. "Is Nora in with him?"

"No. Harold made her go get a sandwich in the cafeteria. She's pretty worried about him. We all are."

Me, too. Julie bit back the words, not comfortable revealing more of her heart. "Is he awake?"

"Still sleeping. Why don't you go in and sit with him? I was on the way to make a call. I need to check in with my husband. Maybe you could cover for me until I come back?"

"Sure. Whatever you need." She could do it. She was Noah's friend. After all, wasn't she wise enough to keep control of her feelings—this time?

Clutching the bud vase, Julie gathered her courage, steeled her heart and stepped into the small room. It was quiet and dim. Noah was asleep on his back, his hair dark against the pillow. Several blankets covered his big masculine physique. Lying there so still, he looked vulnerable.

Oh, Noah. She flew to his side. Her fingers ached to brush across the high cut of his cheekbones and down his face to the strong line of his jaw. She yanked her hand back in time—he wasn't hers to touch.

Lord, please protect him and keep him safe, she prayed. *Because Noah is my heart.*

She leaned over him and pressed a kiss to his forehead. A featherlight brush of a kiss, so he wouldn't wake. Then she set the bud vase with the single bloom on the table where twenty other arrangements were crowded together. They were all elaborate, expensive bouquets, a few with colorful balloons swinging overhead. From friends, she figured.

Her single flower looked unimpressive and lonely. She almost snatched it back, but something seemed to whisper to her to leave it, so she did.

Then, after one final look, she walked out of Noah's room and closed the door behind her.

"Julie!" It was Noah's grandmother, leaving Granddad's side to rush down the hall. "Oh, did you hear the good news? It's not cancer."

"Are they sure?"

"Yes! Isn't that wonderful? Praise the Lord." Nora wrapped Julie into a tight, comforting, wonderful grandmotherly hug. "I am about to dance a jig of joy. My beloved grandson is going to make a full recovery!"

"I'm so thankful." Julie stepped away, trembling, and Nora pushed into the room. As the door closed, Julie could see the older woman settling into a chair at Noah's bedside, taking his hand in hers, tenderly.

Julie ached with gratitude. Tears stung her eyes.

Thank you, Lord, for sparing him, for holding Noah in the palm of Your hand.

There was no need for her to stay. So she retrieved her overnight bag from the waiting room, said goodbye to her granddad and walked away.

"Julie?" Noah struggled away from a dream and opened his eyes. The wisps of the dream faded. Impressions of her presence, soft as a new day dawning. Of her kiss, gentle and reverent on his brow. Her scent of strawberries lingered faintly in the air. That was some powerful dream, he decided.

Someone was holding his hand. Nanna. He didn't need to turn his head to know it was her. He squeezed her fingers, and she held on so tightly.

His head was a little woozy and his vision fuzzy. He wasn't feeling so great, but the sight of her was like warm chocolate on a cold day. Okay, in truth, for a split second, with the scent of Julie's perfume in his memory, he'd dared to hope she'd be the one sitting at his bedside.

But Nanna was, and he loved her for it. She looked tired and drained. He was sorry for that, and he held on to her more tightly.

"Nanna, how are you? Are you—?" He squinted to bring her into better focus. Were there tears in her eyes?

It was bad news. He knew it. He felt it like a cold wave that rolled down his spine. *Help me make this easier for Nanna, Lord.* That was his first wish. Then he prayed for himself. *Help me not to waste another single moment I have left on this earth.*

"Oh, my dear boy. It's good to have you with us." Nanna scooted her chair closer.

"How can I sleep for long, with such a beautiful woman at my side? You look exhausted. Where's Harold? He's supposed to be taking care of you."

"He's in the waiting room. There's no need to fuss. I'm fine, just fine. I don't think I've been this good in a long, long time." Her voice trembled, and two tears trailed down her cheek.

"You must have heard from the lab. I don't want you to be sad—"

"Sad? Why, no. The reports came back negative. Negative!" More tears spilled down her beautiful face. "I don't know if I've ever been more grateful. My dear grandson is going to be just fine."

He closed his eyes. It wasn't cancer? It wasn't cancer. Relief washed through him, and he was afraid to believe it. But Nanna was crying again, big, happy tears. It was true. He was being given a second chance. A new beginning to his life.

Thank You, Lord.

One thing was for sure. He was going to keep the promise he made to God. Starting right now, this instant, he wasn't going to waste one more minute.

A woman knocked on the partly opened door,

balancing two rather large florist arrangements. Word sure had gotten out about the "small procedure" he'd told his vice presidents about, and his attorney, just in case something had gone terribly wrong during surgery. Corporate gifts, no doubt, judging by the apparent cost of the arrangements.

"Please, excuse me. I'll just put these over here with the others," the friendly volunteer said as she crossed the room to the table, where way too many flowers had given their lives for him.

Maybe he'd have the nurses give the flowers to people on the floor who would enjoy them.

"Oh, this was obviously delivered to the wrong room, Mr. Ashton." The woman looked embarrassed as she pulled a single glass vase from the vast forest of flowers. "This couldn't be for you. I'll just take it out of your way."

It was a single white rosebud.

Julie. He knew it in a heartbeat, all the way down to his soul. He *hadn't* been dreaming. She *had* been here. Who else would have given him a single white rose?

"Wait. I want that. It's for me," he assured the woman, and she handed it over uncertainly.

The vase felt smooth and cool in his hand. The small white bud was closed tight, but it was perfect. There was no card because it had been delivered in person. He smelled the faint, faint scent of Julie's strawberry hand lotion on the vase.

Nanna patted at her tears with a cloth handker-chief she'd taken from her jumbo-size purse. "Hope told me that Julie brought that."

"She's here?" Play it cool, keep the excitement out of your voice.

"No, she went home. Heard you would be fine and said she had to go. Something about the annual food drive, but I didn't hear it all. She took out of here like a woman in a hurry." Nanna sounded innocent—she was very good at that. "Or like a woman with certain feelings for a certain man. Not that I'm one to name any names."

"Don't take so much pleasure in this," he told her, wincing when awful pain jackhammered through his midsection.

Julie left, did she? Now why would she fly halfway or more across the country just to deliver a single white rose? The same kind of flower he happened to buy her in Colorado?

What would have happened if he'd had the courage to tell her his true feelings on the flight back to Montana that day? And if he'd said those frightening words—*I love you*. Would she have turned away?

He'd been afraid then. But he wasn't afraid now. His past was gone, and he was a new man. And, being a goal-oriented, type A personality, he knew exactly what he wanted from life—Julie. She was the woman he intended to marry, who was going to have his children and, God willing, the woman he was going to grow old with.

His sister had found happiness, after sharing the same childhood. With God's help, so could he.

Chapter Fifteen

"Misty, you are a lifesaver," Julie said into the phone as she padded past the unlit Christmas tree in her living room, through the first meager splash of early-morning sun on the hardwood floor and went straight to the refrigerator. "I'm going to be indebted to you forever."

"Not forever. Only until my wedding reception, when I need someone to make sure everything goes without a hitch. Wanna guess who I'll call?"

"I think I already know." She grabbed the carton of hazelnut creamer and headed directly to the coffeepot.

She thanked Misty again, said goodbye and dug her favorite mug out of the cupboard. The big, double-size one. She needed caffeine and lots of it, enough to get her through the midmorning ceremony. This was her granddad's wedding day!

She savored that first sip, inhaling the rich coffee smell, enjoying the sweetness from the creamer, letting the warm liquid wake her up. Then the doorbell rang, shattering her perfect moment of peace.

She wasn't expecting anyone. Maybe it was Granddad. He could need help with his tie. He'd been a cowboy all his life, and not as experienced in tying ties as men who worked in offices. Like Noah.

Now, see how she'd gone and worked Noah into her thoughts? It just proved she wasn't as over him as she'd prayed to be. What was it going to be like seeing him today? He was supposed to be flying in this morning for the wedding. She wasn't sure how she felt about that. Only one thing was for sure— she was truly thankful he was healthy.

She yanked open the front door. A bouquet of white rosebuds—what had to be two dozen of them—was staring her in the face, practically obscuring the man holding the vase.

"Clifford? Is that you?" She could barely recognize the man who owned the local floral shop. "What are you doing with those? Wait—"

She could see past the enormous arrangement of flowers to the blue delivery van parked in her snowy driveway. The side door was wide open, revealing vase after vase of roses. Every single last one of them was white.

"Oh, no! Clifford, this is all wrong." She couldn't believe it. And after all the care Nora had taken ordering the flowers. Julie should know— she'd gone with Nora and Hope to the florist regularly for the last two months.

"Sorry, Julie, but this order is correct. If you don't mind, I've got to get these delivered. I got a busy day ahead, as you know." Clifford sounded apologetic, yet determined.

Didn't he understand? "The roses are supposed to be blush pink. And why are you delivering them here? They have to go to the church."

"That's not what I have on my delivery slip." Clifford shouldered past her. "Where do you want these?"

"Back in your van." How could a mistake like this have happened? "Clifford, no, don't put them there."

"I told you, I've got a whole van to unload." He straightened, leaving the bouquet on her coffee table. "You sure don't seem very happy about this."

She was still in her sweats and slippers. How happy could she be? "Can I see the delivery order? I'm going to call Nancy. She'll get this straightened out for me."

"Don't bother, Julie. She'll agree with me." Clifford headed out the door, leaving it wide open as his assistant came in carrying two more bouquets.

Julie didn't understand. How could this be? She

grabbed the phone, but the clerk who answered explained that Nancy wasn't available. She was at the church setting up for Nora's wedding.

"Well, that's it, then." Clifford edged the twelfth vase of white roses onto the edge of the end table. "Boy, aren't those something? That billionaire sure must think a lot of you."

"The billionaire? You mean Noah Ashton? He sent these?" She didn't believe it. "Clifford, come back here."

"Sorry. Got more flowers to deliver. See ya!" Clifford hopped off her porch as if his shoes were on fire.

Noah did *this?* She closed the door, turned around and slumped against it. Why would he send her twenty-four dozen roses?

The doorbell rang, and she jumped. Startled, she had the knob turning in her hand before she could think. There he was, standing on her porch, in a pair of worn jeans and a black wool coat, healthy and alive and strong. He looked completely recovered and entirely different from the vulnerable man lying in a hospital bed.

What was he doing here? She'd said goodbye to him. Closed her heart to him. Walked away.

And he dared to give her white roses, reminding her of their trip and how she loved him.

Pain shredded her heart. No, she wasn't going to do this. Pretend that an apology would make it okay, and they could be good friends again. Maybe he was hoping she'd take him skiing. Well, she didn't want to be his skiing buddy.

Mr. Noah Ashton would just have to go and torment someone else. She grabbed the door and gave it a hard shove. Something stopped her.

Noah's foot against the door frame. "If you close the door, then you're going to miss what I've come to say."

"Noah, I've got to get ready for the wedding."

"This won't take long. It's important. Please." He pushed open the door, gently, and walked into her home. Into her life. Into her heart.

"You can't come in here. I've got to—"

"Julie." He took her left hand in his, his grip tender, his touch warm, the deep affection in his voice as real as the floor at her feet. "I know you came to my hospital room, and I know why you didn't stay."

"You had your family there. You didn't need me, and I had to get back—"

"Julie." He brushed a kiss to her cheek, soft and surprising and gentle. "There's something I should have told you when we were standing on the mountain watching the sunrise. After I kissed you, I should have said, 'Julie, I love you.'"

"No." Tears burned her eyes. "You can't push your way in here and say you love me. You can't do that to me—"

"Sure I can. I brought flowers. I'm trying to

make this right." His smile was genuine, his touch sure.

Right? Nothing could ever make her the same. She loved him, and now everything was different. What she wanted, what she needed. And he wanted a romance. Well, she didn't. She wouldn't lay her heart on the line for the wrong man, no matter how wonderful. How perfect.

To her horror he knelt before her, right there in her rose-scented living room, and pulled a black ring box from his pocket.

She stared at the small box that fit in the palm of his hand. No, this wasn't possible. He wasn't going to propose to her. He wouldn't be that cruel. Would he?

She started to back away, but her feet wouldn't move. Her mind was spinning so fast she couldn't object as he took her left hand in his.

"Julie, I love you." He was kneeling before her like a promise kept, steady and dependable.

No, this couldn't be real. She wouldn't believe it, even when she could see the hope in his dark, tender eyes. A horrible rushing filled her ears.

"Please," he asked sincerely, truly, "will you be my wife?"

"No!" How could he do this to her? Him and his jet and his twenty-four dozen perfect long-stemmed roses, and his billion-dollar bank account, or portfolio, or whatever it was rich men had. "You know I can't marry you."

"What?" He looked crestfallen.

That made it worse. She felt horrible and hopeless and broken. She watched the great hope in his eyes fade increment by increment until only hurt remained, and she could see it deep. There was his heart, tender and true.

"What do you mean?" He sounded bewildered.

As if she'd simply leap at the chance to be a billionaire's wife, without looking to the future and to what really mattered. Anger ripped through her like a gigantic claw, leaving her feeling raw and torn apart. "I said no. I can't be your wife. Look at me."

"I'm looking." He stayed on one knee. "I see a beautiful woman, the only woman who has ever beaten me in a competition. The only woman I've been involved with who has kept her promises and never broken a trust. The one woman who stole my heart when I wasn't looking, and so I'm here before you, asking to spend the rest of my life with you. I truly love you."

"Stop saying that." How was she going to go on with her normal, ordinary life now? Once her grandfather's wedding was over and Noah flew on his shining white-and-gold jet back across the continent, how was she ever going to be able to pick her chin off the floor and pretend her heart wasn't shattered beyond repair? He loved her. That only made everything worse.

"Julie." He didn't move, gazing up at her with all those diamonds glittering against black velvet. "I know you love me. I know it. Don't you realize I'm on your side? That from now on, that's where I'm going to stand, and my feet are never going to stray. Where you go, I go. What you want, I want. We have love, and that's everything."

"Sure, you say that now." She wrapped her arms around her middle, holding on tight, but she couldn't comfort herself. There was no comfort for this. "But what about in six weeks? Or maybe two minutes before the wedding?"

"What I say, I mean. You can always count on me, Julie. I will never hurt you like that. Never abandon you at the altar or anywhere else. Not after we're married. For better and worse, I'll be there for you." He stood, pulling her into his arms with such care. "I promise."

She buried her face in the soft wool of his jacket. She breathed in the scents of the spicy aftershave he always wore. She really loved that scent. She truly loved everything about this man. She was safe here, tucked against his chest, and it felt as if she belonged in his arms forever and ever.

It took all her courage to step away. "I drive a pickup. You travel in a jet. I don't see how this can work out. I wouldn't be happy in New York. Montana is my home. This is my community, where I belong. I teach the children here. I go to church here. My lifelong friends are here. My family is here. I can't leave, and you can't stay."

"I can't stay? I think I can. There's no law against it, is there?" He brushed her cheeks with his thumb, brushing away the tears she hadn't realized were there. "You know, I spoke to God before I came. He seemed to think Montana was a good place for me to be."

"Oh, right. For now. But you'll start missing your company and your friends and your apartment." She wanted forever. It wasn't possible. He couldn't see it, but she did. She'd been left at the altar. She had returned three engagement rings. How could she possibly give up Noah's ring?

"What if I told you I sold my company and the jet with it? You don't believe me, do you? Okay, well, I did. I also sold my apartment to my assistant, whom I promoted before I left. As for my friends, *you* are my best friend. Please, be my wife, too."

"I know you think you'll be happy here, and I'm sure you mean it now. But you're going to change your mind."

"Julie." His touch, gentle against her cheek. His kiss, as precious as a new day. "Just say yes, and let me prove it to you. I promise you that I am the one man who will never leave."

She *wanted* to believe him. She really did. She'd give almost anything to say the words he wanted to hear, the words she ached to say.

She couldn't marry him. This small-town life in rural Montana was the path the Lord had chosen for her. But it wasn't Noah's. How could it be? God had given him intelligence and brilliant business sense. Gifts that would go to waste here, where there were no giant corporations to run. Just modest hometown businesses that had been in families for generations.

She couldn't marry him. She refused to watch him grow restless and bored in a town that was too small for him.

Keep me on the right path, she prayed, as she opened the door and said the words she had to say. It was for his own good. And for hers. "Goodbye, Noah."

He snapped the ring box closed, clutching it in his fist. "No. I won't accept this. I hurt you by not saying this before. I won't do it by leaving you now."

"Staying would hurt me more. Just go." She set her chin, all fight, all determination. She was doing the right thing. It was that simple. "I mean it. I want you to leave."

He took a deep breath, as if the fight had gone out of him. His dependable shoulders slumped just a little as he marched past her. His boots knelled on her porch.

When he turned to face her, he was full of hurt. "I love you. You can push me away, but I'll keep coming back. Whatever it takes, I will prove to you that I'm here for now. For always."

He *would* make her believe it. He would show her the true depths of his commitment to her. One day she would see that she was his heart. And always would be.

Simple as that.

At the organ, Marj Whitly began the first strains of "Here Comes the Bride." "Aahs" broke out in the crowded church from the altar all the way to the back row at the first sight of the beautiful bride, draped in a light gray gown. On her arm was her grandson, James Noah Ashton the Third, in a dark gray tux.

"What a dream," Misty whispered, clinging to Julie's arm.

Exactly. Julie steeled her heart. That's what this morning had been. A dream. Surely nothing real, nothing that she ought to build her future on. Noah had been through a life-or-death experience, and he was naturally grasping at whatever he thought would make everything better. Yes, that was it. That's what he was doing by proposing to her. He was at a crossroads in his life, and he was making the choice he thought would bring him happiness.

She was making the right choice for both of them.

He looked so fine, with his dark hair tamed and the cut of the expensive suit perfectly fitted to his wide, muscular frame. No one could doubt the look of pride and love on his face as he escorted his grandmother down the aisle. Or the respect he showed when he gave the bride to her waiting groom.

Granddad. Julie ached with happiness for him. He looked dashing and dear, as he always did, even if he did fidget in the tight-fitting tux. Anyone could see the bride and groom were perfect for each other. Granddad's and Nora's love was the real thing.

Now and then fairy tales *did* happen.

When Granddad kissed his bride, the entire congregation applauded.

The sun chose that moment to smile through the stained-glass windows, casting bright hues over the bride and groom, as if to remind everyone in the church that love was God's greatest gift.

Time for plan B. *If* he could sneak out of the receiving line. Noah shook the mayor's hand, who planted his feet and looked about as hard to move as a cement barricade in the middle of a freeway.

"Mr. Ashton, pleased as punch to hear you're gonna be staying in our town. Prettiest piece that Montana has to offer. Well, we like to think so. After what you did, rescuing the little Corey girl from the creek, why, you're a member of this community already."

"Oh, yes, you may be from the big city," Mrs. Corey chimed from her place in line behind the mayor. "But you're one of us now."

Noah took the woman's words for what they were—a sincere compliment. He intended to live here, close to his grandmother, forever. And since Julie just happened to live here, well, didn't that work out perfectly?

"How are you holding up, son?" Harold asked, after the mayor had finally moved on and was shaking Nora's hand in congratulations. "I hear from my bride that you're still not up to snuff. Recovery takes time."

"I'm fine." He still tired easily, but the fatigue was slowly improving, and he wouldn't let it stop him. He had a new chance at life, and he didn't intend to wait. He spotted Julie at the gift table, talking to his sister. Now would be the perfect chance to—

"Thanks for your confidence in me," Harold said, his voice gruff, looking down at his shoes. "I've done a fair job with my investments. I'll do even better with your grandmother's."

"I trust you." Harold was a good man. Okay, so Noah had been wrong—he could admit his mistakes. He knew without a doubt that Harold would treat his grandmother right.

"My dear grandson." Nanna caught him before he could break away from the crowd. "What a blessing you are to me. I'm so very thankful you are here with us today."

"You are a blessing to me, too, Nanna." He

kissed her cheek. "Did I tell you what a beautiful bride you are?"

"Oh, my dear boy. It's so good to have you here." Nanna sparkled with happiness. "And as it happens, there goes Julie. I wonder where she's going? Maybe she could use some help with something. You had best go check, young man. Hurry along, now."

There was no fooling his grandmother.

Several people stopped him on the way to the door. To welcome him to town and to say that they sure appreciated how he helped out that day, which seemed so long ago now, when the little Corey girl needed help. He'd pitched in like a true Montanan, they said.

He brushed off their words, but appreciated their welcome. This little town was already beginning to feel like home. Now, if he could convince Julie of that, he'd be the happiest man on the planet.

He bolted out the door, but he couldn't see where she went. He tried the set of double doors that led outside. There was no sign of her in the snowy parking lot. The church, then? He strode down the hall, past the reception and into the quiet side entrance.

There she was, sitting in the front row, arms wrapped around her middle, gazing up at the sparkling stained-glass window. The giant cross glowed, as if God were giving him reassurance. This was the right path he was walking.

He gathered his courage, taking his time, searching for the right words. "The wedding was beautiful, wasn't it?"

She looked up, startled. She must have been lost in thought and didn't hear him approach. "It was lovely."

"*You* are lovely."

She covered her face with her hands. "I can't do this. Please just leave me alone."

"Why would I do that? The woman I plan to marry is hurting." He eased onto the bench beside her. "What can I say to make you believe?"

She bolted off the pew, her dress rustling around her. "Everyone is talking about how you're moving to town. Some say you'll stay. Others figure you'll be here for a few years, then head back to the city where you belong."

"And you think that's what I'll do. That a man who built a company that netted a half-trillion dollars in profits last year is someone who doesn't know what he wants. He can't make a good decision. He doesn't know where to invest his time and his effort."

"Maybe that man has had a scare, and he's evaluating his life. Maybe he's reaching for whatever will make him feel secure or happy."

"I have my faith for that. When I make a commitment, I mean it." He stood and gently turned her, so he could see the anguish on her face. "I love you truly."

"I love you, but I—"

"No buts." He kissed her gently, slanting his mouth over hers, letting her feel how he cherished her. "I've been unhappy for a long time. I want you to understand that. These changes I'm making aren't rash. I'm healthy and I'm grateful for it, and I realized when I woke up after my surgery that I had a debt to pay back to God. To live this life He has given me the right way, with love in my heart. I can't do that without you, Julie."

How could she believe him? How could she risk her heart this one last time? "No, I want a man who is right for me and my life. I want a marriage that lasts, not one torn apart by a midlife crisis or something when you decide you miss the excitement of a big city."

"I see." He was patient, his touch loving as he traced her bottom lip with the pad of his thumb. "Wasn't it you who said that the city was wasted on me? Julie, all I ever did was work. I'm tired of meetings and business trips and jet lag and irate attorneys yelling at me all day."

"I can sympathize with those poor attorneys…."

There was the Julie he loved. The one who would keep his life interesting and keep him laughing. "I want to be happy. I want to marry you."

"You keep saying that." Tears filled her eyes, perfect, silver tears that shimmered and fell just for him to catch with his thumb.

"I'm going to keep saying it until you believe me. If it takes one thousand times, then fine. We have all day. If you need to hear it a million, then fine, the church has heat. We can stay here all night. But understand this. I'm never going to make you stand in front of that altar by yourself. I'm never going to make you regret saying the vows that will make us husband and wife."

Julie's eyes were blurring, so it was hard to see the diamond ring when he slipped it on her hand. The band was cool platinum and as soft as a dream. The diamonds flickered and glittered like a thousand perfect rainbows. Promises that Noah intended to keep. He truly did love her.

Peace filled her, as gentle as the sunlight streaming through the windows, as reverent as the silence in the church. The candles glowed, and faint music lilted in from the reception room down the hall. God had led her here to this man and to this moment. She could *feel* it, deep in her soul.

"I'm standing here, in front of God, and I'm asking you again." He brushed away the last of her tears. "Will you marry me?"

"Yes." More joy than she had never known filled her, slow and sure, as Noah pulled her into his arms and kissed her long and tenderly.

Thank You, Lord, she prayed, burying her face in Noah's shoulder, holding him tight, holding him for keeps. They didn't need to speak. They stood in the peaceful sanctuary, with the sunlight and candlelight and their love that would last forever.

* * * * *

Dear Reader,

When I was writing my first book for Steeple Hill Love Inspired, *Heaven Sent,* I fell in love with Hope's brother, Noah. I could sense in him a great loneliness, and I so wanted him to find his happily-ever-after. I was thrilled when I got the opportunity to tell his story. I expected a charming billionaire kind of a guy, and instead met a man of great faith, whose strength of spirit never wavered, even when facing uncertainty, pain and a possible terminal illness.

Noah reminded me of something important. Our time here is precious. There are blessings all around us in this incredible world. I hope you take the time out of your busy life to enjoy them in love and thanksgiving.

Jillian Hart

HEAVEN KNOWS

Dear friends, since God so loved us,
we also ought to love one another.
—1 *John* 4:11

Chapter One

The warmth of the early-spring sun felt like a promise. Alexandra Sims shut the door of her ancient VW, careful of the loose window, and stared at the little town. She could see all of it from where she stood, with shops on one side of the road. On the other, railroad tracks paralleled the town, and beyond, new green fields shimmered.

She'd grown up in a town like this one along the coast of Washington State. So small, her high school graduating class had been thirty-eight. Maybe because of bad memories, she didn't like small towns much. They'd never brought her luck.

But today she felt luck was in the air, and that made her step lighter as she strolled along the cement sidewalk. She'd pulled off the interstate to fill her gas tank and, since she was here, maybe she'd stop to eat lunch and do a little shopping. This was as good a place as any.

This little town of Manhattan was truly no different from the other small Montana towns she'd passed through since recently she'd thrown what little she needed into her car and fled in the dark of the night.

Few of the buildings were new, many dating from the fifties or earlier when agriculture belonged to the family farmer and not huge corporations. The people who lived here took pride in their town—the streets were clean, the sidewalks swept and not a speck of litter could be found anywhere.

Sparkling store windows tossed her reflection back at her as she halted beneath a blue-striped awning. Corey's Hardware, the sign proclaimed in bright blue paint.

She pushed her sunglasses onto the crown of her head and stepped through the doorway. A bell jangled overhead.

"Hello, there," called a polite male voice the instant her sneakers hit the tile floor. "What can I do for you?"

Whoever belonged to that molasses-rich voice wasn't in sight. Head-high shelves of merchandise blocked the way.

"Where are your ropes?" she called out.

"To your right, all the way against the wall." A

handsome athlete of a man came into view behind the long, old-fashioned wooden counter.

She caught a glimpse of dark black hair tumbling over a high intelligent forehead. Brooding hazel eyes, a sharp straight blade of a nose and a strong jaw that looked about as soft as granite. Definitely a remote, unreachable type.

She retreated to the far wall, where everything from braided hemp to thin nylon rope could be found. Lucky thing, because she found exactly what she needed. What she didn't find was something to cut it with.

"How much do you need?" he asked in that voice that could melt chocolate.

"Three yards."

He was at her side, taller than she'd first thought. He was well over six feet, and while he wasn't lean, he wasn't heavily muscled, either. He didn't have much to say, which was fine with her. Really nice and handsome men made her nervous and tongue-tied. Probably because she wasn't used to them— and great guys had always seemed out of her reach.

As gallant as a knight of old, he measured the thin nylon cord for her, giving her an extra foot, before cutting the end neatly and looping it into a tidy coil for her. "Anything else?"

"That should do it."

He was very efficient—she had to give him that.

"I'll ring you up front." All business, he hardly

glanced at her as he tucked away the small pocket-knife he'd used to cut the rope. "Let me guess. You're going camping?"

"Something like that," she hedged. "I had a tent disaster last night, so I need to repair the main nylon cord."

"Been there." He led the way down the aisle of kitchen cabinet handles in every size and color, his stride long and powerful. "Figured you for a tourist. This valley's small enough that sooner or later, you meet everyone in it."

She'd grown up in a town like that, but she kept the information to herself. Her past was behind her and she intended to keep it that way. "This part of the country is beautiful."

"Have you been down to Yellowstone?" He was only making polite conversation as he punched buttons on the cash register.

"Not yet."

"The campsites aren't booked up this time of year, so you don't need reservations." He slipped the rope into a small blue plastic bag. "That will be two seventy-one. If you have your tent in your car, you can bring it in and I'll repair it for you. Free of charge. Company policy."

His offer surprised her. She stopped digging through her purse for exact change to stare at him. A familiar panic clamped around her chest. Patrick was hundreds of miles away and he had no idea where she was, but this is how he'd affected her. Even a store clerk's courtesy frightened her, when there was no reason for it.

The phone rang, and the clerk answered it. "Corey's Hardware. John, here." He spoke in the same friendly voice to whomever was on the other end of the phone.

John, huh? He looked like a John. Dependable, practical, rock solid.

There was no danger here. She had to remember that not every man was like Patrick. She knew it— now, if only her heart would remember it, she'd be fine.

Alexandra relaxed and bent to dig a penny from the bottom of her coin purse.

"Well, now, washers are tricky things, Mrs. Fletcher," John drawled, tucking the receiver against his shoulder. "Maybe I ought to come by this afternoon and put in the right size for you, free of charge, except for the washer, of course. That'd be the best way to get the job done right."

See what a nice man this John was? He helped all sorts of people. There was no reason at all to feel uneasy. She watched as he swept her coins into his palm as he listened to Mrs. Fletcher.

Nodding, he dropped the money into the cash register till. "Sure thing. I'll give you a call before long."

He tore off the receipt and slipped it into the bag.

"I appreciate your business," he told her. "Bring in your tent if you want."

"Thanks." She could do it herself. She zipped her purse closed and reached for the little blue plastic sack. The last thing she wanted to do was to rely on anyone else ever again. She'd learned that lesson the hard way.

A note pinned to the back wall behind the counter caught her attention. Help Wanted. Full-Time Position.

The rest of the printing was too small to read as she swept past. A full-time position, right there, posted for her to see. She'd been praying for just this sort of an opportunity.

Maybe she should ask about it. Surely it wouldn't hurt.

She took a look around at the neat shelving, the tidy merchandise and the polished old wood floor. This wasn't what she had in mind. She'd been a cashier long ago, and she wouldn't mind being one again, but working alongside a man—no, no matter how nice he seemed. Not after what she'd been through.

"Do you need anything else?" John asked from behind the counter, polite, clearly a good salesman.

"No, thanks." She grabbed the doorknob, the bell jangled overhead and she tumbled onto the sidewalk. A cool push of wind breezed along her bare arms.

The advertisement troubled her. Was it coincidence that she'd spotted it, or more?

Unsure, Alexandra unlocked her car door, stowed the rope on the back floor behind the driver's seat and grabbed her hand-knit cardigan from the back. The soft wool comforted her as it always did. Pocketing her keys, she continued down the cracked sidewalk toward the grocery at the end of the block.

The store bustled with activity as weekend shoppers chatted in the aisles and in the checkout lines at the front. Feeling like a visitor in a foreign land, Alexandra headed to the dairy section. The refrigeration cases were the old-fashioned kind, heavy glass doors with handles, reminding her of the small-town store where she used to shop as a girl.

This was not the kind of place where she wanted to live, she told herself as she selected a small brick of sharp cheddar that was marked as the weekly special. She'd left small-town life forever three days after graduating from high school and had never looked back.

Then again, living in a bigger city hadn't exactly worked out well, either.

She wove around two women who looked to be about her age, chatting in the aisle, with their toddlers belted into brimming grocery carts, and felt a pang deep in her chest. What would it be like to live those women's lives? Alexandra found a bag of day-old rolls that still felt as soft as fresh.

The Help Wanted sign in the hardware store kept troubling her. It was frightening not knowing what was ahead of her. Worse, not knowing if she would be able to build a new life. She had to trust that if the job at the hardware store was what God wanted for her, then He would find a way to tell her for certain.

"Why don't you go ahead of me?" A woman with a small girl in tow gave Alexandra a smile. "I have a full cart, and you have only a few things."

"Are you sure?" When the woman merely nodded, Alexandra thanked her and stepped in line.

She'd almost forgotten what small towns were like—the friendliness that thrived in them. A coziness that felt just out of her reach—as if she could never be a part of it. But she enjoyed listening to the checker ask an elderly woman about her new grandbaby.

Everyone seemed to know everything about a person in a small town, she reflected as she placed her cheese and rolls on the conveyer belt.

Why, if she actually were to interview for the job and got it, she'd be easy to locate. If she stayed here, she would probably be known as the new woman in town, even ten years from now.

No, if she took a job anywhere, it had to be in a larger city where she could blend in unnoticed and be harder to track down.

"Did you find everything all right?" the checker asked.

"Yes."

"That will be three eighty-three, please."

Alexandra pulled the fold of bills from her jeans pocket and peeled off four singles.

"Are you enjoying our countryside?"

"It's very beautiful."

"This time of year we don't see too many tourists and Yellowstone is about ready to open some of its entrances, but I think it's the best time to sightsee."

Alexandra hardly knew what to say as the checker pressed change into her palm. "Have a good day."

Even the bagger was friendly as she handed Alexandra a small paper sack.

Taking her purchases, she headed for the electronic doors. Everywhere she looked, she saw people chatting, friends greeting one another, and heard snatches of cheerful conversations.

After the stress and noise of living in a city, she liked breathing in the fresh-scented air. It was so quiet, the anxiety that seemed to weigh her down lifted a little and she took a deep breath. Longing filled her as she headed back to her car. A yearning for the kind of life she'd never known.

Fishing the keys from her pocket, she watched the woman from the checkout line lead the way to a minivan parked in the lot. How content she looked, carrying her small daughter on her hip, opening the back for the box boy who pushed her cart full of groceries. Full of dinners to be made.

No doubt she'd drive to a tidy little house not far from here, greet her husband when he came home from work and never know what loneliness was.

That life seemed impossible to Alexandra. Wishful thinking, that's what it was. Maybe, someday—if the good Lord were willing—she'd have a life like that, too.

In the meantime, she had a lot troubling her. She grabbed her water bottle from the front seat and tucked it under her arm. Clouds were moving in overhead, but the sun still shone as brightly as ever. The weather would hold for a lunchtime picnic.

When she spied a little ice-cream stand through the alley, she headed toward it. At the far end of the gravel parking lot, there was a patch of mown grass shaded by old, reaching maples.

Perfect. There were picnic tables beneath the trees, worse for the wear, but functional and swept clean. No one was around, so she chose the most private one. The wood was rough against her arms as she spread out her rolls and cheese.

A car halted at the ice-cream stand's window. As the driver ordered, she heard the murmur of pleasant voices like friends greeting one another.

Alone, Alexandra bowed her head in prayer and gave thanks for her many blessings.

John Corey knew the look of someone hurting. Maybe because he knew something about that. For whatever reason, he couldn't get the woman out of his mind as the minute hand slowly crept up the face of the twenty-year-old clock his uncle had hung on that wall decades before.

She was beautiful, no doubt about that. Not in a flamboyant, look-at-me sort of way, but pretty in a quiet, down-deep sort of way. And those wounded-doe eyes of hers made him wonder what had become of her. She hadn't been back to let him repair her tent, and that disappointed him.

Only because he wanted to do what he could, that was all. Helping was sort of his calling. Sure, he owned a hardware store in a little town that was so small, a person could blink twice and miss the entire downtown. But being part of a community meant being aware of its needs.

He'd gotten in the habit of helping out where he could, fixing eighty-year-old Mrs. Fletcher's outside faucet, for instance, because a widow on a set budget might not be able to afford a plumber.

He'd also come to believe that the Lord gave everyone a job in this world. And that his job was doing what he could. Like the beautiful young woman—there he went again, thinking about her. She'd looked as if she had the weight of the world on her slim shoulders, and, in a way, it was like looking at a reflection of himself.

Some might say her problems weren't any of his business, and they might have a point. But what if she did need help? What if there was something he could do? Lord knew he had a debt to pay this world, and he'd seen her look at the Help Wanted sign he'd posted behind the counter. Did she need a job? But before he could ask her, she'd bolted through the door and was gone with a jangle of the overhead bell and a click of the knob.

And now that it was long past the noon hour and not one customer had been by the entire hour, he had plenty of time to think on what might have been. Plenty of time to notice the little yellow Volkswagen was still parked outside his front window.

Not any of his business, he reminded himself as he finished his microwaved cup of beef-flavored noodles at the front counter. She didn't want help repairing her tent. Fine. Still, something nagged at him, troubling his conscience.

You're just thinking of another woman you couldn't help. John couldn't deny it, and it left him feeling as if he had to do something, no matter how small, to help even the balance of things.

He was crumpling the noodle container and tossing it into the garbage bin in the back when it came to him. Working quickly, he dug his way through the messy storage room until he found the small kits he'd received a few months ago.

With one of them tucked under his arm, he hurried to the front. Just in time, too. He spotted her through the display window, unlocking her car. Her long dark hair tumbled around her face, a face more beautiful than he'd seen in a long while. Wearing faded jeans and a fuzzy white sweater, she caught his attention and held it.

Like a good Christian man, he ought to be concentrating on his good deed. But what did he notice? Her slim waist and her lean, graceful arms. She'd settled behind the wheel by the time he made it outside and since she'd rolled down her passenger side window, he did what any good man would do.

He leaned on the door and peered through the window. "Need any help, ma'am?"

She squinted at him as she settled her pink plastic sunglasses on her nose. *"Ma'am?"*

"I'm trying to show off the manners my mama raised me with."

That made her smile, and it was a sight to behold. Dimples teased into the creases bracketing her mouth as she flipped a lock of molasses curls behind her shoulder.

What was with him? He had no business trying to make a pretty woman smile. No right to notice her beauty.

He cleared his throat, hoping to sound more gruff. "I've got something for you. Call it a visitor's gift for every new customer through my door."

"I don't need a gift."

"It's a tent repair kit." He handed her the package through the window. "It's got everything you need. Since you've already experienced one tent disaster, you could have another. It never hurts to be prepared."

"It certainly doesn't." She stared at the kit he offered, her soft mouth turning down in a frown. "How much does this cost?"

"Not a thing."

"I'd hate to be indebted to you."

"What debt? I didn't mention any debt."

"Nobody does something for nothing. It's a hard fact of life."

"The kit was a free sample to me from the manufacturer, trying to get me to order a whole batch from them. My storage closet is full of them. You'd be doing me a favor by taking one off my hands."

How wary she looked. "All right. Thank you."

"No problem," he replied, already backing away. "You take care now."

That was that. He'd done the right thing, he figured. Funny thing was, he couldn't seem to turn around and walk away, or even look away as she bent to set the tent repair kit on the floor, her rich brown hair rioting forward to hide her face. Thick, lustrous curls that made him notice. And keep noticing.

He knew it was the wrong thing to do, but he couldn't drag his attention away from her as she straightened. The amazing fall of hair bounced over her shoulders. He stood with his shoes cemented to the sidewalk as she reached for her keys with long slim fingers.

The hurt—he could see it in her, because it was so like the pain within him.

Maybe that was why he couldn't lift his feet and walk away. Why he watched as she blew her lustrous bangs from her eyes with a puff. She slipped her keys into the ignition, but didn't start the engine.

She leaned across the gearshift instead. "It's odd, because I have a hole in my tent, too. I decided not to patch because I was trying to make do."

"On a budget vacation?"

"Let's just say a very tight budget. So tight, I've been praying for no rain, and then you hand me a repair kit out of the blue. It's as if heaven whispered to you."

"Could be. You just never know."

"Thank you. I really mean that." She started the engine, and blue smoke coughed from the tailpipe.

"How much farther do you think this thing will get?" he had to ask her, gesturing toward her Volkswagen.

"I know Baby doesn't look like much." She snapped her seat belt into place. "But she hasn't let me down yet."

"As long as you're sure."

"Absolutely."

He watched her head east through town, taking the back way to Bozeman.

He couldn't say why, but it was as if he'd lost something. And that didn't make any sense at all. The jangle of his phone reminded him he had better things to do than to stand in the middle of the sidewalk. He had his own problems to solve, debts to pay.

Redemption to find.

Chapter Two

Alexandra glanced at her dashboard and the temperature gauge. The arrow was definitely starting to nudge toward the big *H*.

Great. A serious breakdown was the last thing she needed. Hadn't she just told the guy from the hardware store that her car was trustworthy? That Baby wouldn't let her down?

It looked as though she'd been wrong. She glanced in her rearview mirror and watched a trail of steam erupt from beneath the hood and rise into the air like fog. Yep, Baby was definitely having a problem. She nosed the car toward the gravel shoulder alongside the narrow two-lane country road.

There wasn't a soul in sight. Now what? She killed the engine and listened to the steam hiss and spit. It looked serious and expensive. Expensive was the one thing she didn't need right now. She hopped out to take a look.

The relief that rushed through her at the sight of the cracked hose couldn't be measured. It was a cheap repair she could do herself, and she was grateful for that.

A cow crowded close to the wire fence on the other side of the ditch and mooed at her.

"Hello, there." Her voice seemed to lift on the restless winds and carry long and wide. A dozen grazing cows in the field swung their big heads to study her.

Great. It was only her and the fields of cows. The green grassy meadows gently rolled for as long as she could see. There was the long ribbon of road behind and ahead of her, but nothing else.

No houses. No businesses. No phones.

It was sort of scary, thinking she was out here all alone, but she'd look on the bright side. If she walked to town and back, she wouldn't have to dig into her remaining funds to pay for a tow truck.

After locking her car up tight, Alexandra grabbed her purse and started out. Dust rose beneath her sneakers as she crunched through the gravel. It reminded her of when she was little, and she'd hike with her younger brothers down the long dirt road to the corner gas station at the edge of town.

Like today, the sun, hidden by clouds, had been cool on her back and the air had tickled her nose with the scents of growing grass and earth. In that little store she'd traded her hard-earned pennies for ice-cream bars and big balls of bubble gum.

Why was she remembering these things? She'd long put that painful time out of her mind. What was coming over her today? It was being here, in this rural place. She'd been careful for so long to live with the bustle of a city around her. Traffic and people and buildings that cast shadows and cut into the sky.

It was a mistake to head east. In retrospect, maybe she should have headed south, through California. A busy interstate would never have brought these memories to light. But in this place, the fresh serenity of the countryside surrounded her. The whir of the wind in her ears and the rustle of it in the grasses. After fifteen minutes of walking, not one car had passed.

The wind kicked, bringing with it the heavy smell of rain. She tipped her head back to stare up at the sky. Dark clouds were sailing overhead, blotting out the friendlier gray ones. After another ten minutes, she could see the sheets of rain falling on the farther meadows, gray curtains that were moving closer. She'd lived in Washington State all her life, so what was a little rain?

The roar of an engine broke through the murmur

of the wind. Glancing over her shoulder, Alexandra saw a big red pickup barreling along the two-lane road between the seemingly endless fields.

She prayed it was a friendly truck. That it would pass by and keep going. The closer the vehicle came, the more vast the fields and the sky seemed. The more alone she felt.

Her heart made a little kick in her chest. Come on, truck, just keep on going. No need to slow down.

She didn't glance over her shoulder, continuing to walk along the edge of the ditch.

She could hear the rumble of a powerful engine and the rush of tires on the blacktop. The truck was slowing down.

This wasn't good. Not one bit.

Please, don't let this be trouble, she prayed, eyeing the width of the ditch and wondering just how fast she could get through that fence.

She could hear the truck downshift as the driver slowed down to match her pace. Out of the corner of her eye she saw the polished chrome and the white lettering on the new-looking tires. The passenger window lowered.

Alexandra went cold. Did she expect the worst? Or was it simply that old country code of neighborliness that was at work here?

As if in answer, a little girl leaned out the open window and tugged off plastic green sunglasses.

"Hi, lady. My dad says I gotta ask if you need a ride."

At the sight of the blond curls and friendly blue eyes, Alexandra released a breath. She hadn't realized her chest had been so tight.

It just went to show how traumatized she'd been this last year. And that deep down, she expected the worst—of life and of people.

It wasn't something she could brush off lightly. If this past year had taught her anything, it was important to stand on her own two feet. To keep from needing anyone. "Thanks for the offer, but I don't mind walking."

"That's what Dad said you'd say, right, Dad?"

"Yep, that's what I predicted," answered a molasses-rich voice that sounded very familiar.

On the other side of the little girl, behind the steering wheel, a man tipped his Stetson in her direction. Alexandra recognized that handsome profile and those mile-wide shoulders.

"This has to be more than a coincidence running into you twice in one day." John Corey shook his head. "I can't believe this."

"Neither can I." She blinked and he was still there. The truck's door felt steel-cool beneath her fingertips. "I thought you had a store to run. What are you doing out here?"

"Since I'm my own boss, I can close up shop for a few minutes. Folks know to wait or give me a call if it's an emergency. Hailey, here, spent the morning out at a friend's place and gave me a call to come pick her up."

"Yep." Hailey swiped wayward curls from her eyes, waving her neon-green sunglasses as she talked. "We had a barbecue picnic and potato salad for lunch. I didn't like the potatoes one bit 'cuz they were the red kind and Stephanie's mom put in those black rings."

"Olives," John informed Alexandra from across the cab. "We're not olive people. We flick them off our pizza if they get on by mistake. The pizza people hear about it, too."

"Rightly so." Not everyone shared her opinion of olives. Okay, so maybe it was all right to let herself like him, just a little. "It's good to meet you, Hailey. I'm Alexandra."

John leaned over the steering wheel to get a better look at her. "Alexandra, huh? I couldn't help noticing your car alongside the road a few miles back. Figured I might come across you on the way to town."

"You seem awfully sure of yourself. How many women fall for your knight-in-shining-armor act, Mr. Corey?"

"Thousands."

"None." Hailey frowned. "My daddy only dates the TV."

"The what?"

"Now don't be revealing all my secrets. A man's relationship with his sports channel is sacred." He flushed a little. "Hailey, open the door for the lady. It's a long walk to town and it's fixing to rain."

"I'm not afraid of a little rain," Alexandra argued, because it had been so long since she'd accepted help from anyone.

Hailey moved back on the seat, as if to make room. "You gotta come with us. It ain't right to let ladies walk."

"You said it better than I could." Leaning past his daughter on the bench seat, John fixed his deep hazel gaze on Alexandra. "Come on aboard. You'll be perfectly safe with us. If you're worried at all, I just want to put your mind at ease. My daughter doesn't bite, and on the off chance she forgets her manners and does, she's vaccinated."

"Daddy." Hailey scowled, scrunching up her freckled nose. "I haven't done that since last year at Sunday school, and Billy Fields bit me first."

"See? We're as trustworthy as can be."

"Trustworthy, huh?"

"Absolutely." John reached over and opened the door.

"We got lots of room," Hailey added.

"You two make it impossible to say no." It wasn't as if she was alone with a stranger. Clearly John had a daughter, so that meant he was married, right? A dependable-father type, so she figured she might as well spare herself the long walk to town.

Something wet smacked against her forehead. The first drop of rain. Drops pelted the road and she dodged them by climbing into the cab.

"Looks like we came along just in time." Keeping his attention on the road, John flicked on the wipers and put the truck in gear. "I told you your car was going to break down. I won't say I told you so."

"You don't have to look happy about it. You *were* right, but it's only a cracked hose. Easily fixed."

"Really? Did you diagnose the problem yourself?"

"Sure. I've been on my own for a long time. I've had to learn to do minor repairs here and there. It's no big deal."

"Let me guess. You're one of those independent types?"

"Something like that."

He continued watching the road and never looked her way once.

Yep, definitely the dependable-father type. There wasn't a thing to worry about. Alexandra relaxed into the leather seat. She'd never been in such a fine vehicle. Warm heat breezed over the toes of her sneakers.

Hailey snuggled close. "Alexandra, do you got a dog?"

"Not anymore. I had a little terrier when I was about your age."

"Cool. Did you love him lots and lots?"

"I sure did. He slept at the foot of my bed every night and watched over me while I slept." Alexandra sighed, softening a little at the rare good memory from her childhood, and secured the seat belt. "I miss him to this day. When I was eleven, we moved to a different house and couldn't take him with us, so I had to leave him with the neighbors."

"I bet that made you real sad."

"It did." Alexandra swiped an unruly lock of brown hair behind her ear, looking down at her scuffed tennis shoes. She couldn't help noticing Hailey's brand-new ones, already scuffed, with bright purple laces. "Why don't you tell me about your dog?"

"Don't got one. Daddy is really mean and won't let me have one." Hailey grinned.

"That *does* sound mean." Alexandra never knew it was so easy to tease.

John's dark gaze warmed with mild amusement as he lifted one thick-knuckled hand from the steering wheel to ruffle his daughter's unruly hair. "Alexandra, don't get the wrong opinion of me. Hailey isn't quite old enough for the responsibility of taking care of a dog. She still can't pick up her room every day."

"Can, too." Hailey's chin jutted out. "I don't got a lotta time. I'm very, very busy."

Alexandra stifled a chuckle. "Busy, huh? I bet a pretty girl like you has a full social calendar."

"Yep. I got swimming lessons and ballet lessons and piano lessons, 'cept I'm not so good at that, but Gramma says I gotta keep practicing my scales, even if I hate 'em."

"Wise woman, my mother." John found his gaze straying from the road again and in Alexandra's direction. "You can see how lonely a dog would be waiting for Hailey to get done with all those lessons."

"I'm not taking your side." She shook her head, scattering those rich brown locks that seemed shot full of light. "No way. I'm sticking firmly with Hailey. A girl needs a dog of her own. It's one of those rules of life."

"Like death and taxes?"

"Exactly. I'm so glad you understand."

"Daddy didn't have a dog when he was little." Hailey leaned close to whisper. "Don't ya think that means he's *gotta* have one now?"

"Makes perfect sense to me," she whispered back.

"You're getting me in trouble, Alexandra." John guided the big pickup around a curve in the road. "Have pity for a poor beleaguered dad."

"Yeah, you look like you have it tough." She didn't feel an ounce of pity for him—only admiration. For the obviously comfortable and good family life he had. His daughter didn't sit quietly, afraid to make too much noise. No, Hailey wasn't afraid to sparkle. The affection between father and daughter was clear.

No, John didn't have it tough. From where Alexandra sat, she figured he had everything important in life.

Everything she'd never had.

"Hey, enough about us." John cut into her thoughts. "Tell us where you're headed once you get your car fixed."

Alexandra tensed. It was a perfectly innocent question. She knew that. John didn't mean any harm. She knew that, too. He couldn't know he was asking the impossible. She couldn't talk about where she'd been and never where she was going. She had to leave her past behind, and lying was the only way to do it.

The story she'd been rehearsing since that first frightening night on her own was right on the tip of her tongue, but it felt wrong. She couldn't do it. Not to this man and his daughter, who were being so nice to her.

So what did she say? Her stomach clenched as tight as a fist. Simply thinking about where she'd been sent panic lashing through her. She stared at the road ahead, slick with rain. A wind gust roared against the side of the truck and she wished the winds were strong enough to blow away the bad memories she'd left behind, and she was able to find a way to answer him honestly. "I'm not sure where I'm going. I'm just driving."

"You're the adventurous type, is that it?" John slowed the truck as town came into view. "You decide to vacation and go where the road takes you?"

"Exactly." She said nothing more. She was looking for a new life.

And praying she would know it when she found it.

The rain ended and the wind died down as they drove along the main street of town. Modest shops were open for business, and a few cars were parked along the curb, but no one was in sight. Maybe the rain had scared everyone inside.

"Daddy, can we stop for ice cream? Please, please?"

"What do you need ice cream for? You're sweet enough already."

Hailey rolled her eyes. "Gramma says a girl's gotta have chocolate."

"Gramma ought to know. She's a wise woman."

Hailey didn't know what a lucky little girl she was, to have a kind man for a daddy, Alexandra thought as the pickup slowed to turn off the street and into the gravel lot. Then again, maybe like Alexandra's father, this was how John acted in public—polite and deferential.

Home had been a different matter.

She'd learned the hard way it was difficult to really know a person from outward appearances. It was a tough lesson to learn but one she'd never forgotten.

John pulled up to the drive-through window at the same little stand where she'd eaten her lunch in the shade. On friendly terms with everyone, it seemed, he greeted the blond-haired woman by name after she slid open the glass partition.

"Hi there, Misty. We'll have three chocolate cones, double dipped."

Before Alexandra could protest, the woman smiled brightly. "Three it is. I'll be right back." Then she disappeared into the shop.

"Consider it terms of accepting a ride with us," John explained easily. "Where there's Hailey, there's chocolate ice cream. It's best not to fight it. Just accept it as a law of nature."

"Then it should be my treat in exchange for the ride to town." She peeled a five-dollar bill from the stash in her wallet.

"No, it's not my policy to let ladies pay." He held up one hand, gallant as any fine gentleman.

"It's my policy to pay back good deeds when I can." She pressed the bill on the dash in front of John and gave him an I-mean-business look.

"This goes against my grain," he told her, handing the five to Misty at the window in exchange for three huge chocolate-encased cones. "Thanks. Hailey, pass one down."

"These are awesome." The girl's eyes shone with pleasure as she handed the biggest cone to Alexandra. "You gotta be careful 'cuz the ice cream is all melty."

"I see." The rich chocolate smell was enough to die for. Her mouth watered as John put the truck in gear and circled around to the shaded picnic tables.

Random raindrops plopped onto the windshield from the trees reaching overhead. "This looks like a good place to have a car picnic," John announced. "What do you say, Hailey?"

"A truck picnic, Daddy," she corrected with a roll of her eyes. "My Grammy loves car picnics. Don't you, Alexandra?"

"A car picnic, huh?" She'd never heard it called that before, but it wasn't hard to see at all, sitting in this comfy truck with the heat breezing over their toes as father and daughter picnicked right here, out of the weather. It was way too much for her and far too tempting to stay.

A gust of breeze buffeted the side of the truck, reminding her that she was like the wind. On the move, with no place to call home and no reason to linger.

There was nothing else to do but to tuck her purse strap firmly on her shoulder. "You two enjoy your picnic. This is where I go my own way."

"No! Wait," Hailey protested. "You gotta eat your ice cream."

"I will, I promise." Alexandra popped open the door and her feet hit the rain-sodden ground. "I hope you get your puppy. John, thanks for the ride."

"Wait." He bolted out the door. "You don't have to run off. You're going to need a ride back to your car."

"I don't think your wife will appreciate your driving strange women all over town." Alexandra took a step back, putting safe distance between them. "Don't you have a job at the hardware store to get back to?"

"I own the store, and my part-time hired help can handle things while I'm chauffeuring Hailey around." The wind tousled his dark hair, drawing her attention to the look of him, and the way his shoulders looked as dependable as granite. "I'm not married. Not anymore."

"My mommy died when I was just a baby," Hailey added around a mouthful of ice cream.

"I'm sorry." The words felt small against the size of their loss. Somehow knowing John was a single father made it easier for her to take another step away and another, her heart feeling as heavy as stone.

"It's a long walk back," John called after her.

"I don't mind." She waved goodbye across the gravel lot and disappeared before he could say anything else.

* * *

Crunching the last bite of his cone, John had to admit the chocolate didn't taste as good as usual. That was Alexandra's fault.

When he'd happened along her broken-down car on the road, he had to wonder if he was meant to help her out. A woman alone like that... Surely the Lord was watching out for her. Surely it had been no coincidence John had been the one to find her walking toward town. The good Lord knew John had debts to pay and never turned down an opportunity to do so.

It troubled him now. He tried to put thoughts of Alexandra aside as Hailey told him all about her morning at Stephanie's, but his mind kept drifting back. God hadn't intended for people to be alone. That's what families were for, neighborhoods, churches and towns.

He couldn't help wondering if Alexandra was about ready to walk alone back to her car.

The clouds overhead had broken, but the real storm hadn't hit yet. He could feel it in the wind and smell it in the air.

"Let's get going, Hailey. We can't leave Warren in charge of the store for much longer." The high school kid he'd hired was reliable, but he was young. "Look at you, all covered with chocolate."

"I made a real mess," she agreed cheerfully as she rubbed her hands on a wadded napkin. "Is

Grammy gonna come pick me up now? 'Cuz I've got lots of stuff to do."

That was his daughter, always on the go. "Yep. All I have to do is give her a jingle. Turn your head that way. You really smeared yourself up good this time." John grabbed the last paper napkin and wiped the chocolate smudges from his daughter's face.

"It was really melty. Hey, Daddy?"

"What?" He gathered the trash and tossed it into the garbage bin. "This isn't about getting a dog again? You're wearin' out my ears on that one."

"Oh, I don't want a dog. I want a puppy." She climbed into the cab and plopped onto the seat. "A *puppy*."

"That's just a little dog."

"Yeah, but you let me have a horse."

He got into the truck, turned the key and listened to the engine rumble. "That's it. I forbid you ever to visit Stephanie again."

He gave her head a ruffle, and she giggled, light and sweet—his most favorite sound of all.

Back at the store, Warren was helping a customer, so John grabbed the phone and dialed. He counted nine rings—Mom must be outside in her garden.

She was out of breath when she answered. "Hello?"

"Hailey's ready for you."

"Oh, John, perfect timing. I was starting to wonder about her. Say, grab a container of rose food for me. I just ran out."

"Will do. And since I never charge you a penny—"

"Uh-oh, I'm in trouble now. I can hear it coming." On the other side of the phone, his mom had to be smiling. "All right, I'm sitting down. What do you want now? Don't tell me you finally folded on the puppy issue."

"Not yet. I'm still waging that battle. Listen, on your way to town, you'll see a woman walking. She's medium height and slim with dark brown hair and wearing a sweater and jeans. Give her a ride back to her car, will you? Don't take no for an answer."

"I should hope not! A woman walking alone. This country is safe, I'm proud to say, we're a fine community, but a woman shouldn't be left alone. And walking on that long road. Why, I'll leave right now."

"You're a good woman, Mom."

"Don't I know it."

John punched the button, ending the conversation. Problem solved. Alexandra wouldn't be able to refuse his mother. Few people could. Alexandra would get the help she needed, and his conscience could finally stop troubling him.

End of story, he told himself, heading back to the

garden section. The phone rang and more business walked through the door, enough to keep him busy. So, why couldn't he stop thinking about Alexandra and the way her smile never quite reached her eyes?

Chapter Three

"I just can't leave you here." Bev Corey set her jaw, sounding as formidable as a federated wrestler instead of the tiny slip of a woman standing alongside the country road. "What if your car doesn't start? Dear, I truly believe we should call a mechanic."

Alexandra couldn't help liking the woman. Bev Corey may be a stranger, but in the ten-minute trip from town, she almost felt like a friend. "Don't worry. I've done this before. I'll show you."

"That's what men are for—to keep cars running smoothly. And it's my belief that's what we should let them do. My Gerald is a hop and a skip up the road. Let me go hunt him down, and I'm sure he'll be happy to fix this for you."

"Thanks, but I can handle it. All I have to do is replace this hose, and I'll be on my way."

"That simply seems dangerous." Bev took a tentative step forward, as if to keep far from the grease. "Engines explode, metal parts can burn you. There's acid in the battery, you know. I don't think it's safe for you to be touching that."

"The engine is cool and I'm far away from the battery." Alexandra tugged the damaged hose loose. "Now I just fit this on here—"

"I'm not sure about this at all. Why, those are out-of-state plates. How far have you driven this poor car? I don't know a thing about engines, but this certainly looks as if it needs a mechanic's attention." Bev shook her head, scattering the short, perfectly coiffed curls, which slipped back into place. "What were your parents thinking, to let you take off across country in a car like this?"

It seemed natural that Bev should ask, obviously being a motherly type. Still, it hurt to look back. Remembering couldn't change the past or the family she'd been a part of. "I left home when I was seventeen and I've never went back."

"Never?"

"No. I'm happier that way." If it still made her sad, she tried not to feel it. She'd been fine all these years on her own, with the Lord's help, and even though she'd had a rough time lately, that was all about to change. She was sure of it.

She changed the subject as she wrestled the hose into place. "Have you always lived here in Montana?"

"Goodness, yes. My family homesteaded the land in the 1880s. Five generations of Coreys have farmed that land. We grow potatoes and are proud of it. Montana is a fine place to live. Are you thinking about moving here?"

"It's a possibility," she admitted before she realized she'd spoken.

"Are you here looking for work?"

"I'm looking for the right opportunity." Alexandra slammed the hood and tugged on it to make sure it was latched.

"So you've come to interview for a job?" Bev lit up. "Why, that's wonderful. So many of our young people are moving away to the bigger cities. Are you interviewing right here in our town?"

"I don't have an interview, not yet," she corrected, wiping her hands on the edge of a rag. "I'm looking and hoping the right job comes along."

"Trust in the Lord to see to it, dear. What kind of work do you do?"

"I clean houses."

"Honest work. And hard work."

Alexandra pulled her key from her pocket. "Thanks again for the ride. I'm glad I got to know you."

"Don't say your goodbyes yet. We'll wait and see if that car of yours starts." Bev looked doubtful as she eyed the rusty Volkswagen.

Alexandra unlocked the door, settled behind the

wheel and turned the ignition. The engine didn't roll over, so she pumped the gas—but not too much so she wouldn't flood the carburetor.

She got out and once again moved to check the engine.

"Just as I thought." Bev planted both hands on her hips, leaving her fine leather purse to dangle at her side. "That car isn't drivable. Do you realize what a godsend it was that John gave me a call?"

"John called you? But I thought you were on your way to town—"

"And so I was. But John asked me to keep an eye out for you on my way in and give you a ride back to your car. He's my oldest son. Always with a hand out to help, that's our John. Land sakes, what are you doing now?"

"Cleaning off the battery terminals." Alexandra bent over the engine compartment. "That's probably why my car isn't starting."

It took only a few seconds to wipe the terminals down and tighten the connectors.

"Something tells me you've been on your own a long time." Bev eased closer. "No boyfriend? No husband?"

"No husband. Yet." But there had been a man who'd proposed to her after three years of dating. A man she'd been ready to marry.

Panic clawed in her chest and she said nothing more about Patrick. She wanted to forget him, to forget she'd ever known him. She slammed the hood and took a deep breath. "This should do it."

"If it doesn't start," Bev warned, apparently expecting the worst, "then you'd best come with me and no arguments. I can't in good conscience leave you here."

"She'll start." Alexandra gave her car a pat on the dash and turned the ignition. The engine rolled over, coughing and sputtering, but that was normal. "See? I know she doesn't look like much, but she really is a reliable car."

"I don't know about that!" Bev didn't look convinced. "It's Saturday afternoon, and it's sure to be dark soon. What if this car of yours breaks down again?"

"Then I'll fix it. The great part about having a car this old and uncomplicated is that I can fix nearly everything that can go wrong with it." She liked Bev, and wished her own mother could have been more like the woman standing before her now. "I'll be fine, so don't worry. You've helped me more than you know."

"I feel as if I haven't done a thing. Maybe you should come home with me tonight. I've got a little rental cottage out behind the garage. It's as tidy as could be."

Alexandra bit her lip, not at all sure what to think. She'd been too long living in a city and had forgotten what it was like to live in a small town.

Forgotten that in small towns, the world seemed kinder. It was hard to trust in that kindness—in the belief of that kindness.

Her chest ached, as if a part of the defensive wall around her heart crumbled a little. She'd learned long ago that kindness hurt, too, because sometimes it hid pity. "Thanks for the offer, but I want to reach Bozeman by nightfall. Once I'm there, I'll see where my path takes me."

"But you're alone. How old can you be? Twenty?"

"I'm twenty-four."

"Why, my youngest daughter is that age. I'd hate to think of her alone, driving across country in an unreliable car." Bev opened her leather purse, which exactly matched her shoes. "Let me see… where is it? Here, my husband's business card. You promise to give me a call tonight, when you get settled."

"Sure." Alexandra took the card and ran her thumb across the embossed letters.

Gerald Corey, Potatoes And Soybeans, it said, and listed an address and phone number. There were different logos, probably farmer organizations she didn't know anything about, but she did know one thing. Bev was genuine in her caring.

It had been a long time since someone had truly cared about her. A long, lonely time.

Bev was a stranger, and she probably treated

everyone she met this way. With warmth and concern. As if they were family.

"I'll call when I'm settled," Alexandra promised, tucking the business card into her back pocket.

As she settled behind the wheel, she couldn't help feeling hopeful. That this short stop in this little town was a sign of things to come. Good things the Lord had in store for her.

It was hard to say goodbye, but she managed it. Harder still to put the little car in gear and ease onto the road. Waving, she shifted into Second, watching Bev grow smaller in the rearview mirror.

Alexandra felt as if she were leaving something of great value behind, and she didn't know why. Bev Corey climbed into her luxury sedan, and then the road turned, taking Alexandra around a new corner and down a new path.

It made no sense, but the feeling remained.

"Here's Grammy," Hailey announced from the front of the store. "See ya later, Dad!"

"Don't forget your bag." John watched to make sure she grabbed the pink backpack from the counter, damp from the towel and swimsuit inside from her stay at Stephanie's. "And wait up. I've got something for your grandmother."

The bell above the door jangled and the screen door slammed. Hailey hadn't heard him. Through the front-window display, he could plainly see his mom circling around the front of her car, dressed perfectly as always, and greeting Hailey with a big hug.

His pulse skipped a beat—then he noticed the passenger seat was empty. Mom hadn't brought Alexandra back with her. Disappointment washed through him like a cold ocean wave, leaving him troubled.

Had he been looking forward that much to seeing Alexandra again?

Then maybe it was for the best that she wasn't here. He had no right to feel any caring—however remote—for any woman. Not after how he'd failed.

Through the screen door, he heard his mother talking, and his daughter answering. He could hear a hay truck downshift as it eased through town. It all sounded far away at the memory of his failure long ago now, but yet, in an instant, it seemed like only moments ago. When his world had changed. And a pretty young woman had lost her life.

The container felt heavy in his hand. Praying for the memories to leave him, he pushed blindly through the door, stumbling and dazed. He'd do anything to have the chance to go back and change the past. *Anything.*

Mom's merry voice brought warmth to the afternoon suddenly turned cold. "Hailey, that bag of yours is as wet as your swimsuit. We'd better put it in my trunk because I just cleaned my car. Is that everything?"

"Yep." Hailey took tight hold of Bev's hand, as she always did, and climbed into the back seat.

A typical Saturday afternoon, like a dozen others so far this spring. Mom's cheer, Hailey's charm and his life in this small town—the same as ever. The weight of his guilt made his step heavy and slow.

"John, are you all right? You're as quiet as could be, and that's not like you." Mom peered at him carefully. "You don't seem flushed."

"I'm fine. Just wondering if you found Alexandra," he hedged.

Why was his pulse racing when he mentioned the woman's name? It was guilt—plain and simple. As if he could help enough people, that would atone for the one person he couldn't have helped.

"Heavens to Betsy, John, I'm so glad you called me. I found poor Alexandra walking along that road all by herself. That just isn't safe, not at all." A deep look of sorrow passed over Mom's gentle face. She'd always been tenderhearted, caring about everybody.

"I insisted on giving her a ride, and you were right, she was stubborn at first, but that shows sense. A young woman can't accept rides from strangers these days. So I stayed with her until her car started. But do you know she doesn't have a soul in the world who cares about her? No family at all. No one to worry over her arriving safe and sound. It's a shame, it is, a nice girl like that."

"That's why I called you." John's throat tightened until he could hardly speak. "Thanks for helping her out."

"She bought us ice cream," Hailey volunteered from the back seat. "And she had a dog when she was little. Just thought I otta mention it."

"We heard you, Miss One Track Mind." Bev tried to hide a chuckle. "We'll pray Alexandra has smooth roads ahead of her. You were a good man to help her out, John."

"The least I could do, seeing as she came into my store."

"You don't fool me with your modesty act. You're one of the finest men I know, and I'm proud to call you my son."

Not true, but it made some of the pain in his chest ease. "I come from good stock," he told her because he knew it would make her smile, and he turned to his sprite of a daughter playing with the seat belt buckle. "You stay out of trouble, you hear?"

"I'll try." Hailey grinned like the angel she was.

Such sweetness. Love for her filled his heart as he set the bin of rose food in the trunk with Hailey's backpack. She was a good girl, and he was grateful to his mom for the time she spent with Hailey, making up for a mother's absence.

His guilt felt as dark as the storm clouds overhead.

"Bye, Daddy!"

John watched his mother's car pull away from the curb. Hailey's purple-painted fingernails flashed as she waved.

The Lord had forgiven him long ago, or so Pastor Bill assured him time and time again, but that hadn't erased the guilt. John would never forgive himself for his wife's death.

Ever.

Because he'd stopped by Mrs. Fletcher's house, John was late arriving at his Mom's. The kitchen was a flurry of activity. The oven timer buzzed loud and shrill, and the potatoes boiling too hard on the stove spit sizzling water onto the burner.

"Good, you showed up just in time." Mom poured water from the green beans at the sink. "Give your dad a shout, would you? He's out tinkering with that tractor and I can't get him away from it."

"Daddy!" Hailey looked up from coloring at the table. Crayons flew as she tore across the room, winding her arms around his knees. "Grammy's making my favorite potatoes."

"Good. Those are my favorite, too."

The phone shrilled again just as Mom was reaching deep into the oven to rescue the delicious-smelling roast. Halfway to the door to find his dad, John lifted the receiver from the wall-mounted phone. "Howdy."

"Is this Bev's home?"

Wait. He knew that voice—soft, pretty and gentle. "It surely is. This wouldn't happen to be Alexandra?"

"Hi, John."

"How's the car running? Mom told me you were quite the mechanic."

"I managed to make it to Bozeman just fine. I promised Bev I'd call when I arrived safely. So she wouldn't worry."

"That's my mom. I knew she'd look after you."

"I should hold that against you, sending me someone I couldn't say no to. Thank you."

"You're more than welcome. Here's Mom now. Before I surrender the phone—" he held the receiver high so his mother couldn't reach it "—I meant to say something earlier, and since this is probably my last chance, here goes. I noticed you taking a second glance at the Help Wanted sign I had posted. You wouldn't happen to be interested in a job, would you?"

"I'm surprised you noticed. I hardly glanced at it."

"So you aren't interested."

"I didn't say that."

On the other side of the line, Alexandra could hear Bev telling John something.

John chuckled. "Is that so? Mom said you were looking for a job. For the right opportunity."

"How do I know working in your store is the

right opportunity? I have absolutely no hardware experience whatsoever."

"You don't need experience. I'm not looking for help in the store."

"You're not?" Her heart gave a little jump. "You mean you need someone like a bookkeeper?"

"Nope. I need someone to watch Hailey for me during the week. Mom's only filling in temporarily while I find someone new. The last sitter quit to go to Europe with her family, and how can you blame her for that? But it's left me high and dry. I don't think there's anyone available in all of the Gallatin Valley."

"But you don't even know me."

"I know that you like double-dipped ice cream and you're good with kids. That's good enough for me. C'mon—" Hailey's excited chants filled the background as John laughed. "See? Everyone's in favor of it."

The panic returned and Alexandra wasn't sure why. Wait—maybe she did know. The last time she'd been anything more than strangers with a handsome man, it had ended in near disaster.

This was different, she told herself, but the panic remained. Being responsible for a child with all the worries she had about her own safety, that simply wasn't the right thing to do.

"I'd love to, John, but I'm afraid I can't."

"I appreciate your decision, that you might

want to keep your options open in case some better offer comes along. So here's what we can do. Consider it a temporary position and you're free to leave for a better opportunity. What do you think now?"

"I think you're trying to make it impossible for me to say no."

"True," he admitted, warm and deep, like richly flowing chocolate, and the sound was enough to make her stop breathing and remember how masculine and strong he'd been without seeming cruel or controlling. Just like a hero out of a movie.

Well, men like that weren't real, she told herself, sensibly. They really weren't.

"At least tell me you'll think about it?" he asked.

She held the phone tight to her ear, wishing a part of her didn't long to accept. To spend her days taking care of a nice little girl, baking cookies and playing in the sunshine. She wouldn't be alone— at least for a little while.

And that was almost temptation enough.

"I'm afraid I can't." It was hard to say the words. Harder still to think about hanging up the phone. "I appreciate the job offer, really I do, but I don't think I'm what you're looking for. Goodbye, John."

"Wait! Alexandra—"

She hung up. It was the right thing to do. For John and Hailey. And for her.

"If it's a local call, next time I'll let you use my

phone instead of the pay phone," the lady in the office offered as Alexandra swept by.

"Thanks." She smiled at the woman, who then stepped into the back room where she lived with her husband. The aroma of meat loaf lingered.

It was suppertime. Everyone in the campground was settling down to eat. She walked past motor homes, where retired couples chatted over their meals, and tents, where families cooked over open fires. Everywhere she looked, people were gathering in pairs and groups.

One day, that would be her. She was certain of it. Surely the Lord didn't mean for her to always be alone.

Chapter Four

The wonderful thing about camping was that a person never needed an alarm clock. Nature had its own rhythm, one that felt serene and peaceful as Alexandra punched her pillow, nudged awake by the call of birds heralding the coming dawn, and the downshifting of truck traffic on the highway. But Alexandra was content to ignore that as the first rays of the rising sun cut through the nylon tent and into her eyes.

Good thing she was an early riser. Her nose was cold from the chill in the air, and for one second she snuggled deeper into her toasty-warm sleeping bag. The fabric shivered around her as she turned onto her side. Could she manage a few more minutes of sleep?

But already her mind was racing ahead. It was Sunday—she wanted to find a church service somewhere nearby, and then hit the road when it was over. Would she head east, toward Miles City and North Dakota? Or south toward Yellowstone? The checker at the grocery store had mentioned the park was opening some of its entrances.

Maybe she could find an available campsite, since she'd never had the chance to travel before. This was her first time out of Washington State. Wouldn't it be something to see Old Faithful? Well, she'd simply have to see where the Lord led her on this beautiful spring day.

Already the sun was boldly chasing away the chill from the air. So why lay around like a lazybones? She crawled out of her sleeping bag, deciding she wanted to hit the showers before they got busy. A quick breakfast, and then she'd find a nearby church. The day already felt full of promise.

She crawled out of the sleeping bag, already shivering in her favorite pair of sweats. It didn't take long to grab her bag of showering things and her last clean towel from the stack on the back seat of her car. The campground was quiet this time of morning, except for a few travelers beginning to stir. An older woman, opening her door to the pine-scented air, stepped out of a luxury motor home and offered a pleasant good-morning.

Alexandra returned it, feeling better for the momentary connection. The skies were clear and a dazzling blue. The air smelled fresh and crisp, and she couldn't help feeling full of hope. Surely the happy touch of the sun meant good things for the day ahead. It had been one more night that Patrick hadn't caught up with her.

She showered quickly, shivering in the cold water. Apparently the water heater wasn't working terribly well, but she didn't mind. Cold water was good for the soul, right? She certainly felt invigorated as she toweled dry, pulled on a pair of warm sweats and ran a comb through her hair. Now, to dig out her good clothes from the bottom of the duffel bag, and then she'd go in search of an espresso stand. She was on a budget, but a double hazelnut latte was a once-a-week treat she wasn't about to miss.

With her bag slung over her shoulder, she pushed through the doors and stepped out into the new day, where the sun was up, so warm and bright it hurt her eyes to look into it. Surely there was an espresso stand close by, and if she could find a local paper, then she could check the church listings—

"Alexandra!"

She froze in the middle of the dirt path. She didn't know anyone here. For a nanosecond, fear speared through her. Then she realized that it was a child's voice that had called her name, not a man's. Not Patrick's.

"Hey! Alexandra. Remember me?" A little girl skipped along the low fingers of light slicing through the pine trees lining the gravel driveway.

Alexandra warmed from head to toe. "Of course I remember you, Hailey. What are you doing here by yourself?"

"Oh, Daddy and Grammy came, too, but I can run the fastest."

John was here? And Bev? What were they doing here? Confused, Alexandra squinted into the long bright rays of the rising sun, but she couldn't see anything. Another flash of panic sliced through her—was she really that easy to track down?

Hailey skidded to a stop, her hair tangled and her purple ruffled dress swirling around her knees. Her neon-green sunglasses were perched on her nose and hid her eyes, but her grin was wide and infectious and adorable.

"How did you find me?" Alexandra tried to keep the panic from her voice. She'd paid cash for one night, and the manager hadn't asked for more than her car's license plate number. That didn't make her easy to track down, right?

"Grammy hit the dial-back thingy. That's how we knew where to come get you." Hailey slipped off her sunglasses. "It's Sunday and you can't *not* go to church. Grammy was real worried 'n' stuff, so Daddy said we'd take ya with us. Right, Daddy?"

"That about sums it up," answered a deep rumbling voice.

John. Alexandra felt his presence even before she heard the first pad of his footstep. Even before she caught the faint scent of pine-scented aftershave on the sweet morning breeze. The sun rising in the great sky behind him shot long spears of golden light, casting him in shadow as he strode closer. His broad shoulders were set, his Stetson tipped at an uncompromising angle, his gait slow and steady. Confident.

He looked like a hero out of a movie, the tall, dark silent warrior too good to be real. He strolled into the shadows, the change of light transforming him from shadow to flesh-and-blood man. He looked different today in his Sunday best, still rock solid and powerful, but remote. For the moment, unreachable.

Alexandra's breath caught, and she was very aware of her long hair wet from the shower and tousled by the wind. She'd run a comb through it once. Who knew what she looked like? She was wearing her favorite pair of gray sweats, of course, the old ones that were baggy and had holes in both knees.

It doesn't matter, she told herself. It certainly wasn't as if John Corey was looking at her like a man interested. And shouldn't she be panicking instead of hoping he did like her?

Right. Except she knew there was no danger here. John was a widower with Hands Off practically pasted to his forehead.

"How about it, Alexandra? Seems we owe you for treating us to ice cream, and Coreys always

make good on their debts. We can't let this favor
you did us go unpaid, so here we are, asking you to
ease my conscience and let us take you to church
with us."

"It was only ice cream, John. Not a debt to be
paid."

"That's a matter of opinion. Come to the service
with us. You would make Mom happy. She loves
to fuss over everyone. It gets tough on a guy. Think
of it this way. You would be doing me a favor."

"Oh? A favor now? I thought you said it was a
debt!"

"Semantics." It was easy to see the good in him,
the easy charm that he kept rigidly veiled, but it was
there, lurking in the friendly grin that would put
Robert Redford to shame. "If you came along, then
Mom would fuss over you instead of me and
Hailey. Believe me, it's a lot to endure, and we
need a break. Isn't that right, kid?"

"Yep." Hailey bobbed onto her tiptoes.
"Grammy's real mushy. She says it's 'cuz all her
kids are all grown-up. And I get too much fussin'.
Are you really gonna come, Alexandra? Please? I
can show you my horse."

"Well, I'm not sure—"

Hailey's face fell. "You don't wanna see my
horse?"

Now what did she do? "Well, sure, but—"

"Don't bother to fight it, Alexandra." Amused,

John eased closer. "It's best just to give in. Mom and Hailey together are a powerful force. They scare tornados away. It's best to do what they want."

"And I don't get any say in this?"

"Nope."

It would be easier to say yes if he didn't look so strong and dependable. She wasn't sure she liked how she felt when she was around him. She certainly noticed he was a man. The trouble was, she hadn't planned on making connections of any kind. The fewer people who remembered her, the less chance Patrick had of finding her. "I'll come on one condition."

John lifted one brow, as if intrigued, leaning a fraction of an inch closer. "Name it."

"This settles the score. There's no more debts, no more favors. I don't need any charity."

"Good, because I'm not giving out any."

She couldn't imagine a man as polished and probably as financially sound as John Corey would know much about camping. Or about getting by. Nor could he possibly understand how she felt, that she didn't need help the way he thought.

She could stand on her own two feet, on the path God had made for her. And she ought to tell him so, but she didn't. She was tired of feeling so lonely.

For a handful of hours this Sunday morning, she wouldn't be alone. That was blessing enough. A special gift on the Lord's day.

* * *

The church parking lot was full by the time Alexandra made it back to the small neighboring town, nestled in the rolling foothills of the Rocky Mountains. The day was dazzling, and the sky endless. The sunshine smiled over her as she squeezed into a space along a tree-lined curb, shaded gently by the first buds of an ancient, sprawling chestnut tree.

"Alexandra!" Hailey dashed across the street, all long limbs and swishing skirts and brilliance. An equally coltish little girl ran at her side, in a white pinafore dress that was every bit as nice as Hailey's high-end department-store jumper. "You made it! You made it! Grammy was afraid you'd get lost."

How wonderful it was to be welcomed! "Me? Get lost? No way. Is this your friend Stephanie? The one with the puppy?"

"That's her!" Hailey bounced to a stop.

"That's me," the girl agreed easily. "You have really pretty hair. Can you do mine like that?"

"Yeah, mine, too?" Hailey begged.

"No problem. It's just a French braid. It's a cinch to do."

"Cool!"

Hailey grabbed one hand and Stephanie grabbed the other, and Alexandra found herself tugged across the street. The two girls began skipping.

"C'mon, Alexandra!" Hailey urged. "We're in a hurry."

"I don't think I can go any faster." Her heels were a little rickety, and her right ankle wobbled. But sandwiched between the kids, she gave it a try.

She hadn't skipped since she was a child. Her feet felt so light. And her hair bobbed up and down with her gait. She felt fantastic, like singing, and she hardly realized she was laughing until she leaped onto the sidewalk with the little girls and skidded to a stop in front of John Corey.

Oh, no. He was squinting at her, and he probably thought that was no way for an adult woman to act, skipping like a child right there in the church parking lot. She was a guest of his, too. She hadn't meant to forget herself like that.

Feeling a little embarrassed, she swiped a lock of escaped hair behind her ear. "Thanks for the escort, girls."

"Guess what, Daddy? Alexandra's gonna make my hair like hers." Hailey bounded over to tug on his hand. "Can Stephanie sit with us? Can she, please?"

"As long as it's fine with her parents." John watched as the girls dashed off, in search of Stephanie's family, skipping hand in hand, leaving them alone.

The wind gusted, cool and strong, and Alexandra shivered. Her feet felt heavy again as she took a step toward the church, where families grouped together in conversation. She was sharply aware of being alone and a stranger. On the outside, just as she'd been as a child.

And as an adult, keeping a firm distance away from men. From John as he swept off his Stetson and raked his fingers through his dark hair. A contemplative gesture as he watched the other families, his face an unreadable mask.

Not that whatever he was thinking was any of her business, but she wondered. Several people shouted out greetings to him as they passed. Apparently John was well woven into the fabric of this community, where everyone knew him by name and reputation, and welcomed him with looks that said John Corey is a good man.

"Alexandra? Ready to head inside? It's got to be better than standing around here. I feel like I'm in the way."

"Sure. Hailey told me Bev will be singing in the choir this morning."

"Yep, she is. We tried to stop her, but she's stubborn. It's a shame, too." His dark eyes twinkled with a hint of trouble.

What was it about this man? She hardly knew him, but he could make her laugh. She didn't feel as alone as she kept up with John's long-legged stride, which he kept shortening to accommodate her gait.

She wished she could stop wondering about him.

He'd been a widower for a long time. Out of deep love for his lost wife, maybe? That would explain the distance she felt, just beyond his polite friendliness and warm humor. As if he'd closed off a part of himself long ago, barricaded it well and hidden the key.

When the line moved, John motioned for her to take the step ahead of him. He was so close. Too close. The woodsy scent of his aftershave, the faint aroma of fabric softener on his jacket, the faint heat from him made her acutely aware of the six feet of male so close, if she leaned back a fraction of an inch, they would be touching.

That couldn't be good. Alexandra leaned forward as far as she could, creating distance. Still, the feeling, the sensation of closeness, remained.

"I bet you'll like Pastor Bill." John's warm breath fanned the shell of her ear. "He leans toward meaningful but short sermons. Mercifully short. You can't find that just anywhere."

"Then I guess I'm lucky that you and Hailey hunted me down this morning."

"That's right. Afterward, there's Sunday brunch at my house. You're invited."

She had miles to cover, laundry to do and a future to find. Gazing up at John, seeing the strength and male vitality of him as he towered over her, blocking the sun, every cell within her seemed to take notice.

One thing was for certain—John Corey was not her future. She should say no.

"Come join us. We have plenty to share, and this is the Lord's day. If you don't, my mother will hurt me."

"Sure, like I believe that."

"You should. She's a formidable woman. You should know that by now." He winked in a friendly way. "Just be prepared, that's all I'm trying to tell you. She's going to insist. Personally, I think she's just looking for someone new to impress since we're all tired of complimenting her cooking. She needs you."

"What can I say? I'm in demand. I guess I'd better stay for a little while."

"You've got places to go and people to meet?" he asked, his gaze narrowing, as if he were measuring the truth of her.

"Something like that. I might hop down to Yellowstone. I've never been, and it's only a few hours away."

"You'll be glad you did." He paused while they moved a step closer to the minister. "I've got some old guidebooks for the park. I don't need them anymore, but they have campsites and information. Might come in handy."

"Has anyone ever told you that you are too helpful?" Alexandra twisted around to look at him, the wind tangling the cinnamon-brown wisps framing her pretty, heart-shaped face, making her look vulnerable. Her slim brows arched over her luminous dark eyes in a playful frown. "There has to be something wrong with someone who's *too* nice."

"I toss my dirty socks on the floor just like any man," he quipped, keeping her away from the truth. She had no idea what she'd said, or what her innocent, light comment made resonate deep down in his soul.

The family on the steps ahead of them moved away, saving him from trying to come up with an easy answer, one that wouldn't reveal the pain deep within. His problems weren't anyone else's, and Alexandra looked down enough on her luck that the last thing she needed was to have to listen to his troubles. A wrong he could blame on no one else but himself.

"Pastor Bill." John offered his hand, clasping the older man's warmly. "I'd like you to meet Alexandra."

"What a pleasure." Pastor Bill took Alexandra's slim hand, welcoming and warm. "I hope you enjoy our humble service this morning. We're short a singer in the alto section, if you happen to be willing to join the choir."

"Me? No, but thank you." Alexandra spoke as gently as lark song, her grace unmistakable.

John didn't feel it was good to notice that.

"Daddy!" Hailey called out, as she and Stephanie crowded their way onto the top step.

The girls were laughing, making Alexandra

laugh and the minister chuckle fondly. It was a beautiful morning, this day a gift from the Father above, as were the people surrounding him. The girls who tugged on Alexandra's hand, eager to sit next to her in the church, and Hailey calling to him again to get his attention.

He had more blessings than most. More than he deserved.

"Daddy, Alexandra's gonna braid our hair, so we've gotta hurry. There's Grammy in the front! They're gonna start singing. Hurry! Please!" Hailey's fingers curled around his own, holding on tightly. So very tightly.

Take care of our baby, Bobbie had begged. *Promise me, John. Promise me.*

Pushing down the guilt and a sorrow that had no end, he carefully tucked it away, down in his soul where it belonged.

Steadied, once again back to himself, he managed a smile and squeezed his daughter's hand. Trust glittered in her eyes.

Her hand in his gave him strength as he followed her down the aisle and into the row where Stephanie and Alexandra were already settled.

"Me, first!" Hailey collapsed onto the wooden pew. "Right, Alexandra?"

"Right." She dug through her shoulder bag, bowing her head as she pulled out a comb. Cinnamon-brown wisps, silken and glossy, had escaped from her braid, brushing the soft curve of her cheek.

She's a beautiful woman. The trouble was that he kept noticing that. Over and over again. He found the edge of the bench by feel and dropped onto it. The faint scent of her shampoo—something that smelled like apples and spring—made him dizzy with yearning.

With the wish for a woman to love. Alexandra was so incredibly soft and graceful and everything missing in his life, everything he'd been without for so long. It overwhelmed him. Sharpened the edge of a longing he hadn't felt since Bobbie's death.

The longing for companionship. For the deep, abiding connection of love and intimacy. For that incredibly strange and wonderful way of a woman, of her brightness, of her smile, of her magical softness in his life.

And it was wrong. He squeezed his eyes shut, willing away the longing, just as he'd forced away every other emotion. He tried to focus on the sounds around him—the familiar rise and fall of voices as families settled down into the pews, the strike of heels against the wood floor and the clatter of shoes as the children followed their mothers into the rows.

Hailey's elbow bumped him, bringing him back. He turned toward her, and there was Alexandra. Right there, in his peripheral vision, impossible to miss. She could be an angel, with the colorful light from the stained-glass windows washing over her like grace.

Her slim fingers held and twisted and folded locks of Hailey's sunny-blond hair with deft confidence, fingers that were long and well shaped, feminine and hugged by several silver rings. Nothing fancy or expensive, just artful, and somehow like her.

Her fingernails were short and painted a light pink, hardly noticeable except that he couldn't seem to tear his gaze from the nimble way her hands worked, tucking and folding, and then winding a small lime-green elastic band around the end of a perfect braid.

"Cool! Thanks, Alexandra." Hailey touched her new do, shimmering with happiness. "See, Daddy? I think you gotta hire her now 'cuz not even Grammy can do braids like this."

"They aren't hard to do, not at all," Alexandra argued, stepping in as if to save him from having to answer. "Let me grab one of these hymnals. I don't want to be flipping pages when the choir starts."

Hailey jumped to help, and so did Stephanie on Alexandra's other side, as the organ music crescendoed, and Pastor Bill approached the altar.

With Hailey between them, it wasn't as if Alexandra was close to him. But she was. The apple scent of her shampoo seemed to fill the air. He couldn't stop noticing her. The way she crossed her ankles, the left over the right. He saw that her left shoe strap was held together by one of those tiny brass-colored safety pins.

He ought to feel sorry for her, a woman alone, without family, without means, practically living out of her car. That's what he ought to feel. Obligation, duty and a sense of purpose in the chance to help, to right some wrong, since he had so much on his soul to make right.

But what he felt wasn't pity at all. Or charity. Or the sense of accomplishment that came from helping others. He felt…aware of her as a woman. In a way he hadn't taken notice of any woman since he'd met Bobbie. Shame pounded through him, like wind-driven hail, leaving him icy cold and stinging.

Stunned, he rubbed his hand over his face. This isn't good. It isn't right. He had no business feeling anything but duty toward anyone, much less another beautiful woman. He'd messed up his one chance at love, the beautiful blessing of marriage the good Lord had given him. He had no right to even notice another woman's beauty.

The congregation rose with a resounding rustle that echoed throughout the sanctuary. His cue to stand, too. He held the hymnal and tried to follow the hymn he knew so well. But couldn't seem to remember the words because he heard Alexandra's sweet soprano, so quiet it was barely discernible, but to him, he heard only her.

This strange, warm flutter of emotion…it was something he had to control. Tamp down and extinguish, because he didn't deserve it. He didn't deserve her.

Pastor Bill began the prayer. Bowing his head, John pushed away all thoughts of Alexandra and, with all his heart, concentrated on the minister's words.

Chapter Five

W̲as this the right place? Alexandra pulled into the long curve of gravel driveway that climbed lush rolling fields, and disappeared out of sight. Her tires crunched in the thick, soft gravel as she drove up the incline.

The house swept into view around a slow curve, a two-story log structure with a gray stone chimney rising up into the sky. Smoke puffed from the chimney, and every window facing her sparkled clean and pure with the sun's light. John's house, just as Bev had described it.

At least she was in the right place, although she wanted to turn the car around and speed straight to the freeway. Why? Because she was insane, that's why. She was attracted to John. Attracted—as in liking. As in noticing a man the way a woman noticed a man.

Warning. Danger. Didn't she know better? Remember what happened the last time she felt this way?

She shivered, despite the warm air breezing in through the open window. Trembled all the way down to her soul. If she closed her eyes and looked inside herself, she knew the memories of Patrick would be right there, close to the surface, frightening as he grew angrier and more threatening, his fist raised….

Don't think about it. She took a deep breath and gave the door a push. Warm, grass-scented air caressed her face as she climbed out of the car. The gravel crunched beneath her heels and the wind tousled her skirt hem.

Maybe it was the day, or the way Pastor Bill's sermon had lifted her heart, but she felt as if the world had never looked so beautiful. The sky was a dazzling blue—truer than any blue sky she'd ever seen before. The mountains jagged and snow-capped, awash with sunlight like a row of uncut amethysts, enduring and breathtaking. Like faith.

Good things were in store for her. She simply had to believe.

"Alexandra! Come meet Bandit!" a cheerful voice called out, drawing Alexandra's attention to the shadowed side of the garage, where Hailey perched on top of a chin-high wooden fence. She was no longer in her Sunday best, but in a pair of jeans, boots and a grape T-shirt. "Do ya like horses?"

"I'm sure I'll like yours." John wasn't in sight, so Alexandra gladly headed straight down the cemented path that hugged the long wall of the garage. Lilacs lifted budding lavender cones, brushing her arm and skirt as she swept by.

She still didn't see John. He was probably in the house. Good thing. Considering how she'd been feeling this morning, aware of his presence, of his warm breath on her ear, it was best to avoid him as much as possible. He was obviously a nice guy, but she didn't feel comfortable being alone with any man.

"My horse is named Bandit and I can ride her really good," Hailey called out, swinging her feet. "See how pretty she is?"

Alexandra hardly glanced at the horse. What she noticed were two very big, very male boots visible beneath the horse's belly.

John straightened up, knuckling back his hat to study her over the saddle horn.

She skidded to a stop, her dress swirling around her. She felt melty inside, the way Hailey had described her ice-cream cone the other day. Melty and aware and uplifted. Just from seeing John.

Not good. It was best to ignore it. "You have a beautiful horse, Hailey."

"I know. Bandit's my very, very best friend, next to Stephanie and Christa. Oh, and Brittany, but only sometimes." Hailey flipped her bouncy ponytail behind her shoulders. "Do ya wanna ride? I'll let ya, if you want. I only let my best friends ride Bandit."

"I'd be honored, except I don't know the first thing to do with a horse."

John strolled out from behind the mare, moving with the slow power of molten steel. "You can learn. It's easy enough."

"Gee, thanks. I was hoping it would be really hard. I'm afraid of heights."

"Then I won't torture you. I'll just take you mountain climbing instead." Laughter flashed in his dark eyes. "Hey, I'm glad you found us okay."

John hardly glanced at her. He doesn't feel this same zing of interest that I do, she thought. Why was she disappointed?

John's attention was on his daughter, as it should be. Capable and gentle, he swept the little girl from the high rail of the fence to the soft grass-strewn ground beside the horse. "Want a hand up?"

"Nope, I can do it. I'm big and stuff." Hailey jabbed her toe into the stirrup, reaching high for the saddle horn. She stretched to her limit and struggled to mount up. John stood behind her, ready to catch her if she should fall.

Just like a good father should.

Her heart tumbled in her chest—a sign of doom. Don't start seeing a fantasy where none exists, she reminded herself. That's the mistake she'd made with Patrick. She'd seen all the wonderful things he was, and ignored the not-so-wonderful.

Big mistake. One she wouldn't make again.

"Hey, Daddy! It's Grammy!" High atop her horse, Hailey pointed toward the driveway, already sending her mare into a run. "Gotta go, okay? Bye!"

They were alone. Just the two of them. She pretended to watch Hailey ride off, waving to her grandmother. But she was really trying *not* to notice John.

It was impossible.

Alexandra felt his presence, as if all her senses were honed onto him and nothing else. The sound his boot made when he placed his foot on the bottom fence rung. The whisper of his shirt sliding against the rough wood as he settled his forearms on the rail. The fall of his shadow across her feet.

"I'd better go see if Bev needs any help." It was the only excuse she could think of, but it gave her reason to leave.

Except she felt the unmistakable weight of his gaze on her back, watching her walk away.

Watching her. That didn't sound good. But when she glanced over her shoulder, John was lifting a sun-browned hand to his mother.

Not to her. Heat fired across Alexandra's face. See? More proof that he isn't interested. This reaction to him was probably exhaustion. She was putting in long days on the road. She wasn't sleeping that well at night. She was off-kilter and so were her feelings. Right?

Trying to make herself believe that explanation, she hurried through the shadows and into the blazing sunlight, leaving John behind.

Bev was unloading plastic containers from the back seat of her luxury sedan. "Oh, there you are. I'm so glad you decided to join us. I made my special potato salad, which I usually only make for special occasions, but I was in the mood for it yesterday. Now I know the reason why."

Bev handed over the large container she held, reverently, as if it were priceless. "Heaven above must have known we'd have you for Sunday dinner. Hailey, go tell your father I hope he remembered to get propane for the barbecue."

"But, Gram, I really, *really* need a cookie. I'm gonna starve or something." Hailey leaned over the top rail, while her horse stood placidly. *"Please?"*

"We can't have you keeling over from starvation, now, can we?" Pretending to be stern, although her eyes were twinkling merrily from behind her bifocals, Bev popped the top of a Tupperware container and held the bowl over the fence. "Just one, and it had better not spoil your appetite, young lady."

"I'm as hungry as a horse." Hailey bit the corner off a bright pink iced cookie. "I'll go tell Daddy."

"That's my girl."

Alexandra helped herself to a few of the containers on the back seat. Might as well be useful. See how easy it would be not to think about John?

"Providence has sent you to us, I have no doubt of that." Bev gathered the last two bowls, tucking both of them neatly into the crook of her arm. "I want you to take a look at John's house. You'll see right off how much he needs to hire someone, and fast."

"Ah, now I know why you invited me to Sunday dinner."

"I confess to ulterior motives. But it just seems too perfect, is all. Hailey and you get along pretty well."

"I think she's a great kid."

"See? I knew I liked you."

"I have great taste when it comes to people." Alexandra didn't know how else to say it. "Thanks for inviting me today, Bev."

"My pleasure."

Alexandra's heart felt incredibly light. She'd needed this more than she'd realized. She'd been so unhappy with Patrick, and slowly growing unhappier with every day that passed, that she hadn't noticed how bad it was.

And how much of life she was missing out on.

"See?" Bev pushed wide the ornate front door to John's house and held an arm wide to the living room. "What can I say? Disaster. I've been trying to do what I can, of course, but what he really needs is a wife."

"He's looking to remarry?"

"Oh, I hope and pray. No, Bobbie's death broke his heart clean in two, I tell you. I keep hoping he'll find love again. Then again, who knows when it comes to the heart?"

Alexandra's throat tightened, and she couldn't speak. She felt sad for John and his wife, and surprised at Bev's words. Love like that didn't exist, did it?

"What happened to her?"

"A climbing accident. Something went terribly wrong. John blames himself. He cherished her, you know. She was his everything, and he hasn't been the same since he buried her." Sadness etched into Bev's face, deep around her eyes and mouth, a measure of her own grief and loss.

Real loss. It washed over Alexandra like a tidal wave. Cold and powerful, she was left reeling as Bev tapped away through the foyer and along chinked log walls where framed pictures were the only decoration.

Pictures of family. Of Hailey smiling on top of her pony, her cowboy hat lopsided, grinning while she held a melting grape Popsicle. Pictures of Hailey as a toddler, so small and laughing, cradled in John's protective arms. Images of Hailey as a downy-haired infant tucked beneath a pretty woman's chin—John's wife.

It was impossible not to feel sorry for him. John's

heart was broken irrevocably, Bev had said. Did people really love one another like that? Or was it the fondness of the memory, the sorrow of loss that made the past seem better than it was? She didn't know.

"I'm ready to start grilling." John strolled through open French doors and into the impressive kitchen. "Mom, you're making Alexandra work, and she's our guest of honor."

"Oh, I don't mind—"

He stole the bowl from her arms, standing so close to her that she could smell the comfortable scents of barbecue smoke and mesquite chips clinging to the sweatshirt he wore. Standing this close, she could see into his eyes. How dark they were, instead of filled with light. From grief?

Alexandra remembered the picture of his wife, and how gentle her smile had been. She didn't know what to say as John stepped away and snapped off the plastic lid of the container.

"Mom, you are a wonderful woman. I was hoping you would make this." He inhaled deep. "I'd better sample this. Just to make sure it's good enough for everyone else to eat. I'm a pretty good taste tester. I'm going to get me a spoon—"

"Stop that." Bev playfully slapped the back of his hand as he pulled out a cherry-wood drawer in the center island. "I know what you're up to, and you'll wait to eat like everyone else. Really, John.

You'd think you were a boy again. How is that going to look to Alexandra, when she's trying to decide if she wants to work here or not?"

Uh-oh. Alexandra stepped forward. As gently as she could, she tried to say, "Bev, I'm not—"

"You are?" John interrupted, turning with the bowl in the crook of his arm. "Great. I'm glad you're reconsidering. Look at the mess I'm in. Wait. Don't look. It might scare you."

"I wish I could, but I can't—"

"Just give us a chance, dear." Bev snapped open one container after another. "You could go other places and work for other people, but who could need you more than us?"

"You're pulling my leg. This place is immaculate." Alexandra's throat tightened, looking around at the cozy, well-appointed home.

"Hailey needs you." John scavenged through a drawer for a spatula. "If that makes a difference."

Alexandra didn't know what to say. She'd been looking for a new start. The chance for a new life.

Could it be true? Is this what the Lord had in His plans for her?

"What do you think?" John squinted across the outdoor table at her, shaded by a big yellow umbrella, as she took her first bite.

"Heaven with mayonnaise." Alexandra couldn't help a tiny moan of appreciation.

"See, Mom? I told you." John reached for the serving spoon. "Since it's been officially tested and approved, I'm done waiting. I'm digging in."

"Serve your mother first." Bev winked, holding out her plate, fully aware she was torturing her grown son. "Two big spoonfuls, please. How about you, Hailey?"

"Yep. I want lots." She held out her plate, too.

"In some houses, it's the man who gets served first." Good-natured, John winked, and dumped a heaping serving of potato salad on Bev's plate.

"In some houses, in the fifth century. Don't forget to serve your father. Gerald, only one scoop. We're watching his cholesterol." Bev leaned close to confess. "Alexandra, go ahead and start passing the chicken. Take a nice big piece. You'll love John's marinade. Hailey, honey, pass the biscuits, please."

John and his father were talking about a tractor engine, their voices pleasant rumbles as Alexandra selected a piece of deliciously fragrant chicken and set it on her plate. There was no strained silence, as she'd grown up with. Or the pretense of rigidly polite manners that had been so important to Patrick.

Hailey was chattering away to her grandmother about her horse, and Bev was filling both their plates with wonderful food. Sweetly spicy baked beans and a green salad and biscuits so fluffy they looked like miniature clouds. Ice tinkled in a crystal pitcher as John refilled his glass with iced tea.

"You're pretty quiet." He reached the short distance between them to fill her glass, too. "We're an overwhelming bunch, aren't we? My brother and his wife will be coming along after a while— they're split between two families on Sunday. They usually bring dessert. Then it will really get wild. Ice cream. Cake. Scandalous."

"You do this every Sunday?"

"Pretty much. Sometimes we meet at Mom and Dad's. Sometimes here. Depends on who's in the mood to do the most cooking." John dropped spoonful after spoonful of sugar into the tall glass. "I want you to know my offer stands. The job is temporary if you want it that way. Sort of a test run, if you want. I pay well."

"I'm sure you do." Now she felt uncomfortable. How could she admit why she couldn't take the job? She started to tremble, a quivery feeling that raced from her midsection down to her toes. "This isn't what I'm looking for."

"Then what is?"

How could she tell him what she was really afraid of? "I have my reasons."

"I suppose it's because of my mom. You heard her sing in the choir and the noise she makes scares you."

"Nope. I think Bev has a lovely singing voice."

Bev preened. "Thank you, dear."

John stirred his tea, making the ice cubes tinkle. "You won't stay because of Hailey. She's a wild one with all those lessons. You're afraid you'll run yourself ragged ferrying her to and from. She has a busy social calendar, too."

"I have piano lessons tomorrow," Hailey announced. "Alexandra could take me 'n' stuff."

"Fine, make it impossible to say no." Alexandra knew how to play this game, too. She met John's gaze without batting an eye. "The real reason I'm not sure I can take this job is you, John. I heard you sing in church. I absolutely cannot work for someone who's that tone-deaf."

"She's got your number, son!" Gerald called out.

The family broke into howling laughter.

Wouldn't it be wonderful to stay here? The delicious salad tasted dry on her tongue as she tried to laugh along with Bev's gentle teasing, and John's good-natured banter in return.

Her heart became heavier as the meal ended. John's brother and his family showed up, and dessert was served with great gusto. The Corey family took their sugar intake seriously. Yes, it was sad she couldn't stay here.

After the dessert plates were eaten clean so that not even a crumb remained of the delicious Boston cream pie John's brother's wife had brought, Alexandra retreated to the kitchen. Since she couldn't stay, she'd help out. She planned to be on the road heading south in an hour.

"What do you think you're doing, young lady?"

Bev scolded as she opened the freezer compartment of the stainless-steel refrigerator. "You heard John. You're a guest. You have no business washing our dishes. Unless that means you're going to accept the job?"

Alexandra took one look at the hopeful crook of Bev's brow. "Good try, but I'm only doing these dishes, as a good guest should in return for a delicious meal."

"What about the ones in the oven?" Hailey clomped in, wearing her riding boots and her cowboy hat askew on her head.

Bev frowned. "Don't tell me he's back to doing that." She marched over to the oven and yanked on the door. "Out of sight, out of mind."

Hailey clomped close to inspect the mess. "Ew. They're all gross."

"Okay, maybe John needs hired help more than I think."

"That John." Bev shook her head. "If he keeps hiding them, how am I supposed to find them to wash?"

"You're not supposed to be washing my dishes." John strolled in, carrying a stack of dishes from the table outside. "That's why I hide 'em."

"No way, Dad. You hide 'em because *you* don't want to do 'em. That's what you said last night."

"I'm pleading the Fifth." John set the plates on the counter, so close Alexandra could feel his presence, tangible as a touch, as powerful as a tornado rolling over her.

It's a good thing this is a one-sided reaction, Alexandra thought as she swiped a stoneware plate beneath the faucet and slid it into the dishwasher rack. She'd had enough of romantic entanglements for now. Especially with men who looked too good on the outside.

He's a decent man at heart, too.

That truth bugged her big-time as she rinsed and stacked. She and Bev talked about gardening and the choir. But was it her fault her gaze kept straying to the open glass doors where John was?

Maybe it never hurt to look at a handsome man. Maybe, after the emotional pain Patrick caused her, she needed to see that other men were different. See how gentle John was? She paused, leaving the water running, while she watched him swing his five-month-old nephew into the air, just high enough to make the infant squeal with delight.

He's a good father. He probably wanted a lot of children. How sad he never got the chance.

"You want another one of those, I can tell," Tom, his brother, was saying as Alexandra bent to fill the soap dispenser with lemony dishwashing powder. His deep voice was so like John's, and carried just right, she couldn't help listening.

"This little guy's great, but you know good and well that I'm not going to marry again."

"You never know what God has in store for you," Tom reminded him.

"Broken hearts do mend, John," Nina, Tom's wife, reminded kindly as she took her son into her arms.

They were ganging up on him again. Hurt, he kept quiet. Tom and Nina had everything. They didn't understand. Broken hearts did mend, but not broken souls. Not easily, anyway. John smoothed the palm of his hand over little David's head, the finest silk of baby hair like a blessing against his skin. He and Bobbie had always wanted a big family. It was his fault they'd never gotten the chance.

Closing down the guilt and regret that raged like a century's storm, John turned away, making his excuses, but before he left he caught the look of pity on his sister-in-law's face. The sorrow on his brother's.

John, you still have a life, Tom had said on more than one occasion, and it was as if he was saying it now. John could feel it. He was ashamed, because no one in his family knew what had really happened. He'd tried to tell them at the time, but they'd made excuses. Hadn't wanted to see his failures. Not their oldest son, who'd never failed them. They couldn't believe he was responsible for his wife's death. And couldn't understand why he never deserved another chance at love.

That's the reason he tried to keep his gaze firmly fixed on the floor ahead of him and not straying toward the kitchen. Alexandra was wiping down the counters with an efficient swipe of her slender arm, her chestnut-brown braid bobbing between her shoulder blades as she worked. She looked young and vulnerable. Wisps of escaped hair curled around the faint bumps of vertebrae in her neck. Look how fragile she was.

Hadn't he vowed not to look at her? Angry with himself, John stormed through the family room and up the stairs, taking refuge as the silence of the second story closed around him. Sunlight streamed into the stained-glass windows at the end of the hallway, staining him with green and blue light as he stood gripping his forehead. What on earth was wrong with him?

He hadn't been able to stop noticing Alexandra across the table during the meal. The way she broke her biscuit into small bite-size pieces with her long, delicate fingers, those slim silver rings catching the light, as if to draw his gaze. The way she watched his family talk and banter and even argue over a meal, while her food went mostly untouched. As if a happy, extended family gathered together was a new experience for her.

That made him wonder more about her. What kind of family did she grow up in? Why wasn't she married? What had she left behind her? Where was she from?

Not his business. Still, it troubled him as he dug

through the shelves in the extra room. Troubled him because he'd had his chance and blown it. He had no one to blame but himself. God wasn't going to trust him with anything so precious and sacred— not again. Nor would he trust himself.

There it is. He grabbed the battered copy of the travel guide and dusted it off with his sleeve. He stepped over a pile of magazines on the floor, cornered a toppling stack of newspapers and closed the door behind him. He was thinking about Alexandra way too much. Not a good sign. He would work harder to keep his mind where it belonged, give her the book and wave when she drove away.

A part of him didn't want her to drive away. What would it be like if she did stay?

Disaster. Don't even think like that, John. He grimaced, taking the stairs two at a time.

There, washed in sunlight and tousled by a gentle wind, Alexandra was laughing, with Hailey wrapped around her waist in a hug. He skidded to a stop in his tracks, right in the middle of the doorway. Hailey released her, hopping up and down as she always did, taking Alexandra by the hand and tugging her along the deck railing toward the back steps.

Alexandra was protesting, but not really meaning it. Hailey hauled her over to the lawn, where Bandit was waiting, reins dragging, ears pricked, long tail twitching.

"I really can't ride," Alexandra was saying. "I

never had a pony when I was a little girl. I'd fall
right off."

"You just gotta sit up straight. Don't worry. I'll
show ya!" Hailey grabbed the stirrup. "See? It's
easy. Just put your foot right in here."

"Why don't you get up and show me first?"
Alexandra couldn't hide the quiver of panic in her
voice.

Full of grace, she was, and all beauty. The
wholesome kind, the way a sun rose over the
Bridger Range. The kind of beauty that gave rest to
a man's soul.

The man who wound up with Alexandra for his
wife would sure be lucky.

"See?" Hailey stretched on tiptoe to grab the
saddle horn. "You just do this, and then hop real
high. See? I'm up." Hailey eased into the saddle.
"Wanna try?"

"Show me how you steer, first." Alexandra crossed
her arms around her middle, the fear retreating.
Maybe she figured once Hailey was on her horse she
would stay there and forget about teaching Alexandra.

Wrong. Amused, John watched as Hailey rolled
her eyes. "You don't steer a horse like a car. You
guide him. Like this."

It was evident that Alexandra liked children. A lot.
There was no hiding it on her face or the mirth that
made her dark eyes twinkle. She'd be good for

Hailey. The thought whispered through his mind, as if born on the breeze, carried straight from heaven. Hire her.

Well, that would be a mistake. Right?

"Well, son." Mom planted her elbows on the rail beside him. "How are we going to get her to change her mind?"

"We aren't." John figured God knew what He was doing. "She's made her decision."

"Yes, but look how Hailey adores her. Alexandra's good with children, with that gentle nature of hers." Bev fell silent.

Alexandra's gentle nature. That's all John saw. The quiet murmur of her laughter as she failed to hop high enough to climb into the saddle and slid back down to the ground. The veiled look of panic she tried to hide when she finally sat awkwardly in the saddle, staring at the ground in horror. The tranquil music of her voice as she commented, "Boy, that's a long way to fall. It's higher up here than I thought it would be."

Is this a sign, Lord? In one glance John took it all in—his precious daughter and Alexandra astride the little pinto. The rich land that rolled gently out of sight, the beauty of the mountains rimming the valley in all directions. The big house he could afford, and a loving extended family.

Why he'd been blessed so much, he didn't know, but one thing was for sure. Alexandra wasn't as fortunate in life. She was alone, and hurt shone in her eyes. A hurt he understood.

He had great debts to pay, and not of the financial kind. So what if he was attracted to Alexandra—nothing would come of it. The important thing was that the Lord had brought her to his doorstep, a vulnerable young woman in need. This was his chance to make another payment on the enormous debt he owed God. The answer to the same prayer he prayed every night.

The chance to make amends. To earn forgiveness for the unforgivable.

John knew exactly what he had to do.

Chapter Six

"Don't forget this." John's voice rumbled in Alexandra's ear as he dropped a battered book on the kitchen counter. "What are you gonna do? Just sneak off without saying goodbye?"

"No." Although she wanted to. It would sure be easier. "Your mom doesn't seem to want me to leave. And Hailey. She thinks I'm going to stay and take care of her. I'm not naming names, but I suspect someone is hoping that will change my mind."

"Hey, don't look at me. Hailey eavesdrops. It's terrible."

"But you're not, of course."

"Of course not. I would never try to use my daughter's affections to influence your decision." But his look said everything. "I pay well."

As if that were the only objection. Alexandra gazed around the kitchen, large and friendly and gorgeous. It sure would be a pleasure to cook in this kitchen. To spend her days looking after Hailey. "I do like your daughter."

"Ha! A victory. Does this mean you'll do it?"

"No. It means I'd love to, but I can't." Forget that one of the biggest reasons she couldn't accept was standing in front of her in living color, flesh and blood, too good to be true. "I wish it could be different."

"You'd like to stay?"

"Like to stay? I'd love to. Your family has been great to me. I can't remember the last time I felt so welcome anywhere."

"Then it's a sign from above." John smiled at her in that easy way he had, not flirtatious or coy, as he yanked open the refrigerator door. "Just say yes."

"I can't." She took a deep breath. Did she risk telling him?

"Okay, then what will make it easier for you to say yes? How about free room and board?" An ice-cream carton thunked to the countertop next to her. "Think about all that means. Free ice cream."

He lifted the lid, revealing rich chocolate, gooey fudge and fluffy marshmallow.

"Tempting."

"Bribery by chocolate. I knew it would work." He dug a scoop out of a drawer. "How about a sundae to celebrate your new job?"

"Hold the chocolate sauce. I haven't accepted yet." Alexandra took a deep breath. Did she trust John with the truth? Or did she run out of here the way she'd left Seattle, determined never to look back?

"Alexandra!" Hailey rushed in, cowboy hat hanging down her back. "I heard! You're gonna take care of me. I knew it!"

Reed-thin arms flung around Alexandra's mid-section and squeezed so tight. Innocent and vibrant and so incredibly sweet. What a treat to be able to take care of Hailey as a job. She couldn't think of a nicer way to spend her days.

There were more reasons to leave than to stay. Patrick was one of them.

John was another. What was she going to do about the fact that she was attracted to him? Well, she could keep her distance. If she worked for him, then she was bound to be alone with him eventually.

Hailey grabbed a cookie and skipped out the door, chanting "yippee-skippy" over and over until she was out of sight, and out of hearing range.

John scooped fat rounds of ice cream into a half dozen bowls. "Want to start negotiating your wage?"

"Not yet." She took a deep breath, unable to put it off any longer. John had to know the truth *before* he hired her. "I have something to tell you first. Listen, and then you decide."

"Go on. I'm listening."

"A week ago I packed my camping gear and two bags of clothes in the dead of night and drove away from my apartment and my job and everybody I knew. I'm not aimlessly looking for work. I'm running for my life."

Running for her life? Was she in danger? There was no way she was in trouble with the law. It wasn't that kind of trouble.

He hazarded a guess. "Are you married?"

"No." She shook her head hard enough so the cinnamon-brown braid of hair slipped like silk over her delicate shoulders. "He was my fiancé."

"Was he violent? Did he hurt you?"

Alexandra didn't answer. She didn't have to.

She bowed her head. The silken wisps escaped from her braid fell forward, hiding her face, caressing the curve of her cheek. Her silence was more telling than a thousand words could.

Fury punched through him, and he shoved away from the counter, pacing hard, hands fisted. Seeing red, it was all he could do to control his anger. What kind of man hurt a woman? What sort of coward would terrorize someone half his size?

It was no Christian way to think, but he couldn't stop the wild surge of protective fury that tore through him like a rampaging flood. Drowning him so that he was sputtering for air, for control. No man had the right to do that to a woman. Especially one as good and gentle as Alexandra.

For her sake, he reined in his anger. He still shook with it, but raging at a faceless coward who wasn't even in this room wasn't going to help the ashen-faced, lost-looking woman who was staring at him with wide, worried eyes.

"You don't have to run another step. You'll be safe here." That was a promise he meant all the way to his soul. He knew it. God knew it. Alexandra would know it.

"He could be following me. He made threats."

"He won't find you. And if he does, I'm good friends with the town sheriff." John would talk to Cameron Brisbane first thing tomorrow. Cam was a good man. He'd be more than happy to help. With two of them keeping an eye out, Alexandra would be sure to be safe.

"But if Patrick found me, I could be putting Hailey in danger without knowing it. Or you." She held her chin up, a little wobbly, betraying her fear. "Maybe staying isn't the best idea. I had planned to get as far away as I could. Maybe go back East. I don't know."

"Thousands of miles won't keep you safe, not if he wants to find you." John uncurled his hands. Forced the rest of his muscles to relax. He'd seen enough as a member of the rescue team that he knew exactly what Alexandra was running from. He remembered a local domestic violence situation two years ago. He'd been called in to help find the missing wife.

And had found her body instead.

"It's not right to involve you by staying." Her chin lifted a notch higher. All strength and pride and courage. "This is my problem."

"Now it's mine, too. If two friends share a problem, then it's half the trouble."

She tried to frown at him, but ended up almost smiling instead. "Your ice cream is melting."

"Trying to divert me from the truth." He grabbed the carton and snapped the lid into place. "Too bad. It won't work. You're staying."

"Playing the boss already, are you?"

"Sure, why not? Just as long as you don't go running off alone. You have friends here." He shoved the carton blindly into the freezer compartment, hoping there was enough room on the rack. He knew what he had to do. "You don't need to be alone."

"You hardly know me. I hardly know you."

"I'm at the store all day, while you'd be here with Hailey. You'd be answering to my mom, mostly."

"Really?" She sounded cautious, but he could read her interest. She had an open heart that was easy to read and with hurt that was easy to see.

He hated that she was hurting so much down deep. Hated the horrible man who'd done this to her, made her feel unsafe and unable to trust a Christian man offering her a job—just a job. And nothing more.

The anger returned, but he forced it away. She surprised him by reaching out. The soft warm brush of her fingertips against his rough, sun-browned fingers unnerved him. Knocked him off balance and made him forget how to speak. She twisted the jar from his grip, sauntering away with a feminine gait that was simple and innocent and so womanly, he could only stare.

Lord, You've given me a woman to protect and defend. I'm up to this challenge. Really. John knew in his heart it wasn't going to be easy.

He was attracted to her. It was the plain and simple truth. He was a man. One day a woman was bound to come along and stir up feelings. It was only natural. That didn't mean he needed to acknowledge those feelings. Or act on them. Or give them a fraction of control over his life.

He had self-control. That's what mattered. The trouble was, he was going to have to stop noticing she was so beautiful and vulnerable and amazing.

No problem there. He wouldn't look at her.

Averting his gaze, he grabbed the butterscotch chips from the pantry. He could hear the rasp of the silverware drawer, the tinkle of flatware, the metallic twist of a metal lid coming away from the jar.

Having Alexandra in his kitchen was going to take some getting used to. He unwound the twist tie from the bag and laid it on the counter.

She dolloped a meager amount of chocolate

topping over the first bowl of ice cream. "Is this enough?"

"We don't do anything halfway here. We go for the gusto." He took the jar and upended it. The thick syrup sluiced over the ice cream to form a thick, delicious glacier of chocolate. "Anything less than that, and the crowd gets cranky. My mild-mannered dad will throw his shoe at you."

"Then I'd better put on a lot of chips, right?" She reached across him for the bag, bringing with her the scent of sweet green apples.

Not that he was about to notice. "If there's not enough chips, Mom will refuse to bring potato salad next Sunday. She's tough when it comes to punishment."

"I'd hate to get you in trouble. Is this enough?"

"Wow, you're generous with the butterscotch." He poured syrup over the last bowl. "You fit in here. You oughta stay. You seem to like being here so far, and we like having you. 'Do not forget to entertain strangers, for by doing so some people have entertained angels without knowing it.'"

Why did her heart crumple like that? "I'm no angel, John."

"Close enough."

She wasn't going to be tempted. But she knew, as he handed her a bowl with a long-handled spoon in it, that it was already too late.

* * *

Staying here had to be a big mistake. Alexandra could *feel* it. She could admit it—she liked being needed. Even if it was for a job and nothing more.

She'd have to examine her motives later. But for now, as she dug into the depths of her purse for her car keys, she had enough to keep her busy. Hailey was chattering away, telling her exactly when the school bus came in the afternoons and exactly where it dropped her off. Alexandra would be waiting, right?

"Absolutely. I wouldn't forget you." Alexandra found her keys and slung the leather purse strap over her shoulder. "What do you want to do first when you get home tomorrow?"

"Ride Bandit. You can come, too." Hailey clasped her hands in sheer delight. "You did real good for a first-time rider. Well, not really, but you tried real hard."

"Are you kidding? It was a disaster. Maybe I'll do better next time." Trying to forget the way she kept sliding off the saddle, Alexandra grabbed the grocery sack of leftovers from the counter. "I'll see you tomorrow."

"Cool!" Hailey leaped close, wrapped her arms around Alexandra's middle and squeezed tight. Then she was gone, calling over her shoulder, "You're awesome!"

I'm really going to have a hard time trying not

to fall in love with that little girl. What a pleasure it would be to take care of Hailey day after day.

As for John… Alexandra vowed not to think of that as she trailed through the beautiful house and out the front door where the evening was giving way to the gathering shadows. Twilight clung to the far horizon, drawing the warmth from the air but not from her.

The Corey family was wrapped up in their goodbyes. So genuinely loving and happy. They didn't know what it meant to be alone. Not truly alone. Not so isolated and afraid that it felt as if the world were passing you by.

She unlocked her car door and set the sack of leftovers on the front seat. John and his brother were laughing over some private joke, a friendly sound that lifted on the sweet evening breeze and came straight to her.

John was going to be a problem. She kept noticing him. Out of the corner of her eye as she tucked her purse on the floor and straightened. He stood with his back to her, in the fingers of the long shadows from the mighty oaks lining the driveway, standing just outside the light.

He made her so…aware. Aware of the scent of the lilacs on the breeze. The cool blush of twilight air on her bare arms. The creak of the car seat as she settled onto it. The newsprint texture of the travel book's pages against her fingertips.

It was time to be on her way. Quick, while she

could still be rational and could control her feelings. She was tired and road weary and grateful for a place to rest. For now until she decided to move on, Bev's guest cottage would be her home. And these people her temporary family.

After a good night's rest, things would be better. She really didn't feel attracted to John—not real attraction. So she didn't need to worry. Right? He was like a white knight, and what maiden wouldn't gaze upon him with admiration? That's all this was.

He was her employer, and she was not ready to trust another man with her life.

She started the engine and sat waiting until the family's goodbyes were done. *Show me this is the choice You mean for me,* she prayed, as she followed Bev's car into the gathering darkness. With the night surrounding her, and no stars in sight, she couldn't help feeling alone. Afraid. Unsettled.

Maybe accepting this job was the wrong thing to do. Patrick could be following her.

Had she made another life-altering mistake? There came no answer and no peace as she followed the unlit, bumpy road that led through the Corey property. No stars winked wisely, and the heavens were hidden, the sky shrouded in clouds. She felt as if no one was watching over her, although she knew it wasn't true.

Although later she turned to her Bible and read

before falling asleep that night, tucked in the cozy bedroom in the little cottage, the feeling remained.

John counted himself lucky to have a view of the Bridger Mountains from his kitchen windows. He could watch the purple-gray curtain of night lift, giving way to the soft golden light of a new dawn. That could inspire a man, that's for sure. As long as he knew toward what he was aspiring.

Lifting the teakettle from the stove, he contemplated the reverent changes in the sky. Purple slipping away to the deepest blue-gray, and faint pinks highlighting the underbellies of long, paintbrush strokes of the silhouetted clouds. He poured the steaming water into the awaiting cup, and the scent of apple lifted on the steam—sweet apple. The scent reminded him of Alexandra.

She was going to be here soon. In this house. In this kitchen. He panicked. Yesterday he'd been short of obsessed with her, his gaze drawn to her like a nail to a magnet. Helpless to break away.

He carried the cup to the table, where a hardback novel lay open, a weighted bookmark holding the page. The chair creaked as he settled into it, seeing the faint shadow of his reflection on the uncurtained bay window. Sitting alone. Hair sticking straight up, wrinkled shirt hanging crooked. Behind him was a stack of dishes he'd retrieved from the second oven.

The panic was still there. Alexandra. He ought to be relieved he'd finally found a housekeeper he could depend on, but he wasn't relieved. He was terrified. He was incredibly attracted to her. To this woman the Lord had brought to his doorstep. John would not fail her. He'd be as true as the dawn, sure as the sky, as steady as the mountains.

Reaching for the sugar bowl, he caught sight of the pictures nailed to the wall, the faint glow of the small lamp reflected in the brass frames. Pictures of Hailey, mostly. He'd started a collection, the same way his mother had. One picture had Bobbie in it proudly displaying her newborn daughter from her hospital bed. She was weary with exhaustion but beaming with joy. Bright balloons sailed in the air behind her, and flowers jammed the nightstand behind her.

Remembering that day brought tears to his eyes. He didn't want to go back to those feelings. To the time he'd taken for granted. Back then he and Bobbie thought they had all the time in the world. They'd been wrong about a lot of things. Wrong about the kind of man he was. The kind of husband.

Lord, I would do anything to bring her back. To go back in time and change those last few seconds of her life. To find some way to save her. To try harder. Be more. To have held on to her when I thought I couldn't.

He'd loved Bobbie more than his own life back

then. His love had changed over the years, become a distant fondness mixed with the terrible guilt he carried. He knew what it was like to cherish a woman.

So, how could any man bring harm to someone he loved? Gulping down the hot tea, trying to burn away the lump of emotion caught painfully in his throat, John couldn't understand. Alexandra was on the run, and she was afraid. Afraid for her life. Afraid of being hurt again. Afraid to trust in anyone. Whoever this Patrick was, he'd wounded her deep inside. Didn't he know how precious love was? How brief a life could be?

John slammed the empty cup onto the table, launching out of the chair, his hands fisted, helplessness filling him. What he'd give to have the warmth of a wife's love, the music of her laughter, the comfort of her arms.

But it was not to be. He had no one to blame but himself.

In a few hours, when Alexandra walked through his front door, he'd be ready for her. Polite. Professional. A man dedicated to doing the right thing. When he gazed upon her, he vowed not to see a beautiful woman who made him wish.

He'd see an answer to his prayer for forgiveness. Nothing more, and nothing less.

Chapter Seven

Things weren't any clearer in the morning, although it was a beautiful day, the golden rays of sun carpeting the stone walk all the way to John's front door. Reaching into her pocket, she took out the set of keys Bev had given her. Just in case John wasn't home, Bev had said.

It didn't look as though John was home. Relief slipped through her. She hadn't realized how tense she was over this. She rang the bell just in case. No one came to the door. Looked like she was in luck. John was gone, true to his word.

This job could work out, she realized, as she tested a key. It didn't fit, so she tried the second one. The bolt turned, and she twisted the knob. The house echoed around her as she stepped into the hallway.

Serenity gathered around her like a hug. This was a real home, filled with love. She wanted a home like this someday. Maybe it wouldn't be this lavish. It could be a single-wide trailer, for all she cared. She simply wanted *this* feeling. *This* contented peace.

Well, she couldn't stand here dreaming. John wasn't paying her to stand in his living room all day. Tucking her dreams away, she headed straight for the kitchen. He'd probably left instructions on the counter. That's what a lot of people did, in her experience.

She laid her purse on the center island, but there was no list of chores needing to be done. No instructions of any kind. The granite counter shone in the morning light, highlighting crumbs and dust and a sprinkling of sugar, probably spilled from Hailey's cereal bowl.

She decided to start with the dishes stashed in the oven. It would take only a second to load the dishwasher, and a few minutes to deal with the hand-wash items. Already feeling at home in the roomy kitchen, she found the last clean dishcloth in the bottom stack of drawers. She heard a noise the same moment she pushed in the drawer.

Was someone outside? John's house wasn't on the beaten path. Bev had an appointment in town this morning, so it couldn't be her. Gerald was out in the fields, busy with his farming. John was at work.

Maybe it was something else. She turned on the faucet, letting the water warm. Over the rush of the running water, she heard it again.

Someone was outside. Patrick?

Fear sluiced over her like cold rain. Shivering, her palms went damp against the edge of the counter. What had he said the last time he'd threatened her? *You can't run from me. You aren't smart enough. I'll hunt you down like a dog until I find you. Then you'll be sorry.*

It's him. Fear made her certain. She grabbed the phone with trembling hands, but what good would that do? She could call for help, but it would take a good twenty minutes for the police to come. She was in the middle of farmland and wilderness. She could try to run out the back, but what if Patrick was waiting for her? Her car was out front. He would already know she was here.

The front knob jingled and turned. The hinges whispered open. She heard the pad of a man's boot on the wood floor.

Frantic, she searched for something to defend herself with. She didn't know how to use a knife, so she didn't bother with that. There was nothing useful in the top drawers. She yanked open the pantry door and grabbed the first thing she saw. The wooden broom handle fit into her hand perfectly, and she held it steady. Just having it made her feel stronger. At least she had something to fight with.

What if Patrick had a gun? What good would a broom do her then?

The footsteps tapped closer. Leisurely. Quietly. As if he were listening for a sign of where she was in the house.

Adrenaline fired through her. Praying for guidance, Alexandra tiptoed to the wide entry that separated the spacious kitchen from the formal dining room. The footsteps were so close. Maybe if she struck first, she'd be able to knock him down. That would give her enough time to run to her car—

A shadow filled the doorway. It was now or never. Her entire life could depend on this. She swung like a batter over home plate, hoping to get him right in the stomach.

A big male hand curled around her, stopping the swing before it made contact with a very hard-looking, very solid-looking solar plexus. Patrick was a little portly, and this man was sheer muscle.

"Whew. That's what I get for not warning you before I step into a room." John released her hand and took the broom from her. "You have a good arm. There are local baseball teams who'd be proud to have you."

Had she really almost hit her employer? "John, I'm sorry. I was afraid you were someone else."

"The fiancé?" He lowered the broom. "That's all right. I'm glad to know at least you can defend yourself. Armed with a broom. Do you have a permit for this?"

"You're teasing me."

"Absolutely not. You could have broken a rib with the force of your swing. Wow. Come the next church picnic, I'm picking you for my team first off."

"Stop trying to make me feel better." Her face was burning. What did John think of her? She'd been ready to hit him. "Wait one minute. Aren't you supposed to be at work? You told me I'd never really see you. That I'd be answering to Bev."

"Right, well, I forgot this." He pulled a folded square of yellow notebook paper from his shirt pocket. "Went to the trouble of making up a list and then didn't leave it."

"I was looking for that." Her hands were shaky as she reached out for the note. There was no way to hide it, especially since the paper rattled in her unsteady grip. There was never a hole in the floor to sink into when you needed one.

"Hey, I really scared you. I'm sorry. Are you all right?" His fingers curled around hers, warm and strong and slightly callused against her skin. A strong hand, but he held her with infinite gentleness.

Gentleness she was afraid to believe in. It was too good to be true. She knew it down deep. She withdrew her hand, leaving him in the threshold, retreating to the sink where the water was still running. "Sure, I'm fine. Just easily startled, I guess. That's what I get for not locking the door behind me."

"It was my fault. You have every right to be afraid, considering what you've been through."

She didn't want his pity or his sympathy. And if he kept speaking to her in that quiet, steady voice, the one that sounded as genuine as the earth, as real as a kept promise, then she was going to be in big trouble. She grabbed a plate, ran it under the water and fit it into the bottom dishwasher rack.

"You don't have to rinse the dishes." He lifted the next plate from her grip and slipped it into the rack beside the first. "It's a top-of-the-line dishwasher. It'll clean the worst of this mess, no problem."

She felt foolish. Of course, he was right. Top-of-the-line. Just like everything else about his life. She should have known. Boy, this first day wasn't starting out well. "Good. Then I guess I'll get this load of dishes started faster. If I can reach the dishwasher."

"Oh, right." He stepped aside, all six substantial feet of him. "I've got another stack of dishes hidden on the bottom shelf of the refrigerator behind the pizza boxes. Just thought you should know."

"You couldn't put them in the dishwasher yourself, huh?"

"That's right. It's a character defect men have called Dishwasher Avoidance."

"I've heard of that. Sort of related to Laundry Evasion."

"Exactly. I'm glad you understand."

"I'm a professional. It's my business to understand." Alexandra bit her lip. Okay, he was funny and she wasn't going to let herself encourage him with so much as the tiniest smile. How else was she going to keep her emotional distance? "I've got the list now. I'll be fine."

"The list. Right." He jammed his hands deep into his pockets. "I know you'll be fine. I spoke to the town sheriff. He says it would be best if you talked to him. Give him a description of this fiancé."

"Oh, John, I wish you hadn't done that." The last thing she wanted was for other people to know about this. That was the best way to expose a secret in a small town. "I only told you about Patrick because I thought you needed to know. Because of Hailey's safety. I didn't think you'd actually—"

She turned away, too angry to say anything more. Why had he done that? He'd probably thought he was helping. But he wasn't. Now she'd be easier to find.

"Cam will keep it off-the-record. Unofficial. No one will know." His hand lighted on her shoulder, his touch unshakable and solid. As dependable as the man. "He needs a description, so he can keep his eye out. He's on your side, Alexandra. Just like I am."

How could a stranger be on her side? Again, she didn't know what to say. In her experience, people had never been true to their word. Not when the chips were down. Not when it mattered. And the one time she'd thought differently…well, she couldn't have been more wrong.

"I can handle this on my own." She met his gaze, unflinching. Let him see that she wasn't as helpless as he apparently thought. "I appreciate the job, John, you know that. I'm grateful for the chance to stay with your family. But I don't need a white knight."

"I never thought you did." He didn't back down, didn't blink, didn't soften his voice. "But even a brave damsel can use help now and then."

"I'm not brave." She was living by faith. It wasn't always easy. Maybe she shouldn't have accepted this job. Maybe it had been a mistake. "If you don't think I can take care of myself, then are you worrying that I can't take care of Hailey?"

"Whoa. I wouldn't have offered you the job if I thought that." He grabbed an open box of tea left on the counter. "How about a peace offering? We'll sit down and clear the air. How about it?"

"I'm not sure I should associate with the enemy."

"I'm not the enemy. Just your employer. It's not the same thing." He waggled the box at her. "I've got a bowl of my mom's cookies I'll throw in for good measure."

"That's a good bargaining chip. It's a deal." She gazed up at him with a wariness that she tried to hide with the smallest curve of her lips, a smile that was strained.

She wasn't used to kindness. Maybe she'd stopped believing in it. The emotional pain an abusive relationship must exact on a woman must be enormous. John filled two cups with water and slipped them into the microwave.

As the unit hummed, he grabbed Mom's bowl of cookies and dropped them on the end of the counter that served as a breakfast bar. The way he saw it, maybe it was his job to help her to truly smile again.

The microwave beeped, and she brushed past him to whip the steaming cups out of the machine. She was industrious. He had to give her that. Hardworking, kind, she'd be good to Hailey. He couldn't get luckier when it came to a housekeeper. He'd been looking hard for three weeks, and couldn't find anyone who was half as good.

That only proved to him that this was meant to be.

He dropped two spoons on the marble counter. "I trust you with my daughter. Just so you know."

"I wouldn't blame you if you didn't." She climbed onto a stool, careful to leave an empty stool between them, as if she was afraid of getting too close.

Yep. She'd been real hurt. It was too bad. John's

heart squeezed with sympathy for her, a pain so sharp he had to look away to hide it.

"Sometimes I feel like I can barely take care of myself. I suppose I shouldn't confess that to you." She took a tea bag from the box he offered her. Her slim fingers tugged the end of the tea string, her silver rings flashing, and she dunked the bag into the steaming water. "Sometimes this is over-whelming. If I stop and think about it."

"Then my motto would be Don't Think About It."

"Exactly what I'm trying to do. But then this man wanted to hire me, and I had to admit the truth."

"Where is this man? I'll knock some sense into him. Tell him you want to forget the past. Leave it behind you."

"That would be good. Hey, where did that broom go?"

He chuckled. So, she could make him laugh. That didn't mean he was going to like her any more than he'd liked any other housekeeper. "Denial isn't just a river in Egypt, right?"

"It's my preferred state of mind."

"I've spent time there." He plunged his tea bag into the water and watched the liquid froth. The scent of apples and cinnamon warred with his senses. The tea smelled good, but it was nothing compared to Alexandra's sweetness. "You said you left everything behind. That had to be hard."

"I was renting a furnished room in a house, where we shared the kitchen and living areas. I didn't really have much, but I did leave most of what I had. I took my camping gear and two duffel bags of clothes."

She must have been in a lot of danger. "Did your housemates know what you were going to do?"

She shook her head, scattering her molasses-dark hair and making her earrings jangle. She appeared smaller on the chair. More fragile. "No one did. I'd cashed my paycheck that afternoon. Patrick had been watching me carefully, so I didn't want to do anything suspicious. Like closing my account. Packing my car up after work. That sort of thing."

"He was watching you? As in stalking you?"

Her fingers trembled as she wound the string around the tea bag, squeezing the liquid from it. "I'd already given him back his engagement ring. He didn't take it well."

"He wouldn't let you go? Was he violent?"

"He didn't think he had a problem with his anger while he was yelling at me." She kept her voice even, as if an angry yelling man was nothing to be afraid of.

John knew better. He could see it without her words. Sense it as if he'd been able to peek inside her heart. The secrecy of quietly packing one evening, windows closed, curtains drawn, a radio on to hide the noise of dresser drawers opening and metal hangers rocking on the wooden closet rod.

"You're going to be safe here." He resisted the urge to reach out and brush away the lines of worry from her brow with the pad of his thumb. He knew what it was like to be afraid. To hurt. To want peace. "I'm going to make sure of it."

"I can't ask that of you. I'm not even sure I should be here. I appreciate the job, don't get me wrong, and the pay is generous, but you're not my keeper."

"Someone has to be." John offered her the cookie bowl. "Just think of me and my family as your temporary guardian angels. We'll watch over you."

An uneasy chill shivered through her stomach. She kept her voice light, because not all men were like Patrick, right? John didn't mean he'd literally be keeping a watch on her. "A girl can't have too many angels looking out for her."

"Good. I'll have the sheriff drop by, so be expecting him. You won't be in need of the broom." He bit into the edge of the iced cookie.

"Thanks for mentioning that. I'm still embarrassed enough I could spontaneously combust."

"Why? It's important for a woman to know how to defend herself. Cameron will be able to keep an eye out for any strangers in town. With any luck, this Patrick of yours will decide to stay in Seattle where he belongs."

"That's what I'm hoping." She bit into the cookie and let the sweetness melt on her tongue. She thought of her self-esteem, still tender, and tried to put aside the bad memories of Patrick's angry words that always tore her down….

No, she wouldn't think of that ever again. She was strong enough to evade him. To make a new life. With the Lord watching over her and a few extra guardian angels, she couldn't go wrong.

"Didn't you get a restraining order? Didn't the police help you?"

"A restraining order can only do so much, and the police did all they could." She closed her mind against the pain. The wound in her heart hurt like crazy. She'd once loved Patrick Kline with all her being. Where all that love used to be was a dark, aching place that felt as if it would never be touched by sunlight again.

"You don't need a restraining order here. Not with me around." John's gaze met hers, full of promise, as unyielding as the strongest steel. "You're safe with me. You can count on it."

The tension inside her eased. Just like that, like a tangled knot of yarn suddenly pulling loose. She believed in him. "You really are a guardian angel."

"Good, I've got you fooled." With a wink, John slid off the stool with a man's athletic power, taking the mug and cookie with him. "I've been told I'm a good listener. Any time you want to talk, I'm here. You're not alone. Remember that."

"I will."

"If you have any questions about the list I gave you, just give me a jingle down at the store. I wrote down the number."

"Sure thing." It was hard to speak past the tight ball of emotions locked in her throat, but she managed.

He disappeared through the threshold, and his steps tapped through the house. The door opened, then closed, leaving silence in his wake.

For the first time in a long while, Alexandra didn't feel alone. Her spirit had been uplifted after she'd confided in John. She hadn't dared to trust her troubles to many people. Opening up now left her feeling connected instead of isolated and reminded her that God's love was everywhere, especially in the hearts of others.

She took another bite of the delicious cookie and started reading the work list John had left her.

The late-afternoon sun was blazing strong enough to make the inside of the old VW hot as Alexandra pulled into the gravel driveway of the little yellow house a few blocks from the town's main street. It was always a blessing not to have air-conditioning. Otherwise how could she appreciate the sun's heat?

She killed the engine and rolled down the rest of the windows. A strain of piano music lilted from the house's open front door. Hailey's halting rendition of "Moonlight Sonata" was certainly unique. Fondness for the little girl filled Alexandra's heart right up.

What a wonderful day this had been. After a morning spent cleaning John's beautiful house, she'd met Hailey at the bus stop at the end of the mile-long driveway. Stephanie had come to visit, so there were two little girls to entertain. Easy to do with a fresh pitcher of lemonade and the last of Bev's Sunday cookies.

While she'd dusted the plant shelves in the family room, the sounds of their laughter and constant chatter wafted in through the open windows. Happy sounds of childhood that Alexandra remembered from other children's homes. From other children's yards.

She grabbed the dust mop, reaching for the peak of the vaulted ceiling, straining on the top step of the small ladder she'd found in the garage. Those happy, innocent voices drifting into the room made her happy, too. As if, for one moment in time, she was able to step out of the shadows of her troubles and let the sun warm her. It had been a good feeling, and it lingered with her still as she waited for Hailey's lesson to end.

The halting music continued, one wrong note

souring the melody, and then another. She tugged a paperback inspirational romance out of her purse and opened it to the dog-eared page that marked her place. She'd no sooner started reading than she heard footsteps in the gravel behind her.

"Alexandra." It was John's voice and his reflection in the cracked side-view mirror, coming closer.

Oh, he looks good. That was her first thought. Her second was—don't notice. "John. Bet you couldn't resist the chance to hear your daughter play."

A series of sour notes came from inside the house before the melody rang true.

"I'm not sure her true talent is the piano, although Mom sure keeps hoping." John knelt down so they were eye level. "I was down the street delivering a new mower to the Whitlys, and I spotted your car."

Only then did she recognize the big red pickup parked across the street behind her. "Checking up on me?"

"Let's call it Providence lending a hand. The Whitlys have puppies that are just eight weeks old today. They offered me the pick of the litter, since I didn't charge them for the delivery."

"Now you're in a bind—is that it? Seeing as Hailey wants a dog."

"You see my situation. If I say no, then I'm a horrible, terrible father of the worst sort. If I say yes, then I've got a puppy in my house."

"Look at the bright side. You have wood floors and not carpeting. That will come in handy during housebreaking."

"I like your outlook on life. Yep, there's a blessing if I ever saw one." He shook his head, scattering his dark hair, and for a moment those shutters on his soul opened again. It was easy to see all the good in him.

When he caught her looking at him, the shutters closed. She felt embarrassed for looking so deep.

John stood, gazing at the house, feeling distant again. Remote. "Think you're up to coming along and helping us pick out a dog?"

Before Alexandra could answer, the old metal screen door flung open and a pink-and-purple blur streaked out of the house.

"Daddy!" the streak shouted in an excited rush. "What dog? I getta dog? Yippeeeeee! I'm gonna get a dog. Really, really, truly?"

"Nope. Just kiddin'." John's wink brought another squeal as Hailey bounded to a stop against Alexandra's car, jumping up and down with glee.

"What kind of a dog? A baby one, right? It's the Whitlys' babies, isn't it? I *knew* it. My best friend Christa lives next door and she gets to visit them sometimes. She wants to get the white one, but I ain't never seen them even once—"

Hailey kept talking, and John held up one hand, like a crossing guard attempting to halt speeding traffic. "It's not doing any good."

"I see that." Alexandra covered her mouth to hide her laughter.

"You see why I hired you? I need help."

"If I had known that, I'd have demanded higher wages."

"Maybe hazard pay." John took his daughter by the shoulders and guided her around to the passenger side door, while she chattered the entire time.

He opened the door and Hailey plopped into the seat, chasing away all the quiet.

"I won't want the white one, 'cuz it's the one Christa likes, but maybe there'll be one I like. Do you know what? What if there isn't one I like?"

"With my luck, you'll like all of them. Don't worry." John brushed tangles from her face, a wonderfully loving fatherly gesture, before handing her the seat belt. "Buckle up, and give Alexandra directions. I'll follow, okay?"

"Yep. I love you, Dad." She gave him a smacking kiss on the cheek, an open show of affection that made Alexandra look away.

She turned the key, pumping the gas until the old engine sputtered to life. She felt sharply alone, even with Hailey's merry chatter and John waving them off as she backed onto the street.

"Yippee! I get a dog. I really, really get one. Can you believe it? Cool. My dad's so cool." Hailey bounced on the seat, her happiness tangible. She beamed, her hands clasped, all brightness and innocence.

"Your dad is definitely cool." Alexandra could see him in the rearview, walking the half block down the residential street, his athletic gait striking, his hair wind tousled. There was something about him that held her attention—and that couldn't be good.

Don't think about it.

She forced her attention completely on the road ahead of her, following Hailey's pointing finger toward a paved driveway in front of a vintage, Craftsman-style house, where a profusion of bright tulips were cheerfully saluting.

An elderly woman rose from her weeding in the colorful flower beds in the shade of the house, and waved her garden-gloved hand. Her face wreathed into a smile. "Why, it's Hailey. Your daddy said we ought to be expecting you."

"Hi, Mrs. Whitly!" Hailey shot from the car before Alexandra could set the brake.

Alexandra then pocketed her keys, approaching, as the older woman offered a friendly greeting.

"I saw you in church," Mrs. Whitly was saying, grasping Alexandra's hand in a tight hold that felt so sincere. "What a blessing you are to them, I'm sure. That poor widower all alone, and with a child to raise. I already sent Hailey into the house to find the puppies on her own. Didn't think that child could wait a second longer without exploding on the spot."

"Good idea. She's pretty excited."

"So I see." Laughing, Mrs. Whitly held open the door. "Please come in. Can I get you some iced tea?"

"Thank you." Being part of the Corey family made her belong somehow, she figured. Small towns were like that, she knew all too well. It was a nice privilege, to be welcomed without question.

"Go on into the laundry room." Mrs. Whitly gestured to the far end of her perfectly tidy kitchen to an open door, where Hailey sat sprawled on the linoleum floor, surrounded by leaping puppies.

"Alexandra! Look!" Hailey twisted around, hugging one fluffy black puppy beneath her chin, sparkling like all the stars in the sky, like joy unleashed.

In all her life, Alexandra had never been so happy, but it touched her now. Knocked away one stone in the wall around her heart. Forgetting that she was an adult and not a child, she fell to her knees amid the puppies, scooping up a wiggling little brown one that jumped right into her hand.

"He's so soft." She'd never felt anything so wonderful. Fluffy puppy paws were everywhere—her arms, her shoulders, on her jeans, as the little ones tried to get her attention, jumping up to swipe wet warm tongues at her chin.

"I love this one!" Hailey kissed the head of the puppy she cradled. "This one is the sweetest, bestest puppy, right?"

"Right." Alexandra started when a hand lighted on her shoulder. A heavy, broad touch that somehow made the happiness inside her double. Made another brick crumble in the wall around her heart.

John knelt down beside her. "It looks to me like these puppies are all wrong. Now that you girls have looked, let's leave them and go."

"Daddy!" Hailey protested, giggling. "I found the one I want. Looky!"

"I was afraid of that." John winked, acting as if he was greatly pained, but anyone could see the happiness that made him bigger than life. "Looks like you've got yourself a dog, Hailey."

"I know." She said it with such confidence, as if there had never been a single doubt in her mind. She'd known all along how this would work out.

Alexandra turned away, lowering the puppy she held to the floor, stroking its downy little head with her fingertip. A second pup pushed its way in, wanting attention, too.

All her life, she'd been on the outside looking in. Like a child peeking through the window, wistfully wishing to be part of the happy family inside. She'd always wondered if those people she saw were really that happy. Or was it different, with the curtains drawn and the doors closed. Were they as unhappy down deep as her family had been?

It had always burdened her. She wanted to marry. She wanted a family, just like the ones she'd always watched so wistfully as a child while at the same time fearing that nothing could be that wonderful. Not really.

And now she knew for sure. Those families were real. Like John's family. So this dream in her heart *could* really happen—one day. Maybe that was why God had brought her here, on this uncertain journey from her past. To show her this genuine, happy family. To let her see what her future could be.

She hugged another puppy close, closed her eyes and gave a silent prayer of thanks.

Chapter Eight

"I hope you know something about dogs."

Alexandra dug her car keys out of her pocket. "Actually, I do, but you're not paying me for that."

"Getting tough with me, are you?" He crossed his arms over his chest, impressive as always with the shadows clinging to him and the wind ruffling his dark hair. "I knew you were too good to be true. Now I see the real Alexandra."

"Oh, you're one to talk. Hiring me to keep house and look after your daughter, and now this. A hidden agenda."

"Guilty as charged. Except I didn't know we were going to get a dog so soon."

"You must have known you would fold and give in to Hailey's wishes. After all, Mrs. Whitly told me you had asked about the puppies only last week."

"Can't trust anyone to keep a secret. What's the world coming to? Okay, so I had a suspicion, but that's all it was. Mom doesn't know anything about dogs, either, so that leaves us at your mercy."

"You're in luck. I do have some puppy knowledge, but it's going to cost you."

"I knew you were going to say that. Okay, give it to me. How much is this going to set me back?"

"Your mom's potato salad recipe. Hey, don't look at me like that. I know what's important in life."

"Getting you all the gold in Fort Knox would be easier. Do you know my mom guards that secret family recipe with her life? Is there any chance I could just pay you extra?"

"Nope." Alexandra swung her car door open. "Talk to Bev."

"She's gonna hurt me if I ask her for the recipe."

"A big brave man like you shouldn't be afraid of a little pain." She couldn't help teasing. "Still want my help with the puppy?"

He gestured toward the pickup's passenger window where Hailey could be seen through the tempered glass, her cheek to the puppy's cute round head. They were nuzzling, clearly in love, as only little girls and their puppies can be.

"I need all the help I can get," John confessed. "Are you going to make me beg?"

"It's tempting, but I'll spare you this time." Alexandra dropped her purse on the floor. "I'll follow you to the grocery store."

"You're going to have fun spending my money, aren't you?"

"We'll just pick up a few things the puppy needs for tonight, but there's a pet store in Bozeman that could be making a profit tomorrow."

John's fist flew to his heart, as if she'd inflicted a mortal wound. "I'll take it like a man and give you my credit card."

"And how exactly am I going to use your credit card without being arrested for fraud?"

"I know the owner of the pet store. I'll give him a call first thing in the morning."

"Good." She tossed him a smile that could charm the sun out of the sky and slipped behind the wheel of her rusted yellow VW.

Slim and lithe, as graceful as dreams, she lifted her delicate hand in a wave, silver rings flashing, before backing out of the driveway.

"I love you, puppy, yes I do. You're so cute," Hailey cooed, touching noses with the tiny fluffy black dog that gazed up at her with sheer love in those chocolate eyes.

Trouble. That's all John saw as he pulled out onto the street. Next thing he knew the dog would be sleeping with Hailey. And then it was going to be on the furniture. He'd no longer be king of his own castle. The dog would be. Well, queen, since she was a female.

Maybe it wouldn't be so bad. He reached over to rub a hand over the puppy's warm downy back. A pink tongue darted out in a quick, grateful caress. Okay, so maybe he wasn't gonna mind too much.

"I'm gonna need a girl name. A real name," Hailey chattered on over the Christian country station humming in the background. "Something really pretty, just as pretty as my cute baby puppy."

John ruffled her hair, too, and made her laugh. "I have every confidence you'll come up with the best name."

"Well, yeah, Daddy. I'm good." Hailey stared deeply into her puppy's eyes. "How about Ariel? Nope. I know. Alexandra."

"That would get awful confusing with two Alexandras in the same house."

Hailey sighed, exasperated. "I know. Danielle. Nope."

John eased up on the gas. He hadn't realized he'd been speeding, and he'd already caught up with the time-faded yellow Beetle puttering along the road in front of him. He could just barely see Alexandra's cinnamon-dark hair. It was fluttering around her shoulders, whipped by the wind through the open windows.

She's so different from Bobbie.

Where that thought came from, John didn't know,

but he didn't like it. He was Alexandra's protector. That's what he was. He had no right watching the flick of her long hair in the breeze and seeing a woman instead of his duty. His chance to make amends.

"Belle." Hailey tilted her head to one side, contemplating that name. "Belle? Here Belle, girl?"

The puppy kept licking Hailey's chin.

There was traffic in town, since it was nearly quitting time. He pulled up in a space next to Alexandra in front of the grocery. If he leaned out the window, he could make out the hardware store— looked like Warren was just closing up.

"Hey, I'll run in and grab some puppy food." Alexandra leaned against the passenger side window, reaching through to stroke the puppy's soft head.

Her silver rings flashed, drawing his gaze as they always did. Small and fragile hands. So unlike Bobbie, who'd been strong and capable and athletic. Always the tomboy.

Right there showed how wrong he was. If the day ever came when he'd paid enough for Bobbie's death, he wouldn't want a wife so fragile. So delicate. So easily hurt.

He pulled his wallet out of his back pocket, opened it and handed her a twenty. "Will that be enough?"

"For now." Her smile dazzled. She dazzled.

He held his heart steady, refusing to feel anything at all.

"Here, Daddy. Hold Jessica." Hailey handed him the beloved puppy. "Nope. That's all wrong."

"Don't worry." Alexandra's soft, sweet alto rang like the gentlest hymn. "I bet she'll name herself. Trust me."

Hailey put her hand in Alexandra's, and the two trotted off, the taller, beautiful woman and the beloved little girl, and disappeared from his sight.

"John, do you have any more newspaper?" Alexandra breezed into his kitchen, breathless and flushed, a smile shaping her soft mouth. "I'm afraid the puppy has used what I could find on the shelf."

"There's the recycling bin in the garage."

"There is? I didn't see it." She flicked on the oven light and peered inside. "Looks like another ten minutes will do it. Let me get the puppy settled, and I'll set the table for you."

"Your shift ended an hour ago. I'll take care of it. And the newspaper, too."

"Are you sure?"

"It's about time I'm good for something." He winked, forcing a smile.

"Hmm. You seem to be useful at making your daughter very happy." She smiled like a ray of sunlight on a bleak day, warming him straight through. Unaware of her effect on him, she disappeared down the hallway.

What was bothering him? He couldn't put his

finger on it. Whatever it was, it had his stomach in knots.

Was it the way she looked? No, because he'd hardly noticed she was wearing well-worn Levi's and a baggy purple T-shirt with the University of Washington in faded gold letters. He *wasn't* attracted to her—absolutely not. He was in control of his feelings.

Something was bugging him, though. When he figured out what it was, then he'd be able to solve the problem. He wasn't going to worry about it until then.

He grabbed three plates from the cupboard and dealt them around the table. Alexandra might as well stay and eat with them, since she'd stayed late. It was the decent thing to do, a gesture a man who considered himself her protector would make.

It had nothing to do with the fact that she was an extremely attractive woman. Because he simply wasn't noticing.

When he was done at the table, he headed straight for the garage, grabbed a bundle of newspapers from the bin. On the way through the house, he couldn't help noticing the changes Alexandra had already made. The floors shone. The furniture was vacuumed and plumped and tidier. The big-screen television was dust free.

Hey, now there was an improvement. He'd like that the next time the Mariners were playing. No more screen lint.

Feminine giggles trilled like music down the hallway, drawing him closer. Hailey's high bright laughter blended with Alexandra's quieter, deeper chuckle, and that chuckle seemed to be the most wonderful sound he'd ever heard.

"No, puppy, you're supposed to go on the paper." Hailey started to giggle harder. "Alexandra, she's goin' again."

"She's going to be just fine once we're not in here with her." Alexandra was folding an old towel, made soft by wear, into a cozy piece of bedding. "She'll probably cry for a while, because she'll be lonely, but she'll settle in."

"The teddy bear will help." Hailey placed one of her favorite stuffed animals from years ago into the big cardboard box that was now stuffed with so much bedding, there was no room for the puppy. "Maybe she shouldn't sleep by herself. She's awful little."

Yep, here it comes. The plea to have the puppy in her bedroom. John braced himself, prepared to hold out for as long as he could—probably two hours tops. "The newspaper you requested."

"Just in time. The last of it has been properly used." Alexandra snatched the bundle from him and dove into it, hard at work, her hair falling down to curtain her face, so all he saw was the part going straight down the middle of her head.

There was something about that part in her hair.

The way the fine line of porcelain skin was a contrast to the rich brown strands. Something that made him forget that she was vulnerable and alone and in trouble, and it was his job to protect her and instead made him notice she was all woman, grace and poetry.

Stop noticing her, John.

Her slender fingers tucked a satiny lock of her hair behind her ear, revealing the soft curve of her cheekbone and the elegant shape of her small chin. Her bow-shaped mouth curved into a laughing smile as the puppy leaped up on her and then crashed down in the middle of the newspaper she was trying to unfold.

The sharp rustle of newsprint made the tiny creature yip with delight, her tiny, furry body wiggling from head to tail.

"Look at her. She's so cute." Hailey got down on all fours. "I love you so much. Yes, I do."

The little puppy leaped up to touch noses with her.

That was simply too much sweetness for a man to take. John swallowed hard, trying not to feel too much of anything. Sometimes it could be so overwhelming, all this he'd been given, this daughter he treasured, this life he lived, the moments like this that were tiny pieces of forever.

"I'd best go check on supper." He moved away from the sounds of laughter and crackling newspaper and the puppy's yips of delight.

It was only when he was setting the casserole dish on the trivet in the middle of the table that it hit him what was wrong. It hit him as hard as a plane crashing down from the sky to the earth. As desolating as the fire and flame and metal tearing apart on impact.

His knees gave out, his feet went out from under him and he landed in a chair, clinging to the edge, struggling for breath.

This is what it had been like when Bobbie was alive. The low murmur of a woman's voice down the hall. The bright feminine presence changing the house in some vital, undeniable way that could only be felt by the soul.

In a way, that made new all the pain of the past, all the regret and anguish, as if the void in his life had been ripped open again, and there was no energetic Bobbie zipping around this kitchen, laughing while she worked.

There was Alexandra. And he was glad for that.

He'd had housekeepers before, but it had never been like this. He'd never really been in the house at the same time as those other women—young or old—who'd worked afternoons keeping watch over Hailey and his home.

He hadn't realized taking Alexandra into his life would bring him here, to this place of bleak, burning pain.

The grief was over, but not the guilt. It hit him

with the force of an inferno, leaving him weak and sweating, consumed and empty all at once.

He had to find a way to pull himself together.

"What about Maggie? I sorta like Maggie." Hailey's voice echoed through the house—she was in the hallway, coming closer.

John realized his cheeks were wet and he swiped the dampness away. After a few deep breaths his knees held him up when he straightened from the chair.

Just in time. Hailey bounded around the corner, tugging Alexandra by one hand. Alexandra shone, as if the armor she'd been hiding behind had been peeled back, to expose a truer, more open part of her.

It was like looking at her for the first time.

"Oh, no." Alexandra glanced over her shoulder, her cinnamon-brown locks tumbling everywhere, catching the light, catching his heart.

It's because I can help her, when I failed Bobbie. That's why I feel this way. John clung to that, determined to push away every other feeling until the pain and the anguish were gone. His hands still shook, though, when he rescued the salad from the refrigerator.

"Is the puppy all settled?" At least he could keep his voice steady.

"Yep." Hailey dropped into her chair, unaware, as bouncy as ever. "Alexandra said I couldn't bring a dog to the table."

"Probably not a good idea for tonight." John kept his gaze firmly fixed on the tray in the refrigerator door that held the bottles of salad dressing. He grabbed both of them—Ranch for Hailey and Italian for him. Maybe Alexandra would like either one—

There he went thinking of her again. But only in the protective, most noble of ways.

"I should probably head out." Her voice, and the pad of her step on the floor behind him. "I'll leave you two to your dinner."

"Don't think you're getting out of here that easy." He hit the fridge door with his foot. "You made dinner. You should help eat it. It's only fair. What if the casserole tastes bad?"

"You need an official taste tester, is that it?"

"No. We need a guinea pig to make sure your casserole doesn't make us sick."

"If I don't keel over, then you'll risk it?"

"Exactly. It didn't look so good when I took off the lid. Scary."

Hailey repositioned herself, clambering onto her chair with both knees to get a good look at the questionable casserole. "It does not, either, Dad! It's all cheesy. It smells good."

"Smells can be deceiving." He winked.

There he went again, making her laugh, making her troubles disappear like dandelion fluff on the wind. "Fine. I'll be the royal taste tester, since you need one."

"Knew you'd see things my way."

"I'll warn you. This is my favorite recipe, so if you don't like it, I'll have to raid your mom's recipe box. Wouldn't it be too bad if I ran across the potato salad recipe?"

"Dream on." John set the bottles on the table. "It's such a secret, it's not written down. Mom's committed it to memory and will only reveal the great truths of it when she's on her deathbed. Or so she swears."

"Hmm. Getting that recipe is going to be a challenge." Undaunted, Alexandra stowed her purse and took one of the extra chairs at the table.

A terrible, high-pitched wail careened through the house and echoed in the rafters above.

"What is that?" John boomed like a clap of thunder. "Is that the *dog?*"

Alexandra shrank. She couldn't help it. He was a big man, wide and strong, bounding out of his chair as if the house were on fire.

His big hands closed into lethal fists.

She acted without thinking. On automatic pilot, she was on her feet in front of John, blocking him from leaving the kitchen. "She's just a baby. She's crying. I'll take care of it."

"She's *crying?*" He stopped, the fierce look on his face falling away to concern. "I thought she was *dying.* Got trapped behind the dryer or something."

Alexandra took a step back, confused. He wasn't angry?

"Hailey, go check on her, would you?" John shook his head, relaxed, his hands slack. "That sounds like an air-raid siren. I thought we were under attack."

"It's amazing how something so small can make such a loud noise." Lame, Alexandra, real lame. But it was all she could think to say as the belated rush of adrenaline hit. There was no danger. John hadn't been angry. He'd been concerned.

As he was still.

Hailey raced away to check on the puppy. Within seconds, the siren-pitched cry gave way to a yip of delight. "She's okay!"

"Good." John swiped a hand through his hair, standing those thick dark locks on end, before pinning Alexandra with his intense gaze. "You could have told us about the crying thing."

Was he still angry? "I figured you knew that babies cried."

"Yeah, but, well…is it going to happen again?"

"Probably." Alexandra felt an instinctive tightening in her stomach. Her chest felt hot and closed, making it hard to draw in air.

No, John wasn't angry. He was a powerful man, that was all. He'd been ready to help the puppy, not hurt her.

She'd been the one to read the situation wrong. To jump to the wrong conclusions. To assume a man who'd shown her nothing but kindness and generosity would also be capable of violent anger.

A part of her figured any man was. That was the truth, and she hated to admit it.

Remembering another man in her life, and his short-fused temper, she turned away, ashamed and confused and strangely blaming John for being a man, which made him like the others. And that wasn't fair.

"I don't suppose we can muzzle her?" John's eyes were flashing—he was teasing. Not at all angry.

Not every man became angry the way her father had. Or Patrick. The tightness inside her ebbed away and she could breathe deep again.

"I think you're going to have to buy earplugs," she was able to tease. "Or let Hailey keep the puppy with her."

"See? I knew it."

"Tomorrow I'll get a kennel at the pet store so we can train her. Don't worry—we'll put the kennel in Hailey's room."

"Good. I'm hungry. Let's dish up."

"Sure." She was still trembling with the aftereffects of an unnecessary fear. There was no danger. There never had been.

"Hey, are you okay?" His touch was sure and his words gentle. He stood before her, not just any man, but one of strength and goodness. Her very own hero.

How could anyone be so wonderful? So true?

She withdrew her hand and put distance be-
-tween them. "I'm just hungry. Are you still afraid
to try my cooking?"

"Shaking in my boots." John strode easily away
in that powerful, athletic gait of his as if nothing
were wrong, as if nothing had changed.

But something had.

Her hand tingled, warm and wonderful, where
John had touched her. Even hours later when she
was alone in the little bedroom in Bev's rental
cottage, when she couldn't sleep. She sat up at the
open window, remembering the heat of his touch,
the connection of it, and watched a sickle moon rise
into the starlit sky.

Chapter Nine

There was a creaking sound coming from the back of the house. The buzz of the tiny nine-inch television covered it up—almost. Alexandra's spine snapped straight. The sharp buzz of adrenaline fired into her veins and she flew off the edge of the couch.

There it was again. She didn't know where to run. Her feet were taking her into the bedroom. Even in the dark she could see the white curtain snap in the breeze of the open window. A window she'd left shut tight.

The darkness moved. The shadows became a man, and the faint gleam of metal became a gun aimed at her heart.

Patrick.

"You can't run, Alexandra. Didn't I tell you I'd hunt you down?"

She stumbled backward into the hallway, toward the light.

"You can't leave me, Alexandra. I need you." He stalked her, the shadows fading as he followed her into the living room, the brush of lamplight showing the hard anger in his black, unforgiving eyes.

There was nothing she could do to stop him. The front door was so far away. She couldn't run fast enough. She watched in horror as his finger squeezed the trigger—

She tore away, the scream dying in her throat....

There was only the sound of her ragged breath in the tiny room, where the distant floodlight from Bev's garage cast a friendly glow against the window, smeared with rain. The window was shut and locked.

She was alone and safe. It had been a dream. Nothing more.

Relief left her weak. She found the lamp by feel and turned it on. She followed the swath of light to the door, and into the tiny kitchen. The bulb above the sink was enough to work by—she filled a cup with water and popped it into the older-model microwave.

She hadn't dreamed of Patrick since the night she'd left. Cuddled up in the corner of her car, parked in the far end of a Wal-Mart parking lot in the shadow of a retired couple's mammoth motor home.

Although she wasn't visible from the road, she'd slept only a few hours—and fitfully. The fear felt in those dreams from that night remained real and blade-sharp as she rummaged in the drawer for the box of tea she'd brought with her.

Sweet peppermint scented the air as she ripped open the packet, unwinding the string from the bag and dunking the tea bag into her cup of hot water. The welcome aroma chased away some of the tightness inside her. But the fear remained.

It's all right. I'm safe here. She rescued her Bible from the tiny drop-leaf table in the corner and clutched it to her chest. She breathed in and out, slowing the fear, until there was only the sound of wind and rain.

There's no way Patrick can find me here. Not easily, anyway, and not tonight. It was a small town. Anyone could give him the information he needed—someone at the grocery store or someone on the street who went to the same church. Hers was the only rusty, faded old VW Bug around.

I should have headed to Minneapolis. Maybe Denver. Or back East, where the cities were gigantic and no one would remember another brown-haired woman among so many people.

The night's chill crept around her, and the damp from the storm settled into her bones. She shivered. She felt alone. So very alone.

Lightning flashed through the night, a quick illumination of the cozy cottage, and then only darkness.

The electricity had gone out. As thunder pealed like rending sheet metal overhead, Alexandra stood from the chair. Halfway across the living room, another lightning bolt flashed, helping her find her way to bed.

She could only take each day step by step. Just like this. That was faith. That was life. She was not afraid.

Settling onto the bed, she found her tiny battery-operated reading light on the nightstand and turned it on. The small glow was enough to read by. But which passage?

She thumbed through the well-worn gold leafs until the page chose itself. The book of Jeremiah. There was nothing random about the passage that caught her eye. "For I know the plans I have for you," declares the Lord, "plans to prosper you and not to harm you, plans to give you hope and a future."

Faith. It was like groping blindly in the dark, but she trusted the way. Trusted the path beneath her feet.

Hope and a future. I could really use both right now, Lord, she prayed. In the meantime, she was grateful to be staying with the Coreys. With John.

The thought of him was like a sweet wish. The tender longing for the weight of his bigger hand in hers.

She wasn't sure what to do about that. About John. Everything seemed so different. She closed her eyes but did not sleep.

"John." Alexandra skidded to a stop on the stone walkway in front of his house. "I thought you'd be gone by now."

"We're supposed to be. We're running late. It happens." He drank from a cup of coffee in one hand as he tugged a sprinkler into place with the other. "I've got a leak somewhere in the automatic system, so would you mind shutting this off in about twenty minutes?"

"I could be bribed into it. What's that you have there?"

"A fresh cup of coffee. I ground the beans myself. How about a cup?"

"It's a deal."

"Good." John bent to turn on the faucet. "It's warm this morning. Don't you think?"

A spray of cold water gently sprinkled her, and she shrieked, laughing, into the shelter of the covered porch. "You did that on purpose."

"Me? I'm too much of a gentleman. It was an accident."

"An accident, huh? I'm going to remember this. Expect retribution."

"The Bible bids us to never harm anyone."

"I suppose heaven always makes exceptions when a woman has a good case for revenge."

"Revenge of the sprinkler. I'm afraid."

"You should be." Laughing, with the wonderfully cool water evaporating on her bare arms, Alexandra followed him into the house. An ear-splitting yowl met her ears. "The puppy?"

"Every time Hailey gets out of her sight."

"You're in trouble, John."

"Don't I know it." He snared a cup and filled it. "Since you're here, maybe you could watch over her while we're gone. She doesn't like to be alone."

"It's a good thing you're so strict, or that puppy would be in danger of becoming spoiled."

"Now you're making fun of me. I'm a tough guy. I don't take any nonsense. I run a tight ship. Everyone lives in fear of me."

"I've noticed. You're as tough as a marshmallow. I bet the puppy slept in Hailey's arms last night."

"I'd never allow such a thing." He winked. "I couldn't talk Hailey out of it, but there's an upside. The puppy stopped that high-decibel wailing."

"How's the training going?"

"Accidents abound." He held out the cup to her. "We survived, though. You could have an interesting morning."

"I'll see what I can teach her." She accepted the mug, and her fingers bumped his. Heat zinged up her arm.

I refuse to be attracted to him. There. Alexandra turned away as if the collision of their fingertips meant nothing to her and went in search of the sugar. She found it in the pantry. When she turned around, John had left the room. The faint rumbling of his deep voice could be heard from upstairs.

He had a wonderful tone, masculine and strong without being overbearing. The warmth in his murmured words, the caring she heard as he spoke with his daughter, made her heart twist hard.

Not knowing what to do, she gazed into the depths of the serviceable stoneware mug that fit so wonderfully into both hands. The coffee warmed her palms and seeped into her soul. She stared at the dark liquid, wishing. Just wishing.

If she ran, she'd be safe. From the past, from heartbreak, from finding out that her mother was right. That was the real reason she'd let things go so far with Patrick.

She willed away the past with all the strength of her being, but there it was, a boomerang spinning back around for her to catch, gaining speed with its descent. She couldn't stop it. Not even the bold taste of hot coffee could soothe it away.

She heard the same words she had heard as a little girl, then as an adolescent, then a teenager, over and over again, as her mother had slurred them. *Don't think you'll grow up to be no different from me, Alexandra. Men don't have hearts. No hearts. You remember that. If a man says he loves you, then you know he's lyin'. Who's gonna love you?*

The one time Alexandra had dared to hope that some man could really love her, a good and decent man, she'd been wrong. So very wrong.

Cradling the cup in both hands, she breathed in the comforting scent of steaming coffee. Let the boiling hot brew burn down her throat, but still the feelings and the past remained.

"Alexandra!" Hailey appeared on the stairs, carefully cradling a little black bundle in both arms. "You're here! You're here! I'm real glad, too, 'cuz she cries like a baby every time I leave her alone." She bumped noses with her puppy and her voice changed, higher, sweeter. "Yes, you do, don't you, little baby?"

"Have you found a name for her yet?"

"Nope. I sorta like Emma, but I don't know yet." Hailey stopped moving, so that Alexandra could pet the puppy. "She doesn't like to be all alone, so I'm awful glad you're here."

"Me, too." The puppy was warm and content, and wiggled in delight as Alexandra stroked one furry ear. "I'll take good care of her for you."

"I know." As if there were never a doubt, as if Hailey had never had a real worry, she handed over the puppy with a kiss to its silky head.

Safe and beloved, the puppy buried its warm nose in the crook of Alexandra's arm and whimpered as Hailey bid it goodbye.

John came racing down the stairs, a duffel bag

swinging over his shoulder. "I left a note on the counter with the credit card."

"For the pet store. Right." Alexandra could barely think as he swept by, reached out to pat the puppy's paw. John's fingers brushed over Alexandra's bare forearm. The faintest of touches. It could have been warm air whispering over her skin, but it was him. His touch. His heat. His presence burning through her.

"Have a great day," he called out, already striding away, the athletic bag slung over one broad shoulder, his muscled legs stretching out to carry him from her sight.

The front door opened, then closed, and she was alone. Strangely missing him.

She *really* didn't feel attracted to him. Really. John Corey was like a white knight of old, the greatest of warriors and the noblest of men. What maiden wouldn't gaze upon him with admiration? That's all this feeling was.

He was her employer. It was as simple as that. He paid her to clean his house. Their relationship wasn't personal. In fact, they didn't have a *relationship*—they weren't even friends.

Remember Patrick? And the dream she had last night? Wasn't that all the indication she needed? Worry about what's right in front of you, Alexandra. Doing a good job for the Coreys. Keeping safe. Seizing this chance to put a little bit more cash in her wallet. Her thin stack of twenties had already dwindled alarmingly.

The sound of tires crunching on the gravel driveway brought her to the front window. Was it John? Had he forgotten something? Or Bev coming over to use the guest shower—the electricity on the other side of the ranch was still out from the storm.

It was a police cruiser, polished and gleaming in the cheerful morning sun. The uniformed man inside climbed out slowly, looking around. He caught sight of her in the window and tipped his hat with a friendly smile. Alexandra opened the door.

"Miss Sims? John told me to come talk to you. Says you have a problem I can help you with."

"I'm not sure what you can do. Please, come in."

"I'd rather stay out here on the porch, if you don't mind. Spend a lot of my day sittin'." He swept off his hat, ambling into the shade. "I know you're probably skittish, considerin' all you've been through, but you're not the first woman on this earth to be afraid of someone. It's important to know you're not alone in this. Between me and John, we'll do our best to keep you safe."

The sincerity of his pledge felt like the sweetest of blessings.

Taking a seat on the swing on John's front porch, with the puppy warm and snug in her arms, Alexandra told the officer about the charming man she'd fallen in love with. He'd seemed so kind to her, so perfect.

Just like John.

The bell above the shop's door clattered, and from the back room John didn't look up from the thick parts book. "Be right with you," he called out.

"You in the back?" Cameron, the town's only lawman, didn't let the Employees Only sign stop him. "This morning I got time to talk to that young woman out at your place."

"Thanks for taking the time." John found the part number, scribbled it down on the back of a packing slip and slammed the book shut.

"No problem. It's hard to tell. These things can go either way. She may never have a lick of trouble from that fella. Or he could show up here tomorrow." The sheriff helped himself to the old refrigerator in the back corner and hauled out a bottle of iced tea. "She gave me a good description, and if he drives down the main street of this town, I'll spot him."

"Good. Thanks, Cameron. You're a good man."

"I owe ya one." Cam held up the bottle in a salute. "Staying in your mom's extra cottage ought to help out. She'll be hard to find. No phone bill. No utilities. Plus, I'm bettin' you don't mind watchin' over her. She's downright pretty."

"I can see where you're going with this." Old

friends from high school, Cam wasn't fooling John one bit. "She's pretty, but she needs protecting. Not the town cop playing matchmaker for her."

"Hey, you're awful defensive. Maybe you noticed she's pretty, too."

"She's working for me, that's all. Don't go reading something into nothing." John felt his face heat up a few degrees. "She's in a lot of trouble. I want to help her. That's it. That's all. End of story."

"Sure it is. Anyone with eyes can see that. Hey, don't get so bent out of shape. I've known you a long time, John. I know how hard you took Bobbie's death. I'm not saying you shouldn't grieve, but it's been too long. Maybe you oughta think about that."

"Don't need to." Not even Cam understood.

"I've got civic duties to perform. Laws to uphold, and all that." Cam headed for the door.

The bell jangled, and he was alone. Alone with a knotted-up stomach and this strange horrible feeling right smack-dab in the center of his chest.

Cameron was wrong. John didn't feel anything for Alexandra. It wasn't like that.

He couldn't afford to feel too much at all.

Holding down the guilt, shutting off his emotions, he crossed the alley to the warehouse and went in search of a U-joint. It was tough to find the part. He really had to search since his mind was on Alexandra.

She sure could stir him up. Maybe because she needed him and his protection, and that made him feel worthy for the first time in a long while. Since Bobbie was alive.

His knuckles collided with the hard plane of the wood door, sending sharp streaks of pain into the bones. He'd missed the doorknob entirely—probably because he couldn't see.

Thinking of Bobbie and how he failed her could bring him to his knees. Steal the vision from his eyes. The warmth from his soul. *Inadequate* wasn't the word. Neither was *failure*. He could see it over and over again—her glove slipping, feeling the leather stretch to the breaking point, knowing that she was going to fall three thousand feet down the face of the mountainside.

Lord, I failed her. You put her into my care, and I messed up. More than anyone ever could. I failed. His forehead smacked against the door, something solid to cling to when it felt as if God wasn't answering.

John knew one thing for certain—for whatever reason, God had guided Alexandra to him and the shelter of his family. For as long as she needed it, he would be there.

This time he would not fail.

"Where is that granddaughter of mine?" Bev whipped off her glasses with her free hand as she marched up the path to the back deck. "I swear, summer came early and with a vengeance. Whew, is it hot. I'm going to put this in the refrigerator and help myself to some tea."

"Let me get that for you." Alexandra clipped the safety catch on the pruning shears she'd found in a dusty corner of the outside shed. "And since I'm going in that direction, hand over the sack, too. I'll take it in."

"What a dear you are. There are a few leftovers from my Ladies' Aid meeting. We had a potluck. Hmm, it was good." Bev gladly relinquished the heavy grocery bag. "How's the puppy working out?"

"Terrible. It was such a mistake." Alexandra bit her lip when Hailey's shriek of delight and a puppy's happy yip sounded on the other side of the house.

"So I see." Bev dropped her purse on the table, eyeing the tall, overgrown bushes alongside part of the deck with obvious speculation. "Glad to see someone's finally dealing with those roses. They're beautiful, and John can't keep up with them."

"Just doing what I can while I'm here." Alexandra peeked into the sack and spotted several plastic containers. "This is enough for a couple of meals."

"Thought you could use some help. Hailey is a handful." Sparkling with grandmotherly love, Bev caught sight of her granddaughter. "Oh, excuse me. I've got to hug my girl."

"Sure." Alexandra's throat ached as she stepped away. There was something that hurt inside her as she saw Bev hurry down the steps and across the grass, arms held wide.

"Grammy!" Hailey sparkled like the brightest star in the heavens as she ran, tumbling into her grandmother's arms. "Alexandra and me, we went shoppin' for my puppy. And we got to take her right into the store and everything!"

"Is that right? Let's see this puppy of yours." Bev took Hailey's hand, turning toward the little black dog bounding through the grass toward them.

More than anything, Alexandra wanted a life like this. With all that she was, all that she would be, she wanted to step into a world like this. Be a part of a family this openly affectionate and accepting. Where love—and spirits—flourished.

Bev knelt to meet her new grandpuppy, her happy chuckle of delight blending with Hailey's as the dog leaped and licked and wiggled. This was such a safe place, but it felt like a fairy tale. Something Alexandra had read about, and she was glad the heroine in the story found true happiness and love. But after Alexandra closed the book, she was still in her own world. Alone. Not at all sure if she could find the same joy or if she deserved it.

Remember the verse from Jeremiah? She had hope and a future. She had to cling to that. To believe good things were possible.

But the past clung to her like a shadow. Her mother's words and Patrick's polite, very gradual control. Odd how he'd often said the same thing to her, how lucky she was that he'd fallen in love with her. In all her twenty-four years, no one else had. Don't think about the past, Alexandra. Or those harsh, painful words Patrick had said to her. The ones that made her feel smaller, less worthy, less everything.

But here, she felt different. Renewed. The bright cheerful sounds of Hailey's laughter flitted on the wind into the kitchen. Bev's genteel alto voice answered, and the puppy yipped, bringing her back to the present.

"Hey." A man's voice startled her. "Come in. Earth to Alexandra."

"John." She almost dropped the plastic glass she was holding.

There he was, too handsome to look at, even in a simple blue striped seersucker shirt, tucked into comfortable-looking, wash-worn jeans. The sight of him took her breath away. Made her wonder what it would be like to let those rock-solid arms fold around her. Made her wish she had the chance to know the feel of his comfort, his strength and his heartbeat against her cheek.

"Want a glass of iced tea?" It was all she could think of to say, which was better than blurting out what she was really thinking—now there's a good-looking man.

"Sure, but you don't have to wait on me. Here, let me help." He took the glass, his big calloused fingers closing over hers, leaving her breathless and trembling and feeling so incredibly female against his masculine strength. He towered over her as he used the ice maker in the refrigerator door. "Did Hailey make you max out my card at the pet store?"

"We did our best." Taking Hailey to the pet store was another memory she'd tucked into her heart. They were three females on the loose—including the puppy—going up and down the aisles searching for everything they wanted, and a lot of stuff they didn't need. "Hailey is a serious shopper. When she gets to be a teenager, watch out."

"Don't I know it? Mom has taught Hailey everything she knows. Which is, the more the merrier, and you can't have enough shoes."

"At least Bev's trained her right."

John filled a third glass and didn't move aside when Alexandra sidled up to him to open the refrigerator door. They were so close, all she would have to do was reach out and her hand would brush his arm. She would feel that connection, that unique, strengthening power that made her heart soar.

Unaware, John slid the last glass on the counter. "Let me." He reached in front of her, his arm muscled and rock-hard, brushing against her forearm as he lifted the pitcher right out of her hands. "I heard Cameron came out to see you today. Did he treat you right?"

"He sure did." It was impossible not to notice the caring in his voice. "Cameron promised he'd watch the traffic coming through town for me."

"It's a small town. It wouldn't be too hard to spot a stranger matching Patrick's description. We're here if you need us."

"You're going beyond the call of duty to help me. I don't know why, but I appreciate it. I really do."

"What's the mystery? You need help, and we're helping you." John said the words lightly. He pushed his feelings deeper inside where he couldn't feel them and didn't need to wonder what they meant. Didn't need to admit he admired her more with every day that passed. Admired her? Well, it was more than that.

Alexandra stood off to the side with her arms wrapped around her middle, looking so alone. Her chin was up, her spine stiff. She looked ready for a fight. Ready to stand up for herself. Such a frail woman, petite and wispy and as lean as a willow, but there was strength in her. He could see it.

Whatever hardship she was running from, she would recover. She'd come back from it. He *knew* it, down deep. Maybe here could be a resting place for her. He liked knowing that he'd helped to make that possible. That he'd made a difference for her.

She could stay here all summer. No reason why she couldn't. She could watch Hailey full-time and ferry her around to her hundred thousand lessons and social appointments. And then, every evening when he came home from work, he'd have the chance to see her. She was so beautiful and alone and vulnerable, and when he looked at her he saw a future for the first time—

Whoa. Hold on, John. You can't go thinking like that. Pain arrowed through him, deep enough to rock his soul. He thought of Bobbie, laid to rest in the town cemetery and the day he'd buried her in a white coffin. Of three days before when he'd held her lifeless hand in the helicopter, while his friends did everything they could to try and keep her heart beating, to give her the chance at life.

And failed. How the flat line went forever on the monitor, and the nurse put her face in her hands and wept. Everyone said it wasn't his fault. He'd done everything he could to save her.

No one knew that when she'd been falling to her death, she'd locked her gaze on his. Not looking down, but up at him. She'd always looked up to him, always told him he was her very own hero come to life.

Hero? He'd been the worst failure. The worst sort of man that day, who hadn't been strong enough.

He didn't know if he was any stronger now. "I hope you're not getting tired of us already. I told you it was tough being around us. It was Hailey, wasn't it? She wore you out shopping. Made you afraid to hang around and spend the summer with her."

"That was it. Shopping with Hailey and her puppy was the toughest job I've ever had. No one should be made to work under such conditions. Laughter. Giggling. The puppy to snuggle. Ice cream afterward."

"Torture by chocolate. It happens. I get too much of it here. There ought to be a law against that kind of abuse. A person can only take so much fudge sauce."

"Exactly. I'm going to report you to your cop friend. Tell him about the laughter in this house."

"Scandalous. The neighbors complain."

"The neighbors are a couple of miles away."

"Yep. With the wild social life I lead, the noise carries a far distance."

"Right. Hailey says you only date the TV."

"My affection for baseball is only surpassed by my obsession with football, but I'm not ashamed to admit it."

"That's the first step toward recovery." Alexandra snatched two of the glasses, leaving him one.

"You don't approve of sports?"

"Sure, I love them. I'm not sure I approve of sitting on the couch instead of being outside where you can actually participate in a sport."

"You think I'm a couch potato, is that it?"

"You sure look like one to me." He looked about as soft as a hunk of steel, but she didn't need to tell him that. "A serious couch potato. One that's growing roots right into the sofa cushion."

"Yeah? I suppose it takes one to know one."

"What does that mean?" She waited while he opened the screen door. "You think I look like a couch potato?"

"If the sofa fits…"

"I'll have you know I have plenty of outdoor activities. I hike."

"No kidding?" All at once the shutters were down, as John led the way onto the deck. There was a spring to his step, a liveliness that made the shadows in his eyes fade away, like morning mist giving way to the sun. "Me, too.

"The guide I gave you ought to lead you to some great trails in this part of Montana, not just at Yellowstone. But since you're not hanging around, I guess you'll just have to suffer without seeing some of the best backcountry you'll probably see."

"You're trying to tempt me with promises of great natural beauty."

"Sure. It takes a hiker to know one. The question is, can you resist?" John set his glass on the wrought-iron table in the umbrella's shade. "Hailey and I always take a trip when school lets out. We head up into the backcountry and spend the night. Why don't you come with us?"

"You really know how to tempt a girl."

"Then you'd be interested?"

"If the terms were right." She flashed him one of her pretty smiles as she swished away.

Marriage is like this. John wished the thought away, but it remained, steady like a light always burning and as sure as a new day dawning. He'd missed the companionship, the talk and the ease of being with another person who accepted you.

Except this wasn't a marriage; this was only reminding him of that amazing time in his life. That once-in-a-lifetime place, and he had no business confusing Alexandra's friendship with his longing for a wife. To be married again. To have a woman at his side.

Alexandra made him think about what he could never have again. That's what this hard, sharp feeling was in his chest. The longing for a wife one day—the one thing he could never deserve.

It had nothing to do with Alexandra. That's why he couldn't look anywhere else as she gazed up at him with those deep luminous eyes. Why he felt entranced when the breeze caressed a lock of her silken hair against the soft curve of her face. She looked a little better tonight, more relaxed. More assured.

He liked seeing that change in her.

"I'll be right back." Her numerous silver rings

flashed in the sunlight, drawing his attention to those slim hands of hers, so delicate and feminine, so graceful even doing something ordinary like holding a plastic glass full of iced tea.

Beautiful hands. She was beautiful in every way, and it ensnared his heart and broke it all at the same time.

You can't have her, John. And if she knew what you'd done, she wouldn't want you. He squeezed his eyes shut, blocking out the sight of her walking away from him, but he already knew how she walked. He could see it in his mind's eye. The curled ends of her brown hair swaying with her gait. The quiet way she moved, like a morning breeze in an alpine meadow. The way she gave a little flick of her wrist when she reached for the handrail. Her sneakers padded down the steps, and the bottom stair squeaked when she stepped on it.

You're in love with her, John. The single truth ran through his mind like the clear chime of a church bell, leaving no doubt. He wanted to deny it. He wanted to be noble and say there was no way he'd allow himself to feel that way—he had no right, it was not possible, it was only longing and loneliness and anything else he could think of.

But there was no excuse on earth that could change the sharp pain that expanded with every beat of his heart. He loved Alexandra. The way a man loved a woman he wants to marry—truly and deeply.

He felt as if the sun had gone out. The brightness dimmed from the day, and the shadows crept through him with the cold fingers of a winter's night. He felt trapped in a cold dark place he couldn't climb out of, and he watched, as if at a great distance, as Alexandra breezed across the lush green lawn, her voice a dulcet tone that touched his soul.

He couldn't hear what she was saying. She handed the glass to Bev, with that gentle quiet smile that made his soul ache with a longing so intense, he'd didn't know which way was up or down.

He loved Alexandra. It coursed through him like a raging river in a time of flood. Like blinding sunlight glaring off a mountain glacier that had been icing over and thawing, icing and thawing for a thousand years. Like a violent clap of thunder overhead that was the only sound in the world for that one brief instant, so loud and frightening and overwhelming, it made the ground shake.

I can't feel this way. John wanted to pray for this staggering emotion to lift from his heart, never to return. He felt choked and suffocated all at once, holding back the bright hot flood of love from taking over his soul.

He could never let anyone know that he loved her. Especially Alexandra. So angelic and perfect and unbelievable. Look how she smiled. When her smile reached her eyes, and made them shine with light, he could see heaven.

He felt unworthy to the core. To his soul. He could not move, paralyzed on the spot, as Alexandra knelt to pat the puppy's soft head. Every movement she made was gentle and loving—how she ruffled her fingertips through the pup's soft black fur, the tone of her voice and the way she laughed so wonderfully with Hailey when the little girl bent close.

I don't deserve to love Alexandra. She deserves better.

It was tough, burying the feelings deep, but he did. He had no right to her. He couldn't stop the powerful tides of his heart as he watched her steal the extra bubble wand from Hailey's outstretched hand and keep it high as the puppy leaped. Her soft laughter filled his life and his heart like spring did the breeze, like dawn changed the world, and he was changed.

He dared to look long enough to see Alexandra sweep the soapy wand along the ground, creating giant bubbles for the puppy to chase.

"Look, Daddy! She can sure jump high!" Hailey gleefully swiped her wand, too. More iridescent bubbles rose from the ground, lifting into the air. "Did you see that? She can jump as high as an angel."

"Look." Alexandra made more bubbles with the elegant sweep of her slim arm. The puppy leaped into the center of the big bubble, popping it, but for an instant the iridescence enveloped her.

"Angel wings." Alexandra formed another long bubble, and the pup leaped into the center of it again.

"Cool! I know! I know!" Hailey's joy filled the air like heaven's touch. "I'm gonna name her Angel."

"Perfect," Alexandra praised. "A girl can never have too many guardian angels."

"That's right," Bev agreed.

John had never felt so bleak, so disconnected from life, even though he forced his feet forward, pretending nothing was wrong. Pretending he didn't want to draw Alexandra into his arms, hold her against his chest and never let go.

Chapter Ten

With the warmth of the evening still lifting her spirits and the temperate breeze whipping through the open windows of her Bug, Alexandra struggled not to think of John.

Impossible.

They had a connection. She felt it when they touched. When they talked. When he made her laugh. No man had ever made her feel this way. She was afraid no man ever would.

John wasn't going to marry again. He wasn't going to fall in love with her. She knew that. Was she even ready to love someone new, after Patrick? How did she stop her feelings?

John probably had no clue she felt this way about him. He was simply a kind man and a Good Samaritan. It wasn't as if she could ever let him know how she felt. Right?

She rounded the last bumping corner of the gravel driveway and saw the strange car parked in front of the little yellow cottage tucked in a stand of cottonwoods. With the thick evening shadows, she couldn't see what kind of car it was. Except that she didn't recognize it as belonging to any of the Coreys.

Patrick. She stomped on the brakes, the wheels locked up and the tires skidded in the gravel. Dust flew around her as she sat with her fingers gripping the steering wheel so tight, they ached. Her pulse thudded in her throat as she sat stock-still in the road, in plain sight of the house. It was too late to turn around. He would already have seen her.

What do I do, Lord? She took a deep breath, ready to shift into reverse. Wait. Those were Montana plates. A woman stepped out of the shadows, someone about her age, wearing a pair of jeans and a grass-green sweater with a big fish on it. Her smile was friendly and she looked familiar. Oh, Alexandra had seen her in church. She'd been sitting on the pew in front of them.

She looked nice, too, like she'd be a good friend. Hopeful, Alexandra climbed out of her car. "Hi."

"Hi, I'm Kirby McKaslin." She pushed a lock of hair behind her ear, as if she were a little nervous. "I didn't know if you'd be interested, but a bunch of us meet for Bible Study every Tuesday night at the town coffee shop. Would you like to join us?"

"Yes." An evening of fellowship was something

she'd needed desperately. "The coffee shop in town? The one on the corner?"

"That's the one. If you want, you can ride with me. We can go together."

"Great. Let me get my Bible." Heaven was smiling on her today, Alexandra thought, as she raced inside. She felt like she used to, before Patrick, when she was free to do anything she wanted without worrying how he would react. What he would think.

She didn't have to look over her shoulder as she locked the house up tight and followed Kirby to her car.

Later that night, as she finished her prayers and crawled beneath the quilt Bev had dug out of her hall linen closet, and between the softest sheets she'd ever known, Alexandra gave thanks for the best day she'd had in years.

When she woke up with the first rays of the sun smiling through the crack in the curtains, she remembered the verse from Jeremiah. Good things *were* happening to her. Hope began seeping into her heart again, warm and substantial.

She had to deal with this *thing* she felt for John. This infatuation, for the lack of a better word. A crush. She had to recognize it for what it was. It was all one-sided. Anything coming of it was impossible. She needed to concentrate on the problems she already had. She didn't need to go searching for more problems by mistaking kindness for romance—besides, John wasn't interested in marrying a second time.

After she'd showered and dressed for the day, Alexandra grabbed her devotional and her Bible from the nightstand. The kitchen was dim, and she pulled the curtains open. What a view.

She'd been here long enough, quietly in one place. If Patrick were following her, he'd have caught up with her by now. The tension coiled inside her began to unwind as she sipped her cup of coffee and gazed out the small window at such a great, beautiful world.

When she opened her devotional to the marked page, she had to marvel at how many times she found the passage she most needed to see—when she needed to see it. *I am leaving you with a gift— peace of mind and heart. And the peace I give isn't like the peace the world gives. So don't be troubled or afraid.*

She felt stronger. Better.

Peace touched her, not only from the beautiful mountains jutting ruggedly toward the crystal-blue sky and the rolling green meadows in every direction. But from within. She let peace fill up the wounded places within her heart, like light chasing away the shadows, making her whole.

Alexandra opened the window and breathed in the morning air, letting the warm wind touch her face. This is where she was meant to be. Right here. Right now. She could feel it down deep.

The sound of a pickup's engine cut through the serenity of the morning. She figured it was probably Gerald, driving along the main driveway from the farmhouse. When she spotted a bright red truck, she was surprised.

John.

What was he doing? John couldn't begin to explain it as he cut the engine. The little rental house, which had long been the hired man's house, before the harvesting was hired out, had seen better days, but it had never looked quite so charming as he gazed on it now. That had to do with the woman standing in the threshold, the sunlight streaking auburn highlights into her silken hair that framed her heart-shaped face—the face of the woman he loved.

You're in big trouble, John, if you let your feelings get the best of you. He took a steadying breath and hopped out of the truck.

She was coming toward him in slow steps across the porch, hesitant and demure. The light blue denim shorts and dark blue T-shirt made her look like something in a fashion magazine. With her bare feet, she looked so casually beautiful he couldn't make his brain function well enough to figure out what to say.

"This is a surprise." She leaned one slim shoulder against the support post.

The first thing he noticed was that her smile shone in her eyes, bright and true and more amazing than anything he'd ever seen. She made him feel more everything than he'd ever felt. Suddenly he was aware he was slouching a little bit, so he stood up a little straighter. And his hair was tumbling into his eyes—he'd better remember to get a haircut.

Hold on, John. It's not like you're going to start dating her. What you feel is one thing, but there's only one outcome here. She can never be mine.

"I know it's early, I don't mean to interrupt. I just dropped Hailey off at the bus stop. Figured I might as well bring you this, since I had it. Thought you could use it."

"Oh?"

Good thing she didn't look at him like a woman captivated. She seemed friendly enough, but not coy, not interested in him. That made it easier to hand her the small bag as if it wasn't a big deal.

It wasn't, really. He was simply doing his best to protect her.

He liked the way she lit up when she looked inside the bag. It made him feel good, as if he'd done the right thing.

"A cell phone."

"Figured you didn't want to be stranded out here

without a way to call for help. Not that you'll need it. But just in case."

"That was thoughtful of you, John."

"Had an extra one sitting around." That was almost the truth, he thought guiltily, as he moved close. So close, the apple scent of her shampoo tickled his nose. He could see the flecks of black in her brown eyes. He could sense the warmth of her spirit, of her soul, as if it were a match to his.

He jerked back as if burned. Creating distance. Putting enough space between them. Still, he could feel her, as if their hearts beat together. From five feet away.

What was he going to do?

Anguished, he walked away, calling over his shoulder in a strained voice he hoped sounded normal enough. "I'll be late tonight. Got some volunteer stuff in town. Just go ahead and drop Hailey off at Mom's."

"No problem." Her smile was pure sunshine and genuine appreciation. "Thanks again, John."

"Hey, no problem."

The way she said his name twisted him up inside. Her dulcet voice, her warmhearted tone… No, he couldn't do this anymore. He marched across the gravel to his truck, yanking open the door blindly and landing on the seat, breathing as hard as if he'd climbed Pike's Peak.

She lifted her free hand, waving in her dainty,

female sort of way, a beautiful, just-right way that made him hurt even more.

He put his truck in gear and raced away, churning gravel and dust in his wake, but he didn't care. He had to get out of there. Away from her. The image of her grew smaller and smaller in the rearview mirror, a lone woman standing on a crooked porch, watching him go.

Something had gone wrong. She didn't know what it was, not exactly, she thought as she wrung out the mop. Soap bubbles popped in the air as she lowered the mop to the floor. She swished hard, breathing heavy, intending to wash this floor better than any housecleaner before her ever had, but little Angel leaped into the way, growling in play.

John had turned away so abruptly this morning. Was it because of something she did? How could it be? There could be only one logical explanation—he'd stepped so close to her she could feel the heat from his arm on hers. They'd almost been touching. So close she could smell the spicy after-shave clinging to him, and the fabric softener on his shirt.

Her stomach had flip-flopped strangely and for one moment she'd turned to look at him, at the shaved-smooth cut of his strong jaw and his rugged profile.

What would it be like to have reached out and laid her hand on his arm? Would he feel as hard and substantial as he looked? And what was wrong with her anyway that she kept thinking of these things?

She'd like to explain it away, but she couldn't. The plain truth was that her attraction for John Corey wasn't fading away. It was growing stronger every time she saw him.

Just stop thinking about him. You're just looking for a hero, Alexandra. Someone to save you. From the pain of your childhood. From the heartache of being without a family. From the devastation of falling in love with the wrong man. She'd tried to give those things up to the Lord and look to heaven for that level of deep healing.

But faith was sometimes a difficult thing. It was hard to trust in the Father's great love, when she'd never known real love before. She clung to her faith with all she had, but some days it was harder. The Lord works in His own time. She would have to be patient, that was all.

When the time was right, she would fall in love. The Lord would lead her to the right man, one who was kind. Whose love was true. Right?

One thing she knew for sure—that man wouldn't be John Corey.

Did she embarrass herself this morning? Maybe. Did he guess that she was interested in him?

Great. How was she going to look him in the eye again?

Refusing to think about *that,* she went back to work.

"John, you awake?"

Something knocked into his elbow—his friend's fist. That brought John back to the present. "Yeah, sure. I'm wide-awake."

"Didn't look like it to me." Zach Drake had been his friend since kindergarten and winked at him, whispering so he wouldn't distract from the county sheriff giving a talk at the front of the meeting room. "Know what I think? I bet you were daydreaming. You've got a woman on your mind."

"What I have is indigestion. Ate too much chili over at the diner."

"Sure. You just keep telling yourself that. Maybe you'll believe it." Zach didn't take his gaze from the stern-looking man who was now waving a pointer at a chart. "That's a real nice woman you've hired to take care of things at your place. She wouldn't have anything to do with your mood."

"Of course not." John lied flat-out.

"Hmm." As if he knew far too much, being a newlywed himself, Zach winked again.

John's jaw tightened so hard, his teeth clacked together. "How did you know about Alexandra?"

"She went to the coffee shop last night. Word gets around in a small town."

Great. Just what he needed. Everyone meant well, sure, but before long Zach wouldn't be the only one commenting on how pretty Alexandra was. Or how long he'd been a lonely widower. Not that he cared. Nope, he could take it—well, he thought he could. But if Alexandra was the topic of the local gossip, then it wouldn't be as hard for that Patrick fellow to track her down.

He was concerned about her, is all. It was his duty. He took responsibility seriously.

"Isn't that her?" Zach gestured toward the only window in the room. The one that faced the alley way where an old yellow VW was turning into a potholed parking lot.

That was sure Alexandra's car. John sat up straight, straining to watch as she pulled up in front of a run-down place, where a faded sign from what had to be the fifties proclaimed The Wash Tub.

Sure enough, she climbed out, car keys dangling from one hand as she pushed the seat forward and wrestled two bulging pillowcases from the back. Why didn't he think to offer her the use of his washer and dryer?

Too late now. Every one would notice if he sprinted for the door to catch her. Like Zach, would they all be thinking he was in love with Alexandra? That was no one's business but his own. His conscience bit him good as he watched her saunter up to the double glass doors.

She stopped to redistribute her load. The bags didn't look heavy, just bulky. And it was all he could do not to leap out of his seat and help her. She managed okay, and smiled at a woman exiting the Laundromat with a child on her hip. What a smile. John figured a man could look on that smile for the rest of his life and never tire of it.

And even his guilt wasn't strong enough to chase away the love he felt when she slipped through the doors and out of his sight. Leaving a yearning for the sight of her sweetness and her goodness that did not fade.

Alexandra pushed in the money slot and hit the start button. The dryer hummed to life, squeaking a little as the big drum started to turn, tossing her sheets and towels into a colorful whirl. She'd done a quick load earlier in the week so she had towels, but she was wearing the last of her clean clothes. Good thing the Laundromat wasn't busy. She could use three of the four machines.

Digging into her jeans pocket for more quarters, she didn't bother to turn around when the door opened. Looked like she spoke too soon—now there would be a sudden rush for the washing machines, knowing her luck. Well, maybe she'd only use two of the machines, since that would be polite.

"Hey, stranger." John set two disposable cups and a white paper sack on the lid of the washing machine beside her. "I come bearing gifts."

"Again? Hey, I like this." Okay, so she'd add *generous* to the list of John's admirable qualities. "Are those cookies from the coffee shop?"

"Yep. Being the stellar guy I am, I'm even going to share these double-chocolate-chip-fudge cookies with you. For a price."

"I knew there was a catch. Some things are too good to be true."

"Exactly." He popped the top off of one cup. "Do you want peppermint or apple cinnamon?"

"Peppermint." She took the cup he offered. "My favorite. What's the catch? They say nothing is ever really free."

"You're a wise woman, Alexandra. For a cookie and this cup of tea, I'm going to ask you to use my washer and dryer next time you need to. I'm not about to let you go to this kind of trouble."

"This is no trouble. I'm used to Laundromats. I have a book, see?" She gestured to a paperback facedown on top of the dryer. "Besides, how can I use your machines? That would be taking advantage of you."

"The way I see it, we're taking advantage of you."

"How exactly are you doing that? You're giving me shelter and a job. You're watching over me, in case I run into trouble. And you've let me become a part of your family, just for a little while. I owe you."

"Guess it's a matter of perspective. See, I owe you because my floors shine when I walk in the door, and the towels smell really good and they're all clean and folded up on the shelves. And my TV screen has never been so dust free."

"That's why you're paying me."

"Wait. There's more. Hailey is happier with you in our house. Her puppy is housebroken because you took the time to teach her. Hailey told me you agreed to bake cupcakes for the school party next week."

"In a moment of weakness, I said yes. Actually, I've discovered I can't say no to her."

"A common malady when it comes to Hailey. I have the same problem myself."

"I didn't notice a bit."

That made him chuckle, and a dimple dug into his cheeks. A smile that made him open wide, and she could see the heart of him. Struggling to always do right, fearing he always fell short. Vulnerable and strong, and all too human. A man who brought tea and cookies to a woman who'd been down on her luck.

He'd never hurt her. Or anyone. She realized it in a heartbeat, as if heaven had whispered in her ear. Deep inside, where it mattered, behind the dependable father and Good Samaritan and the faithful son and the loyal friend, John Corey was a trustworthy man. Down to his soul.

Paper rustled as he held the bag open for her. "Try one. There's no heaven on earth, but this is about as close to it as anyone can get."

"That good, huh?" She took a bite and sighed as her taste buds detected the rich fudge and real chocolate chips.

"Thought you'd like it." He seemed pleased as he tossed the drained tea bag into the air. It made a perfect arc into the nearby garbage can. "Can you beat that?"

"You look awfully confident. You don't think I can."

"Nope. I was all-state in high school."

"Really? So was I. I was a starter on the girls' varsity." She wound up and sent the bag spinning into the can. "Two points."

"Here. Let's go two for two." He crumbled a napkin and aimed and missed. "Aw. I can't believe it."

"Some of us have it. Some of us don't." She sent a napkin in a perfect arc and it made the metal garbage can ring when it hit. "I guess that extra cookie belongs to me."

"If I would have won, I'd share."

"Sure, go ahead and make me feel bad. I'm a chocolate-cookie hog."

"Hey, I didn't want to say anything because I didn't want to hurt your feelings, but it's a real problem. One I'd sure be happy to help you with. Maybe it'd be best to give me the whole cookie—"

"Here's half, mister, and be grateful." She broke the soft cookie in two pieces and held out the larger one for him.

His fingers brushed hers and there it was, the connection she'd felt before. Like grabbing hold of a high-voltage line. There was no mistaking the power of it.

"After Hailey's last day of school, we always head up into the backcountry for an old-fashioned camp-out. We hike, we bird-watch. We get all the nature we can stand and then we come home where there's running water. Electricity. My sports channel."

"I bet you two have a great time, but I'll miss Hailey." And you. "This works out great. I've been wanting some time to go clothes shopping—"

"No, that's not what I meant." What was he doing? A sane man wouldn't do this, but the words tumbled out of his mouth anyway and he couldn't stop them. Maybe he didn't want to. "I want you to come with us."

"Camping? You and me? Alone?"

"Hailey will come, too. You'll be as safe as a kitten, and I'll be a complete gentleman. You have my word."

She hesitated. Should she? On one hand she'd love to go. She could read it in his eyes, hear it in his voice and feel it in the air between them. He wanted her to go with him. He wanted her company. Not as a housekeeper, but as a woman.

As a woman he cared about?

"I'd love to." She shouldn't have said it that way, but when he smiled, she felt it all the way to the depth of her being.

Days later when Alexandra was waiting for Hailey's swimming lesson to finish, she tried not to let her imagination get away from her. It was too easy during the warm sunny days to believe John might feel for her the same way that she felt for him. Since he *did* invite her on the camping trip.

It was scary to feel this way about a man again. But John was different from any man she'd ever known. He was good to the core. Everyone said so. The friends she'd made in the Bible Study group told her one story after another of his brave rescues on the county's search and rescue team. He was the town's volunteer fire chief, always with a hand out to help.

No doubt about it. John was a good man. He had a good heart. He would make a fantastic husband.

What if John was ready to marry again? Sitting in the shade of a park bench, she closed her book thoughtfully. What if he *was* falling in love with her?

"Alexandra!" It was Michelle from the Bible

Study group. "I thought that was you. Hey, I wanted to tell you that choir practice is today at seven. Kirby and I decided we'd better stop by to pick you up. It'll be harder to say no with both of us pressuring you, right?"

"Right."

"Hey, have you ever thought about a different haircut?" Michelle, one of the town beauticians, ran her fingers through the ends of Alexandra's hair. "When you get a chance, come sneak down to the Snip & Style. I'll give you a courtesy cut."

"Some people might be wary of a free haircut."

"Oh, right. Well, I'll try not to shave you bald or scorch your scalp with the curling iron. I've never done that before, but there's always a first time, I guess."

"Sure. That makes me feel better."

"Thought it would. Sorry, I couldn't resist teasing. See you tonight!" Michelle trotted away.

The distant din of children's voices grew louder as the classes let out. The walkway became crowded as moms and their kids arrived for the next class. Alexandra tucked her paperback into her purse, soaking up the feel of this day. A toddler dashed past, running all-out, while a slim young woman shouted, "Travis, you come back here!" He ran harder, but his mother was faster. Laughing at her renegade son, she scooped the little boy up into her arms and he squealed.

She knew that not all families were like hers had been. It was reaffirming to see it.

"Alexandra!" Hailey skipped into sight, sand- wiched between best friends Stephanie and Christa. "Can you take us for ice cream. Please? Please?"

"Yeah, please?" the girls echoed, all giving the best impressions of Bambi eyes Alexandra had ever seen.

"Ice cream is never a good idea. I highly disap- prove." Alexandra winked, rising from the bench, and Hailey laughed, lunging against her waist, holding her hard in a sweet hug.

"I think you oughta get extra chocolate on your cone," Hailey told her. "'Cuz you're the bestest of them all."

"That's because I have a weakness for ice cream. Lucky for you." She pulled her keys from her shorts pocket. "C'mon, girls. It's my treat."

The three little girls shouted their approval, dashing through the crowd toward the faded yellow old Bug. They climbed in, debating who was going to sit in the back, then who was going to sit in the front, their cheer contagious.

"Hello, Alexandra," greeted a woman passing by, whom Alexandra recognized from the coffee shop.

"Hi, Helen." Surprised, she returned the older woman's smile as they went their separate ways.

It was unbelievable. Was she really starting to belong? It was a wonderful feeling.

"Hey, there, pretty lady."

She'd know that rich, chocolate-smooth voice anywhere. John. She turned around, trying so hard to hold on to her heart. How could she hold back her affection for him? An affection that grew every time she was with him. That doubled with every kind thing he did for her. "Hey, I thought you had a store to run."

"I left Warren in charge. He's working full-time for me now that school's out. I thought I'd sneak out and catch the last of Hailey's lesson." He shrugged one broad shoulder in apology. "I'm late."

"Hmm. Yes. Being late is a terrible offense. You'll have to pay for it."

"Let me guess. Judging by the way the girls are hanging out the window, wanting you to hurry, you're going to torture them with ice cream."

"Yep. I'm tough. You'd better not mess with me."

"I'll surrender without a fight."

"You just want chocolate. You can't fool me."

"It's not the chocolate I want."

Alexandra's heart skipped a beat as their gazes locked. Held. All around them the world kept turning. Kids dashing down the pathway, their towels fluttering out behind them. Mothers shouting to their children to mind the swim teacher and to meet right here when they were done.

The sound of engines starting, and vehicles

chugging past and Hailey's anguished "Hurry up! We're dyin'!" was all part of the background, nothing but static that could not interrupt the single, perfect way John folded her hand in his.

The heat of his skin. The rough calluses that came with hard work. Sun browned, so dark against hers. So large against hers.

John was amazing. Everything he did made the world a better place, whether it was for his daughter or his mother and father or his community. He was good and kind and endlessly patient. Better than any man she'd ever known. And she wanted him with all the depth of her being.

She couldn't help it. She was falling hard and fast in love with him.

Chapter Eleven

❧

As John was packing the tents into the back of his truck, he was still scolding himself. What he should have said to Alexandra was, "I wanted to check up with you and make sure you were all right."

"Dad, are you sure we can't take Angel?" Hailey skidded to a stop on the concrete and leaned against the side of his truck, so little girl in her bright purple T-shirt and her matching purple sunglasses. "We can still pick her up from Grammy's. Please? *Pleeease?*"

"She won't be safe," he told her for the fourteenth time in an hour. "Go get your backpack."

"But—" Hailey sighed dramatically, enough to make any Oscar winner proud, and stomped off to the house.

His patience was wearing thin today, no doubt

about that. Alexandra should be here any minute—
He looked over his shoulder. There she was, driving
into sight. Now would be a great time to grab the
tent from inside the garage—from way in the back
and look really busy.

He retreated, figuring keeping busy would help
him forget how Alexandra kept gazing up at him the
other day outside the ice-cream shop. Exactly the
same way she was looking at him now.

"Hi." She could dim the sun with the way she
looked, dressed in a lemon-yellow tank top and
denim shorts, her slender feet encased in chunky
brown hiking boots that had seen better days. On
her they looked perfect. She looked perfect.

He tore his gaze away. She may be perfect, but
she wasn't right for him.

Remember that, John. He tugged the tent from
its resting place between the rafters. A stake
tumbled loose and hit him in the head. "Ow," he
said as it crashed to the cement floor. "I nearly
KO'd myself. That takes talent."

"John!" She dropped the duffel slung over her
shoulder and jogged over to him, bringing the
sunshine with her. "Oh, you're bleeding. Let me—"

She reached out, and he did his best to duck.
But his ears were ringing a little and his balance
was a little off. Pain pounded through the top of
his skull, but he had a feeling it didn't have much
to do with the blow to his head. It had everything

to do with the woman running her fingertips across his scalp.

"I don't feel a lump. Yet. Let's get you sitting down, and I'll run for some ice."

Now he was really feeling foolish. If he'd had his mind on what he was doing and not on the beautiful lady in his garage, he wouldn't be bleeding right now.

Then again, she wouldn't be at his side. For once, he wanted to let Alexandra fuss over him. To kiss away the pain. To touch him with those fingers that stroked away all the anguish and tension, leaving only peace.

He didn't deserve peace. What he ought to be thinking about was how he was going to help this woman. That was his sworn duty to himself, to Alexandra and to the Lord. What had happened to his self-discipline that he couldn't control his own thoughts? Instead of wanting to protect her, he wanted to haul her against his chest and kiss her.

And she wouldn't stop touching him. Those tender fingers on his brow made him think about how tenderhearted she was. What a fine wife she would make.

See? This wasn't good, and it had to stop. He caught her slim wrist, meaning to stop her from touching him. But instead, he was touching her. Felt the fine bones of her wrist beneath his fingertips and the warm silk of her skin.

She was wholesome and trusting and good and had no idea what he was thinking. She whipped out a folded handkerchief from her pocket and moved in. Didn't she know what she was doing to him? The wall around his heart was crumbling dangerously and her gentle ministrations could be enough to bring the whole thing tumbling down. He squeezed his eyes shut, fighting for control. He *would not* think about kissing her.

"There." She squinted, studying his brow. "The bleeding's stopped. I think you'll live."

Live? She was killin' him! She speared him deep. The defensive wall around his heart didn't stop her none. She made him feel. She made him want to love her.

Love her? Alexandra needed his protection. That's what he had to concentrate on. That's what was important here.

She smiled, and the cracks in the wall around his heart grew bigger. Just like that. You wouldn't think a man like him, who wasn't afraid of scaling mountains with nothing more than a rope, would be so quick to crumble. It sure bothered him.

"Here, turn your head to the right. That's it." She was totally focused now as she peeled back the wrapping on a bandage she'd rescued from the first-aid box on the garage shelf.

He'd do just about anything, so long as she stayed with him. She pressed a bandage to his brow, just beneath the hairline, and her sweet scent enveloped him.

Her goodness shone when she took his hand. "I don't think that blow to the head was enough to give you a concussion."

"I'm a tough guy. I don't get concussions."

"I'm not fooled one bit, mister." Her fingers curled around his and squeezed. "You're not tough. You're tender. Wow."

Alexandra let go, her face flaming. Had she really said that? She couldn't believe it. She high-tailed it out of the garage and headed straight for her car. She dug around for her sleeping bag and pillow and carried both to the back of the truck.

Was it too late to escape? She wasn't ready for this, and she wasn't sure she could believe in it. Was she going to get her heart broken, falling in love with a man like John?

"Let me help you with that." Suddenly he was at her elbow, as dependable as the mountains that rimmed the valley. He lifted the bundle from her arms with ease.

"Wait. You have a spot of blood—" She couldn't resist reaching out to touch him again.

The fine satin of his hair teased her knuckles, and the heat of his skin against her fingertips was amazing. She swiped at the speck of drying blood with the pad of her thumb. It felt intimate, to take care of him like this, and to be so close to him.

His eyes grew dark and his gaze traveled down her face and settled on her lips. Held.

He's going to kiss me. Alexandra couldn't think of anything else. Not the pillow she dropped or that they were visible from the house, where Hailey was. All she could think about was the way he inched ever closer, his gaze a touch that made her bottom lip tingle in anticipation. She wanted to share that sweetness with him.

Closer. His lips parted ever so slightly, and she did the same. She knew that his kiss would be tender and heartfelt. She also knew without asking that he hadn't kissed anyone since his wife.

And he cares about me. Encouraged, she closed her eyes at the first brush of his lips to hers. Gentle. Just as she'd known his kiss would be. Perfect.

The ricochet of the front door slamming broke them apart. Alexandra took a step back, lost in her own feelings as John turned abruptly and rearranged the camping gear in the truck bed.

The kiss had lasted only a few seconds, but it had been enough for her to know for sure. He did feel the same way about her. This wonderful, good-to-the-core man *did* care for her.

It was unbelievable.

"I'm glad you're here," he said.

"Me, too." Her heart felt full as Hailey burst into sight, dropped her backpack on the ground and wrapped her arms around Alexandra's waist. What a blessed feeling, to have this child's affection.

"I'm all packed and stuff. Guess what? Grammy took me shopping last night and I bought stuff for s'mores. I like 'em all mooshy, but not burned. Dad burns the marshmallows."

"He's a marshmallow burner? Shocking."

"I confess it. I'm a real man. If we eat marsh-mallows, then they'd better be charred and crisped." John winked as he scooped Hailey's pack into the back of the truck.

A real man. Yes, he was certainly that. Alexan-dra's spirits soared. This real man, good to the core, wanted to kiss her again. She felt certain of it.

And she was going to let him. It scared her, to think of trusting another man so deeply again. But looking at John as he told Hailey that they weren't going to stop and see Angel on the way out, Alexan-dra couldn't be too afraid. Even when he was annoyed, he kept his calm and his sense of humor. She loved him more for that, her very own white knight.

As if he could read her thoughts, he took her hand to help her into the truck. His touch made her heart soar.

Hailey chattered all the way, nearly nonstop, talking about everything while John drove with a bemused expression. They took the highway toward the mountains that were so close, Alexandra had to tip her head back to see their proud, jagged peaks.

"Sorry you came?" John asked in a split-second pause of Hailey's conversation.

"I'm so suffering." She didn't want to be anywhere else. This was paradise, sheer perfection, and she wanted to cherish every moment.

Then again, any moment spent with John was bliss. The kiss hung in the air between them, the knowledge of it and the tenderness. It could only mean one thing—that he wanted her in his life.

Joy filled her up slowly, the way dawn came to the mountains. Love moved that way, quiet and true. She felt changed because of it. Look what her future could be. John and Hailey could be her family. This could be her life.

"I love my new sleeping bag," Hailey announced. "It's all soft and has stuff inside—"

"Most people call it fleece," John clarified.

"And it's snugly, and my feet don't get cold if my socks get wet, 'cuz I fell in the river or somethin' like that one time…" She went on and on, each story more darling than the next until Alexandra ached with happiness.

This is what a family could be. This right here. It was no fantasy, no daydream, but it was as real as an answered prayer all around her. The sound of a happy child who'd never known neglect or abuse.

The capable presence of a man who loved and lived in accordance to the Lord's word, which he held dear.

We could be happy together, she realized. Everything she'd ever wanted was right here. Within her reach.

Too full to speak, Alexandra didn't say a word. She let the harmony of being with John gladden her. Hailey chattered, John added comments and Alexandra wanted to hold on to each moment forever. She wanted them to add up to a lifetime.

"This is the end of the road. Now the fun begins." John guided the truck off the paved road. Low branches slapped against the truck's high fenders.

"You call this fun? Running into trees?"

"No, the fun is in avoiding the trees. Watch." They were going four-wheeling. One of John's favorite things.

The old logging road was overgrown, hardly visible between the break in the trees that ribboned up the hillside and out of sight. Just the way he liked it.

He put the truck in four-wheel drive. "Hold on."

Alexandra grabbed the door rail, laughing as the truck bumped and rocked over the rugged terrain. Not dangerous, but it was exhilarating. Hailey squealed, straining against her seat belt to watch as a young sapling hit the bumper and slid beneath the truck with a scraping sound.

"Look! A cougar!" Hailey pointed. "Oops. It ran away. There was this one time, when Dad and I hiked, and…"

He listened, delighted, as always, by his little girl and her exuberant spirit. But what he really noticed was Alexandra seated on the other side of the truck, her eyes shining with excitement.

Good. He wanted her to be happy. He sure liked her being here, with them. He tried not to think about the kiss they'd shared. It was brief, sweet. Friendly. Right?

Okay, he was trying to fool himself. There was nothing friendly about the kiss he'd given Alexandra. It had been tender. He'd kissed her with his whole heart. With a heart he had no right to offer her. *Lord, please help me to remember that.*

Resolved, he kept his attention on the faint tracks of the road hidden by thickets of grass and brush. Until the truck followed a curve into a clearing, and Alexandra's gasp of amazement as the perfect peaks of the Bridger Mountains swept into sight. Strong, jagged, enduring.

He tried not to pick out the peak far to the left— he deliberately kept his gaze to the right, toward Alexandra. Maybe that was no coincidence. The fortress walls he'd built around his heart remained intact, but they were weakening. He had the terrible fear Alexandra could make them crumble.

Did he turn away from her? No. He could see

only her. Her sparkle. Her gentle spirit. Her compassionate, loving nature as she climbed out of the truck, according to Hailey's instructions, and held out a hand to help the little girl to the ground.

"Dad and I hike a whole lot," Hailey was saying as she slipped her sunglasses off of her nose. "Did you hike with your dad?"

"Nope. My dad wasn't around much."

"Christa's dad is divorced and lives in Missoula. He ain't around much, either."

So trusting, Hailey's fingers crept into Alexandra's hand. John's throat constricted watching the two of them. They could be mother and daughter, with the way they were both slim, both graceful, both sparkling like sunlight on a mountain stream.

"I'm so happy." Hailey tipped her head back, causing her golden blond locks to tumble away from her face. "Very, very happy. Come with me, Alexandra. I know the way."

"What about your dad? I guess we can forget him. He's just the chauffeur."

"We'd better bring him," Hailey gleefully teased. "He's good at packing stuff and he can put up the tent."

"A useful man. All right, then, we'll allow him to come. But only if he can keep up with us wild girls."

"Yeah!" Hailey giggled. "Hurry up, Dad."

"I'm coming. Golly." He locked the cab and swung around to the back. "You wild girls look like you have a lot of energy. Here. You'd better carry the heavy pack."

"But I'm the littlest." Hailey shoved her glasses onto her nose, a precious sprite that smiled up at him with Bobbie's grin. "He's just teasing, Alexandra."

"Me? Tease? I'm dead serious." He hefted the big pack, with the heavy gear, out of the back of the truck bed and offered it to her. "Here, Alexandra. Since I'm just the chauffeur, not the pack mule."

"Oh, you have other uses, too."

It would be so easy to draw her into his arms and hold her sheltered and safe against his chest. Simple to give in to the tenderness he longed to feel for her.

Maybe he could give in. Just a little.

"I'm so glad you invited me." She eased into her backpack. "I can't wait to get started. How far are we going to hike in?"

"About two miles. Can you make it?"

"Me? Sure. The question is, can you?"

"Questioning my strength and endurance, are you? I'm not the most decorated member of the county's search and rescue team for nothing."

"Sure, go ahead and brag. You've never been up against me before."

"Is that a challenge? I have to warn you. I'm a competitive kind of guy. I play to win."

"Ooh, me, too. Last one there has to put up the tents." She quirked one brow, eyeing him up and down as if she wasn't impressed with what she saw. "Prepare to eat our dust."

"It's grassy. There is no dust." He slid his arms into the padded straps, letting the heavy weight of the pack settle along his back. "Go ahead. I'll give you a head start. You're going to need it."

"Awfully confident, aren't you?"

"Sure. I'm an awfully confident guy. I always get what I want."

"Then what are you waiting for?" She held out her hand.

His fingers slipped through hers as if they were made to be there. Hand in hand. Her smaller palm fit inside his perfectly. He felt another rend in the wall protecting his heart. He knew it was wrong, but he held on to her, matching his longer stride to hers as they headed shoulder to shoulder into the forest.

"Hurry, Alexandra! Dad's gonna beat us!"

"I'm hurrying." She was out of wind.

Okay, so John was in excellent shape. One look at his amazing physique would tell her that, but she *had* to win. The climb was uphill, and the rocks kept crumbling beneath her boots. It didn't help that John grabbed hold of her backpack and playfully held her in place.

"No fair." She twisted away, but he took advantage, sprinting past her on the narrow ridge. "You get a penalty for that unnecessary roughness, buddy."

"What kind of penalty?"

"I don't know. You're already in trouble with me."

"Me? In trouble? Impossible. I'm a good guy. Innocent. I don't cause trouble."

"I don't have your mom's potato salad recipe, do I? Nope. Someone broke his word to me on that."

"I couldn't get it. Mom's ruthless when it comes to her secret recipe."

"Fine, but you *are* her son. You have an inside track."

"You might think so, but my mom said she'd give it to me if I married, and not until."

"Well, if that's what it takes." She caught hold of his backpack and tugged enough to slow him down.

He fell in line beside her. "Hey! You're stronger than you look."

"You just remember that when you're putting up the tents, loser." She shouldered past, gaining the lead. "You'll be working to the sweat while Hailey and I soak our feet in the creek. Right, Hailey?"

"Yep. Unless there's bugs 'n' stuff." Hailey led the way, being the experienced hiker she was. "Ooh, that's where we always camp."

"C'mon, Hailey, let's run." She grabbed the little girl's hand, and they laughed together, trying to get ahead as John swept his daughter off her feet.

"Hey, Dad!"

"Maybe we'll be soaking our toes while Alexandra does the tents." John swung his daughter to his chest and held her tight, awkward backpack and all, and her merry giggle lifted on the breeze, echoing across the rugged peaks of the mountains all around them. "C'mon, kid. We're gonna win."

"Oh, yeah?" Alexandra dug down deep. It was hard to admit she was tired from the several miles' walk at high altitude, but she wasn't about to let John beat her. She had her reputation to uphold! She started running. He glanced over his shoulder, saw she was gaining and ran harder.

"Oh, no!" She wasn't going to lose. She sprinted all-out, chugging past him, her backpack clunking against her lower back as she shot ahead and into a mountain meadow lush and green.

An elk lifted its head, heavy rack of antlers pointing into the sky, and took off in a streak of brown into the trees.

"Already scaring off the neighbors." Out of breath, John eased Hailey to the ground. "That poor elk is running back to his family to tell them the neighborhood is going downhill, now that the humans have moved in."

"Or he's telling the hungry bears where to find us."

"Not used to being so remote?"

There was no sign of civilization anywhere. Only the velvety texture of trees on the high slope, the soar of an eagle overhead and the echoing presence of nature that felt vast and powerful. She felt small against such greatness, and enlivened, too. "I've never been anywhere like this, and I'm a country girl."

"Then you like it?"

"Love it." She breathed deep, taking in the crisp mountain air and gazing at God's beautiful handiwork. "I could get used to having elk for my neighbors."

"That's why we come up here all the time." John took her hand in his, big, warm, strong.

She felt the connection between them deep in her heart.

"You go dip your toes in the creek and rest up." John squeezed her fingers gently, tenderly, before he moved away. "Since Hailey and I are big losers, we'll put up the tents."

"I didn't lose," Hailey protested gaily. "You grabbed me up and I couldn't help it."

"Sometimes life isn't fair." John ruffled his daughter's hair, all affection, and all unshakable fatherly protection. "C'mon. Let's show Alexandra how it's done. She might be a country girl, but she doesn't know how it's done in Montana."

When John brushed a kiss on Alexandra's cheek, hope rose within her, growing with every beat of her heart.

"Is she asleep?" Alexandra whispered over the crackle of the fire as John emerged from the dark.

"As soon as her head hit the pillow." He swung his leg over the log and hunkered down next to her. "She ate so many s'mores, it's a shock she could actually sleep."

"Me, too. I'm in the throes of a sugar high." Alexandra reached into the open plastic bag and fished out another marshmallow. "You might as well join me."

"How can I resist the temptation?" He held out his hand, palm up, for the fluffy treat. "Having fun yet?"

"You could call it that." She'd had the best day. Exploring the mountainside with Hailey, searching for the wild roses that bloomed in early summer. Letting John hold her hand as they walked in the meadow, watching an eagle soar overhead and the elk return to see if his grazing spot was still full of humans.

"I'm glad." John pierced the marshmallow with the end of a willow stick he'd carved earlier, one for each of them. "Not too many women like to hang out in the backcountry."

"I'm one of those rare women, I guess," she said lightly, teasing.

"I'll say." He wasn't teasing. "You haven't complained once."

"What's to complain about?"

"No running water, no warm water and no indoor plumbing, for a start."

"I love those things, believe me. But isn't this something?" She gazed up at the sky above, the stars so thick and close she felt as if she could gather them up in her hands.

"This is something." John wasn't looking at the heavens.

He was gazing at her. In the flickering firelight, he was completely exposed. His guard down. She could see past his tender heart into the goodness of his soul.

She could sense his thoughts even before he leaned closer. Before his gaze focused on her waiting lips. His eyes grew as dark as dreams as he waited, the air buzzing between them, the infinite night and the diamond sky witnesses as he dipped to cover her mouth with his.

His kiss was like moonlight, silvered and rare. Like the gentlest brush of nightfall. It was like coming home and finding forever all in one sweet touch. His kiss was pure tenderness and all heart.

His kiss made her ache all the way to the bottom of her heart with a love so fierce and pure, she couldn't stop it. Couldn't deny it. Couldn't make these powerful, wonderful feelings stop. Not even when he broke the kiss, staying close to gaze into her eyes, and their souls touched.

Chapter Twelve

Alexandra snuggled into her sleeping bag, trying as hard as she could not to make any sound and wake Hailey. The little girl slumbered in her own sleeping bag, turned on her side so that all Alexandra could see of her was the fall of blond hair across her pillow.

It was cozy being here like this. Sweet. Humbling. With John's kiss still tingling on her lips, with the connection between them still unbroken, she dared to think about a future with John. With the man she loved.

This really is love, she realized. A love like she'd never known before. A power of love she never knew existed.

It was like the passage from Corinthians. John's love was patient and kind. It did not demand its own way. He was not jealous or proud, boastful or rude.

This was her new day, her new opportunity with John. This was her one chance at a happily-ever-after. At a hope and the future the Lord promised. Was John planning to propose?

Thank you for leading me here, Father. She was grateful with all she was and all she had. If this love she and John shared could blossom and grow into a marriage and a life together, then she would never ask for anything else. What would she need? She would already have everything that mattered. Hailey would be her daughter. Her very own daughter. John would be the love of her life. A true soul mate. And later there would be babies. Precious gifts from the Father above to celebrate their beautiful love.

Sure, she was getting ahead of herself, but she could see the future like a bright glittering star right there on the horizon, ready to rise into the sky and shine brighter than any other star in the heavens. That's how wonderful her future was going to be as John's wife.

Happy tears burned in her eyes and wet her face. Every trial she'd been through in her life was worth it, because it made her who she was. Her hardships had brought her here, to John's loving arms. She had everything she'd ever prayed for. Ever wanted. Would ever dream of.

Love filled her, true and pure, generous and kind, unconditional and infinite. She lay long into the night, dreaming—just dreaming of how her future with John would be—until sleep carried her away.

I shouldn't have done that, Lord. I never should have kissed Alexandra for real. Full on the lips. And meant it. John buried his face in his hands. What had he been thinking? He wasn't thinking—that was the problem. He'd been acting on his feelings. On the bright, singular affection that was too beautiful for the likes of him to be feeling.

I know I don't deserve another chance at paradise, Lord. But if I had the right to take Alexandra as my wife, I'd protect her always. Cherish her more than any man could love his wife. If I could only deserve such a gift as her love.

John couldn't bring himself to ask for such a blessing from the Lord. He didn't have to close his eyes to see the image; it was already flashing through his mind. The rope breaking with a snap. The whip of the broken rope against the sheet of granite and Bobbie's cry as she started to fall. He'd been rehammering a piton because the rock was stubborn and Bobbie hadn't gotten it in deep enough. In the second it took for him to figure out what was going on and grab the safety, she'd already plunged past him. Bobbie! The rope jerked tight with her weight. Saving her.

Adrenaline had electrified him, and he started

dragging her up, hand over hand, thankful the piton held her safe. She dangled ten feet below him, gazing up with fear stark on her face, the plea in her eyes unmistakable. The valley floor stretched out over three thousand feet below.

"Hold on to the rock." But it was too late. The piton broke away, he was off balance and he couldn't keep ahold of her hand. Her glove started to peel away...

Lord, I can't remember this. I can't relive that moment again. John squeezed his eyes shut, praying for the images to vanish. He breathed hard, fighting until the memory cleared.

He'd died that day, too. Every prayer he made, every Sunday service he attended, every time he opened a Bible, there it was. The one thing he could not be forgiven for. The shame and horror that he could not face. Could not bear to look at. And what was worse, was that God knew. God, who knew every failure, right there, hiding in John's soul.

There was no way he could deserve Alexandra or her precious love.

John sat on the log and stared at the embers that had been their campfire. Watched as the glow faded from the embers until there was only ashes and darkness.

Alexandra woke to the symphony of birdsong that proceeded the dawn, as if a thousand birds of every kind were singing to the eastern horizon, calling the sun to rise. Who could sleep through that much noise? Apparently Hailey could. Alexandra punched her pillow and closed her eyes. It was no good. Slumber eluded her because she was thinking about John.

What a kiss. What a man. Remembering, Alexandra felt joy fill her in a slow, warm sweep. A wonderful glow filled her, a contented happiness unlike anything she'd ever known. She couldn't wait to see him. Could he be up this early?

It wasn't sunrise, but she was going to find out. Besides, if she'd lie here tossing and turning, she might wake Hailey. No sense in doing that, so she slipped out of her sleeping bag and unzipped the tent flap.

John's pup tent looked silent as she refastened the flap and pulled her sweatshirt on over her shirt. He *could* be asleep in there. She felt alone. The wind had a bite to it, and she shivered. Maybe she could get a fire going and start a pot of coffee—

Something moved in the shadows. A man's wide shoulders and straight back. It was John. He sat with his elbows on his knees, hands together, watching the eastern horizon. With his back to her, he didn't know she was there.

What a man. She couldn't help admiring him, this good man she'd fallen in love with. He heard the pad of her step and his spine straightened.

"Good morning, handsome." She wrapped her arms around his neck from behind.

He stiffened and for an entire minute, he didn't move. Then his hands braced her forearms and he unwound her from his throat. "Good morning."

He sounded pretty gruff. Alexandra felt slapped. Didn't John want her affection? That hadn't been the story last night. Maybe he didn't sleep well.

Or perhaps he regretted their kiss.

No, that couldn't be true. John had held her with incredible tenderness. It had been no accident, but a deliberate act of love. It couldn't be faked.

But it could be regretted.

Alexandra stumbled. She felt as if the earth had disappeared beneath her feet. Last night she'd thought he would want a life with her. But now...

No, maybe he's tired or not feeling well. She'd *felt* the love in his heart. She *knew* it was there.

What she needed to do was to figure out what was troubling him. She would make it right, whatever it was. She settled down beside him. "Did you get much sleep?"

"Nope."

His gaze was shuttered. So was his heart. Different from last night. He was like he'd been when they first met. Distant. Brooding. Unreachable. What was wrong? "Did the owl keep you up?"

"I'm used to owls."

"The deer were pretty loud grazing in the

meadow. I woke up to the sound of them chewing right outside the tent."

"I'm used to deer, too."

Not a good sign. "Was it our kiss? You regret it. Oh, you do." She watched in horror as he turned away, as if ashamed and weighted down by regret.

"It never should have happened. I wasn't thinking. I had no right to kiss you. None at all. I know what you think. You're hoping there's a future in this. But I have to be honest. I can't lie to you, Alexandra. I never meant—" He turned away, tendons cording in his throat, muscles straining in his jaw. "It won't happen again."

"I see." Her heart began to splinter into a billion tiny shards, so sharp-edged, the pain left her breathless and reeling. John didn't want her. He didn't want her kiss.

Those dreams of a future as John's wife lifted like soap bubbles into the air and popped into nothing at all. She hid her face in her hands, embarrassed and ashamed. Way to go, Alexandra. He had to know she was in love with him. She'd shown him her heart. Why didn't he love her?

Her mother's words reeled into her mind like a whisper from the mountaintops. *Don't think you'll grow up to be no different than me, Alexandra... Who's gonna love you?*

Oh, John. I thought you could. I thought— She launched off the log and fisted her hands, walking hard. Embarrassment burned hot as flame in her soul as she took refuge in the shadows.

Pain slashed through her, sharper than any blade could ever cut. Her hand flew to her chest, but it couldn't stop the agony ripping through her. Nothing in her life had ever hurt like this. Not one thing. Worse, it was all her fault. She'd wanted John so much. She loved him, heart and soul.

She'd needed a hero. A white knight to save her from her past. From the hurt Patrick had put into her heart and from the lost little girl she'd been, craving a bright, sheltering love.

She'd been a fool. At least, that's how she felt. Shame burned her face, and she was grateful for the dark. Glad John couldn't see her.

"Alexandra." His voice came from directly behind her.

Oh, Lord, don't let him see me like this. Don't let him guess how wrong I've been. He can't know how deeply I love him. She desperately needed some scrap of pride to hold on to.

Then he touched her, curling his hand around her shoulder. Making the agony inside her bleed.

"I'm sorry. If it helps, I'd like to marry you. If I could."

"No, that doesn't help." It was worse.

He pulled her into his arms. His embrace was the shelter she'd always craved. His love the soft place she'd always yearned for. She leaned into him, letting him take some of her pain, allowing him to be her comfort.

He smelled like woodsmoke and pine needles, and the soft fleece of his sweatshirt caressed the side of her face. With her ear against his chest, she listened to him breathe and to the rapid beat of his heart. Thumping fast and hard and hollow. She never wanted to let him go.

"You are a wonderful woman." His hand curled around her nape, his fingers tender on her vulnerable spine as he cradled her against him. "You deserve a man with a whole heart to give you."

"I'd take whatever you could spare."

"No." He brushed his lips against her temple, a tender and brief kiss that would be their last. "You don't understand. You don't know what I am."

"You are my protector and my friend. You are the most noble man I've ever met."

John felt as if an ax was cleaving his heart in two. He hated seeing the depth of her love for him, glittering in her like a rare and precious gem. Her heart was so open and so easy to read. How could he turn away? He wanted her love more than anything on this planet. He wanted her with his entire soul. "I'm not so noble."

"Yes, you are. After all this time, you're still in love with your wife."

It would be easy to let her think that. Then he'd never risk losing her love. She'd never know the kind of man he was. Never look at him and see less than the protector she thought him to be.

He loved Alexandra. With his entire being. With all he was and all he had. If he could simply hold her in his arms, keep her nestled against his heart and feel her gentle love wrap around him, then he knew this agony in his soul would end. She could make his guilt disappear. She could be the balm to soothe the mortal wounds in his past.

He didn't need to tell her the truth. All he had to do was to tell her that he loved her. He could still fix this. He wanted to be weak, not noble, to hold on to her forever so this soul-rending pain would end.

But it wasn't right. It wasn't fair. Alexandra deserved a better man than he could be. Ever.

Forcing her away from him felt as if he were ripping his heart out of his chest without the benefit of anesthesia, but it had to be done. He took a deep breath and gathered what remained of his integrity.

"I'm not still in love with my wife," he confessed. "I'm responsible for her death."

"No." Alexandra's denial was fierce and instantaneous.

"I wasn't strong enough to hold her. To keep her from falling."

"John, that's not true. You aren't in control of life and death. Only God is."

"You weren't there." She stubbornly wanted to

believe the best in him, and he wasn't going to let her. "I couldn't find it in me to keep my wife from falling three thousand feet to her death. I should have been able to save her, and I couldn't. My heart fell right along with her, all three thousand feet, and crashed to the ground. I can't love you. I can't."

He marched off, leaving her in the shadows, as the sun rose, a peachy gold smudge over the mountains. Watching John walk away was the toughest thing she'd ever done. God gave her strength as she swiped at the wetness on her cheeks, willing no more tears to fall.

She was strong enough for this. God had led her here to show her that. She took a deep breath, and felt wounded and whole all at once. Loving John had given her a strength she didn't know she had. Strength she would need in order to let him go.

It was over between them. There had never been a chance for them. Ever.

Raw emotion left her trembling as she eased to her knees in the tall grass. Hidden by the shadows, she covered her face with her hands and let the hot, burning tears come. The pain in her heart did not end, even after the tears had run dry.

She knew it never would.

Patrick Kline eased up on the accelerator, not bothering to signal as he cut across two lanes of traffic and zipped onto the off-ramp just in time.

Might as well check this last exit. Being the ambitious attorney came in handy most of the time—
he'd learned to be thorough and logical. He'd
checked the gas stations, convenience stores and
campgrounds off every exit since Seattle.

He'd find her. There wasn't a woman who could
outsmart him, and Alexandra didn't come close to
having his intelligence. One of God's blessings that
Patrick used with great pride.

A sign caught his eye. The Lazy J Campground.
Vacancy. Looked like a dirt-cheap place. Alexandra was on a tight budget. He'd check there first.

Chapter Thirteen

It had been another sleepless night. John filled his travel coffee cup, almost brimming it over because he was so tired. The night on the mountain had taken its toll. He felt raw and wounded and bleeding. He feared not even prayer could make this pain fade.

Ten to eight. It looked as if he'd better get a move on. Alexandra would be here any minute. She always came a few minutes early. With any luck, he'd be in his truck, ready to leave when she drove into sight.

"Dad!" Hailey was already outside on her horse. "Can I go to Stephanie's later?"

"Take that up with Alexandra." Even saying her name was painful.

You're falling apart, John. Don't think about her

and you'll be all right. That was a lie. He was never going to be all right again. No woman had ever burrowed so deep inside his heart. This love he felt for Alexandra was greater than the distance from the earth to the moon. He feared it could reach all the way to heaven.

You can't have her, John. He knew it—and the truth tore him apart. The image of Bobbie's face that last moment he'd been able to hold on to her didn't leave him as he stumbled out the door.

"Know what, Dad?" Hailey guided her horse to the driveway, where she sat bareback in a pair of jeans and a fringed shirt. "I had the best time and stuff, you know, with Alexandra. And if, like, you wanted to get married like Grammy says you should, then you can just marry Alexandra. She's like a real mom!"

Could the blade stuck in his heart dig any deeper? Anguished, John yanked open the door, spilling coffee all over his boots and the gravel driveway. Great, and here came Alexandra. Pulling up in her little car, windows down to enjoy the temperate morning, her hair tousled around her face, making her look wholesome and beautiful and exactly like the kind of woman he could never deserve.

It took all his steely willpower to turn his back and climb into the truck. He lifted a hand in a casual wave to Alexandra, as if she were merely the housekeeper and not the love of his life and the missing piece to his soul.

He couldn't look at her as he drove away.

Their friendship was ruined, too. Sorrow felt like lead as she watched John's truck disappear around the bend. As if he couldn't get away from her fast enough. She parked her car in the shade, waved to Hailey as the girl rode her horse over and tried not to let the sinking feeling in her chest take her mood any lower.

Is it going to be like this from now on?

John's love and a future with him had been devastating to lose. But his friendship, too? How could she go without that? How could she go back to baby-sitting Hailey when she'd hoped Hailey would become her stepdaughter?

What was she going to do?

Just concentrate on your work for today, Alexandra. Trust in the Lord to show you the way. So, after taking a deep breath and gathering her courage, she climbed out of the car. Instead of feeling at peace, she felt on edge. That was a loss, too. She treasured the sanctuary she'd once found here.

"Can I go to Stephanie's?" Atop her horse, Hailey remained at Alexandra's side on the trek across the driveway. "You don't have to drive me or nuthin'. I'm gonna ride over. We're gonna ride the trail down to the river and stuff. Can I, can I, please?"

"Sure. Let me give Stephanie's mom a call first." Alexandra tugged affectionately on the toe of Hailey's riding boot and was rewarded with a beaming smile.

Hailey dismounted, leading Bandit by the ends of the reins.

Something cold snaked down Alexandra's spine. Then it was gone. The morning was pleasant, the ever-present breeze warm. Uneasy, she glanced around her. She'd never noticed how much the giant lilacs and hedges could provide cover for someone lurking about.

Not that there was anyone lurking. It was just a weird way to feel suddenly. Probably more than anything else, it had to do with how raw her emotions were right now. Everything felt off-kilter. Although there was no chance at a marriage with John, he was still watching over her. Keeping her safe. The town sheriff had promised to do no less.

I'm pulled in too many directions, she thought while she waited for Hailey to tether her horse. It's being here in a small town. It's finding out I don't belong after all, just like when I was a little girl. It's this small town. She'd been a fool to stay. Small towns had never brought her anything but pain.

"I gotta get my stuff!" Hailey darted ahead, skipping through the house.

Alexandra's neck tingled again. She didn't feel right about that. She waited in the threshold, watching the world around her. Bandit stole bites of grass from the edge of the lawn, unconcerned. Nothing seemed out of place.

She shut the door and turned the dead bolt. They were probably safe as could be, but it never hurt to err on the side of safety. If Patrick hadn't found her by now, then he'd probably given up, right?

"Corey!" Cameron boomed into the store over the sound of the front door banging open. "You in here?"

"More or less." John straightened from the shelf he was restocking. "What can I do you for?"

"I'm not here as a customer." Cam's face was grim lines and a long, worried frown. "I spotted a car I didn't recognize. In-state plates, but something troubled me so I ran 'em. Stolen plates that didn't match the car. Figure you'd better put in a call to that nice Miss Sims out at your place. Just in case."

"I'll do it now." John's pulse kicked hard as he sprinted down the aisle and snagged the receiver from the wall unit. He punched in his home number, praying for Alexandra to be just fine, for this to have nothing to do with her.

The phone rang on and on. With no answer.

Maybe she was outside with Hailey. That didn't

explain the bad feeling in his guts. Something was wrong. "I couldn't reach her."

"Could be a fair explanation for that." Cameron headed for the door. "She could be outside, or the line could be cut. You comin'?"

In a heartbeat. Without bothering to lock up, John walked out of the store. *Please, let her be safe, Lord. Let this be a scare.*

He couldn't lose Alexandra, too.

He hopped into the passenger seat of the patrol cruiser as Cam put the idling car in gear and tore out onto the street. He hit the lights, not the sirens, sending folks out of their way in a hurry.

Good. They had to get there fast. He had a bad feeling. Something wasn't right. Alexandra would have been in the house this time of morning….

I can't lose another woman I love. John sucked in a ragged breath. The agony in his heart doubled at the thought of anyone hurting Alexandra. The woman so precious to his heart. The one woman he wanted above all else. Above anyone. Ever.

Faster, he prayed as Cam hit the open highway at full speed.

Alexandra was rescuing the flour canister from the pantry shelf when she heard the muffled squeak. Like a floorboard creaking beneath someone's weight. The hair at the back of her neck stood on end. An icy chill whipped through her as she turned from the pantry door, the puppy already barking.

Patrick. Alexandra froze, horror rooting her feet to the floor. Her muscles had turned to stone. She couldn't move. She couldn't think. All she saw was the gun in Patrick's raised hand. The cold gleam of black metal was aimed directly at her.

"No!" The single word was torn from her throat as fear turned to rage. She was across the kitchen floor in two seconds flat, protecting Hailey with her body. "Patrick, stay back. You're not welcome here."

"You don't know what I can do." There was darkness in Patrick's words—fury, anger and the will to do harm. "Do you want to see?"

"No! Don't hurt us." She had to think, and think fast. First priority was to get Hailey away from Patrick. "Please, just lower the gun. You don't need it. I'll do anything you want. Let's just leave, okay?"

"Glad you've finally decided to see things my way." His dark hatred felt as deadly as the gun he shook at her. "Then you're sorry?"

"Y-yes." She fought panic. She wouldn't be afraid of him. He'd taken enough from her, and she'd won it back. She refused to give it up again. "I'm ready. Let's go now."

There had once been kindness in Patrick, but now there was only lethal fury as his thumb dug into the tender flesh beneath her collarbone and his fingertips pierced in her neck. "Move."

Alexandra gritted her teeth against the piercing pain and willed her feet forward. Patrick pushed, nearly lifting her off the ground. She didn't cry out as the pain intensified, because she was too angry. Rage pumped through her as she stumbled toward the front door.

"Alexandra!" Hailey sounded terrified. But at least she'd be left behind. She'd be safe. That was all that mattered.

"Call your grammy," Alexandra choked out before Patrick's thumb squeezed the air out of her throat, cutting her off temporarily.

When he moved his thumb, they were outside and she gasped for breath. She twisted around, desperate to see inside the house. Hailey was so terrified. Was she all right?

Patrick flung her against his car door. "Forget the brat and get in."

"Fine. I told you. I'll be agreeable. Let's just leave." That would be best for Hailey. "Now, Patrick. Let's hurry."

"That's what frustrates me. You don't know your place. Believe me, you're finally going to learn," he said as he followed her into the car. He turned the ignition with his left hand, keeping a solid hold on the gun. Sunlight gleamed on its dark barrel. Patrick gunned the engine, and they flew along the driveway.

What was going to happen to her now? Patrick had slipped past the sheriff's defenses, and John was in town. She was alone. She had no weapon. She had nothing to fight with.

Wait—that wasn't true. She had faith. That's all she needed. God had brought her here, and He'd see her through. Somehow. Some way.

Suddenly Patrick swore. She saw flashing red and blue lights and the white bullet of a police cruiser taking the narrow lane way too fast. There was no room to pass. There were ditches and fencing on either side.

"Patrick!" She squeezed her eyes shut, bracing for the impact.

The car spun to the right, tires spinning dust and gravel. They were on Bev's driveway now, which intersected through the farm. The BMW flew low over the fields.

"Watch out!" Gerald's tractor lurched out of a field and onto the road. It was too late for either of them to stop.

Alexandra held on while the car soared into the potato fields, crushing new green clumps of the vegetable planted in tidy, endless rows as it landed. The seat belt cut into her neck but held her in place. Recovering control, Patrick pointed the hood straight down the field, dodging the rain of irrigation stands as he went.

Alexandra searched for the police car in the side-view mirror. She only saw dust pluming up like a tornado behind them. There he was!

John. He'd come for her. She rejoiced. He'd kept his word. He was her hero, her shining white knight who'd never break his promise to her. A man she could always depend on.

Sunlight glinted on Patrick's gun. The joy diminished. She changed her mind. She didn't want John here. He could be hurt or killed. *Protect him, Lord*, she prayed, watching the police cruiser fall behind and then out of sight in the side-view mirror.

John heard the gunshot ricochet through the river canyon as he leaped from the still-moving patrol car. His feet hit the ground with an impact hard enough to rattle the marrow from his bones, but he was already running past the abandoned BMW. Already fearing the worst. I'm too late. I can't save her. It's too late.

He dimly heard Cam shout his name, but he was beyond anything but getting to where that gunshot came from. He raced past the abandoned car. Alexandra's slip-on sneaker was on the ground. Blood marked the white canvas side. Alexandra's blood.

The sight of it ripped at his soul. If there was any hope, if she was wounded, then as God was his witness he was going to save her from the next bullet. He wasn't going to fail her. He *couldn't* fail her.

He tore along the narrow path, where drops of blood stained the wild grasses. His hopes exploded like a lit keg of dynamite when he saw her on the steep cliffside ahead of him, climbing for cover as the man following her steadied a handgun, aimed and squeezed the trigger.

"Alexandra!"

John's warning reverberated along the river canyon below her. Alexandra's foot slipped, rocks tumbled beneath the sole of her one shoe and she fell, hitting her knees on sharp rock. A bullet stirred the air a few inches from her left ear. More rocks slid out from under her. She dug her fingertips into the earth and rock to keep from sliding.

It was a long way down. All she could see was the sloping crest of the canyon wall falling several hundred feet down to the silver thread of the river below. Exposed and open, there was no place to hide. Patrick had a clear shot.

She'd enraged him when she'd knocked the gun aside when he'd stopped the car. The gun had tumbled to the floorboards and with one quick leap into the field, she was out of his reach, running even as a bullet had grazed her, slicing across her ankle. But it didn't stop her from escaping.

He was angrier now. Determined. She ducked, dropped and rolled. Letting gravity take her. Rocks and dirt scraped her bare thigh.

Faster. Gravity was pulling at her now, and she

groped for a small tree, but the sapling snapped out of her fingers. She kept going, her bare foot striking a rock. Pain glanced up her shin, but it wasn't her main problem. The cliff side was becoming steeper.

She dug in, the earth tearing at her fingers. She couldn't stop. *Oh, Lord, please help me.* She was falling too fast, the grade growing steeper until all she could see was the riverbed below her bare feet. She could taste panic on her tongue, feel it in her wild heartbeat.

I really don't want to die today, Lord.

"Alexandra!" John's voice boomed, full of panic and terror. It reverberated along the canyon walls.

Lord, please hold her in the palm of Your hand. John was already running. No man with a gun was going to stop him. Cam shouted, trying to stop him, but it was too late. All John could see as he skidded down the steep grade was Alexandra tumbling behind an outcropping of rocks and out of sight.

No! She was gone. She was dead. Rage hammered through him as he took the slope at a run, letting his boots ski over earth and rock. The descent was fast—he braced his heels to absorb the shock as he skidded from the open face to a more protected outcropping of rocks. Above the pounding of blood in his ears, he heard the pop of a gun. A cold numb feeling blossomed in his left biceps. Crimson spread in a fast-moving circle on his sleeve.

He didn't care how badly he was shot. He had to get to Alexandra. His life wasn't worth anything if she wasn't alive. She was everything. And if she was gone… Grief lashed him hard as he reached the edge of the cliff, digging in with his heels, throwing his whole body back to stop his descent.

I should have loved her when I had the chance. Reached out and held her to me instead of shoving her away. If only I could have told her how much I love her. Heart and soul. For now and for eternity.

He crept over the cliff on his belly, already knowing what he was going to see. An empty canyon oddly silent with the feel of death.

"John." His name was a ragged whisper. He looked down into a pale, bloody woman's face a couple of feet below him. Her scraped hands were clutched tight around a spindly pine tree limb…one that looked ready to go at any minute.

Alexandra. He felt as high as heaven in one second. He read her fear. He saw the earth begin to move as the tree gave way.

He couldn't reach her. He crept out as far as he could go, stretched and touched air. Inches separated them. "Take my hand."

"I can't." She was on the edge of losing control. Panic flashed in her eyes. She looked up at him. *Help me,* she seemed to say. *Save me.*

Rocks tumbled. The tree gave, the roots breaking off, Alexandra began slipping.

"No!" Horror rose in the depths of his heart, from the breadth of his soul. A terrible image flashed back to him. One moment he was seeing Bobbie falling all over again, her hand outstretched to him, her fingers reaching for his as the distance between them grew. The pleading look in her eyes, the fear of death and pain stark on her pixie face.

As he had then, John dug down deep, asking for strength, gathering every bit of might he possessed, praying that Cam had caught up to Patrick. Tree and rock gave way and he snared Alexandra's wrist as the tree tumbled in a free fall along the jagged cliff wall.

His injured arm trembled with the strain, but he hauled her up and into his arms. Holding her tight and safe, never to let her go.

Thank you, Lord. John buried his face in Alexandra's neck, breathing in the scent of earth and apple shampoo. Tears burned in his eyes and ached in his throat. "I'm so thankful. Oh, baby, I thought I'd lost you."

"Me, too." She held him tight, sobbing now, clutching his shirt with both fists. "You saved me, John. You're so amazing. I love you so much. I just love you so much."

"Oh, my love." He kissed her hair, her cheeks,

her lips. Life and death were in God's hands today, just as it had been those many years ago. It had been God's will, which only He could understand.

And it was God's will that Alexandra was safe in his arms, smiling up at him. She'd never looked so beautiful. So renewed. So serene. "I owe my life to you."

"Yep. You're in deep debt to me now." He kissed her forehead, then her lips. A soft, tender caress. "I'm going to have to think of a way to charge you for saving your life."

"How about free housecleaning for a month?"

"Hmm, I was thinking you might like to clean our house for the rest of your life."

"*Our* house? But you said—"

"Marry me, Alexandra." He kissed her again, feather-soft on her silky skin, and the tenderness inside him doubled. Fierce love burned in his chest for her, in his heart, in his soul. "I have never loved anyone the way I love you."

"I know just how you feel." Tears sparkled in her eyes. Happiness lit her up as she kissed him gently. "How do you feel about a quick wedding?"

"The quicker the better. I can't wait to lift your veil. I want you for my wife."

Love lit him up inside, chasing away every last shadow, and the wall protecting his heart came crumbling down, every last piece as she buried her face in the hollow of his neck, holding tight, so very tight. She was heaven in his arms, so precious and amazing, and he intended to treasure her all the days of his life from this moment on.

Epilogue

"It was a beautiful ceremony." Bev appeared through the crowd, a glass of her special-recipe punch cradled in one hand. As the mother of the groom, she'd chosen a deep rose chiffon that made her look even more elegant. "Alexandra, you make a beautiful bride."

"Love makes any woman beautiful—isn't that what they say?" Alexandra did feel like a princess in her gown of white silk. The wedding ring sparkled on her left hand. A beautiful ring. "I never should have let you do most of the cooking and baking for the buffet, but it's a great success. Thank you."

"Oh, my pleasure, my dear. Goodness." Bev wrapped her in a warm embrace, loving and motherly. "To think you're my daughter now. What fun we'll have. I told John he can't keep you away too long on that mysterious honeymoon he's got planned."

"Trying to find out where he's taking me, are you?" Alexandra was brimming with the secret. John was taking her through the national parks of the West on a luxurious driving tour. He'd bought a new car for the occasion. They were taking Hailey, too. Alexandra's first real family vacation, and they were going to do it right.

Joy filled her heart, filled her soul.

"Here's a little surprise from me." Bev pressed something into Alexandra's hand. "Welcome to our family, sweetheart. Oh, there's Helen. I must speak with her."

As Bev hurried away, Alexandra looked at the bundle in her hand. A stack of handwritten cards tied in a pretty yellow ribbon. "A few of my treasured recipes, since you are now a cherished member of the family. Love always, Bev."

"Hey, it's not right for a bride to be alone." John's voice, John's touch. His tender kiss on her cheek. "What are you thinking? That you should've run for the hills while you had a chance?"

"Yep. Too bad I forgot my tennis shoes. I can't get far in these heels." She leaned into his welcoming arms, savored his strong embrace. "I love you, John."

"I love you." His hand cupped her nape, tenderly. "It's a beautiful day, don't you think?"

"Yes. It's going to be a beautiful life."

The past had faded away, Patrick was in jail, and she'd found a place to belong. Her Bible Study friends waved to her from the table on the back lawn. A few women from the choir were accompanying the church's pianist as she coaxed "Amazing Grace" from the keyboard. Hailey in her lilac maid-of-honor dress raced through the backyard with best friends Stephanie and Christa, while Angel followed, barking with delight.

Alexandra felt whole. God was truly good, for showering her with these precious blessings. And the best one of all took her hand in his and leaned close to whisper in her ear, "You have tears in your eyes. Happy ones? Or sad ones?"

"John." She leaned her cheek on his chest, settling into his arms, where she was meant to be. "I'm happy."

"Good, my love. Because this is just the start of our good life together." The proof of it was in his kiss, in his tenderness and in the brush of their souls. It left no doubt. Theirs was a true love, blessed from above, a bright glowing light that would forever burn.

* * * * *

Dear Reader,

Thank you so much for choosing *Heaven Knows*. While I was writing Alexandra and John's story, I began with the idea of a woman on the run, looking for safety, and ended up with something more. This is the story of a woman who has never known real love and finds it in the arms of a strong and tender man.

Love is one of the Lord's greatest gifts to us, and one of the most powerful forces in the universe. Whether in romance novels or in real life, love does triumph over all.

Wishing you love and peace,

Jillian Hart

Love Inspired®

Fan Favorite
Janet Tronstad

brings readers a heartwarming story
of love and hope with

Dr. Right

Treasure Creek, Alaska, has only one pediatrician:
the very handsome, very eligible Dr. Alex Haven.
With his contract coming to an end, he plans
to return home to Los Angeles. But Nurse
Maryann Jenner is determined to keep Alex
in Alaska, and when a little boy's life—and
Maryann's hope—is jeopardized, Alex may
find a reason to stay forever.

ALASKAN *Bride* RUSH

Available September wherever books are sold.

Steeple
Hill®

LI87620

LARGER-PRINT BOOKS!

GET 2 FREE
LARGER-PRINT NOVELS
PLUS 2 FREE
MYSTERY GIFTS

Love Inspired®

Larger-print novels are now available...

YES! Please send me 2 FREE LARGER-PRINT Love Inspired® novels and my 2 FREE mystery gifts (gifts are worth about $10). After receiving them, if I don't wish to receive any more books, I can return the shipping statement marked "cancel". If I don't cancel, I will receive 6 brand-new novels every month and be billed just $4.74 per book in the U.S. or $5.24 per book in Canada. That's a saving of over 20% off the cover price. It's quite a bargain! Shipping and handling is just 50¢ per book.* I understand that accepting the 2 free books and gifts places me under no obligation to buy anything. I can always return a shipment and cancel at any time. Even if I never buy another book, the two free books and gifts are mine to keep forever.

122/322 IDN E7QP

Name _____ (PLEASE PRINT) _____

Address _____ Apt. # _____

City _____ State/Prov. _____ Zip/Postal Code _____

Signature (if under 18, a parent or guardian must sign)

Mail to **Steeple Hill Reader Service:**
IN U.S.A.: P.O. Box 1867, Buffalo, NY 14240-1867
IN CANADA: P.O. Box 609, Fort Erie, Ontario L2A 5X3

Not valid to current subscribers to Love Inspired Larger-Print books.

**Are you a current subscriber to Love Inspired books
and want to receive the larger-print edition?
Call 1-800-873-8635 or visit www.morefreebooks.com.**

* Terms and prices subject to change without notice. Prices do not include applicable taxes. Sales tax applicable in N.Y. Canadian residents will be charged applicable provincial taxes and GST. Offer not valid in Quebec. This offer is limited to one order per household. All orders subject to approval. Credit or debit balances in a customer's account(s) may be offset by any other outstanding balance owed by or to the customer. Please allow 4 to 6 weeks for delivery. Offer available while quantities last.

Your Privacy: Steeple Hill Books is committed to protecting your privacy. Our Privacy Policy is available online at www.SteepleHill.com or upon request from the Reader Service. From time to time we make our lists of customers available to reputable third parties who may have a product or service of interest to you. If you would prefer we not share your name and address, please check here. ☐

Help us get it right—We strive for accurate, respectful and relevant communications. To clarify or modify your communication preferences, visit us at www.ReaderService.com/consumerschoice.

LILP10R

MARGARET WAY

introduces

THE
Rylance
DYNASTY

The lives & loves of
Australia's most powerful family

Growing up in the spotlight hasn't been easy, but the two
Rylance heirs, Corin and his sister, Zara, have come of age
and are ready to claim their inheritance. Though they are
privileged, proud and powerful, they are about to discover
that there are some things money can't buy....

Look for:

Australia's Most Eligible Bachelor
Available September

Cattle Baron Needs a Bride
Available October

CLASSICS

Enjoy these four heartwarming stories
from your favorite Love Inspired® authors!

Irene Hannon
ONE SPECIAL CHRISTMAS
and
HOME FOR THE HOLIDAYS

Janet Tronstad
SUGAR PLUMS FOR DRY CREEK
and
AT HOME IN DRY CREEK

Steeple
Hill®

*Available in December 2010
wherever books are sold.*

www.SteepleHill.com

LIC1210